SHARAF

Raj Kumar

MYRMIDON

Myrmidon Books Ltd
Rotterdam House
116 Quayside
Newcastle upon Tyne
NE1 3DY

www.myrmidonbooks.com

Published by Myrmidon 2011

A catalogue record for this book is available from the British Library.

ISBN 978-1-905802-33-3

Set in Times New Roman by
Falcon Oast Graphic Art Ltd.
Printed and bound in the UK by
CPI Cox & Wyman, Reading, RG1 8EX

1 3 5 7 9 10 8 6 4 2

SHARAF

Raj Kumar is an artist and designer. He and his wife now live in the southern hemisphere after they met whilst living and working in Saudi Arabia.

For the victims of 'honour' killing everywhere.

GLOSSARY

Abaya – Black cloak worn by women in public
Abia – Traditional winter coat
Addus – Lentil soup
Agal – Black rope headband holding the gutra in place
Ahlan – Welcome
Akd Al-Nikah – Bond of marriage
Alhamdulillah – Praise to God
Allah-hu akbar – God is the greatest
Al-Mabahith al-Amma – Secret police
Amil – Foreign worker
Arak – a tree; also an alcoholic spirit
Asr – Third prayer of the day
Asslam alekum – Peace be upon you
Aurat – Part of a woman's body that cannot be shown
Babaghanoush – a dip made from roasted eggplant and sesame paste
Bishts – Black cloak with gold trim
Bismillah – In the name of Allah
Bismillah al-Rahman al-Rahim – in the name of Allah, the Merciful, the Mercy-giving
Bukarah – Tomorrow
Dellah – Arabic coffee pot
Dhuhr – Second prayer of the day

Eid al-Adha – Festival of Sacrifice

Eid al-Fitr – Festival of Fast Breaking

Estamara – Car registration document

Fajr – First prayer of the day (at dawn)

Gutra – Red and white checkered head cloth worn by Saudi men

Habibi – Darling

Hadith – Saying attributed to the Prophet

Haj – Pilgrimage

Halala – Denomination of Saudi currency

Halwa – Arabic sweets and pastries

Haram – Forbidden

Hava – Wind

Hijab – Refers both to women's head covering and modest Muslim dress in general

Hijarh – Arabic Calendar

Hijaz – A coastal region bordering on the Red Sea

Holy Kaaba – The shrine in Mecca that Muslims turn towards to pray

Hommos – Dip made from chickpeas

Iftar – Breaking of fast during Ramadan

Igama – Saudi identity documentation

Ikhwan – Brotherhood

Imam – Religious cleric

Insha'allah – God willing

Insha'allah bukarah – God willing tomorrow

Isha – Fifth prayer of the day

Jihad – Holy war

Jinn – Spirit

Kabsa – Rice and meat dish

Kayf haalak – How are you

Khad – Police

Khutba – Engagement

Koubz – Bread

Kufiyyah – Black and white checked headscarf

Kuzbaratea – Coriander

8

La – No
Laban – Yogurt drink
Labnah – Yogurt cheese
Maalish, habibi – No problem, darling
Maasalama – Goodbye, peace be upon you
Mabkhara – Incense burner
Maghrib – Fourth prayer of the day
Majlis – Court
Marhaba – Hello
Misbaha – Prayer beads
Miswak – Twig from the Arak tree used as a toothbrush
Mu'assel – A syrupy tobacco mixture smoked in a water pipe.
Muezzin – Person who calls the faithful to prayer
Mujahideen – Freedom fighter
Mullah – Cleric
Mutabbal – Eggplant salad
Mutawah – Religious police
Mutaween – Plural for religious police
Nan – Baked bread
Pathan – Afghan tribesman
Pashtu – Language spoken in Afghanistan
Qadi – Law courts
Qahwah – Coffee
Qauzi – Whole roast lamb
Qur'an – Muslim Holy book
Rababa – One-stringed instrument played with a bow
Ramadan – Holy month when Muslims fast
Rek'ah – Unit of prayer
Riyal – Unit of Saudi currency
Rub al-Khali – Area of Saudi Arabia called the Empty Quarter
Salah – Prayers
Salam 'alekum – Peace to you
Sabbah al-khayr – Good morning
Saluki – Arabian hunting dog similar to a greyhound
Sedeeq – Friend

Sedeeqi – Bootleg liquor
Shahada – Declaration of faith
Sharaf – Honour
Sharia – Islamic law
Shaitaan – Devil
Shawarma – Grilled chicken sandwich
Ya sedeeq – Hey friend
Shiaara – Sirius (the star)
Sheikh – A spiritual master
Ship ship – Traditional Saudi sandals
Shisha – Water pipe
Shukran – Thank you
Souq – Market
Tagalog – Philippine language spoken in the northern islands and in the capital, Manila
Taqdir, Sabr ku – All will be well (Pashtu)
Taweez – Talisman
Thobe – White robe worn by Saudi men
Grand Ulema – Consultative body of government
Umm – Prefix meaning 'Mother of. . .'
Visayan – A southern Phillipine language spoken in the cities of Cagayan and Davao
Wa 'alekum es salam – and on you be peace
Wadi – Dried riverbed
Wahabi – member of a strictly orthodox Sunni Muslim sect from Saudi Arabia
Walad – Boy
Wudu – Ablution
Yellah, yellah – Hurry, hurry
Yellah, khallas – Hurry, finish
Zaffaran – Saffron

PROLOGUE

The air was still this Friday morning but the rustling palms swayed in the searing heat as the chorus of '*Allah-hu akbar*' rumbled from the Grand Mosque. *Dhuhr*, midday prayer, had ended and the congregation slipped out into the sunshine. Collecting their shoes and sandals at the entrance they mingled in the courtyard pressing hands, exchanging kisses with familiar faces – sharing news.

'Make way, make way,' screamed a megaphone and the crowd parted to allow a truck and an ambulance through.

'Baba, Baba, what's happening?' asked a boy, watching the police in khaki spill from the back of the truck.

'There's going to be a show.'

'I can't see. Can we go to the front, Baba?'

The police formed a cordon and the *mutaween* shepherded the crowd, wielding their canes.

'There's to be a beheading,' said a man.

'And a stoning,' added another.

'And a westerner is going to be flogged for brewing.'

'This I must see.'

Hush fell as a white Suburban with tinted windows approached and the police cleared a path.

A black man in a *thobe* alighted and was escorted into the courtyard by two men with machine guns.

11

'Who's the big man, Baba?' asked the boy.

'That's Mohammed, the executioner.'

The police led a dishevelled figure wearing Afghani dress and a blindfold into the square. He was barefoot, with shackled feet and hands cuffed behind his back. The chain clinked along the ground leaving a mark in the dirt as the crowd stared and hissed.

The prisoner halted and turned his ashen face to the sky, smiling as the sun kissed it. He heaved a sigh and began reciting verses from the *Qur'an*, seeking salvation. An official read aloud the prisoner's name and his crime. 'Our country does not tolerate drugs. Let this be a lesson to those who deal in this evil,' he said sanctimoniously in a resonant voice. A murmur of approval passed through the crowd and heads shook in condemnation.

'Kneel!' commanded a policeman and the man fell to his knees and bowed towards the Holy City of Mecca.

The executioner jabbed the scimitar in the man's back and made him jerk his head up. The executioner's arm rose high and paused. Silence hung in the air. The sun flashed across the blade, it arced through the sky and then the man's head tumbled from his shoulders spurting a fountain of blood, its lips still reciting the *Shahada*. The body keeled over raising a puff of dust and its twitching made the chain jingle. The parched earth was quenched by rivulets of blood.

A collective gasp escaped from the crowd and several men fainted. '*Bismillah*' was on every lip followed by silence. The boy screamed and grabbed his father's *thobe*.

'Why, Baba, why?' asked the boy.

'It's Allah's will,' replied his father.

Conversation returned and rippled through the crowd.

'That was quick,' a white-faced man said, dabbing his forehead with a handkerchief.

'Mohammed's good at his job,' replied another man.

'His father was too,' someone agreed.

'The stoning is next,' called out an excited voice from the back and pointed at a pile of rocks.

'I wouldn't miss that for the world,' said his neighbour.

'It's very messy,' said a young voice.

'The adulteress must suffer!' shouted an older man. 'That's the way!'

'I don't have the stomach for that,' came a weak voice.

'A sodomite's going to die too,' cried the voice from the back.

'*Alhamdulillah*,' chorused a group around him.

The boy watched the ambulance drive away with the body and shook his head.

'I don't understand, Baba,' he mumbled.

The father patted his son on the head and they walked away.

ONE

A silk prayer mat unfurled over the marble floor spreading a wave of colour.

Maryam tugged at a corner, positioning it towards the Holy City of Mecca. It had a delicate border of flowers, leaves and tendrils surrounding a turquoise arch that framed a fountain in a rose garden. Her father had given it to her after a trip to Iran before the revolution. She stood back and smiled at the artist's labour of love, probably a child from Esfahan.

A cockerel crowed among the palm trees and a whisper of pink heralded the birth of another day. Fiery, gossamer clouds unwrapped the newborn sun. On the horizon, a jagged silhouette of mountains tore at the sky, their peaks glinting in the morning light. Maryam watched the panorama through her bedroom window on the first floor.

'*Allah-hu akbar.*' God is great. The melodious cry of the *muezzin* floated over the date palms that surrounded the farm and across the sands just as it had done for fourteen hundred years. A flock of doves circled the minaret a few times before gliding back to the sanctuary of their roosts. Maryam composed herself for her communion with Allah. *Fajr*, the first prayer of the day, was a meaningful time for her and she chose to be alone, unlike the other women of the house who gathered downstairs to pray together.

It was always different, even though the words remained the

same and the motions had become automatic over the years. With contained excitement she stepped forward leading with the right foot, her bare feet finding warmth in the rich pile of silk. Maryam recited her *rek'ah* and, as a devout Muslim, she repeated it again.

Today was a special day, more special than all the other days of her life. It was her birthday, and although Muslims never celebrated birthdays, she had kept a secret record of the passing years. She was twenty, and today her father would reveal whom she would wed by year's end. This was a day that most Saudi girls longed and lived for, but some loathed and feared.

The fresh morning air made her shiver. She completed her prayers and rolled up the mat. It was five o'clock but already the sun cast the shadow of the window grill across the floor and onto the bedroom wall.

From a little bed in the corner a child stirred in fitful sleep.

'Mama, Mama,' he cried and reached out an arm. Maryam closed the windows and drew the curtains, shutting out the sun.

'Here I am, *habibi*,' she said.

'You're not my mother, I want my Mama,' he said.

Maryam saw the hurt in his sleepy eyes and kissed his forehead.

'Where's my Baba?'

'He's with Allah, Turki.'

'Can we phone him? Can we, Auntie Maryam? I want to talk to him. Please, Auntie Maryam?'

'Okay, okay, after we talk to Mama.'

Maryam smiled sadly and wistfully to herself.

Turki was Maryam's nephew. His father, Sultan, her elder brother, had been a major in the Royal Saudi Air Force. He had received a commendaton for shooting down three Iraqi jets during the Gulf War but a year ago, when Turki was five, Sultan's F-15 disappeared during a routine mission. It was a shock to everyone and the Air Force had failed to solve the mystery.

Turki's mother, Nourah, had remarried and, as was the

custom, he would now live with his grandparents. Like his father, Turki was inquisitive by nature and every corner and cupboard held intrigue. Maryam had taken it upon herself to look after the boy. In the three weeks they had been together they had grown close. Wherever she went, the patter of his feet followed.

Maryam held Turki close to her bosom and fondled his penis as was traditional. She watched contentment wash over the boy's face as he fell asleep, sucking on his thumb.

A few hours later there was a familiar knock. Turki awoke and rushed to the door.

'Good morning, Grandma,' cried Turki and threw his arms around Aishah's neck and kissed her cheeks.

'And how is my *habibi* today?' Aishah asked. 'Did you sleep well?'

'No nightmares and I didn't wet the bed,' Turki said, showing a row of decaying teeth.

'Good boy.'

'Grandma, Auntie Maryam promised I could phone Mama today.'

'Did she now?'

'And Baba too.'

'Is that so?'

'After that, Grandma, can I play with the horses?'

'You're seeing the dentist today, *habibi*.'

'Do I have to, Grandma?' Turki asked, covering his mouth with his hands. 'I don't like that black lady,' he mumbled.

'You shouldn't have bitten her fingers,' Aishah laughed.

'I want to see the *Ameriki* doctor that you see, Grandma.'

'*Insha'allah.*' God willing.

Turki didn't care much for the dental clinic but loved his visits to the grand hospital in the military city. It was like going to Jeddah where his Mama lived. There were people there from all over the world. Most of all he liked the tall women with golden hair, blue eyes and fair skin. They wore different clothes and never covered their faces or heads. He didn't understand what they said but he always laughed when they struggled with his name. *Turkey*, they called him, pinching his cheeks. His Mama said they didn't believe in Allah and that made them bad – but she didn't say why. She told him that, except for oil, everything from cars and televisions to even his favourite chocolates came from their land.

'*Habibi*, remember what day this is!' Aishah called to her daughter along the hallway as she and Turki went down to breakfast.

Maryam's memory didn't need any prompting. Tormented by questions, she hadn't slept all night. She sat with her feet tucked under her nightgown, as it was rude to show the soles of the feet. She combed her fingers through her hair and massaged her scalp as if to clear her mind.

A shaft of light lanced through a gap between the curtains and pooled onto the marble floor illuminating a dying cockroach. I must speak to Zelpha, she told herself.

Across the room, perfume bottles, lipsticks, pencils and brushes littered the glass top of a dresser. Mirrors shaped like palm trees covered the wall and lights suspended from the ceiling looked like a flock of sea gulls.

The house had a library but Maryam preferred to study in her bedroom in peace. In a corner a wooden desk, with an arsenal of pens and pencils poised in readiness, stood next to a chair. A crowd of books rubbed shoulders on the shelf above.

Fat with knowledge, a dark blue volume bound in leather and embellished with gold calligraphy commanded attention. This was the Holy *Qur'an*, given to her by her father. Bookmarks stuck out from it like plumes of feathers on a bird of paradise. Her rolled prayer mat leaned against the wall beside the desk.

Maryam contemplated the room and wondered where she would be a year from now. A tear rolled down her cheek. She knew her father would have chosen well. It had been arranged before her birth.

She loved him and trusted his judgment. He had his moods, as did all men, but he was a good Muslim and had instructed her in the *Qur'an* as only men are allowed to do. They had grown closer after Sultan's death and he delighted in her success at college. With a mischievous glint in his eyes he would remind her that though she possessed her mother's beauty, she had his mind.

The thought of meeting her prospective husband made her head swim and she giggled, twirling her hair nervously. What should she wear? She had never been one for ostentatious clothes like her friends who had travelled abroad. The malls of Riyadh and Jeddah fulfilled all her needs. It was so important to make a good impression today, she thought. Men had been known to reject brides their mothers and sisters had chosen carefully. Above all, she didn't want to disappoint her father. Her mother had never been enthusiastic; she said it was an agreement between men, trading their women like camels to strengthen bonds and build bridges.

Maryam heard a knock and saw Zelpha, her Filipina maid, at the door.

'Good morning, Madam Maryam. Madam Aishah is calling. Breakfast ready!' she said in her sing-song voice. 'Today a very happy day for you!'

Maryam sighed.

Zelpha noticed the tear-stained cheeks. 'It's going to be okay, madam.'

'How would you know? Have you been married?' Maryam snapped.

'Smile and be happy!' Zelpha replied.

Maryam attempted a smile, brushed the tears from her cheeks and headed for the bathroom. Then she remembered: 'Oh, and there's a cockroach. You know how much I hate them.'

Jets of water eased the tension beneath her scalp and she stepped from the shower with her spirits revived. She threw on a navy dress that covered her from neck to ankles. A border of gold embroidery laced the neckline and trimmed the sleeves covering her arms. Dispensing with make-up and still in bare feet, she rushed down the sweeping marble staircase to the women's quarters.

Like all Saudi homes, the house was divided in two. The living quarters occupied the ground floor; a separate wing for the men and an identical one for the women. As a child Maryam had spent many hours watching guests come and go from behind the latticework of teak and mahogany that screened the balcony above the main hall.

'Good morning, everyone,' Maryam said, entering the family dining room. Kissing her mother on the cheek and smiling at her father, she helped herself to some *hommos* and a dollop of *mutabbal* before settling beside Turki. Dishes adorned the table-cloth, overflowing with goat cheese, an assortment of dips, exotic fruits and stacks of freshly baked *koubz*, and steam spiralled up from freshly filled teacups.

Farhan looked at his daughter seated at the far end of the table, her face a picture of nervous anticipation.

Between mouthfuls of bread and sips of tea, he spoke of the recent bombings in the eastern provinces and the unrest that plagued the country. He worried that a trickle of discontent today could easily turn into a flood as it had done in Iran.

'The King has to make changes, not empty promises,' he gestured, throwing open his hands with a sense of urgency. He sighed at last. '*Insha'allah*, all will be well,' he said as he brushed the breadcrumbs from his beard. 'Nabeel called yesterday,' he announced, changing the subject.

'Is he coming home?' Aishah asked.

'And not alone. He's found someone who'll have him,' Farhan added and shot a disparaging glance at Aishah.

'*Alhamdulillah*, I've missed my boy. Is she *Ameriki*?'

'The girl must be mad, stupid or desperate.'

'It'll be good to have him back. This home feels so empty without my sons.'

Farhan nodded and felt the pain in her voice. He was a military man and had come to terms with the death of his son

Sultan – at least in public. Then Nabeel, the black sheep of the family, had left for America. Soon Maryam would be married, leaving only Turki to while away Aishah's days. There was a steady traffic of friends, military wives, and occasionally Farhan's family would descend from the south, but Aishah needed someone closer to her heart.

Farhan's bushy brows knitted in concentration, he coughed, collected his thoughts and prepared to speak. He noticed Maryam's trembling hand and understood her apprehension. He watched Aishah gulp down some *laban* and squirm in her chair making it creak. He smiled at his grandson engrossed in unwrapping the stuffed vine leaves he loved so much. Farhan shot an annoyed glance at Imelda, the kitchen maid, fretting round the table, waiting for titbits of family gossip. For the past week she and the others had been kept busy making all sorts of cakes and sweets.

'Many years ago, before you were born,' began Farhan, looking at Maryam, 'your Uncle Talal and I were stationed in Jizan near the Yemeni border.'

'Where is Uncle Mahmoud?' Maryam asked, prompted to note her maternal uncle's absence.

'A horse is sick.' Farhan replied curtly. 'Anyway – as I was saying – in those days there was much tension in the South. Those Yemeni dogs were on the warpath – corrupted by that Egyptian scoundrel Nasser and his Pan Arab dream.'

Farhan saw Aishah nod in agreement.

'We were young and foolish – thought the war was a joke. We hadn't seen an enemy soldier in months, and so to kill the boredom we decided to go hunting. I was an officer and should have known better,' Farhan reflected.

'You were a *good* officer, one of the best,' Aishah said.

'That day we bagged some rabbits and a gazelle before dusk. Just before dawn the bandits came, some fifteen to twenty of them. Dirty, hungry and mean.'

Farhan believed the success of a story depended on timing

and he paused for effect, twirling the silver ring set with a black sapphire around his little finger.

'What happened, Grandpa?' Turki asked, looking up from his vine leaves.

'I was taken prisoner. But, by Allah's blessing, Uncle Talal managed to escape and get help,' continued Farhan. 'He returned two days later but the bandits were long gone with our belongings and the jeep. They broke my legs,' he said patting the side of his thighs, 'and left me to the hyenas.'

'What are 'hynas', Grandpa?' asked Turki.

Annoyance flashed across Farhan's face.

'Hyenas are big wild dogs,' answered Maryam.

Farhan watched with growing impatience as Maryam demonstrated their size with her arms wide open.

'Wow!' Turki gasped.

Farhan sipped some tea.

'Are they really that big Grandpa?'

'Yes, *habibi*!'

'Wow,' repeated Turki.

'Now, where was I? Ah yes! I would have died were it not for Uncle Talal.'

'Uncle Talal was brave!' Turki said.

'That he was,' agreed Farhan, pride in his voice.

'Bravo Uncle Talal!' Turki applauded, sending grains of rice flying everywhere.

Farhan and Talal were unrelated but that fateful day cemented their friendship for life. Their respective children grew up calling their father's friend uncle.

'It's a great story. *Allah-hu akbar*,' said Aishah, and heaved herself from the clutches of the chair making it squeak.

'Sit down!' commanded Farhan. 'I've not finished.'

'Is there more?' Aishah asked.

'I've never told you the whole story.'

Aishah looked perplexed and eased back into the chair.

'A few months earlier,' continued Farhan, his voice mellowed and his features softened, 'after giving him six girls, Allah blessed Talal with a son.'

Farhan glanced at Maryam and caught her blushing. He thought he glimpsed a drop of blood ooze from her tightly clenched fist, as if her nails dug into her flesh, but her face showed no pain.

'As Talal carried me across the desert,' said Farhan, 'I promised him that if Allah ever blessed me with a daughter, she would wed his newborn son.' He turned to Maryam, smiling benevolently.

'This cannot be, it cannot be,' Aishah mumbled.

'Be quiet, woman!' Farhan ordered. He shot a glance at his wife and noticed that the colour had drained from her face.

'Has the world gone mad?' Aishah whispered, gasping for breath. She flailed the air with her trembling hands and pulled herself to her feet in panic. Her body swayed and faltered.

'Help me, help me!' she screamed, and grasped the table for support.

'What's the matter?' demanded Farhan.

'It's hot. . . I can't breathe!' Aishah cried.

Maryam rushed to her mother's side. 'Let me help you to the lounge?' she said.

Aishah nodded and draped her arm around her daughter's shoulder. Together they staggered to the lounge where Aishah flopped onto the couch. Imelda followed with a damp napkin and dabbed her Madam's forehead.

From the corner of her eye Aishah spotted Farhan scowling in the background with Turki by his side. She sighed and closed her eyes, shutting out the world she didn't understand.

An hour later Aishah stirred to see the solid figure of her brother Mahmoud striding into the room.

'Come, Mahmoud. Come,' she called, beckoning him with henna-stained fingers dressed with gold rings and arms heavy with bangles. 'I have terrible news! Maryam is to marry Nader. Tell me it's not true, Mahmoud.'

'Nader is a good man,' Mahmoud replied stroking his beard.

'Tell me it's a bad dream!' she implored, reaching for her brother's hand.

'And a devout Muslim,' Farhan added.

'Farhan, tell me it's a joke,' she pleaded. 'Yes! Yes! It must be a joke. Mahmoud, it's a joke!' she cried.

Mahmoud's Pathan face betrayed little. He muttered, '*Taqdir, Sabr ku*,' in Pashtu. '*Insha'allah*, all will be well.'

'My word is my honour and you shall obey me!' Farhan declared, wagging his finger at Maryam and Aishah.

Aishah's pained face searched helplessly for hope in her brother's eyes.

'*Taqdir, Sabr ku*,' Mahmoud repeated softly to his sister.

Aishah laboured a nod and blew her nose on her sleeve.

'*Insha'allah*,' she muttered.

Mahmoud was the elder and her only relative in Saudi Arabia. Their world had collapsed when a drunk ploughed his car into a crowd of pilgrims, killing their parents. Ever since that tragic day in Mecca all those years ago, when she was no older then Turki, he had been her father, her mother and her brother.

'What is it, Mama? Why can't I marry Nader?' Maryam asked.

Aishah glared at Farhan and pursed her lips.

'It's nothing, *habibi*,' she replied at last with a dismissive wave. 'It's nothing,' she repeated under her breath and began to sob.

Farhan looked on puzzled. What was all the fuss about? Nader was from a good family, he held a position of responsibility at the prestigious King Abdul Aziz military hospital and, above all, he was a good Muslim. Hadn't he joined the *mujahideen* to fight in the Holy *Jihad* against the Soviets in Afghanistan when others, including his son Nabeel, had shirked their responsibility to their Muslim brothers and absconded to America? Moreover he, Major General Farhan Bin Mohmoud Al-Balawi, Commander of the Northwest Frontier province, had pledged his daughter's hand in marriage to the son of the man who saved his life and there was no going back. His *Sharaf*, his honour, depended on it. If he broke his promise, how could he live with the shame it would bring the family and the tribe? *Insha'allah*, Aishah would come around in a few days.

'*Insha'allah*, Talal and his family will be here after *Maghrib* prayer,' Farhan announced as he left, angry and perplexed at Aishah's behaviour and Maryam's apparent lack of enthusiasm.

'Women! You can't please them no matter what,' he muttered to himself.

Two

With every puff, Turki sent a stream of bubbles floating through the air. He was their creator, this was his solar system and he was the sun. Poking his finger at them, he made them vanish, leaving a fine spray. He didn't ask or care where they went; he just laughed and blew again through the ring of the bubble maker.

Turki looked lost in the black marble tub that could hold four adults. Water roared from the jaws of a pair of gold lions and swirled around his body. Suds floated like icebergs on the water and the scent of rose climbed on tendrils of steam.

Watching her little prince made Maryam's heart dance.

Insha'allah, soon she would have a son of her own and make Nader happy, she reflected with a smile. Otherwise their marriage would be doomed. The thought of divorce or another wife made her shudder.

She had heard stories of wives driven into the arms of 'the women' in desperation. Women without names or an address but everyone knew someone, who knew somebody, whom *the women* had helped in more ways than one.

Turki paddled around the tub and splashed water on Maryam's face, washing away her thoughts.

'Come, it's time,' Maryam announced, glancing at her watch. 'We'll be late for your appointment,' she said, lifting the boy out of the water and draping a towel around him.

'Do I have to, Auntie Miri?' Turki pulled a face.

Minutes later Maryam had him dressed in a *thobe* and leather *ship ship*, the traditional Saudi sandals.

'There you are,' she said with pride, running a comb through his hair before placing an embroidered white cap on his head.

Smiling, Aishah watched them come down the stairs hand in hand and met them in the hallway. 'How is my prince?' she asked. Turki flashed a toothy grin. 'Now, let me have a good look at you,' she said, and made him twirl. 'You're so like your father, *habibi*!' She fought back the tears.

'Uncle Mahmoud will take you to the dental clinic today,' she said, giving Turki a hug. The morning's excitement had worn her out and she would have to rest if she were to receive the guests that evening. Besides, there was much to do in the kitchen.

Turki looked up at Mahmoud towering above him and felt ready to tackle the dentist, maybe even the black lady. Mahmoud was an Afghan tribesman by birth and like all Pathans he was tall. He had a large aquiline nose and angular cheekbones, his thickset jaw hid beneath a greying beard that rested halfway down his chest, making his head seem larger than it really was. A sweeping handlebar moustache framed his chiselled lips, which drooped at the corners in a permanent scowl, and his deep-set eyes under bushy eyebrows seemed to search into one's soul. The desert wind, the sand and the blazing sun had left their mark on his face.

Turki's hand disappeared in Mahmoud's and together they strolled to the waiting car. Turki looked back at the women through misty eyes and saw the blurred figure of his mother framed in the doorway. She was calling to him with outstretched arms.

'Mama, Mama,' Turki called and rushed back. Maryam hadn't lied. His Mama was here. How could he have doubted her?

Turki's foot caught on his *thobe* and he fell into Maryam's waiting arms. Looking into her eyes, Turki realised his mistake and burst into tears.

'I saw Mama. Where is Mama?' he sobbed, burying his face in her shoulder. 'You won't leave me will you, Auntie Maryam? You'll be here when I get back, won't you?'

'I'll do better than that. I'll come with you,' Maryam replied and felt the tension ease from the boy's body. 'Men don't cry,' she said, dabbing the tears from his cheeks with her sleeve.

Collecting her *abaya*, the black cloak worn by women outside the privacy of the home, she and Turki joined Mahmoud waiting by the Chevrolet Suburban parked in the sunshine.

'Auntie Miri is coming with us, Uncle Mahmoud!' Turki announced, and plonked himself into the front seat.

Maryam climbed in the rear, adjusting her *abaya* over her shoulders. Squeaking and creaking, the Suburban made slow progress negotiating the potholes that peppered the three kilometres of desert track from the farm to Medinah Road, the main highway into Tabuk.

'When are they going to fix the road, Uncle?' Maryam asked.

'They promised a year ago.'

'But that was before the war.'

'It's the same everywhere these days. Once they have your money they stall. Your father has taken the matter to the *Qadi*.'

'*Insha'allah*, they will see to justice,' Maryam replied.

'*Insha'allah*,' Mahmoud murmured without conviction.

'What's a *Qadi*, Auntie Maryam?' Turki asked.

'It's where people who have a disagreement can make a complaint,' Maryam explained.

'Also where criminals are punished,' Mahmoud added.

'What's a criminal, Uncle Mahmoud?'

'Bad people.' Maryam laughed.

The midday sun hammered down on the vehicle and the air-conditioning groaned to keep the interior from turning into an oven. A plume of dust followed them and sneaked through cracks, leaving a tell-tale layer of fine orange dust.

'Auntie Miri, are there many bad people?' Turki asked.

'Most people are good, like us.'

'Do you know any bad people?'

'Can't say I do,' Maryam replied, amused at the boy's questions.

'What happens to the bad people?'

'Sometimes they have to pay some money and sometimes they have to go to jail,' Maryam explained.

'The very bad ones get their head chopped off,' Mahmoud added chopping his hand across the back of his neck.

'Do they really, Auntie Miri?' Turki looked horrified.

'Yes, *habibi*, but only sometimes.' Maryam reassured.

Maryam sat cocooned in her *abaya* taking in the scene from behind the cotton veil, grateful for the protection it gave from the bright light. Her gloved hands lay folded in her lap.

Mahmoud remained silent, deep in thought, digesting the events of the morning. Why was Aishah upset on what should have been a joyous occasion? She knew Nader to be a good man. Hadn't she nursed him like her own son when he and his sister Mona were stricken by smallpox while their parents were abroad? Mahmoud shook his head, unable to fathom Aishah's behaviour. It was so unlike his sister.

'Is anything the matter, Uncle?' Maryam asked as if sensing her uncle's thoughts.

There was a long pause then, just as Maryam prepared to ask the question again, Mahmoud muttered, 'It's nothing, *habibi*.'

The remaining thirty kilometres of the journey were uneventful. Turki spent the time counting cars and camels while Maryam puzzled over her mother's reaction to her engagement to Nader and thought of the changes married life would bring. Mahmoud continued to ponder on Aishah's behaviour, drumming his fingers on the steering wheel to some Pathan rhythm he had heard as a child.

The Suburban swung through the gates of the King Khalid Dental Clinic and eased into the carport marked VIP in bold yellow. On cue, Colonel Abdul-Nasser Halawani, the director of the clinic, opened the double doors and stepped out into the heat dressed in a khaki military uniform with an array of ribbons on his chest. His smile failed to disguise his indignation of having to welcome a six-year-old boy who was an hour late.

'I want to see Dr *Ameriki*!' Turki said to the colonel and skipped past him with Maryam in tow. He wasn't sure what he didn't like about the colonel. Was it the protruding teeth framed by fleshy lips and overhung by a pencil-thin moustache, or was it his goat-like eyes?

Turki and Maryam left Uncle Mahmoud and the colonel to the ritual of handshakes and kisses.

Abdullah, the chief clerk, was a tall man with a stoop and a nervous disposition. He greeted Maryam at the reception desk with the smile he reserved for VIP patients. Nicotine-stained fingers spoke of his weakness for roll-ups enriched with hashish. Bloodshot eyes and whiskey-laden breath betrayed his servitude to Johnny Walker, available at a price. He knew Maryam's family, as did the rest of Tabuk, and ushered them into the doctor's surgery.

Dr Joseph Benjamin Goldman greeted them with a disarming smile. He was a little taller than Uncle Mahmoud, Turki judged, fascinated by the sky blue eyes.

'Call me Joe.' He introduced himself in an American accent and shook Turki's hand.

Turki felt safe.

'And this is Tess,' Joe continued, introducing his smiling dental assistant.

'Are you Dr *Ameriki*?' Turki inquired glancing at Maryam. Abdullah translated.

'Well, I guess you could say that, Turki,' Joe replied, correctly pronouncing Turki's name. 'Are you the mother, Ma'am?' Joe asked, nodding a greeting at Maryam.

'Actually, Doc, she's the aunt,' Abdullah interjected.

'Oh, I beg your pardon. Come, come, take a seat,' Joe said and motioned Maryam to a chair in the corner. Taking Turki's hand, Joe led him to the dental chair that Turki loved to ride. He kicked off his *ship ship* and imagined he was an astronaut about to blast off into space. Joe reclined the chair. Tess placed a bib on him and secured it behind his neck.

Fidgeting with a pen while rehearsing his next move, Abdullah gravitated to Maryam. He struck up a conversation laced with innuendo. Maryam smiled at his boyish antics from behind her veil. Occasionally he injected words of encouragement at Turki in Arabic. Foreign women were much more receptive then Saudi women, he thought. Most didn't wear a veil and that made the game easier.

'So you like to bite, do you?' Joe asked, feigning horror at the contents of Turki's file.

Maryam laughed and Turki looked down at his feet in embarrassment and wriggled his toes.

'Well! I hope you've had breakfast 'cause these fingers aren't on the menu today.' Joe flexed his fingers in the air. Abdullah translated and Turki grinned.

'What's the problem today, Turki?' Joe asked in Arabic.

'You speak Arabic,' Turki said, and pointed to his front teeth.

'Well, just a little.' Joe adjusted the beam from the overhead light and Turki screwed his eyes shut. 'You can open your eyes Turki,' Joe said and picked up a dental mirror from a tray of instruments and explained what he was about to do.

Turki studied both Joe's face, etched with concentration, and his own reflected in Joe's safety glasses. He wondered how Dr Joe would look with a beard and moustache. The men he knew all wore a moustache or beard, if not both. Did Dr Joe have a God or was he like the others that Mama said were bad? He thought about what his Mama had said and decided Dr Joe wasn't bad and so must have a God but he probably had another name for him like the ninety-nine names there were for Allah. Joe reeled out a string of numbers and Tess noted them in Turki's file, occasionally nodding or asking a question.

'Well, that wasn't so bad, was it, young man?' Joe asked when he had finished. Turki noticed Dr Joe liked to start his sentences with *Well* and wondered what that meant.

Abdullah peeled away from Maryam, annoyance written on his face. Joe explained and Abdullah translated.

'The good news is Turki has some healthy teeth. But he also has some decayed teeth that will need treatment. The bad news is some teeth are rotten and will have to go,' Abdullah said pointing to Turki's front teeth.

Turki looked across at Maryam. He didn't understand what Abdullah meant by 'go' but it didn't sound good.

'They are baby teeth and will soon be replaced by permanent ones,' continued Abdullah. 'The bad teeth have to go or they will cause an infection.'

Turki didn't like the sound of that either and began to cry. Maryam came to his side and held his hand. Turki searched the black cloth for comfort but there was none. Maryam sensed the boy's frustration but she was alone in a room with two strange men and hesitated. Turki's wail reached out to her instincts, dispelling a lifetime of conditioning. Glancing at Joe and then at Abdullah, she raised her veil and held his hand. Turki stopped sobbing.

A smile escaped Abdullah's lips betraying the pleasure Maryam's face had brought him and he manoeuvred closer to get a better view. He was disappointed to see a face absent of make-up. For him this was a face of youthful innocence with no hidden promise. A boring face.

Joe, too, had seen many faces but none like the one before him. He paled and felt his pulse quicken. Here stood a vision of crystalline beauty unadulterated by Lauder or Chanel. His eyes drank in the intelligent forehead, the large amber eyes framed by high cheekbones and curving eyebrows that tapered to a point. Her patrician nose, so uncommon in these parts, with delicate oval nostrils, gave the face a striking regal profile. Generous lips hung suspended above her delicate chin. Her fine skin, endowed with the lustre of porcelain, conferred an ethereal quality.

Sensing Joe's attention, Maryam blushed and turned away.

Joe stroked his chin and spoke, breaking the tension. 'Well, we can review the front teeth again at the end of this course of treatment. Best go and think about it, young man,' he said, patting Turki's shoulder.

'You've been a good boy,' Tess said and handed him a bag containing a red toothbrush, a tube of paste and a poster of Darth Vader fighting tooth decay. She stuck a glitzy sticker on his chest that said, *I was Brave!* Turki grinned and jumped off the chair and whispered in Maryam's ear and she chuckled.

'Turki wants to know if you have a God, Dr Joe,' she asked in English.

'Well, err. . . we all have a God. How about you?' Joe inquired, knowing the only religion allowed to be practised in the Kingdom was Islam and that everyone had to declare a belief in a God or were denied a visa.

'Allah, of course!' Maryam replied emphatically. She translated and Turki echoed 'Allah!' and waved good bye.

'*Maasalama*, Dr Joe.' Maryam smiled, dropped her veil and stepped out into the corridor accompanied by Turki and Abdullah.

THREE

The phone rang and echoed through the house. Khadijah swore and heaved herself off the bed.

'Where is everyone? I asked for an extension months ago, no one takes any notice of me these days,' she grumbled. She reached the lounge and the phone stopped ringing.

'*Shaitaan!*' Khadijah cursed. 'Mona, Ameera, Fatmah!' She called to her daughters. She looked at the clock shaped like the Grand Mosque of Mecca and shook her head. 'It's been one o'clock for the past week and no one has bothered to change the batteries,' she muttered.

She collected a glass of *laban* and a plate of cookies from the kitchen and flopped onto the couch. She stabbed a button on the remote and the television flickered into life. A man with a thick beard appeared on the screen seated behind a large book. Words spilled from his lips without emotion, expounding the virtue of children in the Islamic family.

Our children are the joys of life, a gift from Allah and must be cherished, be they girl or boy. The man glanced down at the *Qur'an* and continued, *The Prophet Mohammed, peace be upon him, said that any man who receives tidings of the birth of a female and buries it beneath the dust in shame, then evil will be his judgement.*

'Tell that to our husbands,' Khadijah scoffed and changed the channel, cutting the man off in mid sentence.

The custodian of the two holy mosques, King Fahad, opened a school today in downtown Jeddah, read the newscaster. *Crown Prince Abdullah welcomed the Secretary of State of the United States.*

Khadijah smiled in appreciation of all the work the royal family was doing.

'We need more schools!' she called out.

'*Prince Sultan, First Deputy Prime Minister and Minister of the Armed Forces has opened a new Military Academy in Riyadh*,' the newscaster continued.

'That's what I want to hear.' Khadijah tucked into the cookies and before long the plate was empty. Crumbs covered her dress but she didn't care. She wiped her mouth with her sleeve, belched and settled down for the Egyptian soap she loved to watch. The phone rang.

'*Nam!*' Khadijah barked into the mouthpiece.

'*Salam 'alekum.*'

'*Wa 'alekum es salam*,' replied Khadijah. 'Who is it?'

'*Umm* Sultan!' Aishah answered. 'Is that you, Khadijah?'

'It's *Umm* Nader!'

'We must talk, Khadijah.'

'Not until you address me correctly! *Umm* Nader is my rightful title.'

'He's *my* son, Khadijah.' Aishah said.

'I'm his mother, I am *Umm* Nader!'

'I'll sooner die before I call—'

'Die and be done with it!' Khadijah screamed and slammed the receiver down before Aishah could finish. 'Who does that foreign bitch think she is?' Khadijah shouted. Her flailing arms sent the plate and glass crashing to the floor.

Tears streamed down Aishah's face. 'What have I done to deserve this?' she sobbed, looking up at the heavens, clutching the phone as Maryam and Turki entered the room.

'Why are you crying, Mama?' Maryam asked putting her arm round her shoulder.

'It's nothing,' sniffed Aishah and dabbed the tears from her cheeks with a tissue.

'Would you like some tea, Grandma?' Turki asked.

Aishah nodded, ruffled his hair and Turki trooped off to the kitchen to order tea and his favourite biscuits.

'Don't you want me to marry Nader?' Maryam asked. Aishah stared at her in silence. 'Tell me what troubles you, Mama?'

'It's nothing, *habibi*,' her mother replied and blew her nose. 'It's nothing,' she muttered under her breath.

FOUR

From a basement office in the hospital came the rhythmic creaking of a mahogany desk as Nader's muscles coiled and uncoiled like springs. The sweat dripped from his face as flesh met flesh and bodies fused and separated only to fuse again.

Portraits of King Fahad and his two brothers watched from their elevated positions on the wall, smiles of approval on their faces.

The telephone cried for attention. Nader swore.

'Shit!'

'Don't stop!' Lo screamed, digging her heels into the small of his back and pinching his nipples to infuse pleasure with pain.

A moan escaped Nader's lips followed by a '*Bismillah!*' His body convulsed, wringing the last drops of pleasure.

The phone cried like a petulant child.

Nader snatched it up. '*Nam!*' he gasped.

'*Sabbah al-khayr ya* Nader!' greeted a voice Nader recognised as that of the hospital director.

'*Ahlan, ahlan, ahlan!* Welcome, welcome, welcome,' he mustered between breaths.

'I'm not disturbing you, I hope?' the voice asked.

'Of course not, Colonel Ghasib. To what do I owe the pleasure?' Nader knew what the call was about. The Colonel didn't have time for anyone, least of all Nader, his chief of housekeeping, but even Nader had his uses and this was one of those calls.

'I need a favour. Some VIPs from Riyadh . . .'

'I understand,' Nader said.

'They need to feel welcomed.'

'How many?'

'Can you manage three?'

'Fine!'

'I want Heidi. . .' demanded the Colonel. He waited for a response and continued when none was forthcoming. 'I must have her, Nader! My promotion depends on this.' He needed Nader more then he wanted to admit and he knew Nader knew this.

'*Insha'allah*,' Nader replied, listening to the Colonel's laboured breathing. 'I'll see what I can do, *Ya* Colonel.'

'I'll be most generous.'

Nader offered a non-committal '*Insha'allah*' knowing Heidi was off limits to all but one. He would just have to say she had women's problems – that worked every time.

Unceremoniously the line went dead.

Nader wondered whom he could call upon for the occasion. Contemplating his image in the mirror, he adjusted the chequered *gutra* on his head and placed the *agal* on top to keep it in place.

There was impish Jill from Scotland, who joked her family motto was *In bed we serve*. Then there was Regina from Holland with the mop of red hair and lily white skin who had an appetite for the bizarre. She was much in demand from the top brass, some of whom liked being disciplined by a foreign woman.

Of course, he could always count on Bong from Jakarta with his effeminate ways and tight butt everyone loved. Yes, Bong, Regina and Jill should swing the vote in the Colonel's favour *without* Heidi, he told himself.

Nader gave Lo a peck on the cheek and dismissed her with a pat on her butt. She was his daily morning entertainment but also his recruiting agent.

'How long has it been now, Loretta?' Nader asked.

'You know I hate being called that.'

'But that's your name.'

'I prefer Lo, it's hot and beautiful.'

'Let me guess. . . it must be six months?'

'About that.'

'My, how time flies.'

'I've paid off my father's hospital debt last month.' Lo said with pride.

'Keep up the good work and who knows where you'll end up?'

'Don't you worry, there's a bit of Imelda in me,' Lo snapped with a mischievous glint in her eyes.

'Imelda?' Nader asked.

'. . . was our first lady.'

'Ah, yes. The one with the million shoes?'

'That's her.'

'We need more recruits,' Nader said.

'Oh, I clean forgot. There's a new girl in town,' Lo announced, slipping on her G-string.

'Western?' Nader asked, looking at her with interest. 'You know I like blondes.'

'No.'

'What then?'

'Filipina. . . sort of.'

'Sort of?'

'Half-breed. Chinese–American.' Lo sneered.

Nader raised a questioning brow.

'I hate the Chinese. They are filthy rich and tight-fisted.'

'And what of the Americans?' Nader gave an empty laugh.

'They are generous. . . my cousin is married to one.'

'Where does this half-breed work.'

'Admin. . . she asked for you.'

'For me?'

'Says she knows a friend of yours.'

'Oh?' Nader's curiosity was aroused. He knew Lo was wary of new arrivals – especially ones with connections. She knew in his country the law of supply and demand operated and it was who you knew rather than what you knew that counted. Like him Lo trusted no one: *today's friend is tomorrow's enemy* she had once told him; that compassion is seen as a sign of weakness and strength lies in having money. Plenty of it.

'I'll bring her over.'

'Yeah, do that,' Nader said, wondering whom she knew. Normally, it was the personnel office that would alert him of any new talent.

'Midday okay?'

'Yeah,' Nader replied.

Lo gave Nader a lingering kiss and left. Nader used Lo's weakness for money; he knew she'd never let her personal feelings get in the way of business.

A bluebottle buzzed around the room drawn by the scent of sex. It made several passes over the plastic waste bin before settling to breakfast on the damp tissue. Nader lit a cigarette and watched. He hated all insects, flies in particular, and kicked the bin forcing the insect to take flight. He drew on the Marlboro and aimed the smoke at the portraits on the wall. He hated them more than he hated the fly.

'Gotchya!' In one swift movement Nader plucked the fly out of the air and pulled off the wings. He released it on the desktop and watched it attempt to fly. 'That'll teach you to fuck with Nader,' he jeered.

*　*　*

At midday Lo returned looking important, followed by a girl with silky black hair and clutching a handful of papers. She was in her early twenties, wearing a tight-fitting white blouse that left little to the imagination. She was too tall for a Filipina and her almond-shaped eyes and European face hinted at her Chinese–American lineage.

'I'm Kim.' She extended her manicured hand. 'You must be

Nader.' She smiled recognising the odour of stale sex mingled with smoke and sweat.

'*Ahlan, Ahlan, Ahlan,*' Nader reciprocated with a smile.

'Fawaz spoke a lot about you.'

'Fawaz?'

Kim's heart sank. 'Fawaz from Manila, surely you—'

'Ah, yes! Fawaz. . . Of course I know that scoundrel,' Nader interrupted.

'He gave me this,' Kim said, handing Nader the manila envelope addressed in Arabic.

'Come take a seat.' Nader gestured at the sofa. Lo sat down beside the girl, looking her up and down with suspicion.

'Tea?' Nader asked.

Kim nodded.

'Lo, tea please,' ordered Nader and pulled out the piece of paper from the envelope. He studied the two words on it with a solemn face and looked at Kim. She shrugged her shoulders and Nader understood what was to be done.

* * *

Kim's journey had begun when she met Fawaz at the Firehouse, Manila's famous go-go bar in Santa Monica. He had ordered champagne so that she would benefit from the commission but drank Pepsi.

Over the weeks he became a regular at the bar and they became friends. Soon she began spending her days off doing his laundry, cleaning his apartment and cooking for him. He never spoke of his work and she didn't feel the need to ask. Fawaz was a Muslim, prayed five times a day and never touched pork or alcohol. He was distant but attentive, showed no interest in sex and would disappear for weeks, returning with gifts from Indonesia or Malaysia.

He was gentle and thoughtful in his actions, accepting her for who she was. She took him to Cebu to meet her family and he bought them all presents. One day, while in Cebu City, they had come across a medical lab and Fawaz had suggested she should have a blood test.

'What for?' she had asked alarmed.

'Just to be sure.'

'Of what?'

'You know. . . peace of mind.' He hadn't mentioned the cursed disease but she knew what he meant.

'It's a waste of money.'

'I'll pay.'

'I take precautions,' she lied.

'Do it for *me*,' he implored and she had given in. She could still remember that day. The sea breeze blowing through the coconut palms carried the smell of cooking from street vendors. The sun burned her skin as they walked hand in hand along the beach, kicking up the golden sand with their feet. Disco music belted out of beach bars mingled with the sound of laughter. She thought she was in paradise with a loving man by her side.

All that shattered when she opened the buff envelope containing the lab report. They refused to believe it. Fawaz suggested they try elsewhere, perhaps the University Hospital where they had the latest equipment.

Over the next few days they clung to hope, but were disappointed. The young doctor at the University Hospital was kind but there was little he could do.

'It's only a question of time,' he had said in his American accent.

'How long?' Fawaz had asked.

'Perhaps two or three years.' His clinical voice echoed in her brain. She had screamed at him.

'Two years! Two short years! Christ, do you know what you're saying? I'm twenty-two and you're telling me two years is all I've got?'

'What about drugs?' Fawaz had asked without emotion.

'Drugs help but there's no cure for now. It's terminal.' The sentence hung in the air like an atomic cloud spelling doom.

The next few days were a blur as the enormity of it all crystallized. She couldn't tell anyone. Not even her mother. How could she? They knew nothing about her life in Manila and believed she was a well-paid secretary in a big corporation.

She was angry with herself and cursed the man who had paid extra for sex without a condom. She felt cheated.

In Manila she went back working the bars but every time a man made a pass she freaked out, and in the end she got fired.

Days turned to weeks and soon the money dried up. It was then that Fawaz told her about himself. She wasn't sure how much of it was true but in the end it boiled down to money, fifty thousand green ones. That was more money then she could dream about in a hundred dreams. She would be a peso millionaire with two years to live.

She remembered Fawaz holding her in his arms while she wept in confusion and agreed to everything. He arranged the mountain of paperwork at the Saudi Embassy after a doctor gave her a clean bill of health for a hefty fee.

That evening they celebrated at a restaurant called Galing-Galing and Fawaz looked on in disgust as she tucked into a dish of roast suckling pig.

'The pigs in my country are the two-legged kind, bleeding my country dry. But not for long,' he scowled. That was the only time she had seen him show any emotion.

'Like Marcos?'

'Marcos?'

'He was our president.'

Within a month she was boarding a plane bound for Riyadh with the Saudi emblem of a green palm tree and crossed swords painted on its tail. Her instructions were to seek out Nader on arrival.

Lo knocked and entered with a frown on her face, carrying a tray of mint tea in dainty cups and dates on a glass dish. She didn't like it when Nader treated her like a maid in front of the others.

'Tea!' she said, setting down the tray on Nader's desk causing it to splash.

The cry of the phone cut the tension in the room and into Nader's thoughts.

'*Nam!*' he shouted.

The voice at the other end was accustomed to giving orders and Nader listened.

'Yes, yes, leave it with me, Nader assented. 'He won't be disappointed. I know *just* the person.'

'Thursday.'

'*Insha'allah.*'

'The usual package!'

'Nothing less.'

'Thursday before *Maghrib* prayer,' affirmed the voice. The line went dead. Nader swore under his breath and banged the phone down. He would have the last laugh. He lit a cigarette, staring at the portraits on the wall and at Kim. There was no going back.

'Let me have those,' he said pointing to the bundle of papers in her hand. 'I'll sort them for you,' he smiled.

'Are you happy with your apartment?'

'Yes.'

'If there's anything I can do, just yell.'

'It's too late. But thanks for asking.' Kim yawned. The long flight and jet lag was catching up with her.

'Welcome to Tabuk,' Nader added. 'Hope you enjoy your stay!'

Lo took the cue and the girls left, leaving Nader to contemplate the fate of the fly, the cups of tea left untouched.

Nader shuffled through the forms till he found a slip labelled Immunology. He would attend to this himself. Picking up his ivory *misbaha* – prayer beads – he drew on the cigarette till the end glowed. Muttering '*Bismillah*' he stubbed it out on the fly. Popping a date in his mouth he left for the *Dhuhr* prayer in the hospital mosque.

Nader rounded the corner and saw Heidi striding towards him, oozing arrogance. Her honey-blonde hair was in a plaited ponytail, not a strand out of place, and her white uniform was crisply ironed. White Birkenstock sandals cradled her size 8 feet. She was seldom without her Sony Walkman and red lipstick but always without her nurse's paper hat.

Heidi was tall even by German standards, a shade over six foot. Hours spent in the gym and the swimming pool had paid off. She was groomed to perfection and moved with the grace of a thoroughbred filly, a born winner.

She was every Arab's fantasy, but only one man's reality: the man she endearingly called Mr F. Heidi never mentioned his name but everyone knew he was a VIP – perhaps even a prince. The letter F could have stood for any number of names but the Filipinas just called him her Mr Fortune.

Heidi greeted Nader in the German accent she knew he found sexy and her aquamarine eyes held his attention. They exchanged pleasantries before Nader told her that Suliman, Mr F's secretary, had called.

'Thursday OK?' he asked.

'Yeah, yeah,' Heidi affirmed, nodding her head.

'Before *Maghrib*.'

Heidi winked and headed for the cafeteria, turning heads as she went.

The colonel flicked the channels on his TV monitor with the remote button. Via the hundreds of close-circuit cameras positioned around the hospital, he could view every corridor from his office. He boasted he could follow a fly from the time it entered the hospital to the time it left. No one knew what purpose this would serve but some prince had made a small fortune from the contract.

'Ah yes, here we are!' he exclaimed, squirming in his leather chair watching Heidi and Nader in conversation.

'*Alhamdulillah*, I can start packing for Riyadh,' the colonel said out loud. The promotion was in the bag. He chuckled and lit a cigarette.

45

FIVE

Turki sat cross-legged on the bed watching the point of the pencil trace the outline of the upper lip into the shape of a cupid's bow and continue around the lower lip.

'Auntie Miri. . .'

'Yes, *habibi*.'

'Can I paint my lips?'

'Only women wear lipstick, silly,' she said and giggled at the thought.

'Why, Auntie Miri?'

'Because,' Maryam began, trying to keep a straight face, 'Because, women need to look beautiful.'

Turki watched the lip brush fill in the colour as he did in his painting book.

'But some men are ugly,' he said, wondering if make-up would make them beautiful.

Maryam chuckled. She dabbed her lips with a tissue removing some of the silver highlighter. No point overdoing it, she thought and smiled at the reflection in the mirror.

'Red is my favourite colour, Auntie Miri,' Turki declared and gave her a hug. 'I'll marry you if Nader doesn't,' he whispered in her ear making her laugh.

* * *

A cacophony of sounds greeted them in entered the kitchen. Maryam gave a twirl to a chorus of *Oohs* and *Ahs*. Everyone clapped.

She wore a purple dress in georgette with a border of embroidered gold that circled her neck. Radiating rays of beads fanned across the front to her navel ending in a splash of emerald green bordered by gold. Loose sleeves flowed from winged shoulders culminating in braided cuffs.

Pandemonium ruled in the kitchen. Aishah rushed around orchestrating the final touches, adding a pinch of *kuzbaratea* – coriander – here and some *zaffaran* from her palette of spices. Tasting and sniffing her creations, nodding approval and floating onto another pan like an exotic butterfly sampling the delights of a garden in bloom. Imelda, Zelpha and Josi giggled, stirring this and washing that, peeling this and chopping that, under Aishah's watchful eye. They hadn't had so much fun since the festivities of *Eid al-Fitr* at the end of the month of *Ramadan*.

In the garden the smell of cooking filled the air from lambs roasting in clay ovens sunken in the ground. They would take six hours to cook.

Talal arrived with Nader and his sisters Mona, Ameera and Fatmah. A flock of white doves abandoned their lofts, disturbed by the *muezzin* calling the faithful to prayer.

Talal and Nader joined Mahmoud, Farhan and the farmhands in the *Isha* prayer. Farhan invited Nader to lead the prayer to welcome him into the family.

Nader was no stranger to this role, having played it often with the *mujahideen* and gaining their respect with his knowledge of the *Qur'an*. The party entered the red brick mosque with its tin roof, leading by their right foot, having undertaken *wudu* in the mosque courtyard.

Nader stepped onto the prayer mat, right foot first and began the prayer. He spoke with conviction, reciting the *rek'ah*, ending each verse with a loud *Allah-hu akbar*. Allah is the greatest.

A pager bleated during the second *rek'ah*. Farhan and

Mahmoud exchanged glances. Nader reached into his pocket and silenced the intrusion.

One *rek'ah* followed another, the fourth ending with a rumbling chorus of *Allah-hu akbar* that rolled over the farm marking the end of *Isha* prayer. As a devout Muslim, Nader retired to the rear of the room, with head bowed in concentration, he continued his personal prayer. One by one the worshipers left the mosque, reclaiming their *ship ship* at the gate. They took the short walk back to the house through vineyards pregnant with fruit and the doves sailed back to roost.

Maryam's Uncle Eid arrived and greeted them with the obligatory handshake and kisses, reserving a kiss on the nose and a hug for Farhan, his elder brother.

'The marriage will be blessed in heaven,' Eid said, patting Nader on the back.

'*Alhamdulillah*,' they all replied in unison. The cousins were out in force exchanging news and renewing bonds. Many hadn't seen each other for a while: they were scattered around the country, either serving with the forces or studying at the many universities and colleges built during the boom years of the eighties.

In the lounge they drank *qahwah* – Arabic coffee from porcelain cups without handles. The green liquid released an aroma of ground cardamom and rose water. Trays of dates did the rounds followed by almond cookies.

In the adjoining room Nader and Mona sipped coffee and waited for Maryam and Aishah. Turki came bounding in and announced, 'They're coming, they're coming!'

Nader had known the family all his life and remembered Maryam as a delicate child with a sallow complexion. He had last seen her when she was eleven or twelve – just before she took to wearing the veil, a sign of having reached puberty. Mona and his other sisters had likened her to a fresh flower. They talked of her beauty as women do.

'Oh yes, she is beautiful and intelligent, a good Muslim and a great cook. You'll like her,' they assured him. 'She will make a good wife.'

Khadijah, his mother, had never liked Maryam or her family for as long as he could remember. Perhaps it was their wealth she was jealous of, or Farhan's position. Perhaps she despised Aishah, as she was not a Saudi. She never gave a reason. 'He is not your uncle, and she is not your aunt,' she would admonish waving her henna dyed finger at them. 'I don't want you to have anything to do with them; they're not decent people.' Her behaviour puzzled them but no one questioned her, fearing her wrath. She was their mother and knew best. The girls had attended the same school and later the same college. They often met with Maryam in the *souq* for shopping forays.

When his father Talal announced a week ago what he and Farhan had agreed to some thirty years earlier, his mother had withdrawn, refusing to eat or talk to anyone. The two friends had agreed Nader would wed Maryam and that was that. It was only when he threatened Khadijah with divorce that she relented but refused to accompany them.

Aishah and Maryam arrived and Nader and Mona rose to greet them. Mona embraced and kissed the two women and Nader shook their hands. Maryam didn't wear a veil today, as was the custom. For a moment Nader didn't recognise the girl that he had known years ago. Gone were the sallow complexion and shy demeanour. Her skin glowed with health and her face radiated confidence. In her purple dress and the cream satin scarf that covered her hair, Maryam was a woman of beauty. A woman he could call his own. Untouched by another man. She would be his to have whenever he chose and however often. His sisters had been justified in describing her as a fresh flower. Their failure lay only in not naming the flower. Maryam was a heady mixture of an orchid suffused with the serenity of the water lily, touched by the vibrancy of the red rose, wedded to the delicate jasmine. He knew she was everything a woman should be. Above all she would be his until he chose otherwise.

Maryam blushed and turned away, unprepared for Nader's attention. She had seen him from afar when he came to collect his sisters at the college or visited her brother, Nabeel, but now he was at arm's length and she was without a veil. They exchanged greetings and sat down on the cushioned floor.

'Mama couldn't come. She's been ill,' Mona apologized.

'Sorry to hear that,' replied Aishah coldly.

'May Allah speed her recovery!' Maryam wished.

'*Alhamdulillah*,' Mona and Aishah chorused.

With a practiced movement Nader flipped the ends of his *gutra* over his head and was the first to speak.

'I am chief of housekeeping at the military hospital,' he said with pride.

'*Alhamdulillah*' chorused the women.

Stroking his goatee he continued, 'I work with the *imam* converting infidels to Islam. Our beloved King rewards them with money and the hospital renews their contracts.'

Maryam studied the solemn face, marked with the ravages of smallpox that gave his skin the texture of beaten copper. He had a dark patch the size of a *halala* coin in the centre of his forehead caused through bowing to Allah.

His green eyes, speckled with flecks of amber and grey, reminded her of Uncle Mahmoud. They smouldered with excitement when he mentioned Afghanistan.

'For ten years I was a *mujahideen*, fighting the Holy *Jihad* against the Russian unbelievers.'

'You were so courageous,' Aishah said.

Maryam watched the ivory *misbaha* winding and unwinding around Nader's index finger with a clicking sound that disturbed her.

Relating the tragedy that had befallen the Afghani people, his hands gripped the air, squeezing, moulding, tearing and dismembering it, as though it was the enemy. A shiver ran down Maryam's spine and a subdued *Bismillah* escaped her lips.

Mona glowed with pride as she listened to her brother.

The other women looked at each other, overwhelmed by Nader's personality. Maryam knew men were supposed to be strong but her whole being felt suffocated.

Aishah watched the man she had nursed as a boy. He had changed so much. Then he had been a helpless, frightened child suffering in silence. Now he was a lion with a purpose. For her, Nader would always be the little boy she loved as her own son. There had been something special in his eyes that had touched her and bound them together. She was proud of him when he joined the *mujahideen* to fight for her country, the country that she and her family had left behind so many years ago. At the same time she felt a deep sense of loss. She had prayed for his safety and rejoiced at his return. She watched in frustration, unable to speak out, being a woman in a man's world and a stranger in a foreign land.

The Motorola pager bleated.

'Technology!' he cursed and silenced it once more, checking for any message. There was only a series of numbers.

Zelpha brought fresh coffee, mint tea and an assortment of Arabic sweets and pastries. Aishah had prepared Maryam's favourite *shubbak al habayb* – meaning lover's window – dusted with icing sugar.

'These are the specialty of the house,' Maryam said and offered them to Nader. They all laughed. With the tension eased Maryam spoke in a measured voice, her eyes fixed to the floor in front of Nader's feet.

'I am studying now,' she began. 'I would like to go on to teach one day.'

'Which college?' Nader interrupted, knowing Mona was Maryam's classmate.

'Ideally King Abdul Aziz Girls College.'

Nader nodded his approval.

'I would like to complete my studies before having children. That would mean after a year, if it were convenient,' she added, feeling Nader's gaze.

'Education is so important these days, don't you think, Nader?' Aishah asked.

Nader stopped swinging his prayer beads and adjusted his *gutra*. He folded his arms across his chest and smiled.

'Of course education is important,' he said, brushing aside the idea with his hand. 'A wife must first serve Allah and then her husband, bringing up his children.'

'I study the *Qur'an* every day,' Maryam said.

'*Alhamdulillah*. It cleanses our minds and teaches us how to live.'

'*Alhamdulillah*,' Maryam replied staring into her cup of coffee.

Turki sat crossed-legged beside his beloved aunt, elbows resting on his knees. Every now and then he nibbled at a cookie, tapped it free of crumbs and took a sip of tea imitating the grown-ups. His eyes soaked in every movement Nader made. Some day he too would be seated in front of a beautiful woman, recounting his adventures, achievements and aspirations, hoping to impress her and win her hand in marriage.

Zelpha returned swathed in a cloud of smoke carrying a gilded *mabkhara*. They fanned the smoke from the frankincense towards them and inhaled as she passed by.

'I would like to travel abroad. Perhaps study for my Masters degree in America,' Maryam said, avoiding Nader's eyes.

'*Insha'allah*,' Nader replied. 'America has much to offer,' he continued and chewed the inside of his cheek.

'I'm so pleased you agree. Travel and education are very dear to me,' Maryam said and offered Nader another *shubbak al habayb*.

'I'd like to give you this,' Nader said, pulling out a red box from his pocket.

'It's so beautiful,' Maryam gasped, seeing the diamond perched on a platinum band.

'Put it on,' Mona said, and leant forward to look.

'Let me,' Nader said, and Maryam obliged, offering her hand.

Farhan entered, followed by Eid and Talal. The women turned quickly away and covered their faces.

Seeing the ring on Maryam's finger, they chorused '*Alhamdulillah*,' in unison. This was the *khutba*, the engagement. The *Akd Al-Nikah*, bond of marriage, would follow later, in front of the religious *Sheikh*. Nader would pay part of the dowry now and the rest when he and Maryam wed in a year's time. He was now free to visit her without a chaperone.

The men retreated to the Bedouin tent in the garden and the cool evening air. A miniature replica of the façade of the Treasury at Petra served as a fireplace. On a red carpet, green and blue mattresses littered with cushions hugged the wall. On four platters, mountains of jasmine-scented rice decked with chunks of lamb beckoned them to feast. From each platter a sheep's head surveyed the gathering through bulging eyes and grimaced, its mouth jacked open by a whole lemon. Fresh chilli sauce, steaming okra and lentils in china bowls awaited the diners.

Farhan, Eid, Mahmoud, Talal, Nader and Turki squeezed around one platter while the cousins and workers from the farm gathered around the others. With a *Bismillah al-Rahman al-Rahim* – in the name of Allah, the Merciful, the Mercy-giving – they dived into the food, using only their right hand. Fingers tore into greasy flesh and mixed it with rice and chilli sauce, moulding it into balls before popping it into their mouths.

'Try this, Nader, it's the best part,' Farhan said and offered him a morsel from the cheekbone.

Grains of rice clung to beards and the air was filled with the sound of chewing, punctuated by the occasional belch and *Bismillah!*

Nader's pager bleated again.

'That thing is worst than a nagging woman!' snapped Farhan.

'Nothing's worse than a nagging woman!' Eid said and everyone laughed.

Slices of melon fell victim to the second onslaught. Thumbs and fingers dug out the black seeds and juice trickled down the arms staining the sleeves. They quenched their thirst on water, *laban* and orange juice.

Conversation returned. They joked about the day they had met their wives for the first time. How frightened they had been and so very young.

'In those days you had to trust the judgement of your mother and sisters,' Farhan said. 'You saw the girl's face *after* you were married.'

'Of course there were ways around this. I first saw my wife's face through the keyhole of my sister's wardrobe,' Talal explained.

'You cunning devil,' Eid chuckled.

'She forgot about me for hours. The excitement was too much for my bladder.'

'Serves you right,' Farhan teased and everyone roared except Turki, who couldn't see the funny side.

Rice grains and melon seeds lay scattered like confetti on the plastic sheet covering the red carpet. Bones and date stones shared neat piles with orange pips and grape seeds. One by one they shook their hands free from the clinging food and wandered off into the night to wash their hands.

* * *

Plumes of aromatic smoke climbed skyward from a city of *shisha* pipes, spindly columns of turned wood gilded in silver and gold. The sound of rumbling rose like the hum of distant traffic as air gurgled through cold water. The men relaxed on cushions and made playful conversation between puffs of *mu'assel* – tobacco laced with honey and sips of cardamom *qahwah*.

A sickle moon swept across the night sky harvesting a crop of stars.

Turki lay beside Farhan.

'That's Mars, our nearest neighbour,' Farhan said and pointed to a red spot near the horizon. That up there is the North Star that people used to sail the oceans.' Every twinkling light looked the same to Turki but he nodded anyway.

'I want to go there,' Turki said pointing to the moon.

'*Insha'allah*, when you're older,' Farhan replied and gave the boy a pat on the head. 'You're just like your father.'

'Has anyone been there?' Turki asked.

'The *Ameriki* have and a Saudi prince went into space.'

'Do I have to be a prince, Grandpa?'

'You are, *habibi*.'

* * *

The women feasted indoors to the sound of music and riotous children. Like the men, they sat on the carpet covered by a plastic sheet, eating from platters. Some children sat with their mothers or elder sisters, others protested between mouthfuls and wide-eyed babies latched onto their mother's breasts like milking machines, oblivious to the world.

Aishah's girls were kept busy replenishing empty glasses with water, fruit juices and *laban*. They ran after toddlers while their mothers gorged, washed their sticky fingers and wiped faces, all the while smiling and laughing, practicing their Arabic.

Murmuring '*Alhamdulillah*,' one by one, the guests retired to the lounge after washing their hands. They all inspected and approved Maryam's engagement ring.

'If there's one time that size matters, it's here,' a cousin said pointing at her own diamond ring, 'The bigger the better.'

'You've done okay, Maryam,' said another cousin raising Maryam's hand to get a better look.

Tea and coffee followed and Zelpha did the rounds with the smoking *mabkhara*. She left it in the middle of the room and the guests took turns standing over it, raising their voluminous skirts to let the smoke infuse their fine clothes.

Mona had brought some tapes of Huda and Latifa, two popular Egyptian singers. They all knew the words and sang along, swaying to the rhythm while seated on the cushioned floor, sipping tea. Zelpha, Imelda and Josi improvised a disco version and everyone joined in, infected by their enthusiasm.

Feeling the moment was right, Mona slipped a cassette of rhythmic music into the machine and took to the floor with Maryam. Maryam loved to dance. It was one of the few activities she could do in her bedroom without breaking some *Qur'anic* law.

To the beat of the drums and the melody of the flute her hips swayed from side to side. With arms arched high above her head, her henna-painted hands worked the air with grace. With eyes half shut she escaped into a dream world, smiling. Oh how good it felt to be alive! she thought, letting the harmony of the music flow through her.

Everyone applauded. Aishah watched her daughter with pride and wished Allah had blessed her with another.

'Come, Mama, dance with me,' Maryam called.

'I like to watch you, *habibi*,' Aishah suppressed the anger that welled in her from the morning's events. Why had she not been consulted? Soon a year would pass and her girl would be gone.

'Come, Mama!' Maryam said and pulled her mother on to the floor.

'I'm too old for this!' Aishah protested and wiggled her hips to everyone's delight.

The hours slipped by and the guests drifted away a family at a time. Mona and her sisters were the last to leave.

'Do you like him?' Mona asked Maryam, walking with her arm in arm to the door.

'He's changed so much,' Maryam replied.

'War does that to you.'

'I guess so.'

'But he's a good Muslim.'

'I'm sure we'll get on well,' Maryam said and hugged Mona.

* * *

Turki sat naked in bed, his legs tucked under the bedclothes watching Maryam brush her hair.

'That was a wonderful day. Did you enjoy it?' she asked.

Turki nodded, sucking on his thumb.

'Auntie Miri, I don't want my teeth out,' he said, remembering their trip to the hospital.

'Didn't you like Dr Joe?'

'It will hurt.'

'I am sure he's gentle,' she paused. 'Have you brushed your teeth?'

Turki hid his head under the covers in shame.

'Up you get right now!' Maryam ordered.

Turki jumped out of bed and disappeared to the bathroom pulling a face. Maryam smiled at the sound of his furious brushing.

'Do you like him?' Turki asked after flashing his teeth for inspection and climbing into bed.

'We got engaged today, silly, look!' Maryam showed him her ring.

'He likes you.'

'I hope so.'

'Will you marry him too?'

'Who?'

'Dr Joe.'

'Dr Joe! What makes you say that?' Maryam asked.

Turki thought for a while. 'I just know.'

'Oh, do you, young man?' Maryam teased and pinched his cheeks.

'He likes you more then Nader.' Turki continued. Maryam blushed and laughed at Turki's frankness.

'Now off to sleep,' Maryam said and kissed him goodnight.

It had been an exhausting day. She had thought of Dr Joe on the way back from the hospital. She couldn't deny she had felt the warmth in his voice and seen the sincerity in his eyes that seem to beckon her. He reminded her of Brad Pitt, with well-defined features – and not hidden beneath a carpet of hair. Her classmates, Samar and Sahar, said Brad Pitt was hot. So Dr Joe must be hot too, Maryam thought and giggled to herself. Dr Joe had a personality she found attractive and didn't feel threatened by. Perhaps it was because she was in control from behind her veil and he had nothing to prove.

She knew nothing about him except that he came from America. She gave a whimsical laugh and climbed into bed. Why was she so preoccupied with someone she had met once and would probably never meet again? He was an infidel, a foreigner and, besides, their worlds would never. . . her thoughts drifted off.

In a year's time she would be married to Nader, a devout Muslim and a successful man, chosen by her father. He promised to build a beautiful house for them and to let her study in America. He was handsome in a certain way but there was some-thing very raw about him. She felt unable to look into his eyes, perhaps even afraid to. Yes, afraid, but of what? She couldn't say – only that the feeling had been strong and there was no denying it. Perhaps it was his time with the *mujahideen* that had made him what he was today and Arab men were never at ease with women. Perhaps she might have felt more comfortable had she worn a veil, but at the engagement he was allowed to see her face as the Prophet had decreed. Love would grow through the *Qur'an* and her family and she would come to love him and give him many sons, she told herself.

'You're a naughty boy, Turki,' Maryam whispered and ruffled his hair as he slept. She brushed aside thoughts of Joe and succumbed to sleep.

SIX

Nader cursed and punched the keys on the phone. He let it ring three times and hung up. He redialled and let it ring five times and hung up. He repeated his actions for the third time. On the second ring a voice hissed in Pashto, 'It's a full moon.'

'The stars are bright,' Nader replied.

'There are dark clouds and the leopard stalks tonight.'

Nader knew something was wrong. He shut the library door and headed for the garden.

'Is everything alright?' Aishah called out, catching sight of him in the hallway.

'It's the hospital,' Nader replied, patting the pager in his pocket. 'A VIP is complaining about his room. I'll have to go sort it out.'

'You work too hard.' Aishah shook her head.

It was past midnight when Nader turned onto Medinah Road and headed for Tabuk. He drove with haste knowing there would be no traffic police patrolling the road at this time of the night.

Nearing his destination, Nader cut the headlights and engine and walked the last hundred metres to the entrance of a walled garden: Al-Busteen.

This oasis of tranquillity lay in the shadows of the old Turkish fort. A *shisha* den, a place for men to while away the evenings, relinquishing responsibilities to the gurgling water pipe and the heady mixture of tobacco and other substances that freed the mind from the body. A sanctuary from screaming children and nagging wives. This was the meeting place of Islamic scholars, businessmen and political dreamers.

Under the date palms lay alcoves surrounded by a low wall and furnished with a cheap carpet and sausage-shaped pillows. A gravel path bordered by cobblestones snaked between the trees, a conduit for waiters and guests. Fluorescent tubes threw out a cold, blue glow.

Nader walked through the bougainvillea-covered archway and spied a few lingerers. He nodded a greeting to the waiter and made for the tent leaning against the fortress wall. Raising a flap at the rear, he stumbled into the darkness, waited a moment for his eyes to adjust and picked his way along a narrow passage and down some steps. He heard voices, recognised words and then sentences.

Nader turned a corner and entered the dungeon. Darkness evaporated with a hiss. A gas lantern in the middle of the floor threw long shadows onto the damp walls. There were five men. Two were seated on their haunches around the lantern, puffing at cigarettes, another propped up the wall and another lay on a mat with his legs crossed. They all wore baggy trousers and long shirts, the traditional costume of Afghanistan.

Nader recognised them all – except for the one huddled in a corner, gagged and with his hands tied behind his back.

The seated figures rose and greeted him in Pashtu. Abdul Haq and Abdul Kabir were identical twins. Abdul Kabir was the elder of the two by a few minutes and that was why he was named *Kabir*, meaning big. Yusuf was the quiet one who picked his teeth with a broken matchstick while the hulking giant Ahmed Shah leaned against the wall chewing a wad of tobacco. Every now and then he spat a reddish liquid, adding a splash of colour to the yellow sandstone.

'Who is this?' asked Nader, tossing his head towards the stranger.

'The boy came to me with a pair of new shoes for re-soling.' Abdul Kabir said. 'I thought he must have forgotten the money so I placed the usual package inside them and asked for the money when he returned.'

'You dumb ass!' shouted Nader.

'The boy went crazy, shouted abuse, grabbed the shoes and fled before I could recover the package. He must have found the drugs and followed me here,' Abdul Kabir explained.

'How can you be so stupid? I've told you, no money no deal!' Nader bellowed, and his anger reverberated through the walls.

'That's not all,' rumbled Ahmed Shah, and threw a wallet to Nader. 'He's one of them, *Al-Mabahith al-Amma*. The secret police.'

'It can't get any worse,' Nader mumbled, examining the contents of the wallet and the photo ID card.

'There's three thousand *riyals*,' said Ahmed Shah.

Nader let out a whistle, 'They must be desperate to recruit schoolboys and pay so well.' No one spoke. Nader assessed the damage. He walked over to the huddled figure and stared into his frightened eyes.

'How much does he know?' Nader barked in Pashtu.

'Enough,' replied Yusuf in a gravelly voice.

'He's a boy.' Abdul Kabir stated the obvious.

'Shut the fuck up! This is all your doing! When did you go soft?' Nader spat.

'We can't take any chances, he has to go,' Yusuf said with the coldness of an assassin.

'There's no choice,' Abdul Haq added.

'No knives,' Nader ordered, looking at Yusuf who had a penchant for using the stiletto. 'Make it look like an accident. Don't fuck up.' With that he left, muttering insults at them. 'And don't touch the money!' his voice echoed down the passage.

Two days later Nader heard through his informant, a police lieutenant, that a boy's body was found in the reservoir behind the Armour Institute with a large sum of money. Foul play was not suspected. It seemed he had drowned.

Poor fucker, Nader thought and dismissed the whole thing.

Seven

Turki sobbed through the night, clinging to Maryam for comfort, his face buried in her bosom. Tears soaked through her nightdress, wetting her breasts. Maryam fondled his penis but that didn't help. The pain would subside for a moment, she would feel the tension ease and then, with a shudder, he would let forth another pitiful wail that would have moved a murderer.

Dr Joe's predictions had come true. There was no other solution; the front teeth would have to go. Maryam decided they would have to see him first thing that morning.

Breakfast was a hurried affair. Turki refused to eat and Maryam threw on the rudiments of make-up before leaving. They found Mahmoud waiting for them in the Suburban to drive them to the hospital.

The journey was slow. The police were checking car registrations and personal credentials. A private would look at Mahmoud's documents and ask some questions, then pass them on to a corporal who would repeat the performance, then hand them to an officer who would wave them through with a look of indignation.

Mahmoud cursed under his breath.

In the back seat, Turki sobbed and sucked on his thumb.

When they arrived at the clinic, Abdullah escorted them into Joe's surgery and left.

'Sorry we're late, Dr Joe,' Maryam said.

'Checkpoints?' Joe asked.

Maryam nodded and raised her veil. For a moment shorter than a heartbeat, their eyes met and a whisper of a smile crossed Maryam's lips. Deep inside her a candle flickered into life. Joe extended his hand and Maryam offered her gloved one in return. Theirs was a slow firm handshake, unlike the usual brushing of the palms that Saudis practiced to perfection.

Maryam drew up a chair and held Turki's hand.

'Have you had breakfast, young man?' Joe asked, remembering Turki liked to bite. Turki attempted to laugh but tears trickled down wet cheeks.

'It'll be all right, *habibi*,' Maryam said, stroking his hand. Turki's lips trembled.

'Well, let's see what we have here,' Joe announced picking up a dental mirror.

'The front teeth are in bad shape. We really need to do something about them today,' he said, looking up at Maryam. She nodded in agreement.

Joe showed Turki a mask and explained what it did.

'It is like the ones that pilots wear,' Turki mumbled.

'That's right. You can be a pilot, Turki. Take some deep breaths,' Joe asked and placed the mask over Turki's nose. A few moments later the trembling stopped and the pain evaporated.

'Thank you, Dr Joe.' Maryam smiled.

The rest of the procedure was simple and soon Turki was sitting up, a gauze pack where his front teeth had been and free of pain. Maryam offered her gloved hand and Joe took it, each giving the other a squeeze that transgressed the realms of courtesy. Their eyes spoke a common language.

'Well, I think we should complete the rest of the treatment sooner rather then later,' Joe advised. Maryam nodded, she didn't want another sleepless night.

'Feeling okay, young man?' Joe asked his patient and Turki nodded. Tess offered Turki a sticker saying 'I was brave.'

'*Shukran*, thank you, Dr Joe,' Maryam said in her dulcet voice and left with Turki in tow.

'She's beautiful,' Tess said from the back of the room over the clatter of instruments being washed.

'She's all that and more,' Joe responded, hardly realising what he was saying.

'Do you know her name, Dr Joe?'

'How should I? I've just met her.'

'Oh, come on, doctor, you've more than met,' Tess said with a twinkle in her eyes.

'I suppose you do. . . know her name.'

'As a matter of fact I do. How much is it worth to you?' Tess taunted.

'Money, money, money. It's always about money.'

Tess smiled. 'It's Maryam,' she whispered.

'Maryam. What a perfect name!'

'Be careful, doctor.'

'Careful?'

'Yes, very careful. They play by different rules here and you're a long, long way from home. Besides. . .'

'Besides what?'

'Oh, nothing, doctor.'

'Tell me. Besides what, Tess?'

'Besides you're not one of them, doctor. You're not a Muslim. It's *haram*. It's forbidden.'

EIGHT

A plume of smoke rose as the wheels of flight SV1638 from Jeddah hit the tarmac and thundered down the runway. The 735 eased to a crawl before turning towards the cluster of buildings that was the airport terminal.

In the arrival hall Farhan and Mahmoud craned their necks to catch a glimpse of Nabeel and his new wife.

All he had said was that he had married an *Ameriki* and they would be home soon. They heard of his arrival that morning when he phoned from Jeddah airport prior to departure. Nabeel hadn't changed; still inconsiderate and self-centered. Of course they were all delighted that he was returning home and Aishah was looking forward to having him back. She knew it was un-Islamic to have a favourite child but she would explain herself on Judgement Day. When she heard Nabeel had found a wife she was overjoyed. This would put a stop to the rumours that had circulated over the years.

Two foreign workers in orange boiler suits manoeuvred the stairs under the open aircraft door, directed by the female Egyptian flight attendant dressed in a turquoise and blue uniform. Soon a stream of men in *thobes* with vinyl attaché cases, foreigners in shirts and trousers and women in *abayas* clutching handbags descended the stairs.

Farhan scanned the faces for Nabeel. Perhaps he had grown a beard at last? The trickle of passengers dried up. Perhaps he had missed the plane? Knowing Nabeel, that was not at all improbable.

The crowd was thinning as the hall emptied. A herd of leather suitcases cruised around on the conveyor belt waiting for their owners. Farhan glanced at the plane one last time. Nabeel stood framed in the doorway in a cream suit. He had matching shoes, a black shirt and Ray Bans. To top it all he wore a Panama hat. A diamond stud parked on his left earlobe sparkled in the sunlight. Yes, Nabeel had changed, Farhan could see – but for the worse. He had left in a *thobe* and *gutra* and returned in a suit and hat. America had taken yet another son of Saudi Arabia, reconditioned him and sent him back. As if reading his thoughts, Mahmoud placed a hand on Farhan's shoulder to caution restraint.

Nabeel skipped down the steps clutching plastic bags adorned with the Harrods logo. Farhan stepped onto the tarmac. A solider in airforce blue snapped to attention and saluted. Nabeel hurried over, joy on his face. Dropping the bags at their feet, he kissed and hugged his father and uncle. Farhan's features thawed a little.

'Where have you hidden your wife?' Farhan asked.

A woman in a canary yellow, knee-length dress that hugged her body stepped from the plane. She stood at the top of the stairs and surveyed the view. She shook her head, sending red tresses cascading around her shoulders. Ray Bans shielded her eyes and scarlet lips blossomed into a smile when she spotted Nabeel. She waved and the diamond ring on her finger sparkled in the sunlight.

She tick-tocked down the steps in her stiletto heels, rolling her hips. Halfway down the stairs she paused and waved in Nabeel's direction. Farhan knew that a hundred pairs of eyes would be undressing her, each one feasting on their favoured spot. She stretched like a cat as she reached the bottom of the stairs. 'Oooh!' she purred, 'that feels so gooood! Have a good day, boys,' she said to the two ground staff who were gawping at her.

Farhan was absorbed by her movement. Part of him was

nauseated but another part revelled in the performance. His face hardened as the woman approached.

'Saffron Al Balawi,' she said offering her hand, 'but you can call me Saffron if you like.' She giggled. Farhan couldn't believe his ears. No woman had ever introduced herself using his name and in that manner, yet there was something endearing about it.

'Normally the wife keeps her father's name in our country,' Farhan said, extending his hand. Everyone laughed at Saffron's gaffe and shook hands on the tarmac.

A dumpy man with a scraggy beard, wearing a *thobe* two sizes too short approached them wielding a bamboo cane.

'Get this whore under an *abaya*!' he screamed. He stabbed his finger into Nabeel's chest and grabbed his Armani jacket. 'What do you call this? Where is your *thobe*? Have you lost your identity?' He sprayed everyone with his spit like an angry camel. 'No self-respecting Muslim would be seen dead with this whore,' he said and spat in Saffron's direction. 'Aren't Saudi women good enough for you?' The glint of gold around Nabeel's neck caught the man's eye.

'And what's this?' he shouted and snatched the chain off Nabeel, scratching his chest.

'It's *haram* by Allah. When did you last read the *Qur'an*?'

A crowd of soldiers and airport workers gathered around hearing the commotion. Farhan had seen and heard enough. When the man attacked his son, that was an attack on him and when he attacked Saffron that was an attack on his family too. He knew how to deal with this *mutawah*. A good Muslim would not behave in such a manner.

He greeted the man like a brother, welcoming him with open arms, shaking his hand.

'What's your name?' Farhan asked and led him away from the crowd.

'Mohammed,' replied the man.

'Do you know who I am, Mohammed?' Farhan asked and Mohammed shook his head.

'I thought not! I am Major General Farhan Al Balawi, Area Commander of the Northwest Frontier Province and right now you are trespassing on my turf.' Farhan watched fear seep into Mohammed's eyes. He babbled an apology as a soldier escorted him away.

'Ten days away from his wife should instil some manners,' Farhan said and climbed into the car.

With Mahmoud at the wheel the DeVille d'Elegance cruised down the airport road with its rows of date palms and clusters of lights. It wound past King Faisal Air Force Base and round an aging Lighting fighter jet stuck in the middle of a roundabout pointing heavenward. They turned right past the white-walled palace onto Medinah Road and headed home.

The state of the art climate control did nothing to thaw the frosty silence that filled the car. Saffron stared out of the window feeling isolated and vulnerable after the commotion at the airport. Everything was a blur. Mahmoud pointed out the new building that had gone up during Nabeel's absence. Nabeel grunted and continued to sulk. Farhan fiddled with his *misbaha*.

This was not a good start in this very foreign country with strange rules, Saffron told herself. What had she signed up for? Her mind went into overdrive and damage control.

'Nice Cadillac,' she said, turning to face Farhan.

'I prefer my Land Cruiser,' Farhan replied flatly.

'They are my favourite too,' Saffron gave an endearing smile. She preferred a Merc SL with a soft top but that was in California.

Farhan's features softened and he stopped fidgeting with his *misbaha*.

'I'm really sorry. . .' Saffron began, crossing her legs, causing her skirt to ride higher.

'It's over, there's no. . .' Farhan began.

'No! No! It's my fault.' Saffron interrupted.

'And how's that?' Farhan asked.

'Nabeel insisted I wear. . . that, that black thing but. . .'

'*Abaya*,' Farhan added.

'Yes, that's it, but. . .'

'Why didn't you?' Farhan snapped.

'Because it's so hot,' she said throwing up her arms, putting on her best I-am-just-a-helpless-woman performance. It never failed and it worked like a charm with Farhan.

'No need to apologise.'

'But I must, I really must, Mr. . . sorry, General Al Balawi.'

Farhan caught sight of her garters. Saffron saw him smile and knew she had won. You may be a general but you're a man first and you've lost the battle before it's begun, she told herself.

'These things happen,' Farhan muttered and continued to fidget with the *misbaha*. There was an audible pause; the ball was in Farhan's court and Saffron could feel his mind ticking, weighing up the offer.

'We'll have to get you something to cover these,' Farhan said patting her knee. 'At least in public,' he added as an afterthought.

They smiled, each thinking they had won.

Her mother always said, '*Life is a trade-off,*' and she wasn't far wrong as long as you had something to trade. '*If you're a woman you've power,*' she used to say. '*Just be sure you know how to use it.*' The words brought a smile to Saffron's lips.

They sat back and enjoyed the ride, the tension gone, both planning their next move, making small talk, feeling the other out.

* * *

The car pulled up in front of the house and two women and a boy came out to welcome them.

'Holy shit, this is one hell of a pile you've got here,' Saffron exclaimed, turning to Farhan.

'Come, let me introduce you to my family.' Farhan took her by the elbow.

'This is my wife Aishah, and my daughter Maryam, you must

be around the same age. And this is my grandson Turki.' He picked up the boy and put him on his shoulders.

'*Ahlan, alhan, alhan*,' repeated Aishah kissing Saffron on the cheeks over and over again. Nabeel had warned her of this custom and she reciprocated. Saffron tried out the Arabic greetings Nabeel had taught her.

'*Asslam alekum*. Peace be upon you. *Kayf haalak?* How are you?' Turki giggled at Saffron's attempt from behind Farhan's head.

'*Alhamdulillah, Alhamdulillah*,' Aishah praised Allah for Nabeel's return. Putting her arms around the two she marched them into the house and out of the heat.

'Stand still, *habibi*, let me have a look at you! You're all skin and bones. Don't they have *kabsa* in America?' Aishah asked. 'Sit beside me and tell me about your adventures. When did you get married? Where did you find her? Is she pregnant yet? You must have lots of children,' she said eyeing Saffron.

'Mama. . .' Nabeel tried to get a word in but couldn't.

'She is strong. She will give you many sons like I gave your father. My goodness, what happened to you?' she asked seeing the welt on his neck. Nabeel didn't know where to start. Farhan came to his rescue.

'Questions, questions, leave the poor boy alone, woman. Can't you see he's tired?' Farhan said.

Maryam took Saffron's hand and offered to show them to their rooms in the guest wing.

'Freshen up and we'll have lunch, I've made *kabsa*,' Aishah called after them.

*   *   *

The guest wing had three apartments, each with two bedrooms, a lounge, kitchen and dining room.

'Christ, this place is like a hotel!' exclaimed Saffron throwing herself on the king-size bed. I could force myself to like this, she told herself, gazing at the mosaic on the ceiling.

Nabeel shut the door behind him and screamed. 'You could've ruined everything, bitch! For fuck's sake do as I say next time. . . I pay you enough!'

For Saffron, enough was two hundred and fifty grand a year for four years plus expenses, no babies, no sex or taxes. Not bad for playing wife at twenty-two. She knew Nabeel had absorbed the *Ameriki* culture and all its facets. Swearing was one of his fortes and he practiced it whenever he could.

'I'm tired of all this shit, I'm going to have a nap,' Nabeel shouted and escaped into the adjoining bedroom slamming the door behind him.

Saffron gave him the middle finger salute. 'Up yours!' she hissed.

* * *

A few hours later Nabeel and Saffron entered the dining room together. Nabeel in a *thobe* and Saffron in a loose fitting black outfit trimmed with gold that Nabeel had bought her in Jeddah. Saffron caught Farhan's expression of approval mixed with disappointment and Aishah endorsed Saffron's choice of dress after hearing about their morning's adventure from Mahmoud. She had heard *Ameriki* girls were wild and vowed to keep a close eye on Saffron for the sake of her son and the family *Sharaf*.

NINE

A white Mercedes slid into King Abdul Aziz military cantonment without being challenged and made its way to the female quarters.

Two women in *abaya* slipped into the back seat. Heidi had been here many times; over the last few months it had become her second home. Kim didn't know what to expect and the nervousness showed on her face. Asking questions was dangerous. To survive in this game discretion was the key, a smile on your face and a clear head. Heidi had never worried about other Filipinas but Kim was not like them.

Blue velvet curtains screened them from the outside world as the car sped along King Abdul Aziz Avenue, down Al Imam Abdul Rahmen Road and along Airport Road to their final destination.

Towering walls and armed guards signalled they had arrived. An archway opened on to a courtyard and the two women disembarked.

A man appeared and relieved them of their *abaya*. Suliman, a man in his mid-fifties and Mr F's personal assistant of many years, greeted them in the hallway. Eyeing Kim up and down he approved of Nader's choice. He had seen them come and go but none had survived for long. Young boys, always very young, and foreign girls all came to stay only to be discarded eventually. There had been a Saudi boy called Nabeel who had lasted a while some years back but, like all the others, a younger model had replaced him.

Italian marble, Persian carpets, portraits of men in *bishts* and a chandelier was all Kim remembered of the hallway. There were no other paintings or works of art, only mirrored columns reflecting their every movement.

'I love all this,' Heidi said glancing over the room. 'It's a new experience every time.'

Kim took in the surroundings and frowned. She had experienced the luxury of five star hotels in Manila's Makati City. To her this was just another place for a sordid transaction. What was on sale remained the same.

Mr F stood five foot six inches in his handmade shoes and wore a neat moustache. He had an aura of arrogance that came from a belief in his destiny. His was a family that had survived where others had failed. They had murdered and been rewarded, stolen and been cherished, lied and been exalted, deceived and been forgiven. He was a man who smiled easily and welcomed the girls in English tinged with an American accent. His *thobe* of Egyptian cotton, gold Rolex watch and the Cartier pens in his breast pocket spoke a language both girls understood. He fondled his *misbaha*, a string of Tahitian pearls.

Heidi beamed at Mr F across an ocean of Persian carpet.

'Lovely to see you again, Heidi,' Mr F said greeting her with a kiss. 'And you must be Kim. I've heard so much about you.' He kissed her too.

'How do you like my country?' he asked. 'I am sure you will come to love it. You both look stunning!'

He clapped his hands and announced, 'Drinks.' A man waiting in the background materialized to take their orders. 'What would you like? We have everything!'

'I'll have my usual: Tequila Sunrise,' Heidi said in her German accent. The curtain was up and the performance had begun.

'And you, my dear Kim, what would you like?'

'I'll have the same, sir,' replied Kim.

'Sir? Kim, we are all friends here,' Mr F said, faking hurt.

'I'm so sorry, it's my first time.' Kim apologised.

'And it shan't be your last, my dear.'

'So you work at the hospital,' Mr F said, knowing full well that all his girls came from there. It had been Suliman's idea to tap into the ready supply of willing participants.

'They screen for everything under the sun – including HIV,' Suliman had explained to his boss. 'You can't be too careful these days.'

The Tequila Sunrise and Scotch on the rocks arrived on a silver platter with a complement of nuts and dried fruits.

'There's no finer drink on earth than single malt Scotch,' Mr F said raising his glass in a toast.

'Friends!'

They made conversation and Mr F practiced the Tagalog that he had learned from previous Filipina entertainers.

Kim felt her legs weaken and clung onto Mr F's arm making their way to the dining room. She must remember not to have the Tequila. . . whatever next time. They towered above him but he liked that. It gave him a real thrill to control tall, beautiful people.

Under crystal chandeliers they sat at a table that could accommodate fifty. Gold goblets danced with the Rosenthal porcelain and silver cutlery stretched out on a linen tablecloth. The scent of smouldering frankincense filled the room.

'Do you like champagne, Kim? Of course you do! Everyone I know likes champagne! If they don't, they soon acquire a taste or they don't know me.' Mr F thought this funny and laughed. 'Heidi can't get enough of the stuff, can you, darling?'

'I love it,' Heidi purred. 'Would bathe in it if I could.'

'Now that's a thought,' Mr F added and winked.

'It would be just divine, swimming in the drink of the Gods,' she said and winked back. Heidi believed sex without eroticism was a waste of energy. She couldn't remember who had said that what distinguished man from beasts was that the former did it to recreate and the latter did it to procreate. The actual act was great but it was the mental fuck that blew her brains out.

There were dishes from India, Lebanon, Pakistan and Thailand and they gorged themselves, readying for the orgy that was to follow.

After dinner they retired to the lounge for coffee and sweets. There was so much of everything, enough to feed her whole family for days, thought Kim. Mr F was on his third Scotch and Heidi stayed with the champagne. Kim took to the Arabic coffee. The hours ticked away as one cigarette died, another was lit. Tramlines of white powder on golden plates evaporated up nostrils distorting reality. Kim didn't try any.

Midnight came and went. Heidi had said things got started around one. Mr F read her thoughts and wobbled to his feet. With a girl on either arm, they headed for the bedroom.

They stepped into a room with a circular bed that took centre stage. A bank of TV screens covered one wall surrounding a mammoth screen in the middle, there were mirrors everywhere and dim lights created an illusion of warmth.

Kim's felt the rough embrace of Mr F's lips on hers and tried to pull away. His hands tore at her dress, ripping it from her, and in his eyes she saw his hunger and was afraid. She caught the reflection of her naked body in the ceiling mirror and gasped as she became the receptacle of Mr F's lust. For her it was always an act of deception, a performance measured in the number of moans and groans.

Exhausted but dissatisfied, Kim pulled away and watched as Heidi took charge. She performed under a spell, changing the tempo, to suit her needs, teasing, toying, speeding and slowing. Kim saw the pleasure written on Heidi's face and knew this was not the performance as it had been for her.

At sunrise, the *muezzin*'s call roused them from their slumber. After breakfast Suliman escorted them to the Mercedes, bidding farewell and inviting them again. A manila envelope awaited them on the leather seat. It was Mr F's way of saying thank you.

'We're a team.' Heidi squeezed Kim's thigh and kissed her cheek. Kim managed a smile, nauseous with guilt. She pulled back the curtain and peeked out as the car sped along tree-lined avenues and headed back to the military cantonment. This was her first glimpse of Tabuk.

'I always feel like a pawn,' Heidi said breaking the silence.

'A prawn?' Kim frowned and drew back the curtain.

'No, no. A pawn, it's my accent.' Heidi apologised.

Kim pondered for a while. 'You mean, like a rich man's plaything?' she said with scorn.

'Yah, you could put it like that, here today gone tomorrow.'

'That sounds so cold,' Kim said, looking glum.

'We need. . . they want. . . we supply. It's as simple as that,' Heidi explained.

'Yes. A simple formula,' Kim reflected.

'I think of it as a performance, helps me sleep at night,' Heidi said.

'Make believe you're someone else.'

'Right! That's how it is, an out of body experience.'

'And this erases our minds,' Kim said, tapping the envelope nestled in her lap. Heidi patted Kim's hand and they laughed.

Colonel Ghasib's party for his visiting VIPs went well. Regina, Jill and Bong were a hit even though the colonel was upset by Heidi's absence. Regina had saved the day with her leather gear, whip and Nazi uniform and the Iron Cross that hung over her cleavage. The VIPs loved her and invited her to Riyadh.

TEN

The hum of the air-conditioning filled the classroom as thirty girls dressed in a blue uniform and wearing headscarves listened to a man on a television screen conducting a chemistry experiment. An austere woman watched over them in silence from behind a desk. Maryam sat taking notes with Samar and her twin sister Sahar at the rear of the classroom.

'I wish he could show us in person,' Samar complained, fidgeting in her seat.

'What difference would that make?' Maryam hissed from behind her hand.

'It's more informative, I think, and besides, that's how they do things in America,' Samar replied.

'I've sent him a letter,' Sahar whispered in Maryam's ear.

'Sent who a letter?'

'Him,' she said pointing to the man on the screen.

'How did you do that?'

'I put it with my homework. No one knows except you and Samar.

Maryam looked shocked.

'You won't tell anyone will you?' Samar added, concern showing on her face.

'Of course not, silly, but what did you say?'

'Oh, the usual, you know,' Sahar said.

'The usual?'

'Told him he was handsome.'

'You what?'

'And that I came off every night thinking of him.'

Maryam blushed. 'You didn't?'

'Yes, she did,' Samar added, nodding.

'Why did you do that?'

'Maryam, *habibi*, you're so innocent. I want him and there isn't anyone else right now,' Sahar explained.

'Oh.'

'Besides he's Egyptian,'

'So?'

'They're supposed to be good.'

'Good?'

'Yeah. Good, as in good in bed, you know.'

'What if you get caught?'

'He'll get fired. It's so easy, *habibi*.' Samar smiled.

'Yes, of course,' Maryam whispered under her breath.

Maryam had known the twins for a few years. They were born in America when their father, a colonel in the Saudi Air Force was stationed there. They spoke English with an American accent and to Maryam they had that 'something' the others didn't have. She couldn't put her finger on what it was but they were different.

'What if he agrees to meet?'

'That's a dumb question, Maryam. Fuck him, of course!'

'Where?'

'I don't know, I'm sure he'll know somewhere safe. They do it all the time you know.'

'Do they?'

'Yes, of course. They're men.'

'What if he gives you a baby?'

'There's no chance of that. We're on the pill.' Samar grinned.

'Oh. . . I guess it's okay then.'

'You bet it's okay. Sex without a pill is like playing with a loaded gun and you die nine months later. They are ten *riyals* at the Pharmacy downtown – but we pay fifteen and the man doesn't ask questions.'

'It's safer than the rubber,' Sahar added.

'Rubber?'

'Condoms, silly. You've got a lot to learn, *habibi.*'

'Yes, I probably have,' Maryam muttered.

'Tell you next week.'

'Tell me what?'

'His answer, of course, when I get my homework back,' she said. The bell rang and the morning session ended. They piled into the courtyard waiting for their lift home.

Maryam looked at her watch for the tenth time in five minutes. Nabeel had promised to collect her but hadn't shown up. Uncle Mahmoud was never late. Tabuk had changed a lot in the two years Nabeel had been away, perhaps he had lost his way or forgotten, Maryam thought. She walked over to a group of girls deep in conversation.

'How is it?' asked one.

'Is it as good as they say?' asked another.

'Please tell us?' implored the first.

'Has he got a big one?' inquired a third, gesturing with her hands.

Abeer was seventeen and been married for a week. Her wedding night had been a nightmare. Knowing she was a virgin, her husband had forced himself upon her all night long. When she tried to push him away in pain, he had beaten her and her cries for mercy had spurred him on. There was nowhere to hide and no one to turn to. She would bring shame upon the family *Sharaf* if she returned home. Her father would send her back and her mother would shrug her shoulders and say that was the woman's lot. 'It'll get better, *habibi*,' is what she had heard her mother tell her elder sister who had married a year earlier. She would have to suffer in silence; give him what he wanted and bear his children.

Abeer put on a brave smile and told them what they wanted to hear. 'Yes, yes, he is big, and it was better than what they say.' She told them, she couldn't wait to get back home for more. They whooped and giggled. Maryam wasn't fooled. She could see the bruising the make-up had failed to conceal.

The girls left, leaving Abeer on her own. Tears ran down her cheeks. She didn't want to go home. How could life be so unkind? She thought. Her husband was her cousin and yet they had nothing in common except the family name.

Maryam placed a hand on Abeer's shoulder and made her jump. Their eyes met and Maryam saw the pain and hurt in her eyes. Fear had replaced the spark of youth that had glowed a week ago. Maryam tried but couldn't find words to express her sorrow. In the end she held Abeer's hand, her action speaking a thousand words.

A car horn tooted from over the wall, Abeer recognised it and gripped Maryam's hand. It was her husband. She pursed her lips, dropped her veil and walked out through the college gates without looking back.

Maryam felt anger and frustration coursing through her. It was hopeless, she was an outsider and a woman and there was nothing she could do. This was a man's world. They were all as trapped as she was in the college without Nabeel. Where was he? He should have been here half an hour ago. Perhaps he had been involved in an accident? There were no public phones at the college. The religious authorities had banned them, to prevent the girls from communicating with men. Accidents were common in Saudi Arabia: she had read in the newspaper that more people died from car accidents than from all other causes put together. Panic gripped her; she would have to ask the principal to phone home for her.

A familiar car horn sounded. It was Nabeel. Relief washed over her as anger took hold.

Nabeel greeted her with a grin.

Maryam climbed in and slammed the door shut.

'You're late. Where have you been?' she demanded.

'Got held up with friends, you know how it is,' Nabeel replied.

'No I don't know how it is. Tell me?'

'What's the big deal, little sister? You're a woman with nothing to do and nowhere to go.'

'You're selfish, Nabeel,' Maryam shouted.

'And you're an ungrateful bitch,' Nabeel yelled back and laughed.

* * *

Maryam lay in bed staring at the ceiling revisiting the events of the day. She closed her eyes trying to shut out the anger.

A crescent moon crossed her window, looked in, smiled and continued on its way vanishing out of sight. The trees sent messages of love with the breeze that came through the open window. Turki slept beside her, the sound of his breathing betrayed his presence.

She thought of Abeer being abused. Where was love in all this? Families uniting through marriage to serve the tribe. There was no room for love. To love was a crime, it corrupted the mind and led the body into temptation. There was obedience, servitude and loyalty. Disobedience was punished and the spirit of defiance crushed before it was born. How many lives had been wasted and how many dreams unrealised?

Would Turki be like his father, or like the old men with white beards hiding behind the *Qur'an*, with fear in their eyes, watching others watching them?

Maryam wondered what her purpose was. Was she an instrument of trade to repay a debt? Is that all she meant to her father? Was the essence of her being to fulfil the needs of a man she barely knew, bearing his children with the threat of divorce a breath away? What of Dr Joe? Since their last meeting, seldom a moment passed without him intruding into her thoughts. Something drew her to him but what, she couldn't say. They had hardly spoken but it seemed they had known each other forever.

What was she to do and where was it to take her?

Her thoughts turned to Saffron and her carefree ways. Maryam found them appealing. There was a person who didn't know where she was going but certainly knew where she came from. Her easygoing manners were a refreshing change from Maryam's stifled society. She admired Saffron's courage, leaving her home for a love in a foreign land. Maryam was sure she could never do that alone, she had not even seen the borders of her own country. Perhaps Saffron would understand her feelings. She would know if she was in love?

A cockerel crowed in the distance, Maryam whispered *Bismillah*. She sighed and fell sleep, escaping the unanswered questions for another day.

* * *

A fly sat sucking at the wound, draining the essence of his life. Then came another followed by another and yet another. Soon there was a squadron of them filling their hairy bellies with his blood. One raised its head and Nader saw the face of a man from the past who seemed to recognise him. Another fly turned and another familiar face came into view – and it was smiling. One by one, the flies turned to face him and each one had a face that brought back a memory. There were faces of men, women and children, all crying. Then the last fly turned. It was the closest and he could make out the facets of the eyes. This fly had no human head. It moved up his chest and sat preening its wings over his heart, its claws gripping the skin. Then it stopped and millions of blue black unblinking eyes watched and waited.

Nader hated flies: he tried to shoo them away but they hung on, digging their claws deeper into his skin. Why didn't they fly away? He slapped at them but they were still there when he raised his hand. *Leave me alone!* he screamed, *let me be!* Perspiration oozed from every pore of his body. Yellow, creamy liquid exuded a putrefying stench that burnt his nostrils and choked in his throat with every breath. What were they waiting for? Suddenly the nearest fly grew larger, fat on his blood, the head meta-morphosed and turned red. Horns appeared from the forehead and a face, half man, half goat, roared with demonic laughter. It was his face and he was the devil. The other faces, cold and white, formed a circle around the beast dancing and chanting his name. *Nader, Nader, Nader, Nader,* they chanted, slowly at first and then faster and faster until one name fused with another and became unrecognisable. The dancing grew frenzied. A clawed hand tore into his chest and ripped out his pulsating heart, nails punctured the organ and blood trickled down his arm.

Nader let out a scream that reverberated through the house and he sat up in bed shaking.

'Allah help me! Please Allah, help me. Forgive me! Oh please, please, forgive me. Have mercy,' he babbled like a child.

* * *

Tears streamed down Kim's cheeks leaving a damp patch on the pillow. Heidi's smiling face filled her mind and then the hard face of the Japanese businessman who had paid her so well, the man who had written her death sentence. Kim hated him and she hated herself. She was no different. If anything, she was worse.

Money had clouded her judgment and now she had Heidi's blood on her hands. For some reason she felt no remorse for Mr F. He was a man who used people, called them 'friends' to satisfy his needs. She hated Fawaz, the devout Muslim who never drank and didn't want sex. How many other Kims had he recruited? How many lives were at risk and when would it all end? These were desperate people determined to succeed at any cost. Money was not the issue. The prize was something much bigger: it was Saudi Arabia itself.

The thought of this frightened her. She was a pawn in a complex game where there were no rules and anyone who stood in the way got hurt. Nothing would stop them from killing her if they felt betrayed or even kill her family as a lesson to others. The thought of her innocent family slaughtered frightened her. It was too late for Heidi and she was sorry for that. If she could turn back the clock she would. She cursed her American father for deserting them.

*   *   *

Joe sat in his apartment nursing a glass of his homemade apricot wine. It tasted nothing like the real thing, but it was the nearest thing he could get under the circumstances. A little cloudy, he thought, holding the glass to the light, and perhaps a little too sweet for his liking. Maybe next time he would add less sugar and rack it one more time – or just let it settle on its own. He congratulated himself on his first attempt. The important thing was that it had a very pleasant effect on the senses after a long day at the office. A solitary lamp threw an amber glow into the room making it cosier than it really was. A poster by Vernet, titled *La Chasse au Lion*, was the sole adornment on the wall.

The heavy burden of school fees had driven him to Saudi Arabia, where there were no taxes. He had been promised a grand apartment but this had not materialised. Once you were on the plane, the recruiters knew you had no choice but to accept whatever they threw at you. The plane had landed at two in the morning. Tired and hungry he was shown to an apartment and told to sign on the dotted line before he could collapse into bed. That was some six months ago.

Joe sipped the wine and thought of Maryam. He knew nothing about her but felt there was something magical between them that transgressed the boundaries of culture and religion. A feeling he had not experienced since the day he kissed Sara at the back of the synagogue when he was just twelve. There had to be a way they could meet? But where, and how? To give up before he had tried was unthinkable. But then Tess's words returned to haunt him: *Be careful, doctor, you are a long way from home.*

ELEVEN

Ducking under sagging branches pregnant with fruit, Maryam and Nader strolled through the vineyard listening to the dying sounds of the day as the sun dipped towards the horizon. Bees hurried back to their hives and sparrows took their public bath, stirring up puffs of dust, chirping happily, exchanging the day's news in the dusk before turning in for the night. The scent of jasmine wafted over everything carried on currents of warm air rising from the sun-kissed ground.

They had little or nothing in common except that fate had brought them together through their fathers and now they were on a voyage of discovery.

'How was Afghanistan?' Maryam asked, curious to learn more about her mother's country.

'Like Taif. It's very rugged in some parts but not as green and flat and desolate in others. There are deep green valleys and dry sandy deserts just like ours.'

'Is there snow?'

'Plenty in winter, blocks the passes through the mountains.'

'Must be beautiful though.'

'Beautiful but cold. The skin can freeze to the barrel of a gun and come off. . . the old and the weak die in their sleep.'

'Oh, that's terrible!'

'Funny thing is you don't feel any pain and your blood freezes so you don't bleed.'

'How can you be so clinical?'

'It's not the cold that numbs you. It's looking death in the eye every day.'

'What made you go?'

'Our brothers needed help.'

'And you were victorious,' Maryam said.

'The cold, the mountains and our righteous cause defeated the Russians.'

'*Alhamdulillah.*'

'Without Allah we would all have perished,' Nader reflected stroking his beard.

'They're atheists?'

'Godless souls each and every one of them. The only good thing to come out of Russia is the Kalashnikov.'

'What's that?'

'It's a killing machine.' Nader smiled.

'Oh! And what about Tolstoy and Pasternak?' Maryam asked.

'Who are they?'

'Russian authors who wrote beautiful literature.'

'What use is that? Filling women's simple brains with stories isn't going to solve anything.'

'Nader, you big tease, stop being so serious,' Maryam laughed trying to lighten the conversation.

'Words don't bring about change!'

'Did you know it was Tolstoy who thought of bringing change through non-violence?'

'What does that mean?' Nader looked puzzled.

'Change through passive resistance. Like Martin Luther King and Gandhi.'

'Never heard anything so ridiculous,' Nader said sanctimoniously. 'Look what happened to them!'

Maryam bit her lip.

'Change comes out of the barrel of a gun.'

'*Alhamdulillah*, you're back safe,' Maryam said, changing the subject.

'There's much to do here,' Nader said.

'It must be exciting to be back.'

'Things haven't moved forward in ten years, but that doesn't mean it'll always be that way. The wind of change is blowing.'

'I'm looking forward to building a home with you.' Maryam picked a bunch of grapes and offered Nader some.

'Me too,' Nader replied popping a few into his mouth.

'Do you like them?' Maryam asked.

'So sweet.'

'*Alhamdulillah.*'

They entered the house, taking off their shoes at the door.

*   *   *

'Mama Aishah, I think the cookies are ready,' Saffron called. She spotted Aishah in the prayer room, watched a while and left feeling guilty for intruding into a private moment.

Aishah knelt and bowed till her head and nose kissed the floor and muttered her prayers. She sat up and continued praying with her eyes shut.

'I didn't mean to disturb you, Mama Aishah,' Saffron said when Aishah walked into the kitchen a little later.

'*Maalish, habibi.*'

'Is it prayer time already?'

'Not for another few hours,' Aishah replied glancing at her watch. 'Praying gives me strength and helps me to understand.'

'Understand?'

'Allah's will,' Aishah replied patting Saffron on the back.

Saffron smiled and opened the oven door.

'Use these.' Aishah offered Saffron the mittens.

'They smell divine.' Saffron pulled out the baking tray covered in golden cookies.

Aishah smiled, breathing in the aroma, 'I'll make some tea and then we can try some.'

Saffron looked at her creations with pride as Aishah filled the kettle with water. With tea made, they sat in the lounge munching cookies, exclaiming how tasty they were between mouthfuls.

'Have you not baked before?' Aishah asked.

'Never.'

'I have so much to teach you, *habibi*.'

'Mom wasn't one for baking. In America, everything comes out of a packet or a tin. Except for sunshine.'

'They always taste nicer when you've baked them yourself,' Aishah said, and helped herself to another cookie.

'Like picking your own fruit.'

'Farhan's mother taught me to bake in a stone oven.'

'That must have been tricky.'

'We ate burnt cookies for weeks.'

'I'll try my best not to put you through that,' Saffron said and they laughed.

'Farhan even threatened divorce.'

'You're pulling my leg.'

Aishah look puzzled. 'Why would I do that?' she asked.

'It's a saying, means you're teasing.'

'I'll remember that,' Aishah replied with a twinkle in her eye.

*   *   *

Maryam lay in bed that evening troubled by Nader's words: *Change comes out of the barrel of a gun.* Hadn't the world shed enough blood and tears, she asked herself? Could there be purpose to killing another human being? The Holy *Qur'an* forbade killing and advocated tolerance and mercy even for the infidels, so what was going wrong? Why was the world at war with itself and when did war become righteous?

What did Nader mean when he said *the wind of change is blowing*? Just when she thought she was beginning to understand him, he would say or do something that threw her into confusion. Perhaps it was she who did not understand. Perhaps she was young and naive. Perhaps it would all fall into place in time. There were so many *perhaps.*

She would just have to wait and see. Feeling helpless in a man's world, she punched the pillow in frustration as Turki slept. There was no one she could talk to who would understand. With tears streaming down her cheeks she watched the colour drain from the curtains as the day gave way to night. Then there was a knock on her door and Saffron stepped in apologising for the intrusion.

'I was just making a cup of tea for myself when I saw the light under your door. So I made one for you too.'

'You're so thoughtful!'

Saffron made herself comfortable beside Maryam. 'Hey, babe, what's up?' she asked noticing Maryam's damp cheeks. That's what Maryam liked about Saffron, she was genuine and came straight to the point.

The tea felt good and Maryam opened her heart. Safe in Saffron's arms, she sobbed. She couldn't remember when she had last been cuddled; it must have been when she had bled for the first time and run to her mother.

'Gal, I take my hat off to you,' Saffron said taking a sip of tea.

'What do you mean?'

'It's tough understanding a man you love but trying to figure a stranger. . . Well, that's something.'

'You think I should. . .'

'Give him some slack and see what happens.'

'Yes! He's been through a terrible war.'

'Like the Vietnam Vets. Maybe the guy just needs some time to chill out and. . .'

'You're so right. Listening to you I feel a load has been lifted from me.' Maryam sighed.

'This isn't just about Nader though, is it?' Saffron asked gazing into Maryam's eyes.

Maryam bit her lip and shook her head. 'How did you know?'

'I'm a woman. Call it intuition.'

'I'm so. . . confused. My heart says one thing but my head. . .'

'I'd follow my heart, honey.'

'Let it be our secret,' Maryam said.

'My lips are sealed,' Saffron replied and squeezed Maryam's hand.

TWELVE

Colonel Nasser was short on words and big on deeds. He worked on the premise that the more you said the more there was to incriminate you. He stubbed out a cigarette and lit another. He had recruited his nephew, Yahya, to the force and had promised his sister he would take care of him – but he had failed. He would catch those bastards.

A Bangladeshi waiter, dark as mahogany, arrived balancing cups of tea on an enamelled tray.

'That will be four *riyals*, sir,' he said.

'You foreigners think we are made of money,' Nasser cursed, and threw some notes on the table.

The waiter collected the money and beat a retreat with a smile on his face.

'I want these sons of bitches,' Nasser said without emotion. The three men in white *thobes* listened. They had come from Riyadh and Jeddah to help solve the death of the boy found floating in the reservoir.

'Suicide?' asked Kamal, tapping his pencil on the table.

'Would you buy a new pair of shoes and kill yourself?' Nasser asked.

'How about drugs?' asked Ali.

'Drugs? Never! It was murder.'

'But why?' asked Kamal.

'Yeah, and what about the money?' asked Ayman.

'He had rope burns on his wrists!' scoffed the Colonel.

'There is that,' Kamal conceded.

'We found five sets of prints on his driver's license and ID card,' Ali said.

'Any leads?'

'None yet, but we've identified four DNA types from the samples.'

They shook their heads, knowing that the boy had been raped.

Nasser stubbed out his cigarette. 'Secrecy is paramount. That's why you're here. There's something going down,' he hissed. The group talked a while, emptied their cups and left the back-street teahouse.

* * *

Dr Ali poked his head into Nader's office. 'They've arrived,' he mouthed without uttering the words.

'Come in, come in, *Ya* Ali.' Nader looked up from his newspaper and smiled.

'Can't stay long,' Dr Ali said, looking furtive. The Chief of Pharmacy was a short man with rounded shoulders and, in his white coat, he reminded Nader of a penguin. His fleshy lips remained perpetually open, pushed forward by nicotine stained teeth. He had a pug nose and close-cropped hair greying around the temples, and he squinted from behind thick lenses.

'Have you read today's paper?' Nader asked, stabbing a finger at the *Arab News*.

'Anything of interest?' Dr Ali asked.

'Five Pakistanis executed in Riyadh for drug smuggling.' Nader read the headlines in a matter-of-fact manner.

'They've arrived,' Dr Ali repeated. Perspiration appeared on his forehead and around his lips.

'How many?'

'Four.'

'Only four? Are you sure?'

'Yes, yes, I've double-checked.' Dr Ali dabbed his face with a handkerchief.

'Tea?' Nader asked to be polite. He didn't like Egyptians. They were untrustworthy and lazy, but had replaced the hard-working Palestinians and Lebanese after the Gulf War. They would sell their own mothers for a few *riyals*.

'Oh no, cutting down. Diabetes you know,' Dr Ali explained.

'It's a killer?'

'If uncontrolled.'

'When can I have them?'

'Today. Security is lax after lunch.'

'After *Dhuhr* then.'

'Can I have the money today?' Dr Ali asked, fidgeting. 'The wife's been complaining and I have four children. School fees. You know how it is?'

'You've been a busy boy, Ali.'

'*Alhamdulillah*, I have been blessed. Three boys and a girl.'

'Are you sure there are only four?'

'I should know. I'm their father.'

'I'm not talking about your precious children, Ali!' Nader snapped.

'I swear upon my mother's grave.'

'You wouldn't short change me, *Ya* Ali?' Nader said waving an accusing finger.

'Wouldn't dream of it, Nader! You know me.'

'But you dream of the good life in Lebanon with a bevy of blondes.'

'They're just dreams, Nader. From my younger days!' Dr Ali must have wished he hadn't told everyone of his last vacation.

'That apartment in Zamalek must've cost you plenty.' Nader goaded referring to one of Cairo's fashionable districts.

'Oh no, no, no. . . I don't own that. . . It's rented.'

'I want that missing package, Ali. Find it!' Nader barked. 'No package, no money!'

'Perhaps it's delayed and will show up with the next shipment?'

'Find it or your diabetes may go out of control prematurely.'

Dr Ali closed the door behind him and scratched his head wondering where the missing jar had gone. He didn't like Nader's interest in his diabetes. Peddling drugs carried a death sentence – but crossing Nader was dangerous.

During *Dhuhr* prayer, Dr Ali kept watch while Lo collected the dustbin liner as though it was just another bag of rubbish. He dabbed the perspiration from his forehead as Lo left. She ambled down the corridor emptying dustbins under the ever-vigilant cameras and made her way through the hospital to the basement and Nader's office.

Nader examined the four white plastic jars, labelled: AMOX-ICILLIN CAPSULE 500mg.

'Ah, there it is!' Nader exclaimed. *Manufactured in Switzerland* was printed in purple instead of black on the bottom left-hand corner of the label. That's how he could identify their special contents without arousing suspicion.

Nader had hit on the idea of importing the drugs from Pakistan transiting through Switzerland at the same time as the shipment of genuine drugs were being freighted.

* * *

Turki entered the room and announced: 'It's time to go, Auntie Miri! Uncle Mahmoud is waiting!'

'I'll be a minute,' Maryam muttered, and continued applying her make-up.

'You said that ages ago!' moaned Turki.

Maryam wanted to look her best and had spent the morning preparing for their visit. This was to be Turki's last appointment at the dentist's. Besides, Turki was going to Riyadh to visit his mother for a month: she didn't know how he would take it. Turki brushed up to her ear and whispered, 'I think you look beautiful and Dr Joe will too.'

'Turki, you're wicked – but I love you.' Maryam blushed.

'Let's keep it a secret.' With a dash of her new perfume, *Temptations*, on her wrists and one final look in the mirror, she picked up her bag and headed downstairs.

Saffron greeted them in the hall. 'Hey prince, are you taking Cinderella to the ball?'

Turki nodded.

'Maryam, you look one hell of a doll, babe. Are you sure you're going to the dentist?'

'Nader's coming round today,' Maryam replied.

'Oh yeah! Could've fooled me. Is he good looking?'

Maryam shot a disapproving glance. 'Saffron, you promised!'

Turki looked at Maryam and gave a toothless grin.

Was it so obvious? Maryam asked herself. If Saffron and Turki could see through her, then others could too. She would have to work on this.

The journey to the hospital took an hour as the police checked every car.

Joe paced the floor. Tess could feel the tension in the air. Dr Joe was a lost man; he would drown if he weren't careful, she told herself. She wondered if her husband had felt the same at their first meeting. He had showered her with gifts and brought her food he had cooked to the university. That was the Filipino way.

Abdullah ushered them in and left as soon as the formalities were over. Maryam raised her veil, removed her glove and offered her hand to Joe. 'I'm Maryam,' she said.

'I know,' Joe replied, savouring Maryam's words as if they were coated in honey. Joe looked into Maryam's amber eyes, they beckoned and he let himself drown. His pulse raced and his heart drummed a primordial message.

Maryam felt a tingle in her toes that flowed upward, weakening her knees. She was floating on air.

Tess and Turki watched: they both knew they had witnessed a special moment. Turki clambered onto the chair and Tess switched on the overhead light signaling the end of a brief encounter that would be relived for days to come.

Joe tried to concentrate on his work but found himself look-ing up into Maryam's eyes at every opportunity. Turki was with the fairies with the nitrous oxide mask over his nose.

'Do you read?' Maryam asked tentatively, not sure if she should speak while Joe was working.

'Read?' Joe asked.

'I suppose you don't get much time.'

'Well, depends what you mean?'

'Literature.'

'I like a bit of this and that. I read Shakespeare and Tennyson when I was at college. Just finished reading *Anna Karenina*—'

'By Tolstoy,' interrupted Maryam, 'I've heard of it.'

'And have started *Tess of the D'urbervilles* by— '

'Thomas Hardy. I've read it. Such a sad story but he is so gifted. He was English I think?'

'You're right, he was English.'

'Could I borrow the Tolstoy?' she asked. 'When you've finished, of course,' she added. 'It's so difficult to get books here,' she said rolling her eyes.

'Mix!' Joe ordered. 'And a matrix-band, please, Tess. Yes of course, Maryam. It'll be my pleasure.'

'We've gifted Arabian and Persian poets.'

'So I've heard.'

'I'll see if I can find you translations.'

'I would like that.' Joe smiled behind his mask.

'Our prose is also rich.'

'Do you write?' Joe asked and put his hand out. Tess placed an amalgam carrier in it.

'A little,' Maryam answered.

'Poetry?'

'Sometimes, when I am moved.'

'Words are vehicles of expression.'

'Different languages, same emotions,' Maryam said looking into his eyes.

'Like different religions, same God,' Joe said.

96

'Ready?' Tess asked. Joe nodded and put out his hand to receive the amalgam packer.

'Something like that,' Maryam replied after a moment of reflection. 'I like Browning and the Brontë sisters – especially Emily. And of course I adore Pasternak and loved *Dr Zhivago*.'

'Never read the book, but saw the movie.' Joe's hands were on autopilot but his mind was elsewhere.

'I saw it too. Wasn't Omar Sharif adorable? He's a Muslim, you know. And of course Julie Christie was just divine.' Maryam clasped her hands and looked heavenward. 'How could anyone be so beautiful?'

Joe smiled under his surgical mask. If only she knew, he thought to himself. 'Beauty's everywhere; you've just got to know where to look,' he said trying not to sound philosophical.

'I couldn't agree more. There is the magic of colours in the sunsets and there's the beauty of the desert.'

'Beauty comes in many forms.'

'Many think the desert is dead but it's truly alive – oh, I'm boring you!'

'No, no, please go on. I like the sound of—'

'There is beauty in the sound of a lover's voice,' Tess said, adding her own brand of philosophy without thinking. Maryam and Joe looked up and smiled at each other. Tess's prediction had come true, her doctor was drowning and she felt happy for him, happy for them both.

Joe tried to prolong the meeting by taking his time over his work. Was it going to end here today? Turki's treatment was finished and there was no reason for Maryam to return. Had he heard correctly? Had Maryam asked for some books?

Maryam also knew the moment was near. What should she do? Should she follow through with her plan? Would he think the worse of her if she made the first move? He was the man, he *should* make the first move. . . but he might feel threatened as she was a Saudi. No, she would have to take the first step; there was no other way.

Tess sensed the dilemma. 'You must come for a check up one-
day, Madam, Dr Joe is a good doctor,' she said.

'Yes, I must.' They shook hands again, enjoying the touch of
human flesh. Except for her family and Nader, Maryam had
never touched another's hand. 'Oh, I almost forgot, I've
something for you, Dr Joe.' Maryam gave him the *Qur'an*.
'There's something for everyone in here.' she said, and closed the
door behind her.

'Be careful, doctor, she's no child,' Tess said. 'She's not like the
others.'

That evening, while alone in his apartment Joe opened the
book. An envelope fell from it. He laughed. She had planned it
all, he mused, and he opened the envelope and smelt her
fragrance.

* * *

Farhan answered the red phone connected through a secure line
to high command in Riyadh. There were few pleasantries. It was
11.45 hrs.

'Yes, sir! Yes, I understand! Red alert of course, sir! I'll
increase security right away! Roadblocks. No, no they won't get
away; you can count on me, sir! Halat Ammar, Dhuba, Al Wajh
and Haql. Desert patrols, yes of course, sir! Consider it done!
Yes sir, I'll report back!'

The line went dead; this was no time for niceties. Farhan did
not question orders.

A fax machine hummed in the background, spilling details of
the tragedy onto the floor. A car bomb had exploded at 11.30 hrs
in the car park of the American mission on Thalatheen Street in
the Olaya District north of Riyadh. There were six deaths and
sixty casualties. A major read the report and exclaimed,
'*Alhamdulillah*, no Saudis have been killed.'

Farhan responded to the emergency as a veteran of many
wars and particularly the 1979 uprising at the *Holy Kaaba* where

he had distinguished himself against Muslim Fundamentalists. It had been his idea to flood the holy shrine in Mecca and electrocute them, but some prince had taken the glory.

He hated these fundamentalists and their kind. They were like cockroaches crawling out of their mosques, preaching dissent, aiming to destroy the country under their brand of Islam. And like cockroaches they deserved to be crushed and have their lives stamped out.

* * *

Nabeel and Nader sat engrossed in conversation interspersed with laughter, sipping tea, talking about the good old days. They had much in common as they had grown up together, attended the same school and moved in the same circles. Nader was older by some five years but, since a fateful day fifteen years ago, Nader and Nabeel had enjoyed an intimate friendship that had brought them many rewards.

Their destiny had become intertwined when a gang of boys had found Nabeel in the mosque one Friday after midday prayer. At first they teased him about his features. Then one suggested they check he wasn't a girl. They all thought it hilarious. He tried to escape but the door was barred. They chased him around the mosque like a chicken, groped his body and mocked him with laughter. He screamed and struggled but that only spurred them on. Nader, who was passing by, heard his screams and came to his rescue.

After that day, he belonged to Nader. That was until Nabeel had caught the eye of an important man at his brother's wedding feast and after that Nader never came near him again.

'You're his property,' Nader had said in a matter-of-fact way and that was all there was to it. It hurt, but Nader was right, and in the end it had worked out for the best. He had received money and land from the VIP. The land had appreciated in value over the years and in the end he sold it, making him a wealthy man at twenty-five.

Maryam entered the room, the pair stopped talking.

'I'm leaving for Riyadh,' Nader said.

'Oh. Will you be gone long?'

'Depends on how things go. Is there anything you'd like?'

'Thank you for asking.' Maryam didn't want anything from Nader but his respect. Since their last meeting, the demon of doubt had been awakened in her and she was tiring of this pretence.

'Nabeel's coming too,' Nader added.

This was the first time Maryam had heard of Nabeel's plan. They hadn't spoken since the college episode and Saffron had said nothing either. What a pity: she was just getting to know Saffron. Perhaps she'd come over in the summer when Riyadh got intolerably hot.

Saffron sauntered into the lounge, her face uncovered.

'Have you met Nader?' Maryam asked. 'He's going to Riyadh with you.'

'Riyadh! Are we going to Riyadh, Nabeel?' asked Saffron. Nabeel nodded sheepishly and confessed he had just decided to go.

'There's been a bombing in Riyadh with many Americans dead,' Nader said with the detached manner of a TV newscaster.

'How many?' Maryam asked.

'Probably hundreds!' Nabeel announced with glee.

'Riyadh is not safe for *Ameriki*,' added Nader.

'Perhaps in a few weeks when the dust has settled you can come over,' suggested Nabeel.

'That'll be just fine, honey. Mind you be careful,' Saffron drawled. Nabeel grimaced at her accent.

Saffron was contracted to play wife and didn't care where Nabeel went. Her eyes were set on his father and that was all that mattered for now.

THIRTEEN

'This is a fucking nuisance. What the hell do they expect to find?' Nabeel shouted as they waited in traffic.

'Nothing,' Nader replied after a moment.

'I bet it's that bloody bomb in Riyadh!' said Nabeel and tooted the horn. 'These motherfuckers are so slow. Can't they see we're in a hurry?' He wound down the window and shouted to the rookie policeman, '*Ya*, Mohammed! We've got a plane to catch.' Addressing a stranger by the Prophet's name was traditional but produced no response. Nabeel fumed, thumping the steering wheel like a child.

Nader sat composed. It can't be the bomb, he thought. The roadblocks went up weeks ago. His years with the *mujahideen* had trained him to be suspicious. That was how you lived to see another day. Something was not right. His source in the police had said nothing but that didn't mean all was well.

'License and *estamara*, the car registration document, please,' requested the rookie in an official tone. Nabeel handed his driver's license and the faded *estamara* that reflected the age of the car.

The rookie squinted at the documents, comparing the names.

'Whose car is this?' he asked. Nabeel explained the car belonged to his father, Major General Balawi. The name didn't register a response on the recruit's face.

'*Ya*, Mohammed!' Nabeel shouted again, 'Don't you know who Major General Balawi is?'

An officer ambled over and asked what all the shouting was about. Nabeel began to explain but the officer wasn't having any of it.

'I'm sorry, *sedeeq*,' he said. 'We're only following orders, you understand. Your ID?' he said, motioning to Nader. Nader fished out his license from his wallet. The man examined it for a while playing the sunlight on it. He looked at the photograph, then, at Nader and at the photograph again and grinned.

'*Ya*, Nader, you better get this renewed,' he said waving the license in the air. 'It expires next week,' he warned and handed back the documents. Nader thanked the man and scrutinised the date.

'Seems it was only yesterday I renewed it,' he said.

'Get yourself a new picture while you're at it,' advised the officer. So much had happened in the five years since his return from Afghanistan. There was so much to do and so little time to do it, he contemplated to himself.

They were in luck. The plane had been delayed due to the extra security checks. All items were x-rayed and then the security officer examined every case in person, convinced the sophisticated equipment was no substitute for his eyes. At the end of the line a dog sniffed at the luggage with disinterest.

Angry westerners, desperate for a chilled beer, complained they would miss their connections and businessmen lined up at the coin operated telephones to re-arrange their appointments.

'*Insha'allah, bukarah*. God willing, tomorrow,' was the response they got.

'What time?'

'Oh, any time. Just show up.'

Bangladeshi, Thai, Afghani and Sri Lankans cursed under their breaths, re-packing cartons the officer had demanded opened. A man screamed when an officer began to unscrew the back of a television set that represented six months of hard labour. Another officer collected batteries from cameras and radios and dropped them into a bucket.

'Don't you understand the data will be lost?' pleaded an American when an official insisted on removing the battery from his digital diary.

Pandemonium ruled in true Saudi style. One order cancelled another and yet another reinstated the first. To add to the chaos, the airline's computer crashed, leaving passengers waving the blue, green and turquoise tickets like flags on independence day, all pushing towards the counter.

*   *   *

Sahar and Samar giggled, walking down the mall with Maryam in tow. Sahar had got her wish. She received an A+ for her chemistry homework and a note giving a time and place.

'We must stop at a shoe shop first,' Samar said.

'Are you going to buy shoes?' Maryam asked.

'No silly,' the twins chirped. 'Just watch us.'

Around the corner from the car park they found an Aladdin's cave filled with shoes of all shapes and sizes, in every conceivable colour. They tried on a few to please the Pakistani salesman who was hoping to make his first sale of the day.

The girls laughed at the gaudy designs, declaring they were only suitable for Bedouins. They pulled out two pairs of Gucci shoes from a plastic bag and put them on. Their old shoes found their way into yet another bag of a different colour.

Maryam looked on, mystified by the performance. She was about to ask when she noticed the driver walk by, his eyes glued to floor. Why hadn't she thought of it? Women all looked alike in their *abaya* and veils. The only way anyone could identify them was by their shoes and shopping bags. There was much to learn in this game of hide and seek, Maryam noted with a smile.

Samar studied a piece of paper that looked like it had once been part of an exercise book. 'Yes, it's that building there,' she said pointing discreetly ahead.

They followed Samar into a gully that led to the back of the

RAJ KUMAR

building and passed an old mosque with white walls and a tower
for a minaret.

A man with a walking stick, shuffled towards them on the
opposite side of the road. He moved his *miswak* over his teeth
like a toothbrush.

'I don't like this,' whispered Sahar. The man coughed and spat
onto the road before disappearing into the mosque. The girls
looked at each other in disgust. The street was empty. They
hurried up the steps of the five-storey building with a facade of
marble tiles that had fallen off in places, exposing the concrete
beneath.

There was an elevator but they took the stairs, tiptoeing to the
first floor. Someone had sprayed graffiti on the walls in green,
the national colour. It read: *Power to the people.* Another artist
had written: *The end is in sight.*

Samar couldn't control herself and giggled. 'He must have
been coming when he sprayed that,' she said pointing to the
script.

'Shhh, someone will hear you,' whispered Sahar.

There were four apartments on the first floor. They
approached a wooden door with trepidation.

'Are you sure this is the place?' Maryam asked. Samar pointed
at the number four, hanging upside-down on a single screw. She
gave the doorbell a push. They heard the sound echo inside the
apartment.

'Have you the right number?' Maryam asked. Perhaps this was
a joke? They heard a door open behind them.

'Holy shit!' Samar swore under her breath.

'Pss! Pss!' They stood staring at the door, not daring to turn
even though their faces were covered.

'Pss! Pss!' Now more urgent than before. They turned and
spotted the chemistry teacher peering from behind the door. He
beckoned them in and closed the door.

'I thought it was apartment four,' Samar complained.

'Just an added precaution,' he said. 'It's usually empty.

I'm Abdul,' he introduced himself, trying to put them at ease.

A beak of a nose dominated Abdul's face. He had bushy eye-brows and intelligent eyes. His lips curled up at the edges giving the illusion they were ready to kiss. A thick moustache sat on his upper lip. The receding hairline made him look older then he was and a square jaw gave him an air of substance. Hair peered over the rim of his T-shirt like grass over a pavement. Working out in the gym had given him muscular arms and a broad chest that tapered at the waist. A flat butt and spindly legs reminded Maryam of the hind legs of a camel.

'I've made tea,' he said fidgeting with his hands and led the way.

The lounge was furnished with a tired couch stained brown from spilled tea. An ashtray with cigarette butts and used matches sat on a coffee table with the formica top peeling away at the corners.

Curtains with a fading pattern struggled to keep out the sun. The overhead fan distributed the smell of smoke, making a click-ing sound with each turn. A print of the Grand mosque in a frame yellowed by age hung on the wall at an angle. A bulb dangling from the ceiling at the end of a wire gave off an anaemic light. The place made Maryam feel uneasy.

With the pleasantries over, Sahar glanced at her watch and looked at Samar.

'Where's the bed?' Samar asked.

Abdul pointed to a door and the twins headed for it.

'Aren't you coming?' Abdul asked Maryam.

Maryam laughed from behind her veil, 'I think you've got your hands full for the moment, don't you?'

Abdul looked stunned when the twins dropped their *abaya*, revealing underwear more appropriate in a bordello, and helped him out of his clothes.

Maryam heard the girls croon, 'Show us what you can do, big boy.'

Groans and moans overflowed into the lounge. Maryam felt

their excitement flamed by her imagination and fanned by curiosity.

'Shit! He's come!' Samar screamed.

'I'm sorry,' Abdul whimpered.

'You selfish bastard!' Samar shouted.

'Call yourself a man?' Sahar taunted and jumped off the bed.

'Bloody amateur!' screamed Sahar.

'It won't happen again,' beseeched Abdul, hiding his face in his hands.

Samar gave Abdul the 'up yours' gesture.

'Let's go, Maryam!' The twins burst into the lounge, throwing on their clothes and *abaya*. They hurried down the stairwell leaving Abdul framed in the doorway with a towel around his waist.

'The man's a fucking prem,' scoffed Samar when they reached the mall.

'What's that?' Maryam asked.

'Premature ejaculator,' Samar replied, and rolled her eyes.

'That's when they come before you,' Sahar explained and shrugged her shoulders. 'Men! They're all the same.'

For some reason Maryam shared in their frustration. She couldn't explain why she, too, felt cheated. Perhaps it was just in her mind, or maybe it was her body speaking in a language she didn't understand. She felt hungry, but for what?

FOURTEEN

Joe let the scent of Maryam's letter fan his imagination while waiting for Maryam to answer the phone. His finger traced her signature, a series of curves flowing like Arabic calligraphy on the powder pink paper. It was executed in one movement, a sign of continuity of thought, he told himself.

The stack of coins on the metal shelf in the phone booth shook when a truck lumbered by spewing smoke. Joe coughed, held his breath and waited for the smoke to clear. He had chosen to use the public phone to avoid the nosy operator at the hospital. He knew all conversations were monitored in the Kingdom but, here at least, he was just another anonymous voice.

'*Marhaba*,' Maryam greeted, recognising Joe's voice.

'How's Turki?' Joe asked, trying to break the ice.

'He is fine, but my Mother is unwell.'

'Should I call later?'

'No. No. It is okay, she's resting now. It's all the excitement. But she'll be fine.'

'Excitement?' Joe asked.

'. . . It's nothing.'

'I like your perfume.'

'Can you smell it through the phone?'

'The letter. . .'

'Oh, that,' Maryam giggled remembering Saffron's suggestion.

She had said that words only paint a picture, but perfume will drive a man to distraction even when he's asleep.

They made small talk. She wanted to feel the touch of his hand and he wanted to gaze into her eyes and feast on her beauty. She talked about Turki and college and he about work. They reminisced about their first meeting and laughed at Turki's question about God. He told her about the book he was reading and she wanted to know all about his country.

'Do you get snow where you live, Dr Joe?' she asked.

'Call me Joe.'

'Okay, Joe,' she replied, warming to his voice.

'There's plenty of snow in New York in winter.'

'Do you have reindeer?'

'Reindeer? Oh no, not in New York.'

'I've seen them on TV.'

'Must have been Norway,' Joe smiled.

'Is that where Santa Claus lives?'

'So I've heard.' Joe laughed.

'You're making fun of me.'

'I'd never do that, Maryam.'

'I'd love to ski one day and roll around in the snow.' Maryam sighed, knowing it would never happen. Norway – or wherever they ski – might as well be a million kilometres away. She didn't even have a passport and, once married, she was sure Nader would never approve. *The Qur'an says it's haram to ski*, he would say. Besides, she couldn't imagine how anyone could possibly ski in an *abaya* and a veil.

'Will it, and it will happen.' Joe said.

'I can dream, can't I, Joe?'

'Life without dreams is life without meaning.'

'The *Qur'an* gives my life meaning,' Maryam snapped.

'I suppose it does,' Joe mused.

'What do you dream about, Joe? What gives meaning to your life?'

The telephone gobbled up the last coin, leaving the questions hanging in the air.

'Have to go. I've run out of coins.'

'Call again. . . soon, Dr Joe.'

'Tomorrow?'

The line went dead before she could reply.

Joe drove back to the cantonment with their conversation playing over in his mind. He wasn't sure what it was but every cell in his body wanted to dance. Yes, he had a dream, a beautiful dream he told himself, a dream he wanted to share with Maryam.

* * *

Saffron sat on the patio at the rear of the house taking in the sight of the farm. In the distance she could see rainbows dancing in the mist from the irrigation plants that turned a barren desert into green circles of crops. How different it was, she thought, from the mad traffic of LA or the human tide that rushed through the labyrinths of Manhattan.

Since her arrival two months earlier, she had eased into the Saudi rhythm of life where time was measured by the phases of the moon and prayer calls and that was all that mattered. She sipped the sherbet Aishah had made from the limes she had picked earlier that day.

Her thoughts turned to the life she had left behind where she lived from day to day, not knowing what tomorrow would bring. She was constantly on the move with nowhere to call home, and friends were only friends so long as she had money. She barely recovered from one bill before the next one landed on her doormat and her old jalopy gobbled up the rest, but now all that was a distant memory.

'Ah, there you are, *habibi*,' Aishah said, and ambled over from the house.

'What have you got, Mama Aishah?' Saffron asked, eyeing the parcels in her hands.

'A surprise.'

'For me!' Saffron exclaimed like a five-year-old.

'Open them, *habibi*.' Aishah handed them to her and looked pleased.

Puzzled, Saffron opened the larger parcel first.

'It is the Holy *Qur'an*. It is both in Arabic and in your language.'

'So it is,' Saffron said, flicking through the pages.

Aishah took the book and opened it at the front page.

'Sorry,' Saffron said in embarrassment, forgetting Arabic books were read from back to front.

Aishah smiled at Saffron's mistake. 'It will help you understand our ways, *habibi*.'

'I have so much to learn, Mama Aishah,' Saffron said, and opened the second parcel. 'Audiotapes. Just what I need, Mama Aishah. Music!' she exclaimed.

'Now you can learn to speak Arabic,' Aishah said and gave Saffron a hug.

'Oh! It's not music?' Saffron looked disappointed.

'*Habibi*, you will make more friends if you speak Arabic. Nabeel sent them from Riyadh.'

'He did that?'

'He loves you, *habibi*.'

'I'll give it a go, Mama Aishah, if you promise you'll help.'

'You are my second daughter,' Aishah said and squeezed Saffron's hand. 'Maryam will be gone soon.'

'Thank you for everything, Mama Aishah.' Saffron replied thinking of her mother and lost moments.

'We are your family now, *habibi*. You are one of us.'

'Thank you,' Saffron whispered, and began to cry.

* * *

Maryam felt the pangs of loneliness lying in bed without Turki for company. He had been gone a few days but she missed him, they all missed him.

Since Joe's call she had been overcome by euphoria. Her heart raced, the sky was a tinge bluer, the sun brighter, the flowers more vibrant and the water tasted sweeter. . . and yet she felt empty. It wasn't the emptiness of hunger or the desolation she felt when her brother, Sultan, had died.

Her Mother's behaviour troubled her. With every passing day her mood changed and melancholy took a tenacious hold. She asked herself who or what held the key to her troubled heart?

Sleep played hide and seek into the wee hours of the morning. In the end, she sat in bed with her *Qur'an* on her lap. Her fingers flirted with pages soaked in wisdom. Her eyes skipped over the words hoping to find an answer that would bring solace, until she finally fell asleep clutching the holy book.

When she awoke, her body was rested but her heart was consumed by a longing to hear Joe's voice. Saffron said she should follow her heart. But where to?

FIFTEEN

'It must be exam time soon,' Farhan observed from across the dining table as he dusted the crumbs from his hands.

'Two weeks to go,' Maryam replied, helping herself to some *babaghanoush*.

'How do you feel?'

'Getting there slowly.'

'Bumped into your principal yesterday at the supermarket.'

'How is she?'

'Has high expectations of you.'

'I mustn't disappoint her then.'

'You don't have to prove anything to anyone, *habibi*,' Aishah interjected.

'I know, Mama.'

'Whatever you do, do it for yourself.'

'Yes, Mama.'

'I wish she would wear a veil,' Farhan grumbled.

'Who?' Maryam asked.

'Your principal, of course.'

'She's Jordanian, Father.'

'So?'

'In Jordan, Father, they. . .'

'Yes! Yes! I know they are more liberated.'

'She's very knowledgeable about Islam.'

'Then she should know better and set an example for you girls.'

'Wearing a veil doesn't make you a better Muslim, besides her Saudi husband doesn't mind.'

'He should teach her our ways.'

'She's a good Muslim. The Prophet Mohammed, peace be upon him, said nothing about covering the face.'

'I suppose they taught you that at college.'

'The *Qur'an*, if you must know Father.'

'Our Prophet spoke of modesty in dress and wearing the *hijab*,' Aishah interrupted, waving a didactic finger at Maryam.

'Yes, but not about covering the face, Mama.'

'It's all very vague and open to interpretation,' Aishah shook her head.

'Did you know, Mama, one of the Prophet's wives led an army and taught both men and women?' Maryam asked.

'And pray tell us her name?' Farhan asked, trying to catch Maryam out.

'Aishah!'

'Well, I never knew that,' exclaimed Aishah.

'Our Prophet, peace be upon him, was a wise man,' Maryam replied.

'I won't have my daughter parading around without a veil,' Farhan exploded.

'There's no fear of that, Father.'

'Good. I don't want to hear anymore of this liberal talk.'

'Sahar and Samar want me to study the *Qur'an* with them over the weekend. Can I?'

'The Al Shamrani's girls?'

'Yes, Father.'

'Be sure you swot up on the veil,' Farhan taunted with a twinkle in his eyes. They laughed and the tension broke.

'I miss Turki,' Maryam said, tucking into her breakfast, feeling hungry all of a sudden.

'When's he back?' Farhan asked

'*Insha'allah*, in a week or two,' Aishah replied.

'The house is so quiet without him,' Farhan complained and everyone agreed.

SIXTEEN

A man in a *thobe* and chequered *gutra*, accompanied by two figures in *abaya*, alighted from a taxi in the Al Manar district of Riyadh behind the Khurais Hospital and they scrambled over the debris the builders had failed to clear.

The man looked up and down the street and whispered '*Yellah*.' They then entered the dilapidated building. The elevator had stopped working a while back and the well was filled with refuse. They took the stairs to the third floor, feeling their way in the darkness, past walls splashed with graffiti and exuding the stench of urine.

The man knocked on the steel door and waited. A small door opened behind a grill set at head height letting out a beam of light that cut through the dust. The man murmured something and the eyes behind the grill blinked in recognition. Three bolts clanked back in rapid succession, the door opened to let them in and closed behind them.

Men emerged from under their *abaya*. Everyone shook hands and embraced, each asking the other of his health in the customary way, reassuring each other of their wellbeing.

'What took you so long?'

'Roadblocks everywhere. The *abaya* worked a charm and being close to the hospital helped. We are supposed to be visiting our dying mother right now.'

They piled into a room filled with men in their twenties. It was

115

bare except for a rickety table that propped up the fifteen-inch TV and a VCR.

Fight in the cause of Allah those who fight you but do not transgress limits. . . And slay them wherever ye catch them – a passage from the *Qur'an* hung on the wall and a threadbare carpet let through islands of concrete. Cigarette smoke hung in layers. More greetings followed until all hands had been pressed.

Between sips of tea or coffee, the recent bombing was on every lip.

'Was it your doing?' asked a man.

'I wish,' came the reply.

'It was a grand job.'

From a nearby mosque the wail of the *muezzin* entered the room. The men headed to the bathroom for *wudu*.

One by one they filtered back and lined up behind an old man facing Mecca. The room resounded to the sound of prayer, uniting them through their love of Allah. *Isha* prayer ended after the fourth *rek'ah* and conversation returned.

Platters piled with scented rice and decked with spit-grilled chicken arrived with cans of soft drinks, lemons, green chillies, cubed cucumber and onions. Thanking Allah, they attacked the food like a pride of lions, tearing at the meat until only piles of bones remained.

Tea and coffee followed baskets of fresh fruit and they all settled down for the next event, the one that had brought them from the four corners of Saudi Arabia.

A man with a barrel of a chest, on which rested a beard dyed orange with henna to signify his virility, stood up and greeted everyone.

'*Salam 'alekum.* Peace be upon you.'

And they all responded in unison. '*Wa 'alekum es salam.* And on you be peace.'

With the formalities over he burst forth with energy:

'Brothers, you have all heard of the explosion that rocked this city a few days ago and killed five *Ameriki* and injured sixty others. That is five less infidels on our Holy Land.' He paused as everyone expressed delight.

'That explosion,' he continued, 'is the signal for our people to unite under the banner of a pure Islam. Brothers, this is our land. We must drive the infidels out and cleanse our Holy Land of the vermin and parasites who steal as we sleep from the mouths of our children.'

They applauded. The man sat down and another got to his feet. He greeted them all and began, 'We will win, for we fight with Allah's blessing and there is no one greater than Allah.'

'*Allah-hu akbar*,' rippled through the room.

'In the eyes of Allah, brothers, all men are equal. There is no place for kings or emperors in Islam. We, the chosen people of Allah, follow only Him, not men in fine clothes who live in palaces!'

Another chorus of '*Allah-hu akbar*,' followed and the man sat down.

A hush fell, Nader rose to address the congregation.

'Brothers, we have heard promises of reform, of open government, even an elected council. But these are empty words with no substance.' He spoke with clarity and conviction. Nader loved to take centre stage; he believed people could move mountains on words and bullets. He had heard some general say, 'Give a man an idea he believes in and he will die for it.'

'Brothers, we have listened to them for too long. Are we to be fooled like children? Their empty words are to appease the *Ameriki*. They are not for us!' He paused, letting the words sink in and then continued.

'Seventy years ago, Abdul Aziz proclaimed himself King and now his son Fahad calls himself custodian of our holiest mosques. He insults us all – for we followers of Prophet Mohammed, peace be upon him, are the true custodians of our faith and holy shrines, not this alcoholic.'

A murmur of agreement filled the room.

'Allah blessed our country with wealth but now we beg from

Jewish banks with un-Islamic values. Their vile morality corrupts our society. We must cut off the hand that feeds this monster. As good Muslims, it is our duty to free ourselves from this bondage, brothers,' he said, raising his voice.

'Freedom! Freedom!' echoed through the room.

Nader smiled, they were his but this was only an exercise. There would come a day when he would address thousands, perhaps hundreds of thousands, and make history.

'We put our trust in them and they have abused it,' he whispered and the room fell silent, every ear straining to catch his words. 'We swore our allegiance to them and they deceived us. They have turned brother against brother and father against son.' His voice rose again with each word. He compressed all his feelings and theirs into his fist until his knuckles whitened and then he punched the air. 'This has to end!'

The room erupted: everyone leapt to their feet chanting, 'Death! Death! Death to Fahad! Death to the Al Sauds! Death to *Ameriki*!'

Nader sat down followed by the rest and the old man switched on the TV and inserted a videocassette into the VCR. The screen flickered into life, a snowstorm raged for a few seconds and then the screen went blank. All eyes stayed glued to the screen. Suddenly, a figure appeared with his face hidden in the shadow of the *gutra*.

They knew this was their leader, the man they called the Father. Each word he spoke was measured for value. First he thanked them for their contribution to the cause and praised those who had executed the bombing that signalled the beginning of the end. He said, those who gave their lives to the cause were martyrs and seventy two virgins awaited them in paradise. He promised them victory and a brighter future for all.

'*Allah-hu akbar*' rippled again through the gathering.

The Father bid them farewell. Moments later an image of a building appeared. They watched as each second was stretched – warped by the electronic wizardry of the camera set on slow motion, recording the last few minutes of normality on Thalatheen Street. At precisely 11.20 the camera shook and the picture blurred for a second. From a car they saw horns of fire reach towards a building, ripping off the facade and leaving a billowing inferno and a pall of smoke.

Silence enveloped the room, the screen went blank but the image remained etched in their minds, firing imagination and strengthening their resolve. Suddenly they all leaped to their feet with boyish exuberance, congratulating each other.

The old man pressed the eject button and passed a magnet over the videocassette to erase the recording.

SEVENTEEN

Seated at the rear of the classroom, Maryam whispered, 'It's on,' in Samar's ear.

'Did you tell him?' Samar asked.

'Yes.' Maryam grinned. 'He didn't question.'

'How easy is that?'

'I'm a little. . .'

'Don't worry, I was too the first time but it'll all work out.'

'Are you sure?'

'Trust me, been there, done that,' Samar declared triumphantly.

Maryam soon discovered that when you are waiting, one hundred and twenty hours seem longer than five days. Saffron was the first to notice the change.

'You okay, honey?' Saffron asked one day when they were alone in the lounge.

'I'm fine, just exam nerves you know.'

'Can't say I do, wasn't at school long enough to suffer them.'

'Without education Saudi women have no future,' Maryam explained.

'The way I see it, you guys cut a raw deal either way.'

'How so?' Maryam asked perplexed, trying to understand Saffron's English.

'They aren't crying out for women architects or engineers. With or without education there are no jobs. Here, have a look for yourself.' Saffron pushed the *Arab News* towards Maryam.

'Things change.'

'As sure as pigs will fly.'

'Saffron, we don't mention that animal in this country,' admonished Maryam.

'Hey, no offence, Maryam. I clean forgot it wasn't kosher.'

'Change just takes time.' Maryam pushed back the newspaper without reading it.

'Yeah! Hundreds of years, perhaps thousands.'

'I can live in hope.'

'If hope's all you've got, honey, you're going to be mighty disappointed.'

'Why are you being so obtuse? I thought you were on my side.'

'I'm just telling it as it is. What was it your father said at breakfast?' Saffron asked, just as the phone rang beside her.

'My father?'

'Didn't he say he wouldn't want his daughter parading around without a veil?'

'Sure but. . . Are you going to answer the phone?'

'What's with you guys? Women aren't sinners and men aren't saints. Life's not black and white, it's full of greys.'

'How would you know? You've only been here a few months,' Maryam retorted.

'Get real! Your father isn't going to change his mind anytime soon,' Saffron replied, ignoring the phone.

'So why are you here, Saffron? Why don't you go back to your land of milk and honey?'

'Now who's being obtuse?' Saffron shouted and picked up the phone.

'It's for you,' she said, and slammed the receiver down on the table.

'It'll be Nader, I'll take it in the library.' Maryam smiled and skipped out of the room.

That was the first smile Saffron had seen on Maryam's face all day. How wonderful it was to be in love, she thought to herself.

'Hello Joe!'

'Joe? Who's Joe?' Nader asked.

'Oh, hello, Nader.' Maryam struggled to contain her disappointment

'Who is Joe?'

'No one!'

'How can he be no one when you called his name?' Nader yelled.

'It's a bad line. You must have misheard. How's Riyadh?' Maryam asked politely, changing the subject.

'Hot, very hot!'

'What's new and how's Nabeel?'

'Isn't he back?' Nader asked.

'I thought he was with you.' Maryam said, pacing the floor.

'Haven't seen him in ages.'

'When do you get back?'

'I want to know who this Joe is?'

'There isn't any Joe. It's a pretty bad line. I can barely hear you.'

'Rang to tell you I am off to Jeddah tomorrow. I won't be back for a few weeks,' Nader said and fed another coin into the slot. 'I haven't been able to get through to the family.'

'Be careful!'

'Of what?'

'Don't you listen to the news?'

'Not to government propaganda.'

'They said on the news today. . .'

'Don't believe everything you hear,' Nader interrupted.

'They defused a bomb at the airport.'

'In Jeddah?'

'Yes.'

'It's all Al Saud propaganda.'

'Just take care.'

'Okay. Let Mona know I'm off to Jeddah.'

'Call me soon.' Maryam added, in keeping with etiquette, and sighed with relief when the phone went dead. She would have to be careful in future. She was sure Nader hadn't accepted her explanation.

EIGHTEEN

The old man who the Brotherhood called their Father sat in a wheelchair beside Nader. They were in a vestibule with soaring walls that converged in the centre like a tent. The morning light streamed through the arched windows and pooled on the chequered marble floor. Two bodyguards sat at a distance, cradling Uzis in their laps, glancing periodically in their direction.

'I have something to show you,' Nader said. He clicked open the catches on the attaché case and pulled out a cardboard box with the red and yellow logo of Pizza Sheikh. The old man strained his ears to hear Nader.

'What you have here is a plane, the size of a saucer,'

'Give it to me,' ordered the old man.

Nader gave it to the old man and continued. 'It's the most advanced micro plane of its kind in the world.'

The old man's fingers moved over the surface and gave the propeller a spin, letting the memories of his childhood surface.

He frowned and asked, 'So what does it do?'

'It flies using batteries and has a miniature camera with a laser which helps it to target.'

'Yes, yes, but what can it do for us?' the old man asked pursing his lips.

'It *kills*,' Nader said.

There was a moment's silence. The old man stroked his silver goatee, letting the words sink in.

'How?' barked the old man.

'I'm coming to that.' Nader knew he had the old man's undivided attention. 'There is a pencil-size titanium tube that runs the length of the plane. That's the barrel of the weapon.'

'What do you propose to kill with this peashooter, a fly?'

'These are the eyes of the plane,' Nader said and handed over a pair of video goggles. 'Careful with this.' Nader gave the old man a black box with a joystick that had a moulded grip for the fingers and a red button on top.

Nader saw the scepticism on the old man's face and knew it was time for a demonstration. 'Bring me a horse and I'll show you what this toy can do,' he said.

One of the bodyguards wheeled the old man through the French doors into the winter sunshine and the other went to fetch a horse from the stables. Nader wandered off with the plane beyond the walls of the house until he was a speck in the distance.

'He's half a kilometre away, Father,' relayed the bodyguard and the old man nodded.

The plane flew a metre above the coral shore, blending with the background. Approaching the villa, it banked to the right and climbed, clearing the walls. It flew between the palm trees and rocked a little. Nader switched on the laser and watched a red dot dance over the horse's neck. He pressed the red button on the joystick and fired the cannon.

The horse jerked its head and whinied. Moments later, it snorted and kicked the earth. Saliva and blood drooled from its jaws and froth foamed around the mouth. The hind legs gave way and it collapsed onto its side, throwing up a cloud of dust. The horse's eyes rolled, it struggled to breathe and its legs twitched as the poison took effect.

'What's happening?' asked the old man, hearing the commotion.

'The horse is dead, Father!' exclaimed a bodyguard.

Nader arrived with the plane in his hand, looking pleased. They watched the horse fighting for life in disbelief. Flies buzzed around its nostrils trickling with blood and settled on its gaping mouth. The horse raised its neck one last time before it flopped lifeless.

'How did you do that?' the old man asked.

'It's called the Black Widow, after a spider,' Nader replied, waving the plane in front of them. 'A drop of the poison is enough to kill a man in less then twenty seconds.'

'Poison, you say?' asked the old man.

'Yes, it comes from the Golden Arrow frog that lives in South America.'

The old man turned towards Nader, his unseeing eyes sparkled with excitement. His mind pondered the potential of the Black Widow. He hadn't heard of the frog or the spider but he was glad Nader was working with and not against the Brotherhood – for he would make a formidable enemy. He would have a talk with his daughter Azizah. There were not many men like Nader around.

That evening the two men sat sipping tea from gold-rimmed cups in the rock garden overlooking the Red Sea. The sea breeze washed over them and the last rays of the setting sun kissed their faces. The sound of breaking waves on the coral beach and the smell of salt and seaweed played on their senses, evoking different memories for the two. Jeddah was pleasant in winter, free from its usual humidity and suffocating heat.

A ribbon of smoke rose from a cigarette nestled between Nader's fingers.

The old man took a deep breath and continued feeding the prayer beads through hands crippled with arthritis.

'It's bad for you,' he said, wrinkling his nose at the smoke.

Nader stubbed out the cigarette.

The old man gave a nod and continued to ruminate over the report of the meeting in Riyadh that Nader had attended. There was no doubt, Nader was a good orator and commanded the respect of the men. He was also a sly fox with an abundance of imagination. Recruiting infected whores and smuggling drugs were his ideas – and now this Black Widow thing. The Brotherhood needed men like him to win the war. He could be more effective in Jeddah or Riyadh than hidden away in Tabuk.

Weary eyes with grey circles stared at some point beyond the wall and across the blue waters, seeing nothing. He was a blind man with a profound vision.

'What do you see there?' the old man asked pointing to the west with a gnarled finger.

'Sea and sky.'

The old man looked at Nader and barked, 'Is that all?'

'I see the setting sun and fiery clouds,' Nader replied, and the old man smiled.

'Now look again,' he commanded with annoyance in his voice. Nader stared into the distance rubbing his jaw.

'Tell him!' ordered a woman's voice. Nader spun round to see a young woman wearing an aquamarine ankle-length dress and matching scarf. She was not more than twenty-five with well-defined features and sharp black eyes that missed nothing. 'Go on, answer him, my father doesn't like to be kept waiting.'

Nader didn't like to be told what to do by a woman but bridled his anger. He realised the old man didn't want to know about the clouds or the sea or the sun. He wanted to know what his heart saw, the symbolic meaning behind the events unfolding before him. He paused for a moment, taking in the whole picture and spoke with the same clarity that had brought the Brotherhood to their feet.

'Dying with the sinking sun, abandoned by the West, I see the death of the House of Saud. I see the fire of our revolution in the clouds.' Nader looked at the old man and saw his eyes close and his head rock to and fro.

'Yes! Yes! And what else?' The old man snapped. 'Look around you, open your eyes!' he commanded. Nader's eyes scanned the heavens for inspiration and saw the new moon rising in the East behind the date palms.

'I see the birth of the new order of Islam under the banner of the crescent moon, the symbol of our Brotherhood,' he said emphatically. Calm settled over the old man's face. The woman gave a hollow laugh, draped a woollen shawl around the old man and wheeled him into the house away from the winter chill.

Nader didn't understand the purpose of the exercise but was sure the woman had the answer.

'I'm Azizah.'

Nader frowned. Azizah sensed what was on his mind. 'Our Prophet said a woman's hair was *aurat*, not her face. The veil is a product of our culture, not our religion.'

Patting Azizah's hand, the old man chuckled. 'There is much wisdom in a woman's head. It's a foolish man who thinks it empty. Remember son, it's the lioness that hunts, the praying mantis devours her mate after mating and the scorpion stings her mate to death. Fear the woman, for it is she who carries our sons and daughters and our future.'

NINETEEN

Guilt played tag with Maryam's conscience until dawn. Sleep failed to tether her restless mind as it struggled to bridge the ever-widening chasm between fact and fiction, right and wrong, good and evil and men and women.

Saffron was right, there was no denying it. There weren't any jobs that meant anything in the real world. Sure there were the token gestures in hospitals, banks, schools and universities but it was a pipe dream to think that if she wanted, she could be a pilot in a country where driving a car was forbidden or be a politician when women weren't allowed to vote.

Her mother was right, too: she didn't have to prove anything to anyone but herself; but even then the cursed veil got in the way and the shadow of men fell across her world blocking out the sun. Black was black and white was white. There was nothing in between.

Change wasn't going to come anytime soon. A revolution was possible if not probable, but change for women was in the realms of fantasy and fiction. The King and his brothers made promises that were forgotten as soon as they were uttered.

Hope was not the instrument of choice to bring about change. Living in hope was living a life in purgatory. Saffron didn't need to sit exams; she could read the writing on the wall without knowing the alphabet. Was Nader right when he said, 'Change comes out of a barrel of a gun?' She was sure he hadn't believed her about Joe. He would ask again and she would just have to be resolute and see what happened, she told herself.

Dawn brought with it solace and the morning prayer brought salvation to her troubled spirit.

* * *

After breakfast she bid farewell to her father and gave her mother and Saffron a big hug.

'Exams aren't all they are made out to be,' Maryam whispered in Saffron's ear.

'I know,' Saffron replied, and gave a knowing wink.

'Thanks for telling it as it is,' Maryam said, offering an olive branch.

'Have fun, honey!' Saffron shouted and waved goodbye.

Mahmoud drove her into town and dropped her off at the Al Shamrani home on the airbase.

* * *

That evening Sahar's driver dropped Maryam outside Pizza Sheikh next to the Astra supermarket. Joe met her at the rear of the building, away from prying eyes in his Chevy, and spirited her across town.

Al Busteen was an unusual restaurant tucked away among the farms off Medinah Road, far from the city centre and closer to the foreign compounds. It was a sprawling place dotted with squat palms and thatched pavilions with reed walls and tents. Moths danced around naked bulbs throwing out a glow that failed to penetrate the darkness.

A string of blinking fairy lights, draped on a white building that served as the kitchen, competed with the glow-worms and fireflies. The place had an easygoing ambiance with an emphasis on privacy. Patrons came and went unnoticed.

'The *mutawah* don't go there,' Maryam remembered Sahar

saying. 'It's just too far for them to bother. Besides they have to get past security.'

The word security had rung alarm bells in Maryam's head but then Samar had reassured her.

'We've been loads of times, the food is great, discretion is free and the security is there to keep them out.'

A kerosene lantern perched on the rickety table threw out a golden glow from a sooty flame. The incessant hum of crickets filled the air and the evening breeze, scented with jasmine and the aroma of food, carried titbits of conversation and laughter.

They sat in silence. Neither could believe the other's presence. Moist hands entwined, dispelling the notion that this was an aberration of their minds. They gazed through the windows of their souls watching the embers glow within.

'I can't believe you're here,' Joe whispered, fearing the wind was listening and would tell the world their secret.

'I'm excited, frightened and confused all at once,' Maryam confessed.

'My heart is beating ten to a dozen.'

'Mine too. Feels like it's about to explode,' Maryam replied and adjusted her scarf over her head hearing the hurried footfall of the waiter on the gravel path.

He was a lanky, dark-skinned man – probably from the Indian subcontinent, Joe surmised from his accent and genteel manner. He wore a white shirt and black trousers. The bow tie looked out of place in the Arabian setting. He apologised for the intrusion, grinning from ear to ear, and presented them with a faded menu in Arabic and English that was hard to read in the dim light.

Seeing their dilemma he reeled off the dishes, stopping only to catch his breath.

'Very good everything, sir,' he said in the end, shaking his head in the classic Indian way, and took their orders. With a wave he disappeared, hurrying to the next tent.

'Very good everything, madam,' Joe mimicked, shaking his head from side to side making Maryam laugh.

'Thousand apologies,' Joe continued putting on his best Indian accent and they both guffawed like two naughty kids on a school outing.

They quenched their thirst on laughter and filled their bellies with a diet of words and emotions blended with curiosity. For dessert they plucked kisses from lips ripened by desire.

The food was good but they scarcely touched it, much to the waiter's disappointment.

He looked hurt and asked, 'Madam no like?'

'It's very good but we're not hungry,' Joe explained. The waiter shook his head and removed the platter.

'Thousand apologies, maybe madam in love,' he said and gave them a big smile that made them blush.

'I have a secret,' Maryam said under her breath.

'That sounds exciting, show me a woman who doesn't.'

'Be serious, Joe!'

'Thousand apologies, madam!'

'Joe!'

'Okay, okay.'

'I want to share it with you.'

'Is it about us?'

'No, not really. . . not right now. . . But it might be if you behave.'

'Oh, it's like that?'

'Afraid so, Dr Joe.'

'I promise to behave,' Joe replied, raising his right hand and pretending to take an oath.

'You're impossible.'

'And you're divine,' Joe whispered, clasping Maryam's hand. He studied the patterns of the veins on the back of her hands, letting his fingers caress her olive skin, and listened to her lyrical voice.

'That's incredulous,' Joe exclaimed when Maryam finished.

'Incredible yes. Incredulous, no.'

'So you are betrothed to. . .'

'What's betrothed?'

'Betrothed. . . let me see. . . it's like an old-fashioned promise to wed.'

'In that case, yes, I am betrothed.'

'But before you were conceived, let alone born?'

'Our traditions go a long way back. We're very old fashioned.'

'You don't say? And do you love him?'

'*Insha'allah*, I hope to in time,' Maryam said, playing with her engagement ring, thinking back to Nader's phone call.

'You hope. What kind of answer is that, for Pete's sake?'

'We believe love grows through companionship.'

'The point is, do you believe in all that?'

'I think so!'

'But you're not sure?'

'Perhaps. . . It's all very confusing.'

'And you don't know this. . . this Nader. . . he could be anybody off the street.'

'My father has known his family for years.'

'Your father gave you away to his friend's son?'

'This friend saved my father's life.'

'A life for a life! Can't you see it's a trade?'

'Is that how you see it, Joe?'

'People are not objects to be offered as gifts, Maryam.'

'You don't understand.'

'Damn right I don't. . . care to help me out?

'Shhh! Keep your voice down,' Maryam pleaded. She blushed and looked away. How could Joe understand her feelings? Ever since their first meeting her mind had been possessed by him. She felt torn between her loyalty to her father and her desire for freedom.

'What are you doing here?' Joe cut into Maryam's thoughts. 'Why are you risking everything?'

Maryam looked into Joe's smouldering eyes and whispered. 'Don't you know? Have you ever been in love, Joe?'

'As a matter of fact I have, Maryam.' Joe replied without thinking.

'How does it feel?'

'Well, it feels like. . .' Joe hesitated, collecting his thoughts. 'It feels like an emotional volcano exploding in your head. Your heart thunders like a herd of galloping horses and your spirit soars with the eagle one minute and dives down the next, only to soar again.'

'Hmm. . . I like the sound of that,' Maryam said.

'You definitely know you're a lost cause when you can't say no to the object of your love and people think you're certifiable. It's something like that and more. . .' Joe explained, seeing the hesitation on Maryam's face.

'But that's so beautiful, Joe,' Maryam gasped.

'And so are you, Maryam.' Joe watched the lantern's flame dance across her glazed eyes.

'Now do you understand why I can't say no? I love my father.'

Joe frowned, wondering why life was always so complicated, and Maryam sensed his mind wrestling with the conundrum as she caressed his hand.

In her heart lurked uncertainty abetted by guilt. The rumbling volcano that Joe had described was threatening to shake the very foundation of her world, a world that had seemed so secure and ordered not so long ago. Silence joined them at the table and seconds coalesced into minutes.

Joe's fingertips traced the contours of Maryam's face, mapping a terrain untouched by any man's hand. His finger faltered over her lips, teasing them apart.

With eyes closed, Maryam let the magic of his touch wash over her in waves of ecstasy. Throwing caution to the wind she sent silence scurrying back into the darkness. She murmured, 'Let's soar with the eagles, Joe,' and she kissed his fingertips.

'Let's fly away,' Joe whispered, and kissed her lips.

* * *

The driver was waiting for them in the car park under the rustling eucalyptus trees when they pulled up behind Pizza Sheikh.

Their lips brushed and eyes locked for a tantalizing moment.

'I think we're certifiable, Dr Joe,' Maryam teased and then she was gone, blending into the shadows hurrying to the car.

Joe watched the car turn onto the main road and it was lost, speeding away in a battery of tail lights.

TWENTY

Saffron read the letter again. Her hand shook and the piece of paper slipped from her fingers to land at her feet.

'You don't look well,' Aishah said.

Saffron seemed too look at Aishah, but saw nothing.

'Have you heard from America?' Aishah asked, seeing the envelope on the table.

Saffron remained silent.

'What is it, *habibi*? Is it bad news?' Aishah asked.

Saffron nodded and chewed her lip.

'*Insha'allah*, it will all be all right,' Aishah said. She put her arm round Saffron and held her close. 'Is it from your uncle?' she asked.

Saffron shook her head and began to sob. 'It's from the police,' she said after a while.

'Police?'

'Uncle Jim's dead.'

'Dead? How?'

'He was shot during a robbery,' Saffron explained in between sobs. 'He worked in a bank.'

'America is such a violent country,' Aishah said, stroking Saffron's head.

Saffron sobbed louder, remembering how her first husband was gunned down by a drug-crazed hobo as they left a nightclub.

'We are so safe here. It is our *sharia* law.'

'He was all that was left of my family and I didn't even make it to his funeral,' Saffron mumbled, shaking her head.

'Hush, *habibi*, you did not know. You have us now. We are your family.' Aishah wiped the tears from Saffron's cheeks.

'He never forgot my birthday and always phoned on Christmas Day.'

'This is your home now.'

'You're so kind, Mama Aishah,' Saffron kissed Aishah's hand and held it to her face.

'Mahmoud and I were alone too when our parents died. Now we are part of Farhan's family and his tribe. Like you are. We have hundreds of relatives and friends.'

Saffron looked at her feet and said, 'There is nothing left for me in America,'

'What about your tribe?' Aishah asked.

'We don't have tribes in America, Mama Aishah,' Saffron replied and brushed aside her tears.

Aishah threw up her hands in horror. 'No tribes, that's terrible,' she exclaimed.

'We're all Americans.'

'We are Saudis but our tribe gives us our identity. People know where they belong and who their relatives are.'

'Americans come from all over the world. My father was Polish and my mother Irish,' Saffron explained.

'But you all pray to one God?' Aishah asked.

'America is a free country. People worship whoever they want.'

'That must be so confusing.'

'People have a right to choose.'

'What is there to choose? There is only one Allah and his messenger is our Prophet, Mohammed, peace be upon him.'

'I'm sure you're right, Mama Aishah.' Saffron sniffed and blew her nose.

'Do you know what Islam means, *habibi*?'

Saffron shook her head in embarrassment.

'It means submission to Allah and no one else. Our Holy

Qur'an teaches us how to live in peace with ourselves and our neighbours. It gives us our laws and touches every part of our lives. Islam is more than a religion, *habibi*. It is a way of life.'

Saffron saw Aishah's love for her faith glow on her face and realised that there was something in what this simple woman had to say. Catholicism seemed to be more interested in filling you with guilt than in saving your soul. She liked the idea of being one to one with God five times a day. That was more times than in the last five years.

'I promise to read the *Qur'an* you gave me, Mama Aishah,' Saffron said, and kissed Aishah's cheek.

'Would you like some tea?' Aishah asked, getting up.

'I'll help you make it.'

'Remember we all love you, *habibi*. I promise to remember your birthday. But you might have to remind me about your Christmas.'

They hugged and headed for the kitchen.

TWENTY-ONE

Dressed like an Arab, Joe sat in the Chevy van, buried behind a copy of the *Arab News*. He had bought the Hi-Top from a departing Australian contactor who called it his 'Rooting Wagon'. 'It's got everything you want, mate. Except a Sheila. Plenty of them at the hospital,' he had informed Joe.

Joe turned the pages pretending to read, glancing over the top towards an open-air restaurant called Abaya Park that had a section for women. Enclosed by a screen of stained glass, it was a sanctuary where women could relax without being harassed by the *mutaween* who patrolled the malls.

Maryam slipped on a different pair of shoes to step out from Abaya Park, past Mahmoud seated under a eucalyptus tree sipping tea and towards the Chevy at the far end of the parking lot. She smiled thinking of Samar and Sahar and thanked them. She opened the door and slipped into the passenger seat.

'What took you so long?' Joe asked.

'The checkpoints are getting bad and Uncle Mahmoud was busy with a horse that's ill.'

Joe started the engine and headed for the international *souq* on the outskirts of town, which was almost always deserted.

'How I wish we could meet more often,' Maryam said, 'but I'm running out of excuses to come into town.'

'You mustn't take needless risks, *habibi*.'

Maryam gave a wicked smile. 'You've learnt a new word.'

'I'm never sure when we'll meet until you're right here beside me.'

'I'm here now, *habibi*.'

Fifteen minutes later they pulled up a short distance from a cluster of cars and pickups. Many of the shops were empty shells, shuttered and padlocked, a haven for dust and garbage.

They slipped into the rear of the Chevy giggling like kids and breathed a sigh of relief. Though they had done this before, the tension was always there. Joe adjusted a velvet blind that had moved, shutting out the light, and Maryam slipped from her *abaya* and veil looking radiant. They hugged and kissed like adolescents behind a shed.

'I've missed you so much, Joe,' Maryam whispered.

'Me too,' Joe replied, caressing her hand.

'This is so crazy.'

'What's crazy?'

'This sneaking around.'

'Oh that!' Joe laughed. 'Tea?'

Maryam nodded.

'I have your favourite cookies,' Joe said, waving a box just out of Maryam's reach.

'Don't be cruel.'

'I think they are worth at least ten kisses.'

'I'll give you twenty.'

'Done!' Joe laughed, handing Maryam the carton of Scottish Shortbread.

'You're easily pleased, I'd have traded forty.'

'I'll keep that in mind for next time.'

'Can't believe they're back in stock.' Maryam unwrapped the cellophane with glee.

Joe poured the tea from a thermos into two glass cups on the foldaway table.

'You look a sight,' Maryam said, pulling off Joe's *gutra* and drawing him closer.

'Your own *Sheikh of Arabi*,' Joe said, taking a bow.

The aroma of mint tea and shortbread filled the van.

'Do they do this in your country?' Maryam asked, as they cuddled in the back seat.

'Do what?'

'This. . . meet up like we do.'

'Sure,' Joe replied, nuzzling Maryam's ear.

'Really?' Maryam sat up in surprise.

'Mainly high-school kids when they don't have a place to go.'

'You mean even in your free society?'

'Making out in a car is part of growing up.'

'Did you?' Maryam gave a mischievous grin.

'I never grew up.'

'You know what I mean.' Maryam elbowed Joe in the ribs.

'It's part of growing up.' Joe blushed.

'For us it's about growing together isn't it, Joe?' Maryam whispered, resting her head on his chest and smiling.

Joe kissed her forehead.

'I can hear your heart,' Maryam said.

'What's it saying?'

'Let me see. . . Ah. . . yes. It's saying it likes me.'

'That can't be right. Listen again.' Joe faked disappointment.

'Ok. . . yes I hear you, little heart. I hear you well,' Maryam whispered.

'So?'

'It says it's in love.'

'I better listen to yours,' Joe replied.

'Another time, I can't stay long today.'

'Oh?'

'I want to buy this beautiful scarf I've seen for Saffron. It's her birthday soon.'

'Why a scarf?'

'Saffron's very practical. She needs one to cover her hair and she adores clothes.'

'Are you going have a party?'

'Muslims don't celebrate birthdays.'

'But she's not a Muslim.'
'One day I hope she will be.'
'Why?'
'Because I'm a Muslim and I'd wish that upon her. Besides I think Islam has so much to offer her.'
'I can't see that happening.'
'Why not?' Maryam looked puzzled.
'She doesn't seem the type.'
'What type is that?' Maryam pulled away from Joe.
'You need to be passionate to believe in something.'
'Saffron's passionate.'
'About material things.'
'And life,' Maryam added.
'Like you,' Joe said, kissing Maryam's lips, drawing her closer.

Maryam looked at Joe and asked, 'Would you embrace Islam for me, Joe?'

'When you love a person you must. . .' Joe stopped in mid sentence, hearing a car drive up and park close by. Maryam motioned Joe with her eyes to look but Joe shook his head.

'What are they doing?' Maryam whispered in Joe's ear as minutes passed.

'Shhh! Stay still,' Joe whispered. 'You'll rock the van.'

'Switch off the light,' Maryam hissed and Joe reached overhead and flipped the switch of the cabin light leaving them in darkness.

With every passing minute the tension grew. Doors opened and slammed shut. Joe and Maryam held their breaths and waited for a knock on the window.

They heard the sound of *ship ship* scraping on the tarmac coming nearer and then moving around them.

'I can't stand this anymore,' Maryam murmured under her breath.

'Shhh!' Joe placed a finger on her lips.

'The key,' Maryam whispered, pointing to the steering column.

'Shit!' Joe rolled his eyes in despair.

'Nice model,' said a voice.

'Looks new,' said another, and a man pressed his face against the driver's window to get a better look. 'Must've cost a bomb.'

'Don't joke about bombs, brother, the wind has ears,' replied the first voice. They laughed and walked away holding hands.

'That was close,' Maryam whispered, relieved to hear the sound of the voices fading.

'Let's get back,' Joe replied.

Maryam nodded and her trembling lips kissed his. She adjusted the *gutra* over Joe's head and put on her *abaya*. They kissed one last time, a long lingering kiss, and Maryam dropped her veil. Joe peeked from behind the curtain making sure the men were out of sight before jumping in the driver's seat and heading back to the *souk*.

'See you at the Sahara Hotel,' Maryam murmured. She stepped out of the Chevy and made for the mall beyond Abaya Park.

TWENTY-TWO

With monotonous regularity Nader wound and unwound the ivory *misbaha* around his finger with a flick of his wrist. Maryam's nerves were on edge.

'Would you like more tea,' she asked, hoping to distract him.

'How are your studies?' he asked looking down his nose.

'Going well I think,' Maryam replied.

'Mona tells me you have exams soon.'

'Yes, only a few weeks to go now.'

'What subjects are you taking?'

'There's English Language, Geography, History, the Sciences. . .'

'You mean like Chemistry?'

'Yes, also Biology and Physics.'

'Biology?'

'Yes. We study plants and animals and their development and reproduction and how. . .'

'Reproduction?'

'You know, pollination in plants, seed production and germination and. . .'

'That's for farmers. What use is it to you?'

'It's very interesting. We also study cellular and molecular biology and genetics, which is all about genes and cloning.'

'Cloning, what's that?'

'It's producing an offspring identical to the parent by. . .'

144

'Like that sheep I read about in the *Arab News*?'

'Yes! Yes! Like Dolly the sheep. Unfortunately we only study the basic theory.'

'That's Shaitaan's work, you have no business studying this. Only Allah gives life and we have no right to. . ..'

'It's so fascinating,'

'It's *haram*! You hear me, it's forbidden!'

'Think of all those diseases that we could. . .'

'Diseases are Allah's way of punishing evil doers and infidels.'

'Nader! Allah is kind, merciful and forgiving.'

'And how will all this knowledge make you a better Muslim?'

'It teaches me to be humble and appreciate the wisdom of Allah.'

'Is that what they teach you to say at college?'

'No! It's how I feel as a servant of Allah,' Maryam said returning Nader's glare. 'Don't preach to me about what I can say and feel,' she continued trying to control her breathing. 'Allah knows what's in my heart, as he knows what's in yours, Nader! Come judgement day. . .'

'Look who's preaching now,' Nader shouted pointing at her. 'If Allah knows your heart, then he must know of Joe?'

Maryam blushed and bit her lip.

'Well, does he? Answer me!'

Maryam glared at Nader and whispered 'I don't know any Joe.'

'You're a liar. I'll teach him a lesson when I find him. And find him I shall!' Nader stomped out leaving Maryam angry and frustrated. But, for the first time, she felt she had the measure of Nader: she had looked him in the eye and he had backed down. But now she feared for Joe.

*   *   *

Colonel Nasser tapped the ash from his cigarette.

'Remember it's *Haj*, maybe they are away,' said Kamal.

'They'll be back,' said Ali, trying to sound positive. 'These men live and work here. Sooner or later one of them is going to slip up and that's when we'll nab them.'

'You've had no luck with the roadblocks,' Nasser barked abruptly, irritated by what he was hearing.

'Oh! I almost forgot,' said Ayman, handing Nasser a piece of paper. 'It came through this morning. The lab in Riyadh found traces of heroin and shoe polish on the ID card.'

Nasser smiled. 'That's a step forward. We'll check out the heroin users in town. Shouldn't be difficult, they'll have records at the hospitals and the rehab centre. Yahya must have stumbled upon them and paid with his life.'

'He wore a new pair of shoes,' said Kamal.

'A shoe shop could be a front,' added Ali.

'Interesting,' Nasser muttered and gave a wry smile. 'The heroin is probably a long shot, but it narrows the options. I'll get someone on to that right away.'

'And there's another thing,' said Ayman. 'The lab identified syphilis in the samples we sent.'

'So sooner or later these men will seek treatment,' said Kamal.

'We hope,' said Ayman.

'We have to cover pharmacies, doctors and hospitals,' Nasser said, feeling positive.

*　*　*

'You must come, *habibi*,' implored Sahar on the phone. 'It wouldn't be the same without you and you must bring Saffron; we're all dying to meet her. Where did you say she came from?'

'Los Angeles,' Maryam replied.

'We're going to have Egyptian dancers and a Filipino band. It'll be such great fun. The men will be there too but on the other side, in the garden. We'll be around that beautiful pool. I've arranged something special.'

'Let me guess,' Maryam said.

'One of dad's friends is going to check into the hotel. It's so easy at the Sahara, no one cares who comes or goes.'

'I don't believe you!' Maryam exclaimed.

'It was Samar's idea. One minute he'll be talking to my father and the next he'll be screwing his daughters. I get goose bumps just thinking about it.'

'You're impossible.'

'Couldn't be sexier,' giggled Sahar.

'How did you meet him?' Maryam asked, infected by Sahar's enthusiasm.

'He came round to see dad and we bumped into him in the hallway. He's quite old but you know what they say about older men?'

'Tell me.'

'They've got style. I'm sure he's going to be great. Can't get any worse then Abdul.'

'So how did you. . .'

'It was easy,' interrupted Sahar, knowing what was coming. 'I left a note in his car and he telephoned the next day while every-one was busy during *Isha* prayers.'

Maryam couldn't believe her ears. Sahar and Samar never ceased to astound her. But this latest adventure with a man old enough to be their father horrified her. They were so full of energy and guts, living in a world of their own, breaking every rule. That's what this country needed; women with guts. They were going to be nineteen and celebrating in style at the best hotel Tabuk could offer.

'Are you sure about this?' Maryam asked.

'Hell, yes!'

'Okay! Count me in.'

'Promise you'll bring Saffron.'

'I promise,' Maryam replied, thinking of Joe.

TWENTY-THREE

Saffron flicked over the pages with disinterest. The small print made her eyes ache. I would give anything for a racy novel, she said to herself. Tom Clancy and Jackie Collins were her favourite authors but right now anything would do.

'That's enough for today,' Saffron said and slammed the book shut just as Farhan entered the library.

'Reading anything interesting?' he asked coming over to her.

'They're all in Arabic except this one,' Saffron stabbed at the book in front of her.

'Ah! You found the *Encyclopaedia Britannica*, very informative.'

'Great if I was entering a quiz but hardly entertaining. I'm bored out of my mind.'

Farhan laughed. 'Tabuk must be a big change for you.'

'You bet.'

'Don't you have everything you want?' Farhan asked, making himself comfortable on the sofa beside her.

'You kidding? There's no music. I miss my music so much,' Saffron declared.

'Music?'

'Yeah. They say music is the food of love.'

'Who are *they*?' Farhan had a mischievous twinkle in his eye.

'Oh, I don't know, probably Ray Charles or James Brown. It's one of those sayings everyone knows.'

'*Twelfth Night.*'

'Never heard of them. Are they anything like Led Zep? I just loved '*Stairway to Heaven.*' The instrumentals are great but the lyrics are just brilliant. You don't know what you're missing,' Saffron said, patting Farhan's knee.

'The *Qur'an* can show you the way to Heaven.' Farhan played with the ring on his finger.

'Right now I miss my music.'

'If music will make you happy, *habibi*, then music you shall have and perhaps love will follow,' Farhan reached for Saffron's hand.

'Really?' Saffron exclaimed, surprised at Farhan's candidness.

'Heaven can wait a while, I need you now,' Farhan gazed into Saffron's eyes.

'You're a poet.' Saffron smiled and drew closer and brushed against Farhan's knee.

'Has anyone told you lately, you're beautiful?'

Saffron laughed and let her hand trail across Farhan's thigh.

'When is my son coming back?'

'Don't know. He doesn't tell me everything. You know what he's like.'

'Selfish!'

'Then you know him well.'

'So what are you doing here?'

'I though that was obvious.'

'Saffron, *habibi*, you play games with an old man.'

'I never play games and age is a mind thing,' Saffron combed her fingers through her hair, tossing her flaming curls.

'Tell me.'

'You're very naughty, Farhan Al Balawi,' Saffron said and patted his hand, a wicked smile on her lips.

'You're too loyal.'

'Mom told me you can't buy loyalty.' Saffron winked.

'Everything has a price.'

'She told me that too.'

'Then loyalty must have a price.'

'I guess it does. She wasn't wise all the time but I can forgive her for that.'

'Were you close?'

'Nah! She was never around when I needed her.'

'Miss her?'

'Sure. She and Uncle Jim were all I had for family.'

'How long will you stay?'

'What do you mean?'

'Don't you want to go back to. . . ?'

'No, no, it's not like that. . . Mom passed away a while back and Uncle Jim. . . he died recently.'

'I know he doesn't love you,' Farhan looked pensive, slipping the ring up and down his finger.

'Who?'

'Nabeel, of course.'

'How can you say that?'

'He only loves himself.'

'Are you sure of that?' Saffron asked, watching Farhan playing with the ring.

'He's my son, I should know.'

'What makes you different?' Saffron inquired.

'This!' Farhan pulled Saffron close and kissed her.

'I'm your son's wife,' Saffron protested, pushing Farhan away. 'This can't happen.'

'Stop the pretence, *habibi*, I want you,' Farhan attempted to kiss her again.

'How dare you, Farhan,' Saffron shouted, faking anger. She tried to slap his face but he caught her wrist.

'I'll give you anything, just name it,' Farhan whispered and crushed her against the couch, his lips finding hers. Saffron resisted, beating her fists against his chest but gave in. It had been a while since she had been kissed and with such passion.

'You're an obstinate old man,' Saffron pushed Farhan away but knew she had crossed a line.

'Didn't you say age was a mind thing?' Farhan surveyed Saffron's beauty and smiled. He told himself it was only a matter of time before she was his.

* * *

Salem sat picking his nose in the corner of a dingy room at the rear of a restaurant frequented by taxi drivers and itinerant labourers. A grease-covered fan struggled to rid the air of oil and chicken that clung to the walls.

'More tea, *ya sedeeq*!' Salem called, tapping his bamboo cane on the tiled floor, and the Turkish waiter emerged and filled his cup. Salem looked at his watch as a man appeared in the doorway.

'You're late.' Salem said, and greeted Nader with a handshake and kisses.

'This bomb in Riyadh has made life difficult. So many check points and diversions.'

'And all for a handful of *Ameriki*,' Salem added, shaking his head, and snapped his fingers at the waiter for more tea.

'Any idea who did it?' Nader asked, drawing his chair closer.

'Rumour has it, it was the Brotherhood,' Salem replied looking smug.

'You think so?'

'I know these things,' Salem replied tapping his nose. 'I understand congratulations are in order.'

'What do you mean?' Nader asked sipping his tea.

'You're moving up in the world.'

'What have you heard?'

'Come, come, Nader, you can stop pretending.'

'I'm not due for promotion.'

'I heard you've got engaged to the Area Commander's daughter,' Salem said with a satisfied smile on his face.

'A man has got to put down roots sometime.'

'I expect an invitation.'

'You'll be the first, *ya* Salem, I swear,' Nader replied.

'You said you had something for me on the phone?'

Nader fished out a photograph from his breast pocket and slid it across the table.

Salem examined the photo and sipped some tea. 'You want me to teach him a lesson?' Salem asked.

Nader smiled.

Salem laughed and pocketed the photograph. 'Leave it with me, I'll have him quoting the *Qur'an*.'

They emptied their teacups, Salem threw a few *riyals* on the table and they left.

TWENTY-FOUR

Maryam smiled at her reflection in the mirror. Her gaze moved up from her ankles to her calves and onto the thighs that finished at her feminine hips.

She had not been aware of her figure until Saffron raved about it and Joe awakened her feelings. Now she drank in her physical beauty until she became intoxicated. She shut her eyes and let the tips of her fingers run up from her knees to the inside of her thighs. She giggled and imagined they were Joe's fingers.

She let her fingertips map the contour of her belly and come to rest in her navel for a few seconds feeling the warmth within. They continued their exploration up her midriff, rising over her breasts and nipples, tracing a circle over her areola. Cupping her breasts she massaged them and gasped as a tingle rang down her spine.

She examined the curve of her back. 'Perfect,' she purred and patted her buttocks. She tossed her head and turned her hair into a shimmering black wave that bounced with self-possessed energy.

Yes, it was good to be alive. 'I appreciate and love myself more every day.' It had become a ritual for her to make an affirmation every morning. The one she especially liked was, 'I have un-limited potential and I control the present and the future, I am free from my past.' A declaration that Nader was now something of the past and that she had a role to play in a man's world whether they liked it or not. It had been Saffron's idea and, looking back, she wondered why she hadn't thought of it herself.

Today was to be a turning point in her life. She was going to the Sahara hotel with Saffron to celebrate Samar and Sahar's birthday, but it was to be a celebration of a different kind for her. She had decided that today she would give herself to Joe, as a statement of her love and in defiance of everything that she had been nurtured on.

She was wresting control of her life and future from the hands of Saudi men and the establishment. She looked in the mirror and repeated her affirmation, watching her lips breathe life into every word.

This was her day and she was going to be the star. Carefully she examined the item of clothing she had laid out on her bed. Saffron had come shopping with her and they had scoured the souq, discovering hidden boutiques with exotic lingerie that left them gasping.

Saffron said that underwear was like fancy wrapping paper: it made a poor gift attractive and an attractive gift irresistible. Maryam agreed, seeing the transformation in the mirror.

Yes, what you wore affected the way you felt and today she felt on top of the world. She wriggled into one of Saffron's dresses, a Versace creation in scarlet chiffon that hugged the contours of her body like a silk skin. It let her arms and shoulders breathe and plunged down the front revealing the valley of her bosom. Down each side, oval windows exposed islands of olive skin.

Scarlet shoes with stiletto heels and pearls around her neck and on her ear lobes completed the picture.

Maryam gave a twirl and Saffron let off a wolf whistle.

'Hell. If that doesn't do it, nothing will,' she exclaimed and rejoiced in Maryam's metamorphosis into a butterfly. 'He'll cream in his pants when you drop your *abaya*.'

'Cream?' Maryam asked.

'Oh never you mind, Miss Virgin. Just enjoy the ride.' Saffron replied with mischief in her eyes and they laughed and hugged each other. Maryam was learning that the monotony of life could be transformed into one filled with adventure.

* * *

Mahmoud cursed and wound down the window at the check-point. A cadet demanded to see the women's papers.

'You've the brains of a donkey! Don't you know women don't have identifications?' Mahmoud fumed and the cadet waved them through. 'I'll speak to Farhan about this.'

Maryam's thoughts were far away. Joe had phoned earlier that day and given her a number that she had committed to memory.

'Who was that?' her mother had asked.

Flustered she had replied, 'Wrong number.'

The Sahara Hotel sits cradled in a wedge-shaped island between Medinah Road and Airport Road overlooking a round-about, home to a concrete crown the size of a four-storey building. Big, bold and ugly, thought Saffron seated beside Maryam. Tabuk had many hotels but only the Sahara catered for the international traveller and the sophisticated Saudis.

National flags fluttering in the evening breeze proclaimed in Arabic: *There is no god but God; Mohammed is the Messenger of God*, underscored by a scimitar. Tabuk Sahara Hotel blazed in green neon on the roof like an emerald tiara and a necklace of lights ringed the crest of the building.

Mahmoud navigated the Suburban around a fountain spray-ing water onto the road and stopped under the canopy at the entrance. A Filipino concierge in white livery complete with gold-trimmed epaulettes and buttons opened the glass door seeing them alight onto the red carpet.

'Call me when you're done, I'll be at Uncle Eid's,' Mahmoud shouted and drove away, still fuming.

Maryam's heart raced; somewhere in the building Joe was waiting for her. No one took the slightest notice as the two women crossed the marble lobby and waited for the elevator.

This was Saffron's first time at the Sahara and she was surprised to find such opulence after her impressions of downtown Tabuk.

The interior designers had used the same formula found in good hotels: sofas gathered in clusters, a forest of plants in copper pots, walls of tinted mirrors and a galaxy of lights.

In the lounge a crowd of foreigners wearing double-breasted suits and Rolex watches exchanged tales of mega contracts. They all spoke the same body language, one hand buried in their trouser pocket while the other prodded the air. Waiters hovered like vultures, eager to please, waiting for generous tips.

Men in groups of twos and threes, accompanied by the occasional Western woman in casual attire dotted the Al Waha lounge on the other side of the foyer drinking American coffee, a concoction of instant coffee and coffeemate, or sipping Earl Grey tea from china cups. They were from the resident expatriate brigade, swapping tales of recent conquests and alcoholic binges, both in and out of the Kingdom.

The letter G on the brass panel lit up and the doors opened. They took the elevator to the basement and Samar welcomed them by the pool. Maryam introduced Saffron and they pressed gifts and cards into Samar's hand and wished her a happy birthday.

'Where is Sahar?' asked Maryam, walking to their table holding Samar's hand.

'Shhh... She's up there somewhere,' Samar whispered, looking up at the bank of windows. 'I just hope he's up to it. I'd hate to be disappointed on my birthday.'

Maryam looked up at the building and thought of Joe while Samar squeezed her hand. Time was precious; she would have to make her move soon. An opportunity like this might not come again.

They joined Samar's mother at her table and the waiter offered them Saudi Champagne: a concoction of Perrier water, orange and apple juice with a flotsam of mixed fruit garnished with a sprig of mint and a slice of lemon.

Veils and *abaya* lay abandoned on the floor or draped over chairs. The odd mother sat like a black monolith, tsking disapproval under her veil.

There was a gaggle of women by the poolside all eating and drinking. A steady stream of girls paraded to tables with steel platters piled high with food. They heaped their plates and flirted with the waiters, discreetly letting slip a ball of paper at their feet with their phone numbers. They sauntered back to their seats, rolling their hips for appraisal by mothers on the lookout for brides. The atmosphere reminded Saffron of beauty pageants back home where the prize was a cheque for a few thousand bucks and a modelling contract for a year, not a lifetime of servitude to a stranger.

With trepidation, Maryam made an excuse and left for the powder room that was past the elevator. Saffron winked and smiled encouragingly.

The doors to the elevator opened and Maryam froze.

'Good evening, madam,' greeted the concierge. 'Up, Madam?'

'Yes,' replied Maryam sharply and stepped in.

'Ground floor, Madam?'

Maryam nodded. She had to think fast and decided she would use the complimentary phones in the foyer. What could be more normal then that?

She stabbed at the keypad and pretended to speak. She listening to the phone beep and watched the concierge by the elevator.

'Shit! Shit! Shit!' Maryam exclaimed and decided to return to the pool. Just then a car pulled up and the concierge abandoned his position to welcome the new arrivals.

Maryam saw her chance and walked briskly to the elevator. She pressed the button to go up and watched the reflection of the new arrivals alighting from their car in the chrome elevator doors. 'Open,' Maryam hissed and pressed the button again. The doors opened, she jumped in and pressed the button marked three.

Her heart thumped like a jackhammer watching the light

jump from one number to the next. The doors opened on the third floor and a man and a woman stood framed in the doorway.

For once she was grateful for the veil. There was only one way out and that was forward. She recognized the woman's perfume and hurried down the corridor, searching for a number. Suddenly there it was on the door in brass: 301 Al Jazira Suite.

Hearing voices, she knocked with urgency. 'Let me in,' she cried, preparing to knock again. The door opened as two men came into view. In an instant Maryam slipped in and fell into Joe's arms.

They embraced in silence until Maryam stopped trembling. Joe raised her veil, their eyes met and each knew they had found their soul mate. Joe kissed Maryam's quivering lips, and led her to a sofa.

Tea freed Maryam's tongue and words tumbled out. She told Joe of her escapade to get to the third floor and they laughed when she got to the part where she recognised Sahar by her perfume.

Maryam removed her headscarf, releasing her hair to dance like her heart. Joe sat with his arms folded behind his head. He watched Maryam walk away and let her *abaya* slide off her shoulders onto the floor. Spellbound by the flash of colour and toned body, he tried to say something eloquent but failed.

'Wow! You're one hell of a woman!'

Maryam smiled and tormented him, letting the islands of flesh that ran up her side catch his eye. She walked away rolling her hips, back arched, thrusting her breasts forward, and bathed in his attention. She had spent hours in front of the mirror practicing her walk under Saffron's watchful eye, until she got it right.

She combed her fingers through her hair and looked down her patrician nose. The kohl around her eyes made them look large and inviting. Now came the piéce de rèsistance, she licked her lips, leant forward and blew Joe a kiss, inviting him to gaze down her cleavage.

'Holy cow!' Joe exclaimed, getting off the bed. 'You're not the woman I met at the Dental clinic!'

'Yes I am.'

'You can't be.'

'Come over and find out, doctor?' Maryam motioned with her hand.

Joe's head spun, his knees weakened and urgency grew in his groin.

This was the first time they were together without fearing discovery. They relaxed and let their fingers explore.

Clandestine meetings and hurried phone calls had primed them to explode on touch. Passion boiled in their veins, lips sought lips and tongues thrust and parried like French dualists.

Joe held Maryam against his body and let his hands roam over the dress, teasing the flesh beneath. Maryam felt the bulge inside Joe's trouser press against her belly and pulled away in alarm.

'Wait!' she said, looking for direction in Joe's eyes, her chest rising and falling.

'It's okay,' Joe whispered, brushing aside a strand of hair from her face.

'I'm confused and afraid.'

Joe cradled her face in his hands and kissed her.

'I understand,' he said and let the warmth of his body envelop hers. He led her to the bed and they lay gazing at each other. Maryam combed her fingers through Joe's hair and he caressed her face, committing it to memory.

'I want this so much, Joe. I want you,' Maryam whispered, breaking the silence.

Joe smiled.

'But. . .' Maryam shook her head and sighed.

'We don't have to. . .'

'No, no, it isn't that, *habibi*.'

'What is it?'

'I want this to be special, Joe, a beginning of something beautiful, something lasting.' A tear trickled down Maryam's cheek and Joe brushed it away.

'I've waited all my life for you. Without you, life has no meaning, Maryam. It's incomplete.'

'Do you really mean that, Joe?' Maryam asked gazing into his eyes, seeking out his soul.

'You're my moon, Maryam.' Joe replied. Maryam's fingers moved across his lips, feeling his words.

'Then be my sun, *habibi*. Make love to me.'

Their lips met, releasing their unbridled love. Joe nibbled at Maryam's ear lobe and made her giggle. Her perfume filled his nostrils, magnifying his frenzy. His tongue fluttered over her throat setting her alight and his fingers pressed into her buttocks drawing her close.

Maryam dug her fingers into his back in return. She inhaled sharply, feeling his hand slip under her skirt and touch her inner thigh.

Maryam fumbled with Joe's belt. 'Yes!' she said triumphantly when the buckle came loose. She ripped off his clothes and released his erection.

Joe tugged on Maryam's dress and she wriggled her body. Without warning the dress came free and Joe fell backward onto the bed as they laughed.

'Hells Bells!' Joe exclaimed looking at Maryam in a revealing a red G-string.

Their lips met with renewed vigour and hands roamed over their bodies without restraint. Maryam gasped feeling Joe's hot breath on her nipples. They explored each other, showering kisses, and playfully biting.

'I'm ready now, be gentle, *habibi*,' Maryam whispered. Joe's tongue fluttered deep between her thighs. Maryam moaned, gripped by a new sensation.

'I want you now,' she urged and kissed his lips, tasting her own juices on his tongue. Maryam stiffened for a second and received

Joe and then their bodies melted into one. They lay immersed in each other, enjoying the moment, eyes speaking a language only they could understand.

Time stood still. Their bodies began the final dance that would take them over the precipice and into oblivion. Thrust met thrust, Maryam responded to his needs and he to hers. Windows rattled and the furniture shook, their final love song heightened by the roar of a pair of F-15 fighter jets on a night mission.

Out of breath, they lay in each other's arms, soaking in the aftermath of their lovemaking. Neither spoke, for there was nothing to say.

They made love again, without urgency, lingering over each movement and every kiss, knowing that it could be weeks or even months before they would be joined together. . . or perhaps never. Maryam couldn't bear the thought and closed her eyes, hoping to blot it out. Her fingers took a safari, tracing circles, exploring the curly golden undergrowth of Joe's chest.

'I love you so much,' Maryam whispered, looking at Joe. 'Where do we go from here?'

'I love you, too. More than I can say,' Joe replied, knowing the sacrifice Maryam had made and the risk she had taken to be with him.

'Take me away from here, Joe,' Maryam whispered, playing with Joe's earlobe, turning it pink. She knew she was asking the impossible.

'We must find a way,' muttered Joe, deep in thought. The question was *how*? Wasn't love supposed to conquer all and triumph?

They embraced for the last time, the LED screen beside the door counting down their precious moments together: 3. . . 2. . . 1. . . G. . . B. Maryam dropped her veil and stepped out, leaving Joe behind, their fingertips reaching out to savour the last moment.

Saffron welcomed Maryam with a smile and an arched brow.

'I've seen those red shoes before somewhere,' Sahar whispered in Maryam's ear.

'I recognised your perfume,' Maryam replied.

They blushed and giggled, knowing their secrets were safe. Samar was nowhere to be seen. Maryam and Saffron took leave of Sahar, thanking her for a wonderful time.

Everything was available and possible in Saudi Arabia, you just had to have the courage to reach out and help yourself, Saffron reflected.

Mahmoud was in a jovial mood when he returned to collect them. Uncle Eid's *shisha* pipe must have erased his anger. 'Did you have a good time, girls?'

'Yes,' replied the two in concert.

Saffron felt a twinge of jealousy. She wanted to know more but knew the love Maryam shared with Joe was not hers to hold.

Maryam reflected on Joe's manhood and giggled under her veil. So this was what gave Saudi men divine power over women, she thought. It was because of this that Saudi men herded women like sheep, subjecting them to veils and imprisonment behind walls and barred windows. There was segregation in schools, hospitals, universities, public transport and restriction on foreign travel, because of this. They lacked self-control and blamed it on the women when they lost it.

TWENTY-FIVE

'No! No! Push down the clutch before you change gear,' Saffron instructed in frustration. 'Watch me,' she said and climbed into the driver's seat. 'The left foot goes down all the way and then you slide the gearstick like so and release the clutch slowly. Now try it.'

Maryam tried again and the gear stick moved into position.

'That's it, you're doing well,' encouraged Saffron. 'Now ease that foot up a little at a time.'

The car stalled. 'Shit!' shouted Maryam. 'I don't normally swear,' she apologised, glancing at Turki on the back seat. 'I'll never get the hang of this!' She thumped the steering wheel.

'If a man can do it, so can you. Now watch me carefully.' The clutch engaged and the car edged forward. 'See how simple it is.' They swapped seats and Maryam tried again.

'Easy does it. Bring that leg up. Can you feel the clutch bite?'

Maryam nodded enthusiastically and the car moved forward a few feet and jerked to a halt.

'You were nearly there.'

'Well done, Auntie Maryam!' Turki called out, clapping his hands.

'I was so close, *habibi*, let me try again.' Maryam turned on the engine and tried once more. This time the car rolled down the desert road.

'Change into second. No, that's fourth. You want second, it's directly below first.' The car stalled and Maryam thumped the steering wheel with clenched fists. 'Shit! Shit! Shit!'

'Auntie Miri, you said "shit",' Turki said.

Maryam blushed and laughed in embarrassment.

Saffron explained yet again, 'This is first and now directly below is second,' and she pushed the lever down. 'Now this is third and this fourth.'

Maryam put her hand on the gear stick and Saffron placed hers on top to guide the stick through the gears.

'It was so easy!' Maryam exclaimed and memorised the motion. 'How do I know when to change?'

'See this,' Saffron said, tapping the speedo dial with her finger. 'The first gear is just to get the car started and when this reaches five,' she continued tapping the dial, 'you change to the second and when it reaches around twenty you change to third. . . You got it?'

'Sounds so simple.' With that, Maryam turned on the engine and put the car into motion.

'Yes, that's it, keep it up. Good, now try putting it into fourth. Keep your eyes on the road.'

The car stalled but Maryam grinned and kissed Saffron on the lips. 'You're so wonderful and I love you!' she declared before realising what she had done. 'Oh I am so sorry, Saffron,' she said aghast. 'I've never kissed a woman.'

'You're doing just fine,' Saffron whispered and held her close.

'I love you, too,' Turki said, throwing his arms around Maryam from behind and kissing her neck.

Saffron took the wheel and they headed back.

'We must do it again,' Maryam suggested and Saffron agreed.

In the excitement, Saffron failed to notice the white speck in the rearview mirror and the dust cloud growing larger until it was too late. As they alighted from the car, giggling with delight, Nader's truck screeched to a halt, skidding on the gravel, and his angry voice cut through the dust.

'What do you think you're doing?' he screamed at Saffron

and cleared the distance between them with two strides.

'This is not your bloody America! You can't drive here like you own the place!' he shouted, spraying her face with spit, flaying his arms in the air. 'And you!' he yelled to Maryam who was rooted to the ground. 'You should know better than being out here with this *Ameriki* whore.' He gripped her by the arm, causing her to scream in pain.

Turki watched the commotion from inside the Suburban.

'Let her go, you animal,' shouted Saffron coming to Maryam's rescue. She tried to free Nader's grip on Maryam's arm but he was too strong.

'Get inside at once,' Nader ordered, pointing to the gates and shoved Maryam sending her headlong to the ground.

Turki screamed and rushed to Maryam's side.

'Wait till I tell your father and Nabeel!' Nader shouted. He turned on Saffron and crushed her against the door. 'I know what you want, whore,' he said, thrusting his hip hard against hers, planting a rough kiss on her unsuspecting lips.

'Let me go, you fucking bastard!' Saffron fought to free herself. She could see hatred in his bloodshot eyes and smell the whisky on his breath. She spat in his face and with a move learned from her days on the strip, her right knee thundered into Nader's groin. Nader let go and lay on the ground writhing in pain.

Maryam and Saffron grabbed Turki and ran to the gate. They looked back at Nader clutching his crotch hurling insults at them in Arabic.

They hurried into the house covered in dust. Maryam shook with rage and Turki cried.

'We're in trouble,' Maryam muttered.

'He'll never admit he lost a fight to a woman,' Saffron replied. 'We're safe.'

* * *

After dinner Saffron sat in the library, revisiting the events of the day. The library was where she took refuge when she was troubled or wanted to be on her own. She liked the Persian carpet and the walls lined with books. She had never been to a library in her whole life and felt like she was entering an alien world. She wondered how long it would be before women could drive in Saudi Arabia. Perhaps never, if the religious police had their way, she said to herself.

Farhan knocked on the library door and entered. 'I thought I'd find you here,' he said.

Saffron looked up from her book and smiled.

'What are you reading today?' Farhan asked.

'I want to thank you for the music system,' Saffron ignored the question.

'Has it arrived?'

'It's in my room.'

'You like it?'

'I never dreamt of owning a B & O.'

'B & O?' Farhan asked.

'Bang and Olufsen. It's the very best. Didn't you buy it?'

'I know the shop owner and had him send it.'

'Without seeing it?'

'I asked him for the best. I'm pleased you like it.'

Saffron came over and gave Farhan a peck on the cheek. 'Thank you. It means a lot to me,' she added, squeezing his arm.

'I can't have you being miserable.' Farhan clasped her hand.

'That's very thoughtful of you. You must come and have a look.'

'I'll do that,' Farhan replied and kissed Saffron's hand. Saffron felt a tinge of guilt and kissed Farhan's hand in turn.

'What kind of music do you like?' Farhan asked.

'I've an eclectic taste. Depends on my mood. I like rock, soul and R & B when I'm feeling wild, jazz when I'm nostalgic and classical when I'm introspective.'

'What do you like when you're in love?'

'Ah, now that, General Balawi, would be telling,' Saffron replied.

'How about you?' Saffron redirected.

'Music?'

'Aha.'

'We grew up with very little music. The old men sang sagas of battles, journeys, loves and loyalty accompanied by the *rababa* around the campfire.'

'What's a *rababa*?'

'It's a one-stringed instrument played with a bow. A bedouin violin you could say. Would you like to learn?'

'Only if you teach me.'

TWENTY-SIX

Maryam hurried along the brick-paved shopping mall, looking for the Tabuk Pharmacy. She grasped the *abaya* around her face and gripped the leather bag slung over her shoulder.

Maryam saw the pharmacy squeezed between an electronic store and a carpet emporium and hesitated. It had a marble façade that opened onto the street with an aging air-conditioning unit resting precariously above the entrance. One window displayed a sign for 'Tabuk Pharmacy' in Arabic and English with an anaemic snake coiled around a green cocktail glass and spitting yellow venom. From the other window beamed a European baby advertising the latest in disposable diapers and talcum powder.

Maryam hovered at the entrance. Her pulse throbbed in her neck and her palms moistened in panic. She tried to anticipate the man's questions. Was it illegal to purchase these things without a prescription? She should have asked Samar or Sahar, they would have known. Mustering courage, she entered.

She spotted a man at the far end of the shop reading a newspaper. He was seated behind a counter wearing a white lab coat, his hairy arms resting on the formica counter. He looked up, cocked his head, considered her for a moment and carried on reading. Diligently, he moved a toothpick between his teeth. He had curly black hair, bushy eyebrows hiding dark intelligent eyes, a bristly moustache and day-old stubble on his face. Maryam thought he looked Egyptian but he could be Jordanian – hard to tell in the light – but his accent would soon betray him. Unlike the Saudis, the Jordanians spoke with a softer intonation, making their Arabic pleasing to the ear. The Egyptians were more particular and classical in their approach, the Parisians of the Arabic-speaking world.

The shop was a collection of shelves extending from the floor to the ceiling, home to products from shampoos to toothbrushes and insect repellents. A flotilla of fluorescent tubes grouped in threes hovered overhead. Maryam browsed the shelves, like a schoolboy about to purchase his first packet of condoms.

She was the only customer, and that made her feel at ease even though no one would have recognised her. She examined a bottle marked *Head and Shoulders* that claimed to do wonders for your hair. Discreetly she raised her veil and pretended to read the instructions.

'Would you like some help, Madam?' asked the man and ambled over, his toothpick still between his teeth.

Maryam dropped her veil promptly.

'That's a good product,' he said pointing to the bottle in Maryam's hand. 'This one is for greasy hair.' He pulled out another bottle, 'And this one here is for dry hair.' Shrugging his shoulders he confessed, 'If you ask me they all look alike, it's all in the label and perhaps in the mind.'

Maryam laughed at his honesty and decided he was Jordanian. An Egyptian would have been condescending and less helpful. She picked up the bottle the man had recommended and walked over to the counter.

'Do you have those kits?' Maryam asked.

'We have many kits. What kind are you after?'

'To test for pregnancy,' Maryam said blushing under her veil.

The man smiled and Maryam knew he understood her needs.

'We have a variety,' he said as if he were taking about a bar of soap. 'They're much the same.' He pointed to a stack of boxes covered in a fine layer of dust. '*Crystal Clear, Discovery* and this one here is *Clear Blue*. Which one have you used before, Madam?'

Maryam hesitated.

He realised this was her first time and didn't wait for an answer. 'This brand is very popular,' he said, pulling down a carton the size of a pencil case labelled *Clear Blue* from the shelf and blowing off the dust.

'Is this your first baby?' he inquired.

Maryam nodded and the pharmacist opened the carton and read the instructions explaining how to use the various bits and pieces. Maryam looked over her shoulder and saw the silhouette of a figure framed in the doorway looking menacingly like a *mutawah*.

'Okay! Okay! I'll take it,' she said, stuffing the carton in her bag.

'That'll be two hundred *riyals*, Madam.' Normally Maryam would bargain but today the man could have his price. She handed him two rusty coloured notes and made for the door.

'May Allah bless you with a boy!' the pharmacist called out after her.

Maryam found Saffron in Abaya Park, munching into a *shawarma*.

'What did you buy?' asked Saffron between mouthfuls. Maryam showed her the shampoo. Saffron raised a questioning brow and took another bite of her *shawarma*.

*   *   *

Next day Maryam visited Sahar and Samar at their home under the pretext of studying. Sahar propped a chair against the bedroom door to ward off intruders and lit a cigarette.

'Sahar wants to learn how to blow smoke rings,' Samar explained.

Sahar coughed violently. 'It's impossible,' she said and stubbed out the cigarette in a tin box. Samar opened the windows to let the smoke out and turned up the air-conditioning.

The three girls huddled around the plastic cup of golden liquid like Macbeth's witches around a cauldron.

'Do you want to, or shall I?' asked Samar, taking charge.

'I'm not sure it's a good idea,' Maryam said. 'What if the test is wrong?'

'It says it's ninety-nine percent accurate,' Sahar replied, reading the small print on the box.

'But what if I fall into that one percent?'

'We'll repeat it.'

'It's been seven weeks since your last period, *habibi*,' Samar reminded Maryam.

'I know but. . .'

'And you've had morning sickness,' Sahar added.

'Yes, but this test won't change that,' Maryam said shrugging her shoulders. 'I know I am pregnant.'

'Well then, what are you waiting for?' Samar asked.

'Okay I'll do it,' Maryam said mustering up the courage. 'It's my life and I should at least control it.' She dunked the stick into the urine and counted to twenty. A blue line appeared in the round window. They looked at each other and asked the same question.

Samar read the instructions aloud. 'That means the test is over, we have to wait a little longer.' Three pairs of eyes stared at the square window not daring to blink. Three minutes seemed an eternity when each second brought you closer to a verdict that pronounced your death sentence.

A faint blue line, finer than a thread of cotton, materialized in the square window and darkened.

'Holy shit!' exclaimed the twins. 'Maryam you've done it. You're pregnant!' They looked at each other in disbelief, mouths wide open. Then came the aftershock.

'We thought you were joking.'

'Shit! This is the real thing.'

'I thought you were on the pill!'

'I was. . . er. . . I mean, I am, but I forgot a couple of times,' confessed Maryam, looking at her feet in shame.

'You forgot!' the twins exclaimed together.

'I thought it wouldn't matter. I guess I was wrong,' Maryam whispered.

'You've got to do something about it,' the twins blurted out.

A torrent of tears ran down Maryam's cheeks. She began to sob. Yes, she had to do something, but what? Her whole world froze and her body divorced itself from her mind. 'Maryam! Maryam!' echoed through her head but it didn't register. It didn't matter any more who she was. Soon she would be dead and forgotten, buried in an unmarked grave, all traces of her existence washed from the minds of those who had once professed their love for her. Even her mother would forget her – and Turki too. They would repeat some lie until it became real. She would live forever only in Joe's heart.

'Maryam! Wake up, there is much to be done,' cried Sahar shaking her and she came to, her blurred vision focused again on the test stick in her hand.

'What is done is done. It's Allah's will,' muttered Maryam in resignation.

'You have to get rid of it.' Samar said.

'It? How can you say that? I want to keep my baby!'

'Maryam! Listen to us,' implored Samar. 'The baby must go or both of you will surely die. You know the rules. Remember Princess Mishaal. And last year little Huda from our college. They are all gone!'

'But how?' Maryam asked.

'Leave that to us, it's very simple,' Sahar spoke with urgency in her voice.

'I had it done last year,' said Samar 'and I'm still here.'

'We'll arrange it all. There's nothing to worry about,' continued Sahar. 'Now go home and pretend nothing has happened and by next week your problem will be behind you.'

'Do you understand? Speak to no one and we'll be in touch.' Samar said.

Maryam didn't understand but nodded anyway. Sahar's words seemed reassuring, so why was she so petrified? How could she pretend nothing had happened? *Everything* had happened. She was pregnant and life for her would never be the same.

The next few days dragged, she wished she could shake her watch and speed up time. Every time the phone rang she jumped and her heart missed a beat. Zelpha, her maid, noticed her strange behaviour and asked if she was all right.

'Of course I'm all right, can't you see I'm alive,' she had snapped and regretted it. Saffron too had noticed the change but put it down to her period and kept out of her way.

The nights were the worst. She slept little, haunted by visions of faceless men in white unleashing baying hounds, each with a contorted face that seemed familiar. She could make them out under the snarling rage: there was her father and Uncle Eid, and then there was Nabeel and the cousins. They came lusting for her blood in a shuttered room or on a moonless night in the desert to avenge their sacred *Sharaf* that she carried in her womb. Even Turki was there, a little puppy yapping for her blood, weaned on their lies. Only Uncle Mahmoud was absent and she couldn't understand why, perhaps it was because he was not a Saudi and *Wahabi*. The dawn was a welcome respite.

Maryam debated whether she should speak to Joe but decided against it. The hospital phones were tapped and she didn't want him to worry. Sahar and Samar had said all would be fine in a few days and had warned her not to speak to anyone. Once the baby was gone, he would be out of danger.

On the sixth day, the phone rang and Maryam heard Sahar's voice.

'Why don't you come over for tea this afternoon, say after *Asr* prayer, if you're not doing anything important?' Sahar suggested in case someone was eavesdropping on another extension in the house. 'We would love to see you again.'

TWENTY-SEVEN

After dinner, Saffron retired to the library. She was still shaken by Uncle Jim's death. There had been so much life left in him. He had had so much to offer the world in his own special way. She pondered on the unpredictability of life. Uncle Jim would still be alive had he called in sick that day or if the robber had not been born. Why had he moved to LA? Could his death have been prevented or was it predestined?

She thought of her mother and tears wet her cheeks. Her's had been a hard life but had it been of her own making? Could she have broken the cycle of abuse and addiction or was that predestined too? Why did she walk away from an adoring husband to a life on the street and then into the arms of a violent man who said he loved her but drove her towards her death?

The wind whistled through the eucalyptus trees outside and the leaves rustled. Aishah said the change of seasons brought storms. The moon hid behind dark clouds hurrying across the sky.

Saffron sat at the desk in front of the *Qur'an* with her head bowed. 'Why am I here?' she muttered to herself. She opened the book at the bookmark and read with glazed eyes. Her finger crossed the page like a prompter, digesting every word but they failed to make an impression. She read the *Qur'an* to please Aishah.

She had never felt emotional or in the slightest bit moved

while reading the Bible at Sunday school. It was an exercise in penance she undertook because that was what was expected of a good catholic girl. The best part of Sunday School was dressing up in her finest and sitting next to Shaun O'Grady who made her heart flutter. His Irish accent made her giggle and she blushed at his coarse language. He used to pull her red ponytail, call her a carrot and run away.

The thought made her smile, fifteen years on and half a world away. Never in her wildest dreams had she imagined she would end up in the land of Ali Baba and his Forty Thieves.

Thunder grumbled outside and clouds glowed. Gusts of wind galloped past the house howling like a thousand demons.

Maryam had told her that Muslims, Jews and Christians were People of the Book and, through the Prophet Abraham and his sons, Isaac and Ishmael, they shared a common ancestry.

Aishah had explained, 'There is one God and Mohammed was the last of the Prophets.' It all made sense. There was no Second Coming as had been drummed into her as a child. All that baloney that Jesus died for her sins didn't wash with her. She hadn't even been born at the time, let alone committed a sin.

Aishah said, 'Jesus was a Prophet, like Moses and Mohammed, sent to spread the word of Allah. Islam is a living religion guiding people in their daily life.'

'In Islam we don't have stories of supernatural birth, death and resurrection.' Maryam had explained how simple it was. 'There is one Allah, and his messenger is the Prophet Mohammed.'

It all seemed so ordered, Saffron thought, as she flipped the pages with idle disinterest. Then, drunken lighting tumbled from the clouds shredding the night sky. Light drenched the room followed by thunder. Glass shattered, angry hail flung itself at the windows and the wind stormed in.

Saffron shrieked as books and paper swirled around her. The curtains billowed like untethered sails. The lights flickered and died, enveloping her in darkness. She ran for the door and stumbled. A book hit her on the head and landed beside her with a thud. Saffron swore. In the darkness she could hear the pages shuffling, licked by the wind.

Lightning flashed and the word *Allah* jumped at her from a page and then there was darkness. The wind roared through the broken window, tearing at her clothes and hair. She screamed as hail rained down on her. Books fell from the shelves and a table lamp crashed to the floor.

Thunder shook the building and then a mighty flash seared the heavens and *Repent unbeliever* leapt at her from the book. Another volley of hail assaulted her. Saffron whimpered.

With every flash another prophetic word jumped at her and then there was darkness and silence but for the moaning of the wind.

The lights came on, darkness evaporated. The *Qur'an* lay open in front of her. Saffron focused on the page. Thunder rumbled outside. She read, *To Allah belongs the East and the West: whither so ever ye turn, there is Allah's face, for Allah is All-Embracing, All-Knowing*.

A gust of wind ruffled the pages revealing another verse: *This day I have perfected your religion for you, completed my favour upon you, and have chosen for you Islam as your religion.*

A shiver ran down her spine. Saffron knew that Allah was addressing her through this verse. As her fingers traversed over the calligraphy she knew why she had come to Saudi Arabia. It wasn't for the love of money but to find peace and Islam. It had been predestined. She held the *Qur'an* to her bosom and sighed.

Outside, the storm tempered its wrath. Looking into the darkness Saffron sobbed. Tears streamed down her cheeks and her body trembled. Like the pages of the *Qur'an*, the pages from her past flashed at her and she realised how tormented a life it had been. She had lived in a storm with no one to turn to and nowhere to go.

Driven by poverty she had rebelled, using people for all she could get. Money was all that counted in her life and she made it as her mother had done, by selling herself. That was the only way she knew how.

She watched the crescent moon appear through the clouds. It all seemed so pathetic now, far away from the dog-eat-dog world of which she had been part. Contentment washed over her in waves and calm beset the turmoil that had once lived in her. Peace took up residence and filled the void. Looking at the shattered window she realised how fragmented her life was but, like the window, she too could be made new.

'Thank you, Allah,' Saffron breathed, gazing at the sky and watching the dark clouds roll away. 'I am your servant,' she whispered, tears tumbled freely down her cheeks and a peaceful smile rested on her lips.

TWENTY-EIGHT

Joe sat in the Chevy stationed across from Abaya Park. The neon sign shaped like a watch rotated on a pillar outside the jewellers. It was getting late and the time for *Maghrib* prayer was drawing near. The thin air of Tabuk cooled, the shadows lengthened. The sun dipped under the city arch west of the mall. He looked at his watch for the umpteenth time, wondering what was taking Maryam so long. What was so urgent that it could not have waited till to-morrow when they had planned to meet? She had seemed impatient and anxious. *Be careful*, were her last words. The *mutaween* were congregated around a shiny black GMC Suburban parked in the middle of the mall, flexing their bamboo canes in the air waiting for the call to prayer. Joe turned his back on them and focused on the entrance to Abaya Park willing Maryam to appear.

Suddenly the speakers atop the minarets around Tabuk came to life, calling the faithful to pray. He checked his watch again. Shutters rattled down shop fronts and padlocks snapped shut all over the city.

The sound of *ship ship* scraping on the pavement, doing what the expatriates derisively called the Saudi shuffle, migrated in the direction of the mosques.

Joe realized this was not the time to be caught wearing a *thobe* and *gutra*. He prepared to drive away when a megaphone pressed against the window bellowed, '*Salah! Salah!*' He froze. A man opened the door and barked in his ear.

Instinctively, Joe swung round and shoved at the megaphone, slamming it into the man's face, splitting his lip and breaking his front teeth. Without warning, another *mutawah* grabbed his *thobe* and pulled him out from the driver's seat. Joe hit the ground with a thud and his *gutra* flew off his head.

There was a shocked silence. The *mutaween* stared at his blond hair. 'That's him, that's the spy Salem told us about,' a man shouted and a bamboo cane came whistling down on Joe's legs. Joe swore and spun round on the ground, his fists clenched prepared to strike, when another blow caught him on the side of his knee. He kicked out but his assailant was out of reach. A policeman's boot made contact with Joe's ribs, winding him. Two others armed with submachine guns arrived and watched from a distance.

'He must be a spy,' said one.

'Surely not, the Israelis wouldn't send a blonde,' replied the other. They laughed and continued to brush their teeth with the *miswak*.

*　*　*

Powerless, Maryam watched from the other side of Abaya Park, tears streaming down her cheeks. Fear strangled the scream before it was born and anger shook her body. Her impulse was to run to Joe's defence but to challenge the police or the *mutaween* would only put him in further danger and leave her open to all sorts of accusations – a whore, or even an unbeliever – which would carry the death penalty. Even if she were a man, she could do nothing, the *mutaween* were all-powerful.

If only she had been on time or kept to their original plan, this would never have happened. They would now be safe in Joe's Chevy and off the street. She cursed the stupid roadblocks that had made her late.

A policeman snapped a pair of steel handcuffs on Joe's wrists and bundled him into a truck that had appeared from nowhere.

Maryam watched the truck disappear down the mall taking Joe to the *mutaween* headquarters. In the twilight Maryam thought she saw Nader in the distance seated behind the wheel of a car with a satisfied smile, and her face grew hard. What was he doing here? Why was he smiling?

She shook with rage remembering Nader's words, 'I'll teach him a lesson when I find him.'

* * *

The *mutaween* headquarters was a single-storey, whitewashed building squashed between the sandstone Grand Mosque and the courthouse at the far end of what the expatriates called 'Chop Chop Square'. This was where the bloodthirsty, the devout and the curious came in hordes to witness *sharia* law in action and watch heads roll at the end of a sword on Friday after midday prayer.

A short man in khaki uniform with an enormous holster strapped to his side opened a door and shoved Joe into the darkness. Joe missed the steps and crashed onto the stone floor with an audible thump. The door slammed behind him, drowning his scream, and the bolt shot into the stone wall. A sliver of light sneaked into the room from beneath the door, cutting the darkness with surgical precision.

'*Ya, sedeeq!* You okay?' an effeminate voice reached out from the darkness.

'Does this hellhole look okay to you?' Joe groaned.

'*Ya, sedeeq*, I was being neighbourly.'

'Yeah. You keep your bloody neighbourly ways to yourself,' Joe replied and regretted it. 'Hey! I'm sorry I said that' he said eventually. 'I'm Joe, who are you?' There was a strained silence and Joe realized he had hurt the man's feeling. 'Hell! I said I was sorry.'

'They call me Peter Pan, but you can call me Peter.' Without warning the darkness evaporated. Burning white light lanced their eyes, blinding them.

'Christ! What was that?' shouted Joe shaking his head.

'They do that every five minutes, I was going to warn you. It's not so bad if you face the wall,' advised Peter. 'But you never get used to it.'

Gradually an image formed in his head as islands of wall joined together and the edges became defined. They were in a room that was about three metres square and bare of furniture. The only window was at head height and covered by an iron grill, clogged with dust and cobwebs.

Dead cockroaches gathered dust in the corners. A cloud of flies buzzed around a dark patch on the floor in one corner. Peter sat hunched in another corner, his head buried into his knees. He was a small, lean man with a boyish physique, a mop of thick black hair and pair of Reeboks that looked new. He had somehow managed to wiggle his body around his handcuffed arms so that they were in front of him, draped around his knees.

The inky blackness flooded the room once again without warning and a ghostly image of Peter huddled in the corner lingered in Joe's brain for a few seconds. From the red glow Joe could make out four bulbs stuck to the cracked ceiling. A stench of urine permeated the room.

The next time the lights came on Joe was ready. He struggled to his feet and charged the door, screaming at the top of his lungs. 'Let me out of here, you bastards.' The door stayed shut and he tried again, this time his feet made solid contact but nothing happened.

'It's no use, man,' Peter said.

The lights went out and Joe collapsed on the floor with a grunt, anger burning inside him.

'Are there any more surprises?' Joe asked.

'Food and water once a day.'

'Let me guess, toilet once a day,' Joe added.

'You're catching on fast, *sedeeq*.'

'From where I come, they treat pigs better than this.'

'Pigs, I love. But there are none here.'

'That's because they had the sense to leave,' Joe said.

'Going to stay long?'

'Depends on the room service.' Their laughter reached out across the darkness and Joe felt better. The next time the lights came on he was ready with his face buried in the corner. His eyes burned but it was not like the first time.

'Why are you here?' Joe asked.

'Religion.'

'Religion?'

'They caught me wearing a gold cross in the *souq*,' Peter explained.

'A cross?'

'Yeah. Gold and Jesus don't go together. It's *haram*!'

'Sick bastards!'

'How about you? Religion?'

'No. They thought I was one of them in my sheet and tea towel outfit.'

'They probably think you're a spy.'

'Hell! I never thought of that.' They peppered the night with small talk when the light came on and caught snatches of sleep during the moments of darkness. Peter asked a lot of questions but Joe didn't mind at first. He was grateful of the company, besides he felt sorry for Peter who had been in that stinking hell-hole all alone for the past three days. After a while the questions became more personal and Joe became wary.

'Married?'

'No.'

'Got a girlfriend?'

'Yeah.'

'Where?'

'Hey, you with the Feds?' Joe asked sharply, wondering where this was leading.

'Feds?'

'Oh, never mind.' Joe was too tired to explain. His body ached, his stomach rumbled and his head throbbed. The *thobe* soaked up the dampness in the air and clung to his body making him shiver.

They took Peter away just after *Fajr* and that was the last he saw of him. His smiling face haunted Joe; he felt something wasn't right.

* * *

Manicured, sausage-like fingers flicked backwards and forwards through a black book the size of a pocket dictionary, making a rustling sound. Glinting eyes scanned up and down the columns of fine print, pausing a while and moving on, only to linger again over another part of the page.

An old man with a henna-dyed beard and a large bony nose, pencil-thin lips, pointed cheekbones and dried, wrinkled skin that gave him the appearance of an Egyptian mummy, sat sipping a cup of tea.

'*Ya*, Salem! We don't need your book. We have nothing on him,' he said.

Salem, perched on a rickety wooden chair on the other side of the room, took no notice. He was a pugnacious man in his late twenties or early thirties but looked much older, with a Zoroastrian beard that covered most of his face and fanned over his chest. He could have stood in for Karl Marx were it not for the voluminous nose. A cigarette with a head of ash hung from between fleshy lips that drooped at the corners. A neat white *gutra* rising in the middle like a tent was draped over his balding head.

'You heard Beter,' the old man continued, substituting the P with a B as the letter P was absent from the Arabic alphabet. 'He's a doctor,' he said pecking like a hen at Joe's ID with his finger. Salem squirmed in the chair making it squeak.

'Here we are, *Goldman*! I knew it the minute I saw him. It is a Jewish name! I can smell these Jews before I see them!' Salem exclaimed.

'Yes. And I can smell you,' replied the old man in disgust. 'His ID says he's a Christian and that's the end of the matter.'

Joe stood in the middle of the room listening to the interplay of words passing backwards and forwards between the two men. He didn't understand what they were saying but knew from the tone of their voices and barbed looks that he was the subject of their discussion.

'Do you have a tattoo, Goldman?' asked Salem in English.

'Tattoo?'

'Like numbers on your arms.'

Joe realised what Salem was getting at. 'Are you out of your fucking mind?' he shouted.

'Show me your arms if you've nothing to hide.'

'I'm an American citizen, I don't need to take this shit from a fascist bastard.'

'Why are you wearing a *thobe*, Goldman?'

'Is it a crime?' Joe asked.

'Who sent you?'

'I demand to speak to my embassy!'

'You Americans always demand. What's your religion?' Salem shouted, slapping the book on the desk.

'What's it to you?'

'Answer the question, Goldman. You're a Jew! Admit it and we can all go home.'

'Are you mad or just plain stupid?'

'Admit you're a Jew!' screamed Salem, dabbing the perspiration on his forehead with the ends of his *gutra*.

'Enough! Enough! Let him go,' interrupted the old man, embarrassed with the farce he was witnessing. 'This will blow up in our face, Salem.'

'Show me your tattoos,' Salem demanded, grabbing Joe's *thobe*.

'I don't have any fucking tattoos,' Joe shouted rolling up his sleeves.

'Did your father have tattoos?'

'I'm an American, born in America.'

'Jews are not welcome in our country!'

Joe didn't reply, he stared out of the window taking in the cloudless sky. The sleepless nights and hunger had weakened him. His mouth felt like the inside of a kettle and his whole body ached with every movement. The clink of the chain reminded him of his incarceration.

'What have you done with Peter?' Joe asked abruptly. Salem and the old man exchanged glances.

'We ask the questions!' Salem shouted.

'The hell you do. Where's Peter?'

'I have heard enough,' said the old man and stood up to leave. 'Since when did a spy or Jew ask about that worthless Filipino stooge?' He asked Salem in Arabic. 'This man is innocent, now let him go.'

Salem threw open Joe's wallet and fished out a photograph.

'Who is this?'

'It's none of your fucking business,' replied Joe instantly protective.

'Is she Saudi?' Salem thrust his face into Joe's. Joe could smell the onions on the man's breath and saw the venom in his eyes but remained silent.

'She looks like a Muslim. Is she?' Joe said nothing, not realising that the Fifth Amendment didn't exist in Saudi Arabia and silence was implicit of guilt.

'If she is a Saudi, I will throttle you with my bare hands,' Salem shouted in Arabic, gesturing with his hands. Joe didn't understand the words but understood the action.

'See how his silence speaks of his guilt,' Salem said, casting a filthy look at the old man. 'There is more to this, he stays for now.' Salem waved a dismissive hand at the guard sitting hunched in the corner chewing on his *miswak*. Joe was escorted back to the cell.

TWENTY-NINE

Maryam entered the library carrying a tray with cups of tea and a plate of cookies. The library was her favourite place in the house. As a child it was where she disappeared for hours to browse through books while her brothers played soldiers or rode horses. Most of all she liked the history books that told stories of Alexander the Great who had once passed through her country and of the great civilizations of the world from the Egyptians to the Babylonians and the Persians.

'Come, sit with me, *habibi*,' Farhan said, beckoning his daughter to the sofa. 'We haven't talked in ages.'

'It's been a while,' agreed Maryam.

'You barely touched your breakfast this morning.'

'I wasn't hungry.'

'Are you ill?'

'I'm fine, Father.'

'*Habibi*, I'm your father. You know you can always come to me,' Farhan said looking into Maryam's bloodshot eyes and putting his arm around her.

'I know, Father,' Maryam replied, holding back the tears. How could she tell him about Joe? He would never understand.

'Look at the damage the storm caused.' Farhan pointed to the carpet and his desk. 'I've had the window repaired.'

'*Alhamdulillah*, that was all,' Maryam replied. 'Saffron was here when it broke.'

'Do you remember the good times we spent here?'

Maryam nodded, looking up at a wall of books she had helped put back after the storm. She recalled when she was perhaps ten or twelve years old and the occasions when, with her seated on his lap, he would read to her.

'I loved all your stories Father, particularly the ones of King Suleiman and the Queen of Sheba who came to seek his wisdom.' Maryam sat beside him.

She remembered the story about the two women who lived together and had each given birth to a son. During the night, one of them had discovered that her son had died and so swapped his body for her friend's baby. The next morning the other mother had discovered a lifeless body that she knew was not that of her child. The women had fought and argued and in the end they had sought King Suleiman's judgement.

The king had commanded the living child be cut in two: one half to be given to each woman. One mother had pleaded the child's life be spared – that he be given to her adversary – while the other was content that the child be divided. The king had ruled that the boy be given the woman who had begged for his life, for she was his rightful mother.

'He was a wise king, Father.'

'With Allah's blessing we come into this world with nothing and leave with nothing, but it is what we do with ourselves while we are here that is all important.'

'Is it true that the Queen of Sheba came from a land ruled by women?'

Farhan nodded and sipped his tea, enjoying reminiscing with his daughter. Soon a year would pass and she would be gone.

'Isn't that fantastic, Father? Did the wise king fall in love with the Queen?'

'He did. . . I think she gave him a son. It broke his heart when she left,' Farhan added shaking his head. 'Love. It's a mystery.'

'What a beautiful story,' Maryam exclaimed, biting into a cookie.

'How is it going with you and Nader?' Farhan asked, trying not to sound inquisitive.

'He comes round twice a week.'

'And?'

'We talk.'

'Anything in particular?' Farhan asked.

'Not really, a bit of this and that.'

'You don't sound enthusiastic, *habibi*.'

'I don't really have much say in the matter, do I, Father?' Maryam snapped.

'And what's that supposed to mean?' Farhan asked, snapping a cookie in half.

'If you must know, Nader is a bore,' Maryam blurted out.

'Oh. What makes you say that?'

'He doesn't understand the importance of education. He pokes fun at me and ridicules my studies.'

'How so?'

'He thinks it *haram* to study biology and that it's devil's work learning about genes and cloning.'

'Interesting,' Farhan mused, stroking his beard hiding a smile, proud of his daughter.

'Interesting! Is that all you've got to say?'

'There're always two sides to everything, *habibi*.'

'Father, Nader is against all education for women!' Maryam shouted in exasperation. 'That's not *interesting*!'

'Surely not, *habibi*?'

'With the exception of *Qur'anic* studies.'

'I think it was King Faisal who said, 'Educate a man and you liberate an individual, educate a woman and you emancipate a nation.' Farhan reflected, patting Maryam's knee.

'Now that, Father, *is* interesting. Are you sure it wasn't King Suleiman?' Maryam asked with a twinkle in her eye.

'I love to see you smile. Did you know you were born smiling?'

'I had a lot to smile about then.'

'And now?' Farhan asked.

Maryam looked away and swallowed hard as tears welled.

'Hmmm! These cookies are very tasty,' Farhan said, taking another.

'I made them especially for you, Father.'

'I'll talk to Nader, *habibi*,' Farhan promised and hugged his daughter.

* * *

The room shook and the building trembled. Thunder roared across Tabuk. A flash of light and screaming flames climbed into the sky. A blast of hot wind shattered the windows, sending thousands of pieces tearing at the portraits of the King and his two brothers high on the wall.

Salem and the old man lay dazed on the floor surrounded by debris, their *thobes* splattered with blood.

Joe felt the rumble, too, and thought it was an earthquake. He feared the old building would give way. Plaster cracked from the ceiling and spiralled to the floor leaving a trail of dust hanging in the air. The lights came on, flickered and died, leaving him in darkness.

'Let me out of here,' Joe screamed at the top of his voice. There was no answer, only the sound of feet hurrying past his door. He shouted again and kicked it. There was no one to hear him. He was the last person anyone would think of.

Joe tripped on the chain that bound his legs and hit the floor, doubling up in pain. He punched the ground with his fists and clawed at the dirt until his fingers were a mass of bleeding pulp. Exhausted, he collapsed.

Time flowed with the deliberation of treacle. Joe could hear voices, some shouting, others moaning or groaning and yet others screaming or just sobbing. Some begged for help, others gave orders or dispensed comfort. Joe didn't comprehend the words but understood the vocabulary of human suffering. It was the same the world over.

Outside, sirens of every description raged, competing for attention, and penetrated the darkness of Joe's forgotten world.

The sound of boots on concrete reminded Joe of his father's accounts of his experiences in Nazi Germany as a young boy. His father survived only because his quick-thinking grandfather had locked him in a chest of drawers when the SS came, their jackboots eating the stairs two at a time. They had raped his grandmother only feet from where his father was hiding and his grandfather died fighting to save his wife's honour. His father never saw his mother again, and after the war he learned she had died in Auschwitz.

Angry voices grew louder, the metal bolt shot back like a crack of a rifle and the door flew open. Beams of light criss-crossed the cell, seeking Joe's huddled form.

'There he is!' shouted an excited voice.

'You bastards!' Joe yelled, hiding his face.

'That's him! That's the Jew!' barked Salem, pointing into the darkness.

'Get him!' The mob of armed police dragged Joe down the corridor and into the afternoon sun. Joe winced. Random patterns like blazing comets were etched into his eyes. He reeked of urine. He gulped the air like a pearl fisher preparing to dive as they bundled him into the back of a windowless van and sped away towards Tabuk's central police station on Medinah Road – adjacent to Al Bustan, the restaurant.

'Where are you taking me?' Joe shouted at the guards who shared the back of the van. They surveyed Joe in his filthy *thobe*, muttered something and laughed. Salem sat with the driver, nursing his wounds, congratulating himself for catching the Jewish spy and terrorist. The King was sure to hear of his feat and reward him, he mused.

He indulged himself in a monologue punctuating every sentence with a *Wallah, Alhamdulillah* or *Allah-hu akbar*. They passed wailing sirens and men shouting *Ameriki!* It was only then that Joe realised there had been an explosion with American casualties.

* * *

Farhan knocked on the door and waited. He could hear music but there was no answer. He knocked a little louder and reached for the handle but etiquette stayed his hand.

Remembering Saffron's invitation, he opened the door a little and spotted her in the middle of the room dressed in a lycra suit moving to the music. His eyes followed her around the room, mesmerised by her supple body. The music ended and Farhan applauded.

'How long have you been watching?' Saffron asked, blushing.

'Not long enough,' Farhan replied. 'You dance well.'

'It's a great way to keep fit. I always wanted to be a dancer,' Saffron dabbed the perspiration from her face with a towel. 'My body craves music and every note sets me free. It's very primordial, I guess.'

'Will it free me too?' Farhan asked with a twinkle in his eyes.

'For sure, you just need to tune in.'

'Tune in?' Farhan arched a brow, smiling at Saffron's way of putting things.

'We're conditioned by our environment.'

'Like culture.' Farhan agreed.

'Right. It's a superficial layer that can be peeled back.'

'Like an onion,' Farhan said.

'Exactly,' Saffron said, feeling she was getting somewhere.

'It makes my eyes water just thinking about it,' Farhan said with a devilish grin.

'You're making fun of me,' Saffron laughed and slapped Farhan's arm.

'I'd love to peel this skin off you,' Farhan said, plucking at the suit.

'Now you're being naughty.'

'At my age, I'm allowed to.'

'Yeah. And the rest,' Saffron said and gave one of her rambunctious laughs.

'So how do you propose to set me free?'

'Let me show you.' Saffron flipped through a collection of cassettes on the floor. 'There wasn't a great selection downtown but these will do for now. This one is an old favourite of mine,' Saffron said, showing Farhan Mike Oldfield's *Tubular Bells*. 'I want you to shut your eyes and clear your mind. Do you think you can do that?'

'I'll try,' Farhan replied, making himself comfortable on the bed.

'Okay, now let each note make an impression. Let it vibrate within you.'

Saffron pressed play on the remote, Farhan listened for a few minutes and shook his head.

'I don't understand all this.'

'Try and relax. It's supposed to be fun.'

Farhan shut his eyes tight and tried again.

'No, no, no! Relax these,' Saffron interrupted and rubbed the wrinkles from Farhan's forehead. 'You're trying too hard.'

Saffron took Farhan's hand and stroked it. One movement flowed into the next. Farhan smiled.

'How was it?' Saffron asked when the music stopped.

'It's a new experience.'

'Like meditation.'

'You're right. It's uplifting.'

'I'll have you dancing soon, Farhan Al Balawi.'

'And I'll make a Muslim out of you if you tune in.'

'That's a deal.' Saffron laughed.

Farhan kissed Saffron on the cheek and left. Saffron gave a wry smile recalling a conversation with her mom before she killed herself:

'Now, Hon, listen real good. In this world everyone has something to sell, whether it's a Harvard professor or a hooker.'

'I figured that already, Mom.'

'If you're a woman there're always buyers out there and you'll be surprised at what they'll pay. If you've got it, flaunt it, 'cause if you don't, there're plenty who will.'

'And look where it's got you, Mom.'

'Come on, gal, don't talk to me like that. Get real. Life's a trade-off and out there, it's the biggest auction going. The bidding just didn't go my way.'

'You could say that again, Mom.'

'If you've got a pussy, you've got them by the balls and that's as good as having the combination to the safe. They'll do what you ask, when you ask, and that's real power. You got that, Hon?'

With mischief in her eyes Saffron looked up at the ceiling and whispered, 'Yes, Mom, I gotch'ya!' Nothing short of death was going to stop her from enjoying life. Tony, her dead husband, used to say, 'When in Rome, do as the Romans do,' and that was precisely what she was going to do. She'd play the game by their silly rules, but they were going to dance to her tune and, boy, were they in for a surprise.

THIRTY

'Are you sure you have the right address?' asked the Egyptian taxi driver, dabbing his sweaty face with a green rag. It wasn't so much an address but a location that Maryam repeated. The driver nodded, 'Yes, we are there. Madam. This is a bad neighbourhood, *very* bad. Want me to wait?'

'No,' replied Maryam, handing the driver a fifty riyal note as she stepped out. She watched the departing taxi jiggle from side to side to negotiate the potholes. She wished he had stayed, but Samar had told her she was to go alone. She stood in the middle of what had once been a street and looked around. A group of dilapidated buildings huddled together at one end awaiting the developers and their bulldozers. Tabuk was a boomtown and all around this once sleepy oasis buildings were going up.

Maryam picked her way towards the cluster of six-storey buildings along the street strewn with debris. There were no lights in the windows. Plastic bags rustled past like ghostly jelly-fish and she wondered if she had done the right thing. A dog yelped, disturbed by her footsteps, and scurried off.

The building had once been a proud residence of a wealthy family who had long since moved on. The plaster was crumbling off the walls and a smell of dampness hung in the air. Tabuk sat on a bed of water that seeped to the surface soaking into the walls, rotting away the foundations until buildings collapsed.

As she entered the stairwell a black cat skittered past, and she suppressed a shriek. On the first floor, she knocked on a door and listened to the sound echo through the building. Nothing happened. She knocked again, this time a little louder.

'*Nam*,' barked a voice.

'Zubaida?' whispered Maryam.

'Who wants her?'

'Maryam.'

'Are you alone?'

'Yes.' Maryam heard the squeak of a rusty bolt being drawn back. The door opened a little.

'Were you followed?'

Maryam shook her head and the door closed. A chain rattled, the door opened wide.

'Come in,' ordered the voice and Maryam stepped into a corridor lit by a paraffin lamp giving out a dirty yellow light. The greasy smell grabbed her by the throat and made her stomach churn. Perhaps this wasn't such a good idea, Maryam thought.

'You'll get used to it,' squawked Zubaida reading Maryam's mind. 'It's the damp and the paraffin.' She led the way.

'Sit,' commanded the woman, pointing to a patch of carpet on the floor and took up a position on a short wooden stool. 'Arthritis,' she explained, 'the damp makes it worse.'

Zubaida was a slender Negro woman, perhaps six-foot or more. In the light of the lamp her skin took on the appearance of ancient parchment, dry and fragile. She looked like a piranha with her angular face, protruding jaw and bulging, bloodshot eyes. Her cracked lips failed to hold back the front teeth and they splayed out like open fingers. When she spoke her upper lip curled back exposing blue black gums and a patchwork tongue of grey and pink. She had a large flat nose and prominent cheek-bones. Tortuous veins tracked across her forehead and grey, matted hair clung to her scalp like a cap. Tiny welts radiating from around her eyes in concentric circles covered her face and neck. She wore gold earrings that stretched her ear lobes like rubber bands that threatened to snap at any moment.

Rope-like veins bulged on her skinny arms decked with gold bangles, and matchstick legs escaped from a multicoloured dress ending in spade-like feet. A jade disc, strung on a leather thong, hung around her neck. It was difficult to tell how old she was. Time had not been kind and Maryam felt sorry for her.

'I am happy as I am,' said Zubaida reading her thoughts. 'This is the way we all are.'

'All?'

'Us women!'

'Oh!'

'My mother, my grandmother and her mother were the same.'

Maryam didn't understand everything Zubaida said. The Arabic she spoke was tainted with a foreign accent. Samar had told her she came from somewhere in Africa. No one was ever sure where the women came from. That was one of their many mysteries. She had come to perform *Haj* but stayed behind to escape the famine and the war that had destroyed her country. She was, in effect, an alien – even though she had spent half a century in Saudi Arabia.

'So you're with child,' Zubaida said without wasting time. 'Have you been well?'

'Yes.'

'And when did the bleeding stop?'

'Two months.'

'What colour are your nipples?'

'Red! I mean pink.'

'What is it, child? Red or pink?' Zubaida snapped.

'Dark pink.'

'Does your nose bleed?'

'Yes, but. . .'

'But what, child?'

'Only from the right side,' Maryam said wondering what all this had to do with her pregnancy.'

'Are you sure?'

'Yes, yes! It's this side,' Maryam answered, touching the right side of her nose.

'And where do you feel heavy?'

'Here!' Maryam replied pointing to the right side of her stomach.

'Have you any freckles?'

'No.'

'Any nightmares?'

'No,' she lied. The baying hounds and faceless men in white had continued to torment her with regularity.

'Child, you are lying to me!' Zubaida barked. 'Come here and bring that lamp' she ordered.

The stench of *arak* hit Maryam in the face and made her heave. Zubaida peered into one eye and then the other holding up the lamp with one hand and pushing back her eyelids with the other.

'Hmm!' she muttered.

'What is it?' Mary asked.

'Congratulations, child! You're pregnant,' Zubaida proclaimed in her squawky voice. 'It's a boy.'

'A boy! How do you know?'

'What do you want?' the woman asked.

'Want?' Maryam asked. Surely it was obvious why she was here. Did she have to spell it out? She stared at the floor in silence.

'Has Shaitaan got your tongue, child?'

Maryam jumped at the mention of the devil.

'Yes! I mean no!' Maryam blurted out in fright. She knew devil worshipping was a capital crime as was witchcraft, and they would most certainly be put to death if caught. On the other hand, she also knew her father, even Uncle Mahmoud or the self-righteous Nabeel would kill her for bringing shame and dishonour to the family. That was their right as men: she had committed a grave crime not only against the family but also Islam and the state; she had conceived a baby out of wedlock – and to an American infidel at that.

'What do you mean?'

'I don't want it. . . the baby. . . the boy, or whatever it is!' Maryam said panicking. 'I don't want it! I don't want it!'

The woman got up, grunting in pain.

'Come.' Zubaida took Maryam's hand and led her into another room. A candle flickered as they entered and the reek of *arak* made her hesitate at the door.

'Take off your dress and lie down here,' Zubaida commanded pointing to the mattress on the floor.

'What are you going to do?' Maryam trembled with fear.

'Look into the future.'

'The future?' exclaimed Maryam. Why would anyone want to look into the future of a baby that was not even born? It hadn't been a good idea after all and she shouldn't have let Samar talk her into it. This was all very confusing. She had come here to get rid of the baby not to know whether it was a boy or girl and what its future might be.

Pointing to the ceiling, Zubaida said, 'Every living thing has a future and only He controls the future, neither you nor I.'

Maryam removed her dress and shivered on the damp mattress.

The woman took a leaf from a wooden bowl and examined it by the candlelight. She turned it over, rubbed it between her fingers before folding it into a neat square and popping it into her mouth. She chewed for a few minutes with her eyes shut and then spat green liquid into a corner. She towered over Maryam, her breathing slow and deliberate. Waving a fan of peacock plumes over her arms and chest, she stared at a point in the ceiling. Her body began to move to the strange rhythm of the fan. Her breathing grew shallow and her movements became feverish, the fan moved to and fro, her eyes bulged out of their sockets and her lips trembled, frothing at the corners. The woman began to speak in a different voice and in a strange language Maryam didn't understand. Her body shook and perspiration trickled from her forehead down her neck and soaked into her dress. She bent over Maryam and waved the fan from her head to her toes, never touching the body, all the while muttering.

She stopped abruptly and knelt beside her, the fan resting on Maryam's stomach. She remained there for what seemed like eternity, not moving a muscle.

Suddenly she looked at Maryam, her face calm, with gentle eyes and still lips. There was a pause and then it happened. A moment when Maryam's world changed, a moment she would never forget.

The woman closed her eyes and began to speak but this time Maryam understood every word and recognised the voice. It was Sultan, her brother.

'Miri, come hold my hand,' the voice said and the woman extended her hand. No one but Sultan and Turki called her Miri and she reached out and took hold of the woman's hand. It felt warm, alive and strong.

'You are supposed to be dead!' she said, confused.

'Yes, but I have always been with you. How is my son?'

'Turki? He's just fine. Mama says he's so much like you.' Maryam answered.

The conversation flowed between them as if nothing had changed, but Maryam knew nothing would ever be the same. Then Maryam asked about the crash. There was silence and the voice spoke.

'I was shot down by my partner.'

'Not by the Iraqis? But. . .'

'By my partner!'

'An accident?'

'It was no accident!'

'But why?'

There was a pause before Sultan spoke. 'Because I discovered they were plotting to kill the king.'

'They?' asked Maryam.

'The king's family, of course.'

Maryam gasped.

The conversation ended. The woman began to tremble and mutter again in the strange language. Zubaida knelt with her head to the ground, arms outstretched in submission. Her perspiration-soaked dress clung to her body.

Without notice Sultan's voice boomed through the walls. For some reason this wasn't frightening.

'Miri, you and the child are in danger. You must leave this land. No harm must come to him.'

'But how?' Maryam asked. 'I am all alone.'

'You shall name the child Isa, after the prophet.' There was love in Sultan's voice and Maryam felt calm. 'There will be a sign in the heavens. Follow it, and you will reach safety. I will be with you walking in your footsteps. Go now, prepare for the journey.'

Maryam got up and dressed. The woman stopped shaking and came to. She threw herself at Maryam's feet and kissed them. 'I have been waiting for you and now you have come,' she said with tears in her eyes.

'I don't understand. . . why me?'

'You will understand one day – it will *all* become clear.'

'Take this,' Zubaida offered Maryam the speckled disc dangling on a thong from around her neck. 'My mother gave it to me, and she received it from my grandmother – it was left to her by her mother. It must always be gifted. . . to a woman. It has been with the women since the beginning.'

'The beginning?' Maryam asked.

'It came from the heavens.'

'I can't accept this,' Maryam protested. 'I'm not worthy of such a precious gift.'

'I have no daughter,' Zubaida said, holding Maryam's hands. 'I have seen it *all*. . . the fire. . . the girl child. . . the war. *Everything!* My time is near. . . I have no need for it.'

'What use is it to me? Maryam asked. 'Besides, it's forbidden by Islam.'

The old woman gave a dismissive wave and sat down on her

stool. She pondered a while, took a leaf from the bowl and began to munch it. She spoke in bursts that Maryam found hard to follow. 'The circle is the sign of strength. . . green is for life. . . white is for peace. The hole is your window. . . you will see what has passed and what is to come. It will ward off the *jinn*. . . those who steal it will be damned. . . it will protect you.

Reluctantly Maryam took the disc and held it up to the lamp. A ray of light shot through the hole and she smiled for the first time.

'There, child. . . go now!' Zubaida said, placing a reassuring hand on Maryam's shoulder.

Quickly Maryam slipped the gift into her purse and kissed the old woman farewell.

On her way back, Maryam thought about Sultan. His partner on that fateful day had been a prince – the man who killed her brother. Had he really spoken to her or was her imagination playing games? Why had he commanded her to leave the country of her birth and where was she to go? There would be a sign in the heavens. . . but when and where? Her baby was growing fast and soon someone had to notice.

What kind of power did the stone have? Islam forbade the use of magic potions and the wearing of *taweez*. This was against everything she had been taught. How could a mere stone have power, even if it had fallen from the heavens? How could anyone know of the future besides Allah? What did this strange woman mean when she said she had seen *everything*?

THIRTY-ONE

The nightmares were back: more vivid and real. Menacing faces of men in white jeered at her, pointing accusingly, blotting out the sun, leaving her in darkness. Hounds with contorted human heads and fangs dripping blood snapped at her. They came again tonight, entering through the dark labyrinth of her sub-conscious. Beams of light criss-crossed inside her skull, like searchlights arcing through the night sky. She was the enemy: their enemy and the enemy of the state. But today they came looking for her unborn child; he was their enemy too, living proof of her crime and pronounced guilty before he had uttered his first cry.

The baby moved in her womb. Maryam awoke, soaked with perspiration. Soon they would notice her ballooning belly and then the nightmares would come in her waking hours, making life a living hell. Turki lay beside her, sucking his thumb. She had missed him and tried not to think of the day when she would have to leave him forever. Perhaps she would never see him again, or perhaps he would secretly visit her some day wherever she was, or perhaps he would never forgive her for abandoning him.

She wondered if Saffron was awake. She needed to share her thoughts with her cool head and practical mind. She watched the clock ticking away the seconds, like a timer on an atomic bomb counting down her end. Would they let her give birth before they killed her or would they let the shameful evidence die with her?

A tear trickled down her cheek and soaked into the pillow. Was it such a crime to love another human? Surely this could not be the will of Allah but the will of the men in white. Allah was merciful and she was His child, as were Joe and the men in white.

She wondered who would cast the first stone. Would it be her righteous father or her self-centered brother? Maryam remembered reading in the great book how the Prophet Isa had saved a woman from certain death at the hands of a bloodthirsty mob.

'Whore! Adulteress!' they had shouted and chased her through the streets seeking vengeance.

'May he who is without sin cast the first stone!' the great prophet had called out to the mob and none had stepped forward. Where would they find a pure person in this corrupt world? Her unborn child was without sin and yet he would die without mercy at the hands of sinners, a sacrificial lamb to cleanse their conscience.

With tears in her eyes she tiptoed from her room to find Saffron. She often read her *Qur'an* into the early hours, killing time.

'We'll make a Muslim out of you yet,' her mother had said in jest when she gave Saffron the Holy Book. At first the book lay untouched, gathering dust at the bottom of her chest of drawers, but lately, to everyone's surprise, Saffron had become an avid reader and was forever asking questions that left her mother and herself lost for words. Unfortunately, the intimacy that they had once shared had been missing since Sahar and Samar's party.

A light streaked from under Saffron's bedroom door. She heard voices, the bed creak and the thud, thud, thud of the headboard against the wall. Nabeel was back, she thought and turned to leave but a voice drew her to the keyhole.

Kneeling on the floor, Maryam watched the lovers floating on clouds of ruffled sheets. The sound of kisses and moans reached her ears. Suddenly the man swung round and kissed Saffron's breasts. Maryam watched dumfounded. A long moment passed;

her head throbbed, her lungs screamed for oxygen and her body forgot how to breathe. Tears of guilt, hatred and confusion streamed down her cheeks. She gasped for air.

It was her father.

She wanted to barge in and scream at them but instead she fled back to her room. She buried her face in her pillow and sobbed, her body consumed by rage. Her stomach churned, wanting to vomit up the unpalatable reality of what she had witnessed. She pounded the pillow with the fury of a boxer while Turki lay sleeping only feet away.

Anger gave way to exhaustion and she collapsed on the bed, her mind swirling.

This would explain Saffron's aloofness and her sudden interest in the Holy Book, she thought. How long had it been going on and how could she have been so blind?

Was Nabeel aware or did he not care so long as they left him to pursue his boyfriends? Saffron never spoke of how and where they met and where they planned to live and bring up a family. She was always polite and with her disarming smile she would laugh away any inquiries with a well placed '*Insha'allah*' or 'Nabeel knows best.'

She watched the stars through her bedroom window and wondered where she would be a year from now? Would the bars of a prison cell replace the ornate grill of her window or would she be dead, buried in an unmarked grave, forgotten forever? Every night she searched the heavens for the sign Sultan had promised, but where was she supposed to look and for what? The Milky Way stretched out across the window like a stairway to heaven as always.

'What am I to do, Sultan?' she asked aloud. She gripped the grill and shook it. 'Don't forsake me,' she cried.'

A star fell from the sky followed by another. Lamenting her dilemma, she slipped to the floor and sobbed, rocking from side to side. A hand lay on her shoulder.

'Who are you talking to, Auntie Miri?' Turki asked standing

naked, his head cocked at an angle. His lower lip quivered at her distress and a frown creased his forehead.

'I'm here,' he said, throwing his arms around her, he kissed her cheeks. 'I'll protect you,' he puffed out his little chest like his hero, Popeye.

Maryam swallowed the lump in her throat and brushed away her tears with the back of her hand. Turki's antics made her smile. She hugged and kissed her brave prince and carried him off to bed, tickling his feet until the room was filled with laughter.

'I want you to promise me something, *habibi*,' Maryam said, looking into his big brown eyes.

'Yes, Auntie Maryam?'

'When you grow up you promise to be brave.'

'Like Popeye.'

'Yes, like Popeye, and seek the truth and protect the weak.'

'I promise, Auntie Miri.'

'Promise you'll always treat women with respect and as equals.'

'Equals?' Turki asked, cocking his head to one side.

'Like the same as men! Treat them like your sisters.'

'But, Auntie Miri. . .'

'Yes, *habibi*.'

'. . . I don't have any sisters.'

'One day you will understand,' Maryam whispered and watched him fall asleep. 'Listen to your mind but lead with your heart, you are our hope and future. Don't judge in haste those who fail you. We are all children of Allah and only He can judge. I love you, my prince.'

* * *

The cacophony of sounds associated with the morning rituals of the household came from downstairs.

Maryam heard her father's steps on the gravel path and her

Uncle Mahmoud following close behind making their way to the mosque. She looked at the prayer mat leaning against her desk vying for her attention. She hadn't prayed for weeks, finding it difficult to kneel but she couldn't tell Turki why.

Breakfast was a silent affair. Maryam avoided Saffron's and her father's eyes. She wanted to call her a whore and an adulteress, but the story of the sinner and the Prophet Isa reminded her that she too was a sinner and it was not for her to judge.

She barely touched the food on her plate and toyed with the goat's cheese, pushing it around the plate until she got bored. A cup slipped from her fingers spilling the tea over the table.

'Are you not well, Maryam?' Farhan asked, scooping a dollop of *labnah* with a triangle of *pitta* bread.

She had failed to greet him or Saffron this morning with her normally breezy manner. Anger smouldered, knotting her stomach. She wanted to scream *Adulterer! Hypocrite!* She wanted to ask him: *how could you sleep with your son's wife and then feel clean to face Allah in the morning?* Instead, she quenched her anger with a mouthful of *laban*. 'Women's problem,' Maryam muttered, and looked away in embarrassment. 'Besides I am fat.'

'Men like a bit of meat on the bones,' Farhan said, glancing at Saffron. 'Something to hold onto. Remember it's not long before you'll be a bride. You wouldn't want to disappoint Nader, would you?'

Maryam's face turned crimson with anger at the mention of Nader whom she had not seen for weeks. How much did her father know? Was he toying with her like a cat with a mouse? How much had Saffron told him, if anything? Could she be trusted to remain silent about Joe or was she just another opportunist who would capitalise on her trust to gain favour?

'Leave the girl alone,' Aishah said. 'I was all skin and bones when you married me, Farhan, or have you forgotten?'

'I have an announcement to make,' began Saffron,

straightening in her chair and tossing her hair, she paused for everyone's attention. Saffron glanced at Farhan and prepared to speak. Maryam's heart missed a beat. All eyes turned to Saffron. Even Turki stopped blowing into the orange juice through the straw and looked up.

'In the short time I've been with you I've come to love you all,' Saffron said.

Maryam's head thumped, listening to the words that passed the lips that had been kissing her father hours earlier.

'Each one of you is very special to me,' Saffron continued, giving Farhan a fleeting glance. 'When I left America I left behind everything, my family and friends. Now I have you as my family and my friends. I also left behind my culture and my religion and here among you and, with your help, Mama Aishah and Sister Maryam, I have found Islam.' She smiled nervously at the two women. Aishah acknowledged her gratitude with a smile and a nod but Maryam pursed her lips and looked away.

'What I am trying to say,' she said faltering, 'is that. . . I have decided to embrace Islam and become a Muslim. I want to be a servant of Allah the one and only God.'

'*Alhamdulillah!*' they all exclaimed. Farhan and Turki clapped and Aishah hugged and kissed Saffron, saying 'my *habibi*' and showering her with a thousand blessings.

'You'll have to have a Muslim name. What shall we call her?' Aishah asked looking at Farhan.

'How about Hanifah?'

'What does it mean?' Saffron asked.

'True believer.'

'*Alhamdulillah*. It's perfect!' Aishah said. 'After your *Shahada* you'll be Hanifah, *habibi*,' She hugged Saffron again, feeling happier for the first time in weeks.

'Hanifah! I like it Mama Aishah. I like it a lot,' Saffron said, smiling at Farhan.

Maryam remained silent, wondering what manner of sorcery was at play and for what reason? Mahmoud sat stoically. He thought it was easy for sweet words to pass the lips but often they were hard to swallow.

'This calls for a celebration,' Farhan announced and everyone except Maryam agreed.

'Why does Auntie Saffron have to change her name?' Turki asked, tugging at Maryam sleeve.

'Because Auntie Saffron is going to become a Muslim.' Aishah said.

'I want to make an announcement too,' Turki called, standing on the chair and waving his arms to attract attention. Everyone stopped and looked at the boy dressed in his new battle fatigue that Aishah had given him during *Eid al-Adha* as he copied Saffron's performance. With his head held high and nose in the air, he declared, 'I'm going to be a pilot like my father and fight for our King.' They all chorused '*Insha'allah!*' and applauded, rolling with laughter. Turki had stolen the show.

THIRTY-TWO

Nabeel's call surprised everyone except Aishah. Hearing his voice brought a little colour to her face and a smile that diminished the melancholy that had taken hold.

'When are you coming home, *habibi*?' she asked. 'The days are long and my bones are weary, not many years are left in me,' she complained.

'I've not been gone long, Mama.'

'When are you going to give me grandchildren, *habibi*? It's not good for a young wife to be alone for long. It's *haram*. Tongues will wag!'

'*Insha'allah*, I'll be home soon, I promise. Can I talk to Saffron, Mama?'

Saffron took the call in the privacy of the library.

'Have you seen Nader?' Nabeel asked without ceremony.

Saffron detected a hint of urgency in his voice. 'No. Why the hell would I? When are you coming back? We need to talk!'

'Talk! About what?' Nabeel asked.

'I'm going to become a Muslim,' Saffron said in a matter of fact tone. There was silence and Saffron could hear the hum of the static in the line and a faint chatter of voices.

'You're going to what?' Nabeel shouted.

'Become a Muslim.'

'Are you nuts?' Nabeel's voice was an octave higher.

'Thought you would approve.'

'There's no money in it,' replied Nabeel and gave one of his hollow laughs, thinking this was one of Saffron's sick jokes. He had realised early on in their relationship that money was what made Saffron tick.

'What a pity you're not here to celebrate with me.' She was enjoying the moment. Nabeel was not one to handle stress very well and she could just see him pacing up and down, dabbing his forehead with his neatly ironed handkerchief. 'Oh, I almost forgot. . .'

'Is there more? Shit!'

'Yes. You're going to be a father. Isn't that just wonderful? I'm going to have our baby.' She waited for his reaction.

'Are you fucking mad? You can't have my baby and you know it. Remember the contract? No sex.'

'No. Not mad, just one month pregnant,' Saffron laughed, knowing she had his undivided attention.

'I'll divorce you.' Nabeel screamed.

'It's too late for that now. And anyway you can't.'

'I'm a Saudi! I can do what I like.'

'Have you forgotten! You can't divorce me while I am pregnant. That's the law.'

'I'll tell them you are an adulteress, slut!' Nabeel shouted.

'I didn't think you were so dumb, Nabeel. You'll be the centre of every sick joke from here to Timbuktu.' Saffron knew calling a Saudi *dumb* was the mother of all insults. 'Besides, you need three male witnesses.'

'So you've been studying the *Qur'an*.'

'You bet and I'll tell them the whole story.' Saffron knew Nabeel was all talk and when push came to shove he was as weak as dishwater.

'No one will believe you.'

'Try me. I've got nothing to lose and I've got the contract document and. . . photos.' There was no going back now; he was going to have to take the bait.

'Photos? What fucking photos?' Nabeel thundered into the

mouthpiece. There was a pause as his overloaded brain tried to make sense of everything all at once.

'Photos of you and your boyfriends.'

'Fuck you! Slut! Bitch!' He ran out of expletives. 'Whose child is it anyway?' he asked, trying to regain composure.

'Guess?' There was a pause and Saffron could hear his laboured breathing.

Shit, he should never have rung up. Why the fuck hadn't Nader returned his calls? And then it dawned on him. It had to be Nader: he had become impossible to reach and hadn't replied to his messages. It was Nader who had suggested that he should accompany him to Riyadh but had disappeared on arrival. That was just a ploy to get him out of the way so the field would be clear. He also had the opportunity to meet the whore every time he came to see Maryam. It was so simple, so open and clever that no one would ever suspect.

'I'll kill that Nader! It's him, isn't it?' Nabeel screamed.

'Nader! Are you kidding? Try again, *habibi*!' Saffron suggested, repulsed at the thought of being in the same room with Nader let alone the same bed. There was another pause. Nabeel racked his brains for another candidate and then it struck him like a bolt of lightening. There was only one person who it could be. . .

'You're fucking my father!'

'Well done, *habibi*!' congratulated Saffron. 'I thought you'd never get there. Wasn't it good of me to keep it in the family,' she declared, knowing Nabeel was hardly going to kill his father in revenge.

'It can't be! He's a very religious man! He wouldn't do such a thing.'

'Your father's all man! More than I can say for you. And, anyway, does it matter?'

'You're a sick bitch!'

'A bitch, maybe. Sick? Definitely not.'

'Does he know?'

'He's not stupid. Why don't you ask him yourself? Now listen here, pretty boy,' she drawled. 'Like it or not, I'm going to have this baby, so you better get used to the idea fast. This kid could solve all your problems and for that I want another hundred grand a year. Call it maternity pay.'

'You money-hungry bitch!'

'There hasn't been an Immaculate Conception in two thousand years and there isn't going to be one now. So get your ass on the next plane and play at being a loving hubby or people will talk. And we wouldn't want that would we, *habibi*?' Saffron commanded: she was in the driver's seat tearing down the highway of free enterprise and there was no stopping her.

'Fuck you!' Nabeel screamed.

'What's wrong, *habibi*? Can't you shake your boyfriends off for a few days?'

Nabeel thumped his fist on the wall and winced in pain. He hated her *Ameriki* drawl and her sarcasm cut deep into his Arab pride.

'I'll kill you and feed you to the dogs. I'll turn you into dog shit.'

'Sure, bozo. Now, I'm done talking. So get your ass over here if you know what's good for you!' Saffron hung up.

Nabeel's hand throbbed. The pain jolted him back to reality and made him think. Why fight the bitch, he thought? The bloody whore was right. There was Nabeel the husband and now Nabeel the father; no one would ever call him Nabeel the faggot again. His mother wanted a grandchild; now she could have one and let him get on with life. A hundred grand was a small price to pay to get the whore and others off his back.

Saffron stepped out of the library, flushed with victory, triumph written all over her face.

THIRTY-THREE

The festive mood was in full swing by mid-morning and excitement bubbled over in the kitchen. Aishah lifted her spirits and mustered her girls – as she liked to think of Zelpha, Imelda and Josi – into action.

The celebration in honour of Saffron's conversion was a modest family affair. However, Aishah made sure the occasion would be remembered and dispatched Mahmoud and Turki to the animal *souq* to purchase lambs. A celebration feast without the traditional *qauzi* would be unthinkable. 'It would be like having Thanksgiving dinner without a turkey,' Aishah told Saffron, 'and a great insult and loss of face for the whole family.'

They had selected two white-faced *Nedji* lambs that were neither fat nor lean. The Yemeni farmhand had dispatched them ceremoniously with the single stroke of a sharp knife across the neck while murmuring '*Bismillah!*' Hiding behind Mahmoud, Turki had watched the animal kick and roll its eyes until the stream of blood had disappeared into a hole the ground.

The guests arrived soon after *Maghrib* prayer, so they could be present for *Isha* prayer and Saffron's *Shahada*. Mona and her sisters accompanied Nader and their father Talal. Uncle Eid brought Jamillah, his eighteen-year-old wife of six weeks, to meet her in-laws. She was pregnant, bemused by her exalted position after displacing Uncle Eid's first wife, Wafa, who had borne him nine children.

213

Maryam found Wafa, cowering in the background. She was a frail looking woman with dark eyes that sparkled in a weather-beaten face creased with age and peppered with tattoos. Maryam greeted her with the affection and respect reserved for the elderly and sat holding her frail hand as she watched Jamillah hog the limelight.

'Allah has been kind to me, *habibi*. I still have a roof over my head and six sons,' Wafa said, clicking her dentures.

'*Alhamdulillah*,' replied Maryam.

'Aishah is fortunate your father hasn't taken a younger wife.'

'He loves my mother very much,' Maryam answered, choking on her words.

'*Alhamdulillah*. I mustn't be envious of the good fortune of others.'

'Not if you want to be a good Muslim, Auntie Wafa,' Maryam said, and admonished her gently with a pat on her wrist, making the old woman smile.

'You're a good soul, Maryam,' Wafa said, holding onto her hand. 'I've always liked you. I told your Uncle Eid a thousand times you should marry one of our sons but your father wouldn't have any of it.'

'Auntie Wafa, now you're really being naughty,' Maryam exclaimed in mock horror.

'In my day we all married cousins. That way we knew the family. Now it's all changing. Jamillah is from another tribe and it's all about money.'

They talked about the old days when the family wasn't scattered all over the world.

'There have been so many changes during my life,' Wafa reflected. 'We had no television, running water or electricity. I still can't get over how the telephone works. I tell you it's a miracle, a real miracle. It helps me keep in touch with my children.'

'It must've been very different.'

'Look at me, I can't read or write but I recite a bit of the

Qur'an from memory,' Wafa said tapping her head. 'There were no schools for us girls in my days. But now they have big colleges. . . but you know about that.'

'Yes, the government has done much.'

'King Abdul Aziz and his sons. . . may they live to be a hundred and may Allah bless them with many sons.'

'Auntie Wafa, I'm disappointed in you,' Maryam teased.

'Oh, never mind me, I am too old to change, *habibi*.'

'Tabuk must've changed,' Maryam asked.

'Tabuk, Jeddah, all those places. . . *habibi*, there are so many tall buildings with all that glass and people rushing here, there and everywhere. Busy, busy, busy, making money. Oh my-oh-my, it makes my head spin just thinking about them.'

'It's called modernisation,' Maryam smiled at her aunt's perspective on life.

'I don't care what you call it. It's not like it used to be. People don't have time anymore. It's all "I have to do this" and "I have to go there".'

'We have to keep up with the world. It's changing so fast,' Maryam explained.

'There are so many hospitals and all those foreign doctors. All this rushing round must make you ill. *Alhamdulillah*, it's all free,' Wafa said, clicking her dentures.

'You're probably right, Auntie Wafa.'

'I took my daughter, Rasmeyah, to one of those special clinics in Jeddah and now she has twin boys. *Alhamdulillah*, it saved her marriage. But in my day they didn't have all these fancy things. If it didn't happen naturally it wasn't Allah's will.'

'We have some of the best hospitals in the world.'

'An *Ameriki* doctor made these for me at the dental hospital,' Wafa said, fishing out her bottom denture and waving it in the air. 'I'm still getting used to them but it's so nice to be able to chew my food after so many years.'

'You'll put on weight.'

'Now that would be a first.' Wafa laughed. 'When I was young we never saw a fat person but now they are everywhere. I blame the cars. They make people lazy.'

'How did you manage without them?'

'Oh, we had our camels and donkeys or walked. Life wasn't fast like it is now. There was time for everything and everyone; the seasons ruled our lives.'

'What do you miss most?'

'It was a simple life, we didn't have much money and everyone shared what little they had in those days. There was more kinship. I think I miss that the most. If your neighbour killed a goat he would give you the best cut.'

'The oil has changed all that,' Maryam lamented.

'Dowries have climbed, only the old men with money can afford a wife,' Wafa said, tsking in Jamillah's direction. 'This was my dowry,' Wafa showed Maryam the six gold bangles on her arms. 'These days it's every man for himself and we women still have no say.'

'What I'd miss most is the air-conditioning,' Maryam said, changing the subject.

'Yes, I don't know how we ever managed. I guess, *habibi*, you don't miss what you don't have,' Wafa clicked her dentures again.

Maryam laughed as she reflected on Wafa's pearls of wisdom and suddenly realised what she stood to lose.

The cousins were out in strength and their ever-expanding troop of children turned the house into a circus. Girls in frilly frocks and boys in military outfits ran around the house scream-ing and shouting, waving toy guns and plastic swords, stuffing their mouths with sweets and chocolate. Turki enjoyed meeting children his age, shy at first, wondering who they all were and never quite remembering everyone's names. However he soon took on the leader's role. Just like his father used to do, observed Aishah.

Pink-faced babies sucked on nipples for dear life, making squelching noises. Their mothers, decked out in flamboyant costumes, garishly made-up like china dolls and draped in twenty-two carat gold, told stories and updated themselves with the latest hot gossip to come out of the palace.

'Did you know Abdul Aziz Al Ghamdi has taken another wife? She's barely twelve. I swear he's seventy and not a day younger,' said one.

'No! No! We know him,' chirped in another. 'He's our neighbour; I swear he's at least eighty. I've seen him rushing back from the hospital after one of those injections, hanging on to his you-know-what,' and they all burst out in fits of laughter, their fat bellies wobbling like jelly through slits and provocative portholes in their dresses. 'Believe me, his *thobe* looked just like a tent.' They roared again, tears rolling down their cheeks, clapping their henna-stained hands with delight. 'Poor girl,' they all commiserated without any genuine feeling.

'You know Zana, that anaemic girl who thought she was something special at school? Well, rumour has it that the Prince is interested in her,' offered another.

'That can't be true. They only marry among themselves and their relatives and I hear, from a reliable source at the hospital, he's got syphilis,' interrupted another cousin.

'Syphilis!' they all exclaimed throwing up their hands in the air in disgust.

'I bet he got that in Pakistan while hunting.'

'I wonder what he hunts,' asked another, and they all hooted with laughter until their mascara ran with the tears.

'Just because he's interested doesn't mean he's got to marry her,' added another with a wink. And everyone agreed in unison.

'Did you hear about the three sisters and the gardener?' inquired Mona, wanting to contribute to the gossip. They had all heard the story but wanted to hear her version.

'These three sisters were happily watching a six movie one afternoon when they spied this Sri Lankan gardener through the window, watering the plants.'

'That's a sex movie but we call them six,' Maryam explained for Saffron's benefit.

'You can't imagine what happened next!' She looked around the room wide eyed at the smiling faces all creating a vision of their own in their minds. 'They dragged the bewildered man in and had their wicked ways. . .'

'Never!' They all chorused.

'. . . at least two did but the poor man couldn't you-know-what so the third sister bit it off.'

'Oh!' they all gasped and covered their mouths in embarrassment.

'What happened next?' young Jamillah asked, blushing under her make-up, eager to be part of the group.

'Oh! The poor man got such a shock that he ran out of the house and down the street where he collapsed and died.' They all gasped in horror but thought it was hilarious.

'The father paid some blood money and everything was forgotten,' Maryam explained to Saffron.

'You can't imagine how horrified I was when my eight-year-old daughter came home from school saying she wanted a circumcision like her friend,' complained another cousin. 'I thought this barbaric practice had been banned but obviously it goes on.'

Everyone shook their heads in dismay and complained the government wasn't doing enough. This was another way to control women, Maryam thought silently. If you didn't enjoy it you wouldn't go looking for it. So they found a way to make it unpleasant, attached a religious label to it and sold it to the masses.

'I wouldn't want my clit cut off for anything. It's the only thing that keeps our marriage alive,' added a young woman from the back with a giggle.

'You were always the horny one. Remember the time I caught you with a cucumber in your bed and you were only fourteen?' disclosed her sister.

'That was when I was a vegetarian.'

'Ha!. . . and now you're a meat eater.'

They had a great time exchanging family secrets without fear. Saffron felt left out, unable to share in their stories. She had a tale or two of her own that would have gone down well but her Arabic was not up to it.

* * *

The men sat in the garden under the Bedouin tent sipping tea and thimbles of clove and cardamom scented Arabic coffee, eating dates and cookies and watching the television blare out the virtues of Islam on Channel One. *Misbahas* of every colour whirred through the air to wind and unwind around their owner's fingers. They talked about the poor returns on the wheat these days and how the government was giving financial incentives to encourage them to switch to barley.

'I'm off to the Philippines soon,' Talal announced and enthused about how cheap it was to live there in style. 'The women are so receptive.' He made an obscene gesture with his hands. 'And always available. It's paradise for men. *No* is a word you never hear – only *how much*? Some hotels are so full of Saudis that you think you're in Jeddah. You should try it, Farhan. It'll do you a world of good. You'll come back a new man – that is, if you come back at all.'

'They eat pigs, dogs and even live monkeys,' complained Farhan. They heard the Saudi newscaster fumble with the names of the two British nurses convicted of murder and shook their heads. The king, in his infinite wisdom, had shown clemency and pardoned them.

'There is no justice these days. The British have only to send their Prime Minister and the king bends and kisses his arse!' exploded Nader. A murmur of support rang around the gathering.

'I overheard an English doctor saying the king had intimated that a promise of a football match with our national team at Wembley would help secure their release.'

219

'We have become a nation of beggars and a football game is the price for our pride!' Nader declared.

'There should be one law for everybody – besides, the British need us more then we need them,' expounded one young man.

'This king is not just ill, he's weak and they should replace him,' interjected another young man.

'A weak leader means a weak country,' voiced yet another and a rumble of approval greeted his donation.

'What we need is a queen,' declared Farhan trying to keep a straight face. They all fell about laughing at the joke, knowing a queen in Saudi Arabia would make them a laughing stock.

'Didn't the Prophet say man was the superior and that he was there to look after the women?' Eid asked.

'He did indeed. But what we need is young blood with young ideas and Islamic values!' countered Nader with passion.

'Someone like young Saud!' suggested Farhan in a serious tone.

'He's an excellent foreign minister, respected by many heads of state,' Eid said.

'Yes! Saud would be a good choice, people still remember his father Faisal,' Mahmoud added. Except for Nader, they all endorsed young Saud's credentials.

'What we need is a revolutionary council like in Iran,' Nader said after a moment's reflection, and everyone laughed.

'I'd prefer a king to an Ayatollah any day,' Talal replied, and everyone agreed.

The cry of the *muezzin* announcing *Isha* prayer ended their spirited conversation, much to Nader's annoyance. . . and Farhan's relief – the desert had ears and everyone had his price, family or friend. In the old days the family and the tribe came before all and loyalty could not be bought. Farhan reflected on the old saying, 'I and my brothers against my cousins; I and my cousins against the stranger.'

Today money pervaded the hearts and minds of the young and there was no loyalty to the tribe or the family. Nader had a volatile temper and aspirations that spelled trouble. Such loose talk was tantamount to treachery and he knew where that would lead. Pushed out of a plane over the Rub al-Khali, the empty quarter, at six thousand feet without a parachute or a slow lingering death in some prison, forgotten for years.

* * *

Saffron had heard the call to *Isha* prayer and stood on the prayer mat facing Mecca in a room filled with women. Today she had worn a plain lemon dress in the Arabic style that added a warm glow to her pale Celtic features. Her locks of fiery red hair lay imprisoned in a cream satin scarf that Maryam had given her and it was drawn tightly around her face.

Saffron looked reverential. Without a hint of make-up, Maryam observed from a distance. Was this apparition really the woman she had heard demanding fulfilment in the throes of adultery? Maryam shrugged her shoulders. Who was she to pass judgement when her own credentials were suspect?

Maryam had explained the five pillars of Islam and Saffron was about to begin the *Shahada*. In a clear and resonant voice with a hint of tension, Saffron called out in Arabic, '*La ilaha illa'Llah*,' and then repeated in English, 'There is no god except God. *Mohammedun rasulu'Llah*,' she pronounced in Arabic and then affirmed in English, 'Mohammed is the messenger of God'. With the conviction of a devout Muslim, Saffron performed her first prayer in public. At prayer's end the other worshippers welcomed Saffron into the sisterhood of Islam, calling her by her Muslim name, Hanifah.

Dinner followed and the guests gorged themselves until the seams of their dresses stretched to bursting point and the stitching protested. That was the desert way: feast today for there might be none tomorrow, and when it was free every morsel was tastier then the last. The children gulped down gallons of Pepsi and Miranda and abandoned spoons, preferring fingers that

RAJ KUMAR

squelched through trifles and puddings. Food debris lay everywhere and Zelpha and the other maids shook their heads in
dismay at the wastage.

It was well past midnight when one family after another
gathered their slumbering princesses and soldiers and made their
way home. The men decided when to leave because only they had
the authority to drive. The bachelors dragged their feet and hung
around in the garden nursing *shisha* pipes and ridding the world
of all evil with one word: *Islam* – followed by '*Insha'allah.*'

Aishah, with Saffron by her side, entertained the guests but
Maryam, weary, retired to her bedroom. Turki joined the men in
the garden, enjoying being the centre of attention. He sat in
Farhan's lap and followed his hand across the blackboard
littered with stars.

'Do you remember which is the North Star?' Farhan asked.
Turki nodded, pointing to the brightest star he could see.

'That's *Shiaara*. Now over there,' Farhan pointed, 'is the
North Star.'

'It's used by travellers,' Turki interrupted, bringing a smile on
Farhan's face; the boy had remembered something and that
pleased him.

'Over there is Mars which is also called the red planet. . .'

'Because it's red. It's my favourite colour,' Turki added.

'. . . and up there is Venus, the brightest of the planets. . . oh,
and look over there above the city lights! Can you see the long
fuzzy streak of light?'

'I see it, Grandpa,' Turki said, pointing to the horizon.

'That's a comet, visiting us. Soon it'll be gone for thousands of
years.'

'What's a comet?'

'Let me see. . . a comet is a huge chunk of ice that goes round
the Sun.' Farhan said, stroking his beard and predicting the next
question.

'Does it melt and disappear?'

'It's very cold in space.' Farhan smiled.

'Why doesn't it stay?' Turki asked.

'Everything in the universe is moving.'

'Like the moon.'

'Yes, just like the moon,' Farhan replied, delighting in his grandson's company.

'How long is a thousand years, Grandpa?'

Farhan thought for a while and contemplated the night sky. 'Hmm,' he said stroking his beard. 'It's a very long time, *habibi*.' He couldn't explain time because the Muslim calendar began with the flight of the Prophet Mohammed from Mecca to Medinah, fifteen hundred years ago; before that, time had stood still.

'Is a thousand years older then you, Grandpa?'

Farhan chuckled. 'A thousand years is. . .' he began and hesitated. '. . . a thousand years is older than the oldest trees, but it's not as old as Islam.'

'How old are the stars?' Turki asked. 'Are they older then a thousand years?'

'The stars. . . well, now you've really got me,' he said with a big grin. 'They're older then the Earth and the Sun and. . .'

'Are they older then Islam?'

Farhan didn't know how to say it and so he did his best. 'First Allah made the stars, the Sun and the Earth and then he made us humans and sent us our Prophet Mohammed, peace be upon him, and through our Prophet, Allah gave us Islam and the Holy *Qur'an*.'

Turki nodded. After some reflection he concluded, 'So Allah must be very old!'

'Indeed he is,' Farhan replied.

Turki sighed, cocked his head and contemplated the heavens sucking on his thumb. 'Grandpa?'

'Yes?'

'Who made Allah?' Turki asked looking at the stars twinkling in his Grandpa's eyes.

Farhan let the question hang in the air for a while. 'Nobody made Allah, Turki. Allah is the creator of all things. Now, it's time for bed, young man!' he said. They walked to the house hand in hand along the lantern-lit gravel path. Shadows followed them, eavesdropping, and the full moon watched over them. Farhan felt a mixture of emotions, it made him happy that Turki had inherited Sultan's questioning mind. He had always been close to Sultan and he still felt the pain that his elder son's his life had been cut short in the line of duty.

THIRTY-FOUR

After the *Isha* prayer the men filed out of the mosque, collected their footwear and wandered back to their tin shacks to feast or play cards.

Nader and Farhan returned to the Bedouin tent to enjoy the cool evening air.

'I'll catch up with you,' Mahmoud called out and headed for the stables.

Turki arrived, balancing three cups of tea and a plate of dates and cookies on a tray.

'Well done,' Nader said, and kissed the boy on the cheeks.

'Look, Grandpa, I did not spill the tea today.'

'You're learning fast,' Farhan said, and pulled Turki to his side. 'Uncle Mahmoud tells me you are riding well.'

Turki grinned. 'I can trot now but soon Uncle Mahmoud is going to teach me to canter and then I want to learn to jump.'

'Which horse did you ride?' Farhan asked, delighted by his grandson's adventures.

'I love Hava. He is the best, Grandpa. The others are slow and they don't do what I want. Sometimes I have to whip them.'

'Have you tried talking to them, *habibi*?'

'They don't understand Arabic, Grandpa.' Turki giggled.

'Next time, whisper in their ears and see what happens. You'll be surprised.'

225

Turki laughed at the suggestions but promised to try, then bit into a cookie.

'Do you ride, Nader?' Farhan asked.

'Not lately. But I did in Afghanistan.'

'How forgetful of me. Of course there aren't many roads,' Farhan said, taking a sip of tea.

'Mules and ponies more than horses – and none like our magnificent Arabs.'

'Ah yes! The Arab, he is a majestic beast. Did you know the thoroughbreds of Europe are descended from just two Arabs?'

Nader shook his head and sipped his tea.

'We Arabs have given so much to the world,' Farhan said.

'That we have,' Nader agreed. 'We have spread the word of Allah to all four corners of the globe.'

'There are even Muslims in Outer Mongolia,' Farhan added.

'Where's Outer Mongolia, Grandpa?' Turki asked. He sat cross-legged, his head resting on his hands.

'Do you remember I showed you where our country was on the map?'

Turki nodded. 'The yellow one in the middle.'

'Do you remember the other big country in yellow I showed you?'

'China!' Turki shouted.

'That's right, and just above China is Mongolia.'

'But Grandpa, I thought that was Russia.'

'Mongolia is close to Russia, *habibi*. Where were we?... Ah yes! Al Khwarizmi, an Arab, invented algebra and the numbers that are used all over the world – even by the Europeans and the *Ameriki*. And we were great sailors because of our knowledge of astronomy and navigation.'

'Stars and planets!' Turki piped in. 'Grandpa has taught me their names.'

'Did you know we gave the world the zero?' Farhan asked Nader.

'That is nothing!' Turki interjected.

Nader shook his head and continued to twirl his prayer beads. Farhan frowned.

'Tell *me* the story, Grandpa,' Turki begged. As always, Farhan loved to tell stories and so took a sip of tea, brushed his moustache and began.

'In the old days when they used pebbles to count, someone noticed that when the pebble was gone there was nothing left in the sand but a hollow and so we use a dot for nothing.'

Turki went to the edge of the carpet and picked up a pebble in the sand and his eyes lit up seeing the hollow where the pebble had been.

'Grandpa, look! It works!' he shouted.

'Well done!' Farhan applauded.

'You have a clever grandson,' Nader said.

'*Alhamdulillah*, he has Sultan's mind, always yearning for knowledge, just like Maryam. Education is such a wonderful thing don't you think, Nader?' Farhan raised an inquiring brow.

Nader nodded and twirled his beads with gusto.

'It can unlock the mind. You should try it,' Farhan suggested.

Nader stopped playing with the beads. 'You're a wise man,' he said, and folded his arms across his chest.

'An inquiring mind is like a tiger; cage it and it will hate and despise you.'

'Tigers are heading for extinction.'

'Only because of ignorant men.'

'That's the law of the jungle.'

'Fight a tiger on his terms and you'll soon know the law of the jungle,' Farhan laughed.

'We are smarter,' Nader replied with a smirk.

'You're right! We are smarter because we have knowledge and that, Nader, is power.'

'It's a double-edged sword,' Nader retorted, but knew he had lost the argument.

'Ah, but only in the wrong hands. The Holy *Qur'an* gives us direction. Our Prophet, peace be upon him, said that the search for knowledge is a duty of every Muslim and we must seek it from the cradle to the grave.'

'The Holy *Qur'an* gives us much wisdom.'

'My daughter, Maryam, is a devout Muslim. . .'

'And you have taught her well,' Nader acknowledged.

'She has an inquiring mind. . .'

'That I know,' Nader interrupted and started twirling his beads again.

'I'm very proud of you, son,' Farhan said, patting his back.

* * *

The cane swished through the air again and again to connect with the soles Joe's feet. He screamed.

Joe lay strapped across the table face down, an arm chained to each leg. 'Ah! And what have we here,' whooped the captain, fondling Joe's buttocks.

'You bastards!' Joe yelled. Fear gripped him, for he knew what was to come. His indignity was complete and his humiliation total. The portraits of the King and his two brothers looked on from their lofty positions, their smiling faces seemingly condoning the act.

The captain raised Joe's *thobe* and exposed his behind.

'Please God, no!' Joe screamed.

'Your God doesn't live here, Jew,' the captain sneered as he penetrated Joe.

Joe thrashed like an animal caught in a net. The chains cut into his flesh and the pain ricocheted around his brain like a pinball.

Satisfaction crossed the captain's face and a wave of approval rolled through the room. A lieutenant took the captain's place and they cheered him on with crude gestures and obscenities until he too retired to be replaced by another. . . and another.

'We fuck you to instil respect and obedience, Jew.' The captain spat in Joe's face. The room spun with jeering faces and half-naked men until it became a blur that sucked Joe into an ever-speeding vortex. When there seemed no end in sight, Joe's brain abruptly severed all communication with his body and he passed out.

THIRTY-FIVE

Maryam stood by the roadside silhouetted against the sky, her *abaya* flapping like an untethered sail catching the breeze. Long before she was born, Tabuk had been an oasis village through which locomotives trundled carrying pilgrims on *Haj* from the Ottoman Empire. Since then it had become both jaded and careworn and so was now the target of vigorous redevelopment.

She watched a herd of bulldozers at work, leaving behind destruction in their wake. Zubaida's building was a mountain of rubble and Maryam's heart sank.

'Have you seen the woman who lived there?' she shouted to a labourer over the deafening noise.

Suspicious eyes peered from between the folds of his *kufiyyah* like a Tureg warrior and appraised her fine *abaya* and gloved hands. A moment passed and then he turned and walked away without uttering a word. Drawing a note from her purse Maryam ran after him.

'Tell me!'

The man stopped, looked at her for a long while, drew closer and shouted, 'A black woman!' More a statement than a question.

Maryam nodded.

'Was she a friend?'

'A friend?. . . Oh yes, yes, a friend,' replied Maryam, startled by his question. Her instincts told her something was wrong. There was a pause as the man weighed Maryam's reply.

'Your friend's gone,' the man said with a dismissive wave.

'Gone where?' Maryam asked, thrusting the note in his hand.

'She's dead. They sealed the doors and set the building on fire.'

'No!' gasped Maryam. Her baby kicked as if he had heard the terrible news.

'Who are *they*?' Maryam fought back the tears.

'The *mutaween*!' The labourer crumpled the note, crushing the smiling face of King Fahad, and stuffed it into her hand, leaving a smudge of dust on the black cloth. 'I don't want your filthy money! Now go!'

With tears streaming, Maryam jumped into the waiting taxi and slammed the door.

'This isn't your father's car,' protested the driver.

Maryam ignored his comments. '*Yellah!*' she snapped. 'What are you waiting for?'

The taxi driver dabbed his face with a towel, muttered something and drove back. He remembered Maryam; she had tipped him well the last time, so he tried to be nice. Perhaps this was going to be his lucky day.

In the back seat Maryam sat, dazed. Zubaida had known the end was near. That's why she had entrusted her with the stone. She had said that she had seen the fire, but why hadn't she run? Perhaps that is what she wanted, with no family to wash her body and give her a proper burial. Now Maryam was one of them, chosen to wear the stone of the women and carry the seed. She was also on her own and would have to face the world alone.

Listening to Maryam's sobbing, the taxi driver looked over his shoulder and asked, 'Is there anything I can do?'

Maryam didn't respond but tried to regain her composure. Perhaps this man could help after all. Could he be trusted? He hadn't seen her face, so couldn't identify her.

'Take me to the vegetable *souq*,' she ordered in a firm voice, trying to quell her apprehension.

Maryam knew the vegetable *souq* was always busy. She had only to step out of the cab and melt into the crowd of women if something went wrong. Besides, hadn't Sahar and Samar said 'an Egyptian's word counted for nothing and was worth less than that of a Saudi woman?' Her mind worked on how to pose the question and from his response she would be able to gauge how far to go.

'Stop here,' she commanded, pointing to one of the stalls where a group of women were busy selecting fruit. Maryam thrust a hundred *riyal* note over the driver's shoulder.

'I want to go to Egypt,' she said, gripping the door handle ready to flee.

'Egypt? I thought you said the vegetable *souq*,' exclaimed the driver.

'I want to go to Egypt tomorrow. Can you take me?'

'Impossible! Impossible! Impossible!' replied the driver.

'I'll pay you well.'

The man digested the sentence. 'How well?'

'Well enough,' replied Maryam. The man thought again for a moment, playing with the note.

'Tomorrow. . . er. . . that's impossible. Totally out of the question. I can only go as far as the Jordanian border in this taxi. But. . . let me think. Perhaps I could take you in two week's time when I leave for Egypt with my family. That's if you don't mind waiting that long and it might be a bit of a squeeze in the back of the car.'

Maryam looked at the man's bloodshot eyes and watched him mop his face. He had a nervous tick that made him screw up his eyes every few minutes and a large mole resided besides his left nostril. On his breath she could smell tobacco tinged with a fruity odour, the telltale sign of a diabetic. She remembered a Saudi saying: 'Trust a snake but never trust an Egyptian.' Perhaps he would hand her over to the border guards and keep the money. Then she remembered the second part of the saying: 'You can buy an Egyptian but never the snake.'

'How much?'

'Let me see. . .' The man stroked the stubble on his double chin for a second or two. 'Where in Egypt did you say you wanted to go?' he asked, buying time to think up a figure that would fill his pocket but at the same time not frighten the woman.

'Cairo.'

'We're from Aswan but I guess we could make a detour for you,' he lied, and dabbed his forehead with the towel. 'It'll add another two thousand kilos to my journey and an extra two days of travelling and hotel bills. Benzene is very expensive in Egypt, not like here. How about four thousand riyals?' he asked, trying to keep a straight face. He knew Maryam could fly to Cairo and back twice over for that amount of money.

'I don't have a passport.'

'Oh! That's makes it difficult. . . er. . . *very* difficult. . . but not impossible. . . just maybe, and I can't promise you anything right now but. . . there might be a way.' The man rubbed his chin and chewed on his lip. 'I'll let you know after tomorrow, *Insha'allah*. Meet me at the taxi rank after *Maghrib* prayer.' With that the man stuffed the money into his shirt pocket and drove Maryam back to the city centre. 'Remember, after *Maghrib!*' called out the driver.

'*Insha'allah,*' Maryam replied, and melted into a sea of bobbing *abaya*. She felt alone and isolated in a street filled with people oblivious to her torment. That was the Arab way, emotion was to be controlled and to display it was a sign of weakness.

She passed a battery of orange phone booths, thought of Joe languishing in jail and reached for the change she always carried in her purse.

The operator put her through to Joe's apartment. The monotonous trill taunted her and she banged down the phone in fury. They still had him. But where, and for what? He had broken no law and the hospital would have done something by now.

She phoned the Dental Clinic to hear Tess confirm her worst fears. 'I rang the American embassy but they wouldn't listen to me. To them I'm just a Filipina. They'll hear *you*, Madam,' she said and gave Maryam the number.

Maryam dialled the number and waited for someone to answer.

'American Embassy, Riyadh!' answered a woman with a chirpy voice. 'Arminda speaking, how may I help you?'

For some reason Maryam had prepared herself for a man's voice and the woman's voice threw her off guard. She hesitated, wondering what to say. Would a woman be able to help her? She had rehearsed her lines but now at the crucial moment her mind went blank.

'Hello! American Embassy, Riyadh! Can I help you?' repeated the voice.

'Dr Joe is in prison!' Maryam blurted out.

'Come again, Ma'am?'

Maryam repeated the sentence a little louder.

'Who is Dr Joe, Ma'am?'

'Dr Joe Goldman. He is an American.'

'Where does he. . . ?'

Maryam didn't let her finish. 'Tabuk! Please do something!'

'To whom am I speaking, Ma'am?'

Maryam panicked, slammed the phone down and burst into tears.

*   *   *

Maryam joined Hanifah in Abaya Park as agreed.

'You've been gone a while,' complained Hanifah, looking suspiciously at her empty bag.

'Didn't find what I was looking for,' Maryam replied, lifting her veil.

'How I hate these flies,' Hanifah said, waving her hand over the glass of mango juice she had bought for Maryam.

'It's warm,' Maryam said, taking a sip.

'You've been crying.'

'How did you get on with the tailors?' Maryam asked, turning away.

'What's happened?'

'Will they be able to follow the designs in the book?'

Hanifah shook her head. 'They can only copy dresses.'

'You'll have to wait till you get to Jeddah. Tailors there are more experienced.'

'I need a whole new wardrobe now. It's so different being a Muslim.'

'They can copy my dresses.'

'What a good idea and I can make some subtle changes.'

'They should be able to manage that.'

'I hope so. What were you looking for?'

'Let's head home, it's getting late. I want to buy Mama flowers, she's not been herself for some time.'

'We'll ask Uncle Mahmoud to stop at Astra supermarket, they always have fresh roses.'

'We'd better hurry,' Maryam said, looking at her watch. 'It's almost prayer time.'

THIRTY-SIX

Every movement from her baby reminded Maryam that time was running out. She thought of nothing but her flight from a land where it was a crime to love and be loved and the penalty was death. But where was she to start and how was she to flee when she didn't possess a passport! Only her father or Nabeel could obtain one and that was as likely as a Saudi woman winning an Olympic medal in gymnastics.

The taxi driver had come up with a plan that had filled her with revulsion and had her questioning the very value of life. The man explained his daughter would remain behind and she could take her place.

'Remain behind! What do you mean by that?' she had asked.

'She will marry a Saudi,' he had replied.

'Marry a Saudi?'

'I know a nice old man who's been asking for her for some time.'

'How old?'

'Difficult to say, but he's rich and I'm sure he'd treat her well.'

'How much will he pay you?'

'Enough.'

'How much? I have a right to know.'

'Ten.'

Anger had flowed like molten lava through her veins at the thought of some poor girl trading places with her. So ten thousand was the price of a human life, no doubt calculated on the basis of supply and demand. She felt ashamed of being a Saudi and nauseous at the thought of being a party to this trade.

'*Shaitaan!*' Maryam had exploded. 'Have you no shame? She's your flesh and blood!'

The man had laughed and simply shooed her out of his taxi with a dismissive wave.

For days she could not bear to look at herself in the mirror. Her self-esteem lay in tatters and every time she thought of escape, she broke down in tears. She tried to convince herself that her death would be a blessing, but realised it would solve nothing. Only the love for her baby infused her with determination and a sense of purpose.

There were regulations preventing women from travelling alone to protect their family *Sharaf*. A woman by herself would raise eyebrows and officials would seek answers.

Men would refuse to sit beside her if she managed to board a plane. An old Arab proverb came to mind: 'when a man and a woman are alone together, Shaitaan is their chaperone'. Temptation lurked everywhere, ready to strike, even on a plane.

Everyone had heard the story of the pregnant girl who escaped with her lover using his sister's passport. Sahar or Samar might furnish her with a passport but they had no brother to accompany her. Besides, Tabuk wasn't blessed with an international airport. Maryam recalled a story she had heard at college of a pregnant girl from Dhahran who escaped across the King Fahad Causeway to Bahrain hiding in the boot of a taxi, but Bahrain was as far as she got: without money, passport or friends, the police caught up with her and that was the last anyone heard of the girl.

Another daring woman escaped aboard a food lorry from Dhahran bound for Bahrain and got as far as Paris, but she had a passport and money. Since then, the authorities on the causeway had become vigilant, causing delays on Wednesdays when the Saudi men went to live it up, drinking, whoring and night-clubbing. Bahrain was the Mecca for the East Coasters, only a twenty-minute ride to a bottle of Johnny Walker.

Maryam discounted this avenue of escape. Dhahran was on the other side of the country and getting there would be a feat in itself.

On a map in the library Maryam studied the yellow mass of the Arabian subcontinent, shaped like a shark's tooth and surrounded by the Red Sea, the Indian Ocean and the Arabian Gulf. This was the land of her ancestors.

Her eyes searched the northwest corner for Tabuk, the gateway to Egypt, Israel and the ancient Hashemite Kingdom of Jordan to which it once belonged. Sultan had told her King Hussein was a direct descendant of the Prophet Mohammed and his ancestors had been the custodians of the Holy Mosques of Mecca and Medinah for a thousand years. The treacherous British had changed all that when they wooed Abdul Aziz Al Saud and sold out the Jordanians in the final hours of the Second World War.

One day, she told herself, she would like to visit Jordan and admire the Roman colonnades of ancient Jerash she had heard so much about. She would love to walk through the famous entrance of Petra she had seen in a movie at Sahar and Samar's house. One day she would be free to go wherever she chose without asking a man's permission.

Her eyes traced a red line going southwest. She estimated Tabuk was two hundred kilometres from the fishing port of Duba. On many occasions during the *Eid* festivals her father and Uncle Mahmoud had taken the family there to swim in the Red Sea and picnic on its coral shores. It had been Sultan's favourite place: he would disappear for days, living under the stars, enjoying the vastness of the desert or listening to the rolling waves. He used to say it was as close to paradise as you could get on earth.

Perhaps she could bribe a fisherman to smuggle her across to Egypt. Once there, anything and everything was possible with a purse full of money. She was sure an official would furnish her with an Egyptian passport if enough money crossed his palm.

'Money talks in Egypt,' Sahar had said, 'like nowhere else on earth. . . Well, except the Philippines,' she had added on reflection. 'Many Saudis go to Egypt to buy wives,' she told her, 'because they are so cheap, prettier and some are even educated. Of course Egyptian education is really of no value in our country when women are not free to work,' Samar had added wryly. 'Besides, their education doesn't come up to Saudi standard. You know, most are bought to work as housemaids by old men who already have two or three wives and enough children to field a football team, but not enough money to employ a Filipina or Indonesian maid.'

There was another option. Her finger traced the red line going northwest to Haql, a town on the Gulf of Aqabah. The mountains of Egypt were visible across the blue water. The Israeli City of Elate and the Jordanian port of Aqaba lay round the corner out of sight. She had seen the grey-blue gunboats of the Saudi Coast Guard that patrolled the area flying the sap-green flag with Allah's message. Haql was ideal but, with many roadblocks to negotiate, the drive through the mountains was dangerous. If stopped, her escape would end scarcely after it had begun.

The more she thought of it, the more depressed she became. First she would have to find a fisherman who would risk his life for a stranger, let alone a woman. If caught, they would make an example of him to deter others. Where and how would she find this man without arousing suspicion and how long would it take? Once they found her vehicle it would become impossible, with nowhere to hide.

As a woman, she could not check into a hotel. And even if she could, the *mutaween* came looking for illicit lovers. She had seen them in Jeddah at the Khaki Hotel inspecting their records and the documents of the guests.

Everything hinged on a man's loyalty. Could she trust a man who could be bought? What would happen if she couldn't meet his price? Would he hand her over to the police or walk away?

What was there to stop him from taking her money and pushing her over the side with a chain around her neck to disappear into the depths of the sea?

Loyalty was hard to quantify in her people, Maryam thought. When money meant everything, loyalty could usually be guaranteed; but with religion added to the mix uncertainty reigned. The wrong man would hand her over to the police. After that. . . she could not bear thinking of the consequences. Her father would be humiliated by the shame she had brought to his name. He would lose his job, perhaps even be punished for her crime. She would be imprisoned and, once they discovered she was pregnant, her fate and the fate of her unborn child would be sealed. The men in white would have their public persecution one sunny Friday after midday prayer and the world would be rid of a sinner and be a better place. A better place for whom?

No. The way through the towns was too risky and fraught with danger. But there had to be a way and it was up to her to find it. She followed every red line out of Tabuk but none led to freedom. Maryam affirmed to herself: *I have unlimited potential and I control the present and the future, I have the power to succeed.* The lack of a passport wasn't going to get in her way. After all, no one ever asked the Bedouins for a passport. The cogs of reasoning jammed in mid-thought.

'Yes! *Alhamdulillah!*' she cried and punched the air as Saffron often did. Why hadn't she thought of it earlier? For centuries the Bedouins came down from Jordan during autumn to winter in Saudi Arabia and returned in the spring. It was their birthright: people without boundaries, camels for transport, sheep for food and tents for homes. That was the way to go: across the sands on foot, following the Bedouin trail.

Her finger followed a red line travelling north to Jordan, forking at Bir ibn Hirmas. The right arm led to Haql. That was not the way to go. Maryam's finger followed the left arm north to Halat Ammar on the border with Jordan. With her heart pounding, she measured the distance and checked against the scale.

'Ninety kilometres, *Alhamdulillah!*' she exclaimed. She heard a squeak and the door opened. A tense moment crystallised and vaporised just as quickly. Turki's face appeared and lit up. He ran in and threw his arms around her, squealing with delight.

'You're a naughty boy, you gave me such a fright,' Maryam admonished and pinched his cheeks until he protested. She kissed away the pain and took in the softness of his skin and the warmth in his dark brown eyes. She ruffled his hair and let it slip through her fingers. They looked at each other and Maryam reflected on how she had shared the same silent language with Sultan. Words were always so artificial and meaningless between the two who had shared the same womb and suckled the same breasts.

'I bet you cannot guess what Grandpa showed me last night?' Turki asked, barely able to contain his excitement.

'Let me think. . . he showed you how to make a paper aeroplane?' she offered.

'Nope! That was days ago. Try again?'

'I give up,' she said, throwing up her arms in defeat.

Turki loved this part because he knew something that Maryam didn't and he burst out laughing. 'Grandpa showed me a very special star,' he said. 'Come on! Let me show you!' He took Maryam by the hand and dragged her out into the garden.

For a few minutes he craned his neck looking at the evening sky, not quite sure what he had seen and where. He pointed at the brightest star and said, 'That's it, there. That's *Shiaara.*' Maryam knew, but faked ignorance to Turki's delight. Then Turki remembered his Grandpa had pointed above the yellow glow of the city lights and he stared hard, his heart thumping with excitement. 'There,' he said after a while, pointing low on the horizon. 'That's the special star that Grandpa showed me,' he declared. 'Can you see it, Auntie Miri?'

Maryam played along and stared towards Tabuk.

'Look over there,' he said again, pointing. The heat haze blurred everything but she didn't want to disappoint Turki and searched a little longer. Suddenly she saw a beam of light crossing the sky like an arrow, outshining all the wonders of the heavens. She gasped and gripped Turki's hand until he squirmed. This was the sign Sultan had spoken of and it was pointing northwest.

Towards Jordan.

She trembled and wept tears of joy mixed with sadness. She smothered Turki with kisses. She knew her days with him were numbered and the next time they met he would be a man and it would be forbidden to hold him. If there was to be a next time.

'I want you to know I love you and will always love you, whatever happens,' she whispered.

Turki nodded, pressed her nose with his thumb and grinned.

They stared at the comet, holding hands, and then returned to the house.

THIRTY-SEVEN

'We're here! We're here!' Turki shouted, clapping his hands. Mahmoud turned off the main road and cruised past a battery of stalls selling dates and parked opposite the vegetable and fruit stalls.

'I want to see the fish.'

'*Insha'allah*,' Aishah replied. She took the boy's hand and ambled towards the stalls. Turki watched her inspect the fruits, squeezing some and smelling others before haggling. When a price was reached, she would nod at Mahmoud who would fish out a wad of notes from his pocket and complete the deal.

'I want to taste those,' Aishah asked, pointing at a polystyrene container overflowing with purple grapes.

'What shall I tell the boss, Madam, if you eat my profit?' The Indian man grinned.

'If I can't taste, I don't buy,' Aishah replied from behind the veil and walked away.

'Okay, okay, come back, you win, Madam,' the man said, throwing up his arms in resignation, and offered Turki a few grapes.

'What do you think, *habibi*?' Aishah asked Turki.

'They are sweet, Madam!'

Turki nodded his approval, with juice trickling down his chin.

'I told you they were sweet, Madam.'

243

'Two kilos,' Aishah ordered with a flick of the wrist and left the rest to Mahmoud.

'I'll drop these off at the car and catch up with you at the fishery,' Mahmoud said, picking up a clutch of plastic bags.

They worked their way around the market, finally stopping at the Saudi fishery outlet for Turki to watch the Tilapia swimming with the lobsters and crabs in a tank.

'I want this fish,' Aishah ordered the Filipino assistant waiting behind the counter.

'That's mine, I was here before you,' a big woman standing beside her protested.

'So why didn't you buy it?'

'I was thinking.'

'I offered to buy it first, so it's mine,' Aishah snapped and grabbed the fish by the head and the other woman grabbed its tail.

'I want it. Give it to me!' shouted the other woman. The shop assistants watched in amusement. Suddenly one of the women lost her footing, dragging them both to the wet floor. The fish went sliding across the shop. Laughter erupted from the assistants.

'Shouldn't we help them or something?' one of them asked in Visayan.

'Lay hands on Saudi women? We'll be on the first plane back to Davao. Or worse. Besides, this is hilarious!' The women tried to scramble to their feet and failed miserably. A veil lay at the big woman's feet.

'It's you, Khadijah!' Aishah gasped.

'Aishah!' exclaimed Khadijah.

'I want to talk to you.'

'I've got it, Grandma. I've got the fish,' shouted Turki cradling the fish in his arms.

The women stared across the room at Turki and then at each other and again at Turki. They scrambled towards him on all fours.

'Ten riyals the smaller woman gets the fish,' said the older Filipino assistant.

'I'll bet twenty on the one without the veil,' countered the other.

Aishah reached Turki as Mahmoud entered the shop.

'Take it! Take it! But in the name of Allah give me back what's mine!' Aishah shouted, throwing the fish at Khadijah's feet.

'I have nothing that's yours.'

'You know that's a lie.'

'The lie is what you're living.'

'Why are you doing this?'

'Why? You ask why? What gives you the right to ask why?' Khadijah screamed. 'How can you, a mother of two sons, understand why?'

'What's going on?' Mahmoud asked, picking up Turki.

Khadijah covered her face with her *abaya*.

'This woman wants our fish, Uncle Mahmoud,' Turki explained, pointing at Khadijah.

'You'll never have what's mine as long as I live,' hissed Khadijah and kicked the fish sending it skidding across the floor. She spat at Aishah, picked up her veil and stomped out, slamming the door.

'What was that about?' Mahmoud asked in Pashtu. Aishah didn't reply.

The journey home was filled with silence interspersed with sobs. Aishah brushed aside Mahmoud's questions and Turki wrinkled his nose and complained of his smelly hands.

* * *

'American Embassy, Riyadh,' answered Arminda. This time Maryam was prepared and asked for the ambassador.

'What, may I ask, is it concerning?' Arminda asked in her official tone. Maryam had made up her mind that nothing was going to stop her today. She was going to speak to the ambassador however busy he was and he was going to listen.

'It's regarding Dr Joe Goldman. Put me through at once,' Maryam replied putting on her most authoritative voice.

'Did you phone earlier, Ma'am?'

'Many times! I keep getting cut off!'

'I'm putting you through now.' The phone went dead.

'Shit!' Maryam exclaimed. I've been cut off again,' she shouted and was about to hang up when a mellow voice slipped into her ear.

He introduced himself as John Braxton and said, 'I'm the ambassador's personal secretary. How can I be of assistance?'

'I asked to speak with the ambassador,' Maryam said politely.

'Ma'am, the ambassador is not available right now. He doesn't take personal calls.'

'It's not personal.'

'May I ask what it's regarding?'

'You don't understand. I must speak to him. It's a matter of life and death'

'Perhaps I can help, Ma'am?'

'It's about Dr Joe,' Maryam sighed.

'What's his family name?'

'It's Goldman, Joe Goldman.'

'Is he an American citizen?'

'I wouldn't be phoning you otherwise!' Maryam snapped.

'Is he registered with us?' Mr Braxton asked courteously.

'How should I know?'

'I'll check.'

Maryam drummed her fingers on the glass partition listening to Neil Diamond singing *America* in her ear.

'I'm sorry to have kept you, Ma'am,' Mr Braxton's voice interrupted. 'We have a Joseph Goldman registered with us. Do you have a name?'

'Questions, questions, questions. Mr Braxton, I must talk with the ambassador.'

'Ma'am, the ambassador. . .'

'It's very urgent. Dr Goldman has been arrested by the *mutaween*.'

'How do you know?'

'Because I saw it with my own eyes!'

'Oh, I see.'

'No, you don't see. He's in grave danger. You have to do something now, Mr Braxton, before it's too late. He might even be dead.'

'Come now, Ma'am, surely. . .'

'. . . The *mutaween* think they are above the law. They are evil. People disappear all the time,' Maryam sobbed.

'What did you say your family name was?' Mr Braxton asked, remaining calm.

'I didn't, it is not important.'

'How do you know Dr Goldman?'

'How? When? Where?. . . what matters is that you find Joe. He has no one but you.'

'Let me take down some details, Ma'am, and we'll look into it. When did this occur?' Mr Braxton's friendly voice instilled confidence in Maryam. He made encouraging sounds and let her continue until she had told him all that he needed to know.

'I'm much obliged for your help, Ma'am. Where do you suppose they have Dr Goldman?'

'Somewhere in Tabuk. Find him please, Mr Braxton,' Maryam pleaded. 'I'm running out of money.'

'Could I have your name and contact number?'

The phone went dead.

THIRTY-EIGHT

A man of about six feet two, with a cloud of silver hair parted down the middle, listened to the grim statistics, eyebrows knitted in concentration. His tanned face, athletic body and Ralph Lauren suit reflected the good life that came with the job.

A hand buried in his jacket rolled the two marbles he had found in the gutter as a young boy growing up in the Bronx. They had lost their lustre a long time ago and made a grating sound rather like an arthritic hip connected to a loudspeaker. He always carried them with him; they helped him concentrate and reminded him of his own humble beginnings and of the American dream come true.

He believed people remembered you if they could identify you with something simple. Mao had his red book, Hitler his moustache, Gandhi his round spectacles and Jesus had his crown of thorns and cross. Like Churchill he favoured a bow tie and Paratagas cigars, and was seldom seen without one poised between the tips of his fingers.

Diplomacy was a game to him, one where the players changed with regularity, as did the rules. He was a survivor, knew the game plan and played for keeps. That's why they had sent him to keep the Saudis happy and make sure the balance of power and sentiment stayed tilted in America's favour. These days it wasn't so much the oil that was the primary concern but the armament contracts – and of course propping up the Al Saud family.

Fundamentalists, terrorists and liberators lurked under every rock like deadly scorpions and sidewinders. It was his job to keep his ear to the ground and his eyes open. They couldn't afford to have another debacle like Iran. The overthrow of the Shah had been a political disaster of immeasurable magnitude as the CIA failed to assess the fallout Khomeini would generate.

The Al Sauds were scared both of their own people and of the Shiites in the Eastern province. They were living on borrowed time and knew it. Gone were the days when the people could be bought by handouts of scraps of land or pickup trucks. Now they hungered for something the Al Sauds didn't want to share: power. He had learned very quickly that the Arab was a mercurial individual whose loyalty could be bought so long as it benefited him, and ended when it didn't.

Religion was the glue that bound the Saudis together while petro-dollars lubricated their palms. But that was all changing. In diplomatic circles, many whispered that the country was ripe for revolution. The Al Sauds had long used the Shiites and Saddam as scapegoats but now they themselves were trapped under the microscope. These days, every day was the Fourth of July. The fireworks had begun and he was sure that before long Al Saud blood would spill. His job was to do his best to stop that from happening – whatever the cost.

'Fourteen dead, twenty-seven wounded and five on the critical list, Mr Ambassador, sir.' Colonel Kozlowski brought the ambassador's mind to focus on the immediate situation.

'How in God's name did it happen?'

'A bomb, sir.'

'Colonel Kozlowski, I'm not a total imbecile,' snapped the Ambassador adjusting his bow tie.

'Pardon me, sir. It was a *car* bomb. Judging by the crater and the damage, we think it may have been somewhere in the region of a thousand pounds of C4, sir.' The colonel spread out a number of twelve-by-eight photographs on the table.

'Holy shit!' exclaimed the ambassador. His eyes jumped from

one mangled scene to another. 'Where do the motherfuckers get that kind of muscle?' His clothes may have changed but his language reflected his origins.

'Yemen, sir.'

'The President isn't going to like this one bit. He's got his hands full with mid-term elections and the soaring trade deficit. Madam Secretary is flying in tomorrow with a team of Feds and the Saudis aren't cooperating.'

'Nothing new there, sir.'

'If they hadn't executed those they claim did the Riyadh bombing, we might have been able to prevent this one. You know, I'm not even sure those four suckers were guilty.'

'They've been holding out on us, sir.'

'Egomania! That's what it is, Kozlowski. Egomania!'

'Sir, the two Saudi guards were missing when the terrorists left the vehicle in the parking lot,' explained the Colonel pointing at an aerial view of the carnage.

'That figures. Overpaid and underworked. I want a full report by ten hundred hours tomorrow so I can brief Madam Secretary before she meets with the Crown Prince. The King is in hospital again.' He gave a wry smile at the vision of the old battle-axe clashing with the scimitar.

'Yes sir. Mr Ambassador.'

'Koslowski, there is one other thing I want you to look into.' The two listened to the short conversation on the tape for the second time.

'What do you think, Colonel?"

'It could be a hoax, sir!'

'The woman sounds distressed. Braxton thinks she's genuine.'

'What's her angle?'

'She wouldn't say.'

'You think Goldman's. . .'

'Who knows?'

'It won't be the first time they've used a foxy female as bait.'

'There's a Dr Joseph Goldman on our database working in

Tabuk. That's your turf. Look into it and keep me informed.'

'I'll do my best, Mr Ambassador, sir.'

'You'll do better then that Colonel. Goldman's an American citizen. My butt's on the line if anything happens to him.'

'I understand, sir.'

'The last thing we want is one of our boys rotting in a Saudi jail. The president hardly needs more bad publicity right now. Keep me posted.' They shook hands and parted.

As George Kozlowski stepped out into the scorching Riyadh heat in his dappled battle fatigues, he pondered that if a B-movie actor could make it to the White House then Mr Ambassador in his air-conditioned ivory tower would surely go a long way. He hated politicians and diplomats. He was a career solider and had no time for these college boys with their fine clothes and fancy talk.

THIRTY-NINE

George Kozlowski should have made brigadier general but all too often his principles and downright cussedness had got in the way of promotion. Though of average height and average build, there was nothing average about his intellect. An astute tactician, he knew the Saudis well and, above all, how they thought. This was something he knew the top brass and the over-funded CIA didn't have a clue about. He had majored in psychology and often reflected on how this had helped him penetrate the ever-smiling Arab mask that deceived the politicians so easily.

And it wasn't just politicians who said 'maybe' when they meant 'no,' and 'no' when they meant 'maybe': the Arabs were masters at double talk and, with '*Insha'allah*' punctuating every other sentence, they kept even the most accomplished diplomat guessing at what was agreed and what was presumed to have been agreed. So it came as no surprise to Kozlowski when the young Saudi police lieutenant, informed him from behind a desk the size of a pool table that he had no knowledge of anyone by the name of Joe Goldman.

'This Goldman, what he do wrong?' The lieutenant asked in broken English, without looking up from his desk.

'You don't need to break the law to be in a Saudi prison!' To Kozlowski's way of thinking, Saudi Arabia had one of the poorest human rights records on earth; the international community choosing to ignore this in its thirst for oil.

The lieutenant didn't like the implication. He pretended he hadn't understood and continued doodling as before. George Kozlowski's palm came crashing down on the table, sending the pens and pencils flying. Silence reigned, everyone in the room stopped in mid-sentence and looked stunned There was one thing that annoyed Kozlowski more then anything, and that was insolence and bad manners.

'Look at me when I am talking to you, boy!' He boomed into the lieutenant's face. 'I know you've got Goldman and I want to see him right now! You hear me, boy?' The lieutenant knew he was outranked, but more to the point this was an *Ameriki* who, they had been told, was on their holy soil at the personal invitation of their King. A strained silence hung precariously like a guillotine waiting to fall. The lieutenant tried to find a way out of this without losing face in front of his subordinates.

'Would you like tea?' the young man asked, now in impeccable English.

Kozlowski's square jaw hardened and his icy blue eyes narrowed, boring into the frightened young man. Tense moments passed as they glared at each other like tomcats, weighing up whether Saudi arrogance would triumph over American might. In the end, the young man lowered his gaze and gathered his arsenal of pens and pencils. Kozlowski knew he had won: age, experience and sheer force of personality had triumphed. When push came to shove, the Saudis were all talk and no action, all show with no results, eloquent rhetoric with empty promises. That was also the Arab way.

'I will see if anyone has heard of your Mr Goldman,' said the lieutenant, avoiding Kozlowski's glare. He spoke animatedly on the phone in Arabic for a few minutes and hung up and tried another number. After the third attempt Kozlowski had heard enough and stabbed his finger on the phone, terminating the conversation.

'I want to see your commanding officer,' he ordered. 'I want to see him now!'

The lieutenant gathered himself up, glanced in the direction of his staff and beckoned the colonel to follow.

They entered a large office with a red carpet and comfortable sofas hugging the walls. The Saudi flag stood in one corner and the air-conditioner was going full blast.

A bank of phones and a mountain of paper surrounded a hawkish man with a slight stoop, deep-set eyes and a brusque manner. Dark rings around his eyes spoke of sleepless nights and the face had stress etched all over it. A gold crown and two stars attached to the epaulettes of his khaki uniform identified him as a colonel. A ribbon of smoke rose from a cigarette balanced on the rim of a brass ashtray crowded with butts. The ever-present portraits of the 'three wise men' of the Saudi Royal family looked down over his shoulders.

'Colonel Nasser Al Khatani,' he said, offering a limp hand-shake across the desk, and touched his heart in the customary of sincerity. He ordered tea with a wave of his hand and invited Kozlowski to sit.

Tabuk had once been a lazy little town hiding in the northwest corner of the country but was becoming a dangerous place to live. Six months earlier two Scandinavian girls had disappeared without trace after getting into a taxi at the airport. A Pakistani woman was abducted a couple of months after from a car, and two days later her husband identified her mutilated remains. A disgruntled father shot a captain dead at the Military City when he refused to marry his daughter whom the captain had im-pregnated. Since the murder of his nephew and now this bomb at the American Military Mission, the burden of responsibility that came with his rank had weighed heavily. The roadblocks had failed to produce results and inquiries at the hospitals, drug rehab centres and private clinics had drawn a blank. He was inundated with a barrage of questions from the generals in Riyadh who were trying to save their skins. There was always a fall guy somewhere and the higher you got, the more precarious your existence became.

With the pleasantries over, Kozlowski came straight to the point. He had already wasted time and he could see this Nasser was a busy man. 'We're looking for an American doctor called Joseph Goldman. You haven't come across him by any chance?' Kozlowski asked, as if he was inquiring about a mutual friend.

Nasser flicked at a lighter, drew hard on the cigarette and looked concerned, reading between the lines. The last thing he wanted at this critical time was a missing *Ameriki*. 'You think he could be one of the bomb victims?'

'We have reason to believe he may be in custody,' Kozlowski began, not wishing to make any accusations or insinuations.

'Oh? And where did you get such information?' Nasser took up the offensive, exhaling smoke towards Kozlowski's face, testing how far he could push his visitor.

'Someone reported him missing,' Kozlowski said, without taking his eyes off Nasser.

'If he's in custody, he won't get very far,' Nasser cracked with a dry smile. 'Leave it with me,' he said, stubbing out his cigarette and as if to close the meeting. 'He'll show up soon. *Insha'allah.*'

'*Insha'allah*, he'll show up today!' Kozlowski retorted, letting the colonel know he expected results. He wasn't happy with the colonel's attitude but, as the commanding officer of US forces in the Tabuk region, he was the man in the driving seat and Nasser knew it without being told.

'Go easy on the cigs!' he added, getting to his feet.

'Thank you for your concern,' Nasser replied, managing a wry smile as the two men shook hands.

* * *

Along the dusty road lined with date palms and eucalyptus trees, Turki walked with purpose to the stables in his jodhpurs and carrying his hard hat. He pulled Maryam by the hand. She was dressed in her *abaya* and scarf

'Slow down. The horses aren't going to fly away.'

'Grandpa told me of a horse that had wings.'

'Pegasus.'

'How did you know?' Turki asked in surprise.

'He told me the same story, too.'

'Could he really fly, Auntie Miri?'

'It's a legend.'

'What's a legend?' Turki asked, cocking his head to the side.

'It's a story. Like a fairy tale.'

'Like the *jinni* in a bottle that you read to me?'

'Yes just like that.' She ruffled Turki's hair.

'I know Hava can fly. He's so fast.'

'That's why he's named after the wind,' Maryam smiled and reflected on her childhood when she used to come with Sultan to watch their father ride. Like most Arabs, he loved horses. It was in his blood, a passion that he shared with her uncle Mahmoud who had a way with horses too.

They met Mahmoud by the gate to the arena.

'I want to ride Hava, Uncle Mahmoud,' Turki said.

'He's ready, for you, *habibi*.' Mahmoud opened the gate.

They walked over to the centre of the arena where Hava stood saddled and waiting.

'Here you go, Hava,' Turki patted the horse's neck and fed him cubes of sugar.

'He likes you,' Maryam said. 'See how he looks at you.'

'I like you too, Hava,' Turki said, stroking the horse's head.

Mahmoud lifted Turki onto the saddle and adjusted the stirrups. 'Now, remember what I told you last time, hold the reigns up and keep them short. That way you have more control. Walk him round the arena a couple of times and do your exercises before you trot.'

Turki nodded, kicked and Hava responded.

Maryam and Mahmoud sat on a wooden bench and watched Turki ride Farhan's favourite stallion.

'He's so like his father,' Mahmoud said as he mended a broken bridle.

'Every day he sounds more and more like him,' Maryam agreed.

'Did you ever want children, Uncle Mahmoud?' Maryam asked after she had waved to Turki.

There was silence, and she turned to find her uncle staring past the arena into the distance, his brow knotted.

'I'm sorry,' Maryam said.

'It's all right, *habibi.*' Mahmoud worked the leather strap through the buckle. 'There, that's done,' he said with satisfaction. They watched Turki at the far end of the arena turn and trot towards them, rising and falling in perfect rhythm with the horse.

'He's a natural,' Mahmoud said. 'Even better then Sultan. See how he changes his rhythm when he turns the corner. Perfect, just perfect.'

'Well done, Turki!' Maryam called out as he passed them, beaming.

'He's so in tune with the horse. Watch how he controls with his heels, he's telling Hava what he wants.' Mahmoud explained, his eyes alive with passion.

'Hava is a magnificent animal. So noble,' Maryam said, watching the grace and power in motion, muscles rippling.

'He's beautiful and he knows it. You can tell by how he carries his head. Nostrils flared, ears cocked and alert.'

'He is saying: *watch me dance.*'

They watched the horse and rider in silence for a few moments.

'I chose not to marry because of your mother,' Mahmoud began, picking up the bridle again. 'When our parents were killed, she was Turki's age and I was a few years older. In a blink of an eye, the world that promised everything vanished. It was Allah's will.' He continued fiddling with the buckle.

'That was tragic,' Maryam said. Her uncle was normally a man of few words and lived in a world where emotions had no place. So she was surprised when he continued.

'Imagine trapped in a foreign land without your family, not understanding the language or customs.'

'It must have been so hard for you both.'

'When she married I stayed with her because I was all she had and she was all I had. Love is a very precious thing given to us by Allah. We have to treasure it, nurture it and make it grow.'

'So you sacrificed your own happiness for my mother's?'

'It's not a sacrifice when you love the person. It was more an offering. A gift. And Allah has blessed me with happiness.'

'Mother's been so unhappy since my engagement. I thought she would be happy for me.'

'You're her only daughter. She's going to miss you, as will I.'

'You were like a second father to us, as you are to Turki.'

'You're my children. When Allah took Sultan, a part of me died.' Mahmoud turned away and stared into the distance.

'Look at me! Look at me, Uncle Mahmoud! Auntie Miri!' Turki cried out as he trotted by.

'Sit up straight in the saddle and look ahead!' Mahmoud called out.

'Be careful you don't go too fast!' Maryam added.

'There goes my grandson. What more could I want?'

'You're a very special person, Uncle Mahmoud.' Maryam reached out and squeezed his hand.

'So are you, *habibi*. Don't you ever forget that. Now, tell me, what's on your mind?'

Maryam blushed and looked away. Tears welled in her eyes and her lips trembled. Words choked in her throat. Mahmoud reached out and held her hand and waited. Together they watched Turki execute another perfect turn and waved to him.

'It's nothing, Uncle.' Maryam played with the ends of her scarf.

'Life is like a horse, a wild and wonderful thing that you ride with Allah's blessing and guidance. But you have to tell it where you want to go. Otherwise it will buck and kick and fly with the wind, leaving you behind.'

'I think I know what you mean, Uncle Mahmoud.'

'Of course you do, *habibi*. You've been on a wild stallion the past few months.'

'You noticed?'

'How could I not, *habibi*?' Mahmoud brushed his handle-bar moustache, looking intently into Maryam's eyes.

'I don't know how to ride this stallion,' she whispered.

'When you love someone, I mean *truly* love someone, then everything else – besides Allah – is secondary, including yourself.' Mahmoud sighed.

'What if love cannot find a home?' Maryam looked down at her feet.

Mahmoud raised her head by her chin and looked into her eyes. 'Put your faith in Allah and trust in your heart.'

'I'm afraid of falling.'

'Everyone falls. It's painful sometimes but you have to get back on and ride again. Allah will be there to catch you, *habibi*,' Mahmoud said. 'He is always there.' He brushed away Maryam's tears with his thumb. She sniffed and mustered a smile.

'Thank you,' she said softly. 'You're so wise, Uncle Mahmoud.'

'Now go and ride with your heart, *habibi*!'

'Uncle Mahmoud, can I learn to jump next time?' Turki interrupted and pulled Hava up beside them.

'You must learn to canter first.'

'Is that faster than trotting?'

'It certainly is,' Mahmoud replied. Maryam and Turki waved goodbye to Mahmoud and Hava and headed home.

Turki skipped from one stone to another on the way back in a world of his own. He was always animated after his riding sessions.

'What are you doing?' Maryam asked.

'I am stepping across a river.'

'I can't see a river.'

'The stones are the rocks and the sand is the river. Uncle Mahmoud told me when he was a boy that is what he did when he crossed a river. He says in life we step from one stone to another.'

'So I am in the water now,' Maryam said looking down at her feet placed firmly in the sand.

'Quick, get on a stone, Auntie Miri, or you'll be washed away,' Turki said, leaping on to the next stone and balancing with his arms.

'Can I play, too?' Maryam asked.

Turki grinned, took Maryam's hand and together they skipped to the house laughing and carefree.

FORTY

An amber flame sent a ribbon of soot spiralling from a red candle. Wax flowed like lava down the side and set in miniature terraces. Across the wall, like a protective eagle, the light stretched the shadow of a cross made from a broom handle. The flame flickered and with it wavered Kim's faith in a battle raging for her tormented soul. She gazed with reverence at the jigsaw puzzle of Salvador Dali's *Jesus on the Cross* that she had smuggled in a box with a picture of the Swiss Alps on the cover. A rosary slipped through her fingers as she offered the Lord's Prayer and asked for forgiveness. She kissed the crucifix and crossed herself.

Faces from the past were her companions at night. They came to torment her soul and left her drenched in perspiration. The smiling face of her Japanese client with his gold-rimmed spectacles and thick fish-eye lenses came to haunt her, thrusting his fistful of dollars in her face for that extra special service that his wife had refused.

Then came her mother's face filled with tears, weeping for a child born out of wedlock, conceived in the back of a GI jeep for a ticket to the US of A that never materialised. The face of Mr F visited her, flashing his white teeth and hungry eyes that unclothed and raped in one swift glance.

Then there was Fawaz the pious, with his bushy beard and moustache, never touching pork or alcohol, ever courteous, always attentive, religiously praying five times a day, but forever scheming. She hated him, but understood his passion for revenge.

Heidi was a victim like herself. Watching her beautiful body filled with the energy of youth, yet knowing all the while that she too had perhaps two or three years to live, broke her heart. They shared all their free time together, feeling a sense of empathy that comes with sharing a lover and a deep secret that no one could ever know.

Heidi was an accomplished swimmer and had taught her to swim. 'My father used to take me to the pool and being in the water reminds me of him,' she said one day in a moment of reflection. 'He died in a car crash when I was five – or so they told my mother – and with him went all our hopes.'

Kim liked to hear Heidi's laughter, the essence of her free spirit, and it lingered in her mind. In a short time they had erased the boundaries of culture, class and language with the force of their personalities to form a sisterly bond in a foreign land where money was the only common denominator.

Having a Chinese mother and an American father, Kim was regarded with suspicion by some of her compatriots. Their smiles were often laced with the poison of envy and their words carried the venom of a snake.

Heidi, too, was something of an outsider, being the sole German in the hospital. British nurses were well represented there and though the expressions 'stuck up Kraut' and 'lanky Hun bitch' were initially bewildering to Kim it didn't take her long to realise who they were levelled at.

Kim and Heidi had no illusions about the world they inhabited and it was this that drew them ever closer. Heidi marvelled at Kim's resourcefulness for a girl who had dropped out of school. They were still in demand from Mr F and the envelopes awaiting them on the back seat of the Mercedes grew ever fatter, occasionally accompanied by a gold watch or a gold chain and matching earrings. He called them his 'pleasure machines' and that summed up his total lack of appreciation for their feelings or needs.

Kim watched Heidi munch a spring roll she had made. Heidi was going on vacation and this was to be their 'Last Supper' together. The whole of her insides churned. She knew she had betrayed Heidi's trust and love.

'This is so delicious,' declared Heidi in her clipped, accented English as she wiped flakes of pastry from her lips with a paper napkin while helping herself to another. 'You must show me how to make these when I get back,' she said, talking with her mouth full.

Kim managed a smile and played with her food.

'This wine is not bad, even if I say so myself.' Heidi took a mouthful. She had made it from grape juice, sugar and baker's yeast. 'We will call it Chateau Tabuk and sell it downtown.' She let off one of her infectious laughs.

Kim was finding it hard to make conversation, knowing all the while that whatever she did would be wrong. She had spent many sleepless nights looking for a way out and in the end had decided it would be better to come clean and tell all. She wasn't sure Heidi would understand, but at least she could seek treatment in her country and, perhaps, a cure. She had planned it to the last detail but her tongue refused to cooperate with her brain.

She busied herself with washing the dishes and fought hard to keep the tears at bay. Words gushed forth from her lips with a purposeful urgency but said very little. A wineglass slipped from her hands and crashed on to the floor. Heidi cut herself picking up the pieces. Kim placed a Band-Aid around the finger and held Heidi's hand in hers, feeling the warmth of their friendship. A tear rolled down her cheek and Heidi brushed it away, reassuring her that the two weeks would fly by and they would be together again.

They hugged and held each other like sisters and walked hand in hand to the waiting minibus that would take Heidi to the airport. Kim returned to her room feeling empty, lonely and confused. She had wanted to tell Heidi how much she loved her but now that moment had slipped by like water through her fingers, lost forever and never to return.

FORTY-ONE

Joe gasped as the cold water numbed his naked body, then he scrubbed hard with the sliver of carbolic soap left behind by the last bather. The rusty water trickled from a chrome showerhead that had lost its shine a long time ago. Since he hadn't bathed in a month, the dirt flowed off him like a mudslide and accumulated at his feet.

He reflected on how much he had taken for granted and, despite the leering guards less than ten feet away, treasured the feeling of every drop that struck his body. Dirty nails were one of his pet hates; to him a sign of self-neglect and low esteem. He picked at them fastidiously until he rid them of the black line.

'*Yellah, khallas sedeeq!* Quick, finish, friend!' shouted the corporal growing impatient and throwing him a threadbare towel that still bore its *Made in Pakistan* tag. He felt a change in attitude towards him but he couldn't be certain. Perhaps it was a trick of his mind or perhaps he had succumbed to the Stockholm syndrome that psychologists rave about on television during hostage crises. Maybe being clean made him feel congenial and coloured his view.

They didn't shackle him after his shower or return him to his cell, but instead escorted him to a room with windows that looked out onto Medinah Road and the Sahara Hotel.

His eyes welcomed the sunshine and the blue sky whose intensity and clarity he had previously overlooked. A man brought him a cup of tea and a plate of almond cookies. They tasted divine and revived his taste buds. An unvaried diet of nan bread and *addus*, a concoction of chickpea, had taken its toll on his weakening body.

The men talked between themselves with lowered voices. It was then that fear seeped into his brain and fanned by his past experience, took hold with the intensity of a bush fire. Were the nightmares going to begin, he asked himself? Were they going to rape him again? In the past they hadn't bothered about his appearance but perhaps this time he was going to get dicked by a VIP.

'Why am I here?' Joe asked in Arabic.

One of the men scowled, pursed his thumb and fingers together, meaning 'take five,' and carried on with his conversation. It was one of those gestures that Joe found objectionable. He had a version of his own with his middle finger that expressed what he wanted to say but he refrained. Instead he turned his attention to the last cookie. The door opened and a man with an air of authority strode in clutching an olive green file and a manila envelope. The corporals jumped to attention and saluted.

'Colonel Khatani, Nasser Al Khatani,' the man introduced himself in a matter of fact way and their hands met for a fleeting second in what passed as a weak handshake. 'How are you, Dr Goldman?' he asked and proceeded to answer the question himself. 'You look well. We believe in looking after our guests,' he added, seeing a frown on Joe's face. A tray bearing tea and more cookies arrived. The Colonel lit a cigarette, took a few deep breaths, glanced at his watch and opened the olive green file without further ceremony. 'Ah! Here we are,' he exclaimed after fumbling with a sheaf of papers. He fished out a document in Arabic stapled at one corner. 'Please sign here, Dr Goldman,' he said in a persuasive tone, offering Joe his pen and pointing to one of the four dotted lines at the bottom of each page. 'It's just a formality, you understand,' he added, trying to sound reassuring. 'Then you are free to go.'

To Joe it all seemed far too simple after a month of incarceration and beatings, not to mention the sodomy and humiliation. Joe narrowed his eyes and stared at the man seated in front of him. It was incredible that a man he hadn't seen before was offering him his freedom in exchange for a signature on a document that he couldn't read. No explanation or apology, only: 'sign here and walk out a free man.' Simple, clinical – as though nothing had happened.

'Why am I here?' Joe demanded. 'I'm not signing anything until you give me an explanation and an apology.'

The colonel swore under his breath in Arabic and drew hard on the cigarette.

'Dr Goldman,' he began in earnest, 'you've been charged with a serious crime that carries the—'

'Charged with what and by whom?' Joe interrupted. 'No one has told me what I'm supposed to have done. I've been denied a call to the US embassy and now you walk in here after I've been rotting in this shit-hole for a month and order me to sign some goddamn piece of paper that I can't read and everything is going to be fucking dandy!'

'Dr Goldman! Please listen—'

'No! You listen, pal, and listen real good.' Joe pushed the papers away. 'I'm not signing a damned thing without an embassy official present. And I want an English translation of this,' he said, pointing at the document. 'Otherwise there's no deal.'

The colonel puffed on the cigarette for the last time and ground the stub into the saucer. 'There is no need for this kind of. . . excitement.' he grimaced and kept glancing at the two corporals in the corner.

Joe didn't need to be a medico to read the signs. The artery that snaked across the colonel's temple pulsed and his flushed face told him this was one proud and angry Arab who wasn't going to apologise anytime soon – that would be an admission of guilt and loss of face.

'Listen to me, Doctor. Hear me out,' the colonel cajoled trying hard to maintain a steady tone. 'You're a reasonable man,' he said. 'These are *routine* release papers, you understand. May Allah be my witness.'

'I want a translation,' Joe said.

'Sign now and you walk free. Tomorrow the matter will be out of my hands,' the colonel said, dusting his palms. 'You will have to deal with the *mutaween*. And you know how unaccommodating they can be.'

The image of Salem's malevolent face flashed across Joe's eyes and he flinched. The words 'Do you have a tattoo,' came to mind. He was a fascist thug, a man with a grudge against all non-Muslims but Jews in particular. If these papers were what the colonel said they were, then he had nothing to fear. But how could he be sure? If they weren't, what were they? Was this a trap to ensnare him after failing to break his spirit after a month of physical and mental torture?

The colonel saw the confusion on Joe's face and pushed the papers across to him. With a disarming smile and a nod he urged, 'Please. . . do it and go.'

Joe eyeballed the colonel and considered his options. He had none. After a short, thoughtful pause, he picked up the pen and flashed his signature over the dotted line. All of a sudden he felt lighter, almost euphoric, but at the same time drained.

At last he would be able to phone Maryam and discover what was so urgent for her to change their meeting arrangement.

FORTY-TWO

To avoid the heat, Maryam ventured out in the evening to watch the routine of the farm. There was much planning to do and many obstacles to overcome. On one such outing with Turki, while walking through the vineyard at the rear of the house, they heard a sound that stopped them in their tracks. Turki clung to Maryam's dress and screamed. A snarling shadow came bounding towards them. It stopped, crouched and darted from side to side.

Men came running to their rescue waving bamboo staves. Maryam stood her ground, the beast snarled and melted into the darkness, leaving them dazed. They had just met Zaki, the guard dog, a German Shepherd her father had purchased from the neighbour after he had broken loose one night and savaged a dozen sheep.

Maryam carried the sobbing boy to the house, accompanied by the two men.

'I was about to feed the beast when it charged and the rope broke,' a man explained, fearing for his job. He showed Maryam the wound on his forearm.

'Madam, you were very brave. Never show fear. They can smell it and that's when they attack,' said the second man.

At the house, Mahmoud doused the man's wounds with iodine and dressed it with a bandage. 'We don't need the dog,' he said. 'We have Basheer.' He shook his head in dismay and took the farm worker to the hospital with his arm in a sling.

That night, lying in bed with Turki curled up beside her, Maryam realised the beast had changed everything. He was feared by all except Basheer, his keeper and the night watchman.

During the day Zaki lay in the shade tethered to a palm tree, his head resting on the ground and a paw over his head as if to deflect insults and the occasional date stone aimed at him. At night he was feared and no one ventured out. Maryam spent hours lying in bed listening to his bark trying to find a solution. She even considered poison and hated herself for such a thought. There had to be a way; there was always a way, she told herself.

One moonlit night, Maryam spotted Zaki from her bedroom window. She felt a further pang of guilt at wanting to kill him and realised their lives were not dissimilar: both were shackled to the home, at the mercy of men and unable to drive.

Inspired by the stars, she remembered a story her Bedouin grandmother had told her of a runaway slave who had removed a thorn from the paw of a lion while hiding in a cave.

Years later, this slave was caught and thrown to the lions, as they used to in the days before the Prophet Mohammed. The lion refused to attack the slave who had shown kindness and so the emperor had them both set free. There was her answer, she thought. Kindness was the key and not fear.

Friendship was a slow process with a suspicious animal. Maryam persevered, threw leftovers from her window, softly calling out his name until a fragile trust grew. Before long, Zaki took to sitting under her window after midnight and whining until she had fed him. Sometimes when she ventured on to the veranda in the night, Zaki would recognise her footfall and come to her side, wagging his tail. It was a kind of game to him and Maryam had become a source of companionship.

Maryam discovered there was another obstacle to be overcome. The keys to the pickups hung in the gatehouse where Basheer, the night watchman, kept guard.

One night, while the house slept, Maryam slipped out through the kitchen door that opened out to the backyard. Hearing her footsteps, Zaki appeared, and together they crept from one shadow to another to spy on Basheer – only to find him missing from his post.

In the kitchen the next morning, Maryam heard Basheer's name mentioned in an animated conversation in Tagalog. Josi and Imelda listened wide-eyed to Zelpha's story, accompanying it with giggling and exclamations. The following morning she was again rolling out the account of her night's adventure. One day, while combing Maryam's hair, Zelpha declared she was in love.

'Anyone I know?' Maryam asked, as was expected of her.

'Oh no, no one you'd know, Madam,' Zelpha replied. Maryam wished her happiness.

Nothing more was said again until one morning Zelpha burst into her room crying.

'My boyfriend. . . the one I love. . . he wants to end it,' she sobbed.

Maryam's heart missed a beat. The words exploded like bombs threatening to destroy her plans. She had to think fast and sound convincing but at the same time be discreet and diplomatic. 'Why?'

'He wants me to become a Muslim first,' she confessed. It was obvious Basheer had got what he was after and now wanted out without losing face.

'That's rubbish!' Maryam declared. 'Look at Madam Hanifah, she became a Muslim through her own free will. In Islam, Muslim men may marry non-Muslims. It's only Muslim women who can't marry outside the faith.'

'Thank God for that!' Zelpha exclaimed. She crossed herself and hugged Maryam. 'I owe you one, Madam.' Zelpha left and Maryam flopped on the bed exhausted. She had salvaged her plan and acquired an accomplice who would help make her escape easier.

FORTY-THREE

The family sat at the breakfast table exchanging news and making plans. Farhan complained about the bombings. Mahmoud talked about the horses with Turki. Nabeel was in a world of his own and Hanifah practiced her Arabic with Aishah. Maryam ate in silence, planning her escape.

'There's a call for you, Madam,' Zelpha told Maryam.

'Who is it?' Maryam asked, without looking up from her plate.

'It's a man.'

'That'll be Nader. Tell him I'll call back.'

'He said it was urgent.'

'I'm having breakfast,' Maryam said tucking into her *babaghanoush*.

'Sounded American, Madam,' Zelpha muttered in Maryam's ear and her heart leapt.

'Is anything the matter, *habibi*?' Aishah asked.

'It's just a phone call.' Maryam looked flustered.

'Nader?' Farhan inquired.

'Yes, Father.' Hanifah gave a knowing smile.

'Talk to him, probably wants to apologise.'

'About what?' Aishah asked.

'Oh, nothing, woman.' Farhan gave a dismissive wave and Mahmoud arched a questioning brow.

Maryam took the call in the library, closing the door behind her.

'Joe?' she whispered, holding the handset hard against her ear. There was no reply.

'Joe, talk to me. Is that you?'

'Yes, it's me,' Joe replied. 'I can barely hear you.'

'Is that better?' Maryam asked, speaking up.

'A little.'

'Where are you? Where have you been? Are you okay? What happened?'

'Whoa! Not so fast.'

'I've been worried sick.' Maryam paced the floor.

'They know about you.'

'How?'

'Your photo, I had it in my wallet.'

Maryam digested this information. 'We need to talk, Joe,' she said, feeling increasingly cornered.

'Not on the phone.'

'I have so much to tell you,' Maryam glanced over her shoulder at the door.

'I'm being watched,' Joe said, looking out from the phone booth.

'Shit! Who by?'

'I don't have much time,' Joe replied, and pushed the last coin in the slot.

'Call me tomorrow at ten. I'll arrange something,' Maryam said, taking a deep breath.

'I've missed you. And thank you,' Joe said.

'I've died a thousand times.'

'Talk to you tomorrow.'

The phone went dead.

* * *

Lo and Nader lay entwined on the sofa in a passionate embrace watched over by the portraits of the 'three wise men'.

'They give me the creeps,' Lo said, coming up for breath.

273

'Never mind them, they're just envious,' Nader laughed.

He heard the knock at the door but ignored it. A moment passed and there was another knock, this time a little louder and Nader cursed. A minute lapsed, then a sharp metallic rat-ta-tat on the door made them jump.

'Who is it?' Nader shouted. He straightened his *thobe* and Lo composed herself on the sofa, patting her hair in place.

Nader opened the door.

'I'll come back later,' Kim said, seeing Lo across the room.

'Why can't you use the phone?'

'I'll come back later,' she repeated, but it was too late. Nader pulled her in and shoved her onto the sofa, slamming the door.

'What the hell do you want?' he barked. Kim paled. Nader's clenched fist was inches from her face. Kim's humiliation made Lo smile.

'I want out,' Kim said. 'I can't go on anymore.'

'You want out? What of the money we've paid you?' Nader asked.

'Please, Nader.'

With a quick toss of his head in the direction of the door he motioned Lo to leave. The door closed and Nader erupted.

'There is no out for you! That was never an option!' he shouted, stabbing a finger in her chest.

'I'll give back the money.'

'We made a deal and you'll keep it or I'll stamp out your life!' he screamed, banging his fist on the table. 'Now get out and remember you've an important appointment this weekend.

Kim left the office feeling drained. Nader's venom had poisoned her soul and she knew the end had come.

* * *

The point of the pen rolled across the paper, each word wrung from a wretched heart, spelling out her confusion and confessing her guilt. Tears fell onto the paper, washing away the ink. She

274

sobbed as images swirled in her head and the pen ate up the paper until the well of emotion ran dry.

Begging your forgiveness, Heidi, with all my love, rolled from Kim's pen, ending with her stylised signature, a circle, dotting the 'i' like a halo. The pen flashed across the page compressing all her love in a single X.

In the basement of the hospital that evening, Kim dropped the envelope into the letterbox marked *internal mail*. It would be waiting for Heidi on her return. She sighed and slipped the letter and bank draft for her mother through the opening marked *foreign mail*. Now she had passed the point of no return.

The smell of death travelled through the air-conditioning ducts and alerted her neighbours, but it was a week before Nader realised that he had not seen or heard from her. They found her curled up in bed, her rosary locked in her hand and a smile on a face free of anguish. Photographs of her mother and Heidi lay beside her and a trace of a red candle remained in a saucer beneath the cross. Kim's life was extinguished when the candle flickered and died. The valium had eased her passage to heaven and closed the door, shutting out her melancholic past and Nader's vengeful world. She had escaped where he could not follow.

FORTY-FOUR

Maryam made an excuse to visit at Sahar and Samar's to study but accompanied them to an engagement party that evening at the hotel.

Joe drove to the main *souq*, crossed the mall, dived into a restaurant he knew, exited by the rear door, ran down the alley and took a taxi to the hotel.

They met as before on the third floor of the Sahara hotel.

'Let me look at you,' Joe said, holding Maryam at arm's length in the sanctuary of his room.

'You've lost weight.' Maryam ran her hand over his gaunt face.

'A month in a stinking hole does that.'

'I know. I rang the American Embassy.'

'Ah. . . that explains everything.'

'Did they harm you?'

Joe ignored the question. 'You look stunning as ever,' he said.

'I feel like shit,' Maryam replied, using one of Hanifah's expressions.

'Are you unwell?'

Rubbing her stomach, Maryam blurted, 'I'm pregnant.'

'You're pregnant!' Joe exclaimed.

'Feel!' Maryam placed Joe's hand on her belly.

Joe felt the baby move. 'Wow! Why didn't you tell me?' Joe asked.

'How could I?'

'Is that why you wanted to meet earlier?'

Maryam nodded. 'That was a bad idea.'

'I'm so happy, we're having a baby. It's fantastic!' Joe said and punched the air.

'Is it?' Maryam asked in a vacant tone.

'Isn't that what you want?' Joe cradled Maryam's face in his hands. 'Aren't you happy, my love?'

Maryam bit her lip. 'Of course, but, Joe. . . this is Saudi Arabia.'

'Is it forbidden to love?'

'We've broken a cardinal rule,' Maryam said, searching for hope in Joe's face. 'The penalty is death.'

'For God's sake, we're not living in the Middle Ages, Maryam!' Joe held her to his chest but Tess's words replayed in his mind: *be careful, you're a long, long way from home.*

'Last year a classmate disappeared after they discovered she was pregnant. I think her father. . .' Maryam began.

'Okay, okay. I believe you. Let's think this through.'

'I'm so frightened,' Maryam said, squeezing Joe's hand. 'I want to keep the baby.'

'It's an affirmation of our love,' Joe declared and Maryam nodded in agreement.

'They'll kill us both.' Maryam clung to his sleeve, her eyes welling with tears. 'What am I to do, Joe?'

'There's only one way out.' Joe raised Maryam's head by her chin and looked into her frightened face.

'What's that?' murmured Maryam.

'Come away with me. Away from here.'

'Away where?'

'I don't know. But it has to be soon!'

'But how? This is not America.'

'I'll think of something.'

'How about Jordan?' Maryam suggested.

'Why Jordan?'

'Because the border is only ninety kilometres from here.'
Maryam managed a feeble smile. She wanted so much to place
her hopes in Joe's confidence and resourcefulness and in Sultan's
words she had heard through Zubaida, but the machinery of the
state and the power and authority of her father made her feel
impotent.

'Where did you get this?' Joe asked, noticing the green disc
around Maryam's neck.

'It was a gift. . . from a woman. . . a friend.'

'It's beautiful. Everything will be fine,' Joe said, touching the
stone.

'*Insha'allah*,' Maryam mumbled and buried her face in Joe's
chest, hiding her shame and ridden with guilt. How could she
have thought of killing their baby? She would have been
murdering their love.

They spent the next few hours in each other's arms saying
little, just happy to be together, periodically glancing at the clock
on the bedside table. Two F15's roared over the hotel on a
mission and made the window panes rattle.

'Will there ever be peace?' Maryam asked.

Joe frowned. 'Insecurity breeds the fear that politicians feed
on,' he reflected, stroking her forehead.

'They cloud our minds with words and poison our hearts,'
Maryam said. She tugged at his beard. 'This makes you look old
and wise.'

'I'll let it grow and join the *mutaween*.'

Maryam laughed. 'Don't you dare, Dr Joe.'

'Laughter becomes you, Maryam,' Joe said, and kissed her
lips.

Maryam glanced at the clock and whispered, 'It's time, Joe.'

They embraced, said their farewells and took the lift down to
the basement.

'I have this for you,' Maryam said, giving him an envelope.
'Whatever happens, Joe, I'll always love you.'

They kissed for the last time, Joe lowered Maryam's veil for her and she stepped out, confused but with hope in her heart.

Back in his room, Joe opened the envelope and recognised the work by Erté entitled: *Bird in a Gilded Cage*.

'You have impeccable taste, my darling,' Joe murmured. As his eyes travelled over the flowing script his fingers trembled and tears ran freely.

Flow through my hair like the wind
Light up my life like the flame.
Torment my soul like the Devil
Dance in my heart like a spirit.
Ignite my desire with a spark.
Quench my thirst like a mountain spring.
You are I, I am you and we are one.

'I will free you, my love,' Joe whispered, 'we shall soar together as one.'

* * *

George Kozlowski took the call in his offices in the Al Kareem compound off the Medinah Road. The USMTM had moved there for security reasons after the bombing of their head-quarters in downtown Tabuk. He was surprised to hear Colonel Khatani's voice on the line and even more surprised to hear him in a jolly mood.

'I'm pleased to inform you we have no one by the name of Joe Goldman as our guest,' he declared. 'Your informant must have been mistaken,' he added, gloating.

'Happy to hear that, Colonel,' Kozlowski replied, reading between the lines. 'I guess he'll show up for work sooner or later.'

'*Insha'allah*,' the Colonel replied, and hung up.

Kozlowski dialled the embassy, got John Braxton and left a message for the ambassador that would make him happy. 'Another mission accomplished without casualties,' he said to himself, and grinned.

FORTY-FIVE

A kaleidoscope of colour danced across Turki's eyes as he rushed past shelves decked with toys. Every time he spied something he liked he yelped, spun on his heels like a dervish and pointed.

Maryam hurried behind taking delight in his adventure, her own happy face hidden behind the veil. She had promised him an outing he would remember and he was in his element. The Indian salesman, watchful of any damage that he would have to pay from his meagre wage, followed them.

In the end, Turki selected a battery-powered helicopter with flashing lights and spinning rotor blades that sounded just like the real thing. They dropped in at the tailors with Mahmoud to get Turki measured for another *thobe* and the El-Faleh sports shop where he picked out a flash pair of football boots. Some days Turki wanted to be a pilot and on others he wanted to play football for the national team.

Happy but exhausted, they drove home with Mahmoud at the wheel, arriving in time for lunch and a well-earned siesta.

Running her hand over the floral pattern, Aishah admired the silver picture frame that Maryam had found at Samir, Tabuk's foremost Kodak photographic lab. Yousuf, the soft-spoken Jordanian assistant, had offered her a discount since it had been the last one.

Aishah pored over the photograph of Turki and Maryam that

Hanifah had taken with her camera on the day of Sahar and Samar's birthday party and declared: 'In my day, photographs were forbidden. They said the camera stole your soul.'

'Things are different now, Mama, thanks to King Faisal,' Maryam replied.

'You look so beautiful, *habibi*.'

Maryam smiled, remembering that day. She had glowed with confidence wearing Hanifah's dress that had left Joe speechless. It was the day she had lost her virginity and the day they had conceived the baby boy she carried. That day was to change her life forever and the lives of all around her.

'I'll keep it in my bedroom with Sultan's,' Aishah said, putting it aside.

'Can I have one of you, Mama?' Maryam asked. 'Hanifah can take it for me.'

'Why?'

'I want one of Father, Uncle Mahmoud, Turki and all the maids.'

'The maids?' Hanifah asked. 'Are you sure you're all right?'

'I want one of you and Nabeel too,' Maryam replied. 'I want you all to be part of my new home.'

'*Insha'allah* tomorrow,' Aishah said, and turned on the television. They held hands and watched the melodrama of an Egyptian soap opera unfold, interrupted every ten minutes by advertisements for hair shampoo or cartoons tempting children with mouth-watering ice creams or chocolates. Every afternoon around five this was Aishah's ritual.

Turki sat at Maryam's feet, sucking on a lolly and playing with his helicopter. Maryam watched, knowing these daily events she had taken for granted would be treasured memories in years to come.

Hanifah flicked through the glossy magazines, nauseated by the ostentatious hairdos of Arab Madonnas decked out in clothes from European fashion houses. The publications came from Lebanon, Egypt, Jordan and the Gulf countries where the dress codes and censorship laws were not so strict. Images of coarse decadence created by pouting lips, heavy eyeliners and baroque jewellery jumped at her from the pages. The Arabic script was a mystery but the photos spoke for themselves.

'Look at this,' Hanifah said, showing Maryam a page defaced by a mass of black ink covering every inch of visible flesh.

'That's so the men don't get excited,' Maryam explained.

'It's hardly *Playboy* material,' Hanifah muttered to herself.

'Samar told me she'd seen a man on a flight from Jeddah with an erection while seated beside a western woman with no *abaya* or headscarf.'

'Men are so weak!' Hanifah replied, wrinkling her nose in disgust.

'The *Qur'an* says they should avert their gaze.'

'It says that?' Hanifah asked in astonishment.

'Sure. The sight of naked skin is an open invitation.'

'But what of the women newscasters?'

'They're Syrian or Jordanian.'

'Don't they count?' Hanifah asked, a little bemused.

'In my country they buy people. Surely you know that by now?' Maryam answered.

Hanifah gave a pursed smile and went back to her magazine, marvelling at the elegant bridal gowns with metres of exquisite fabric and acres of delicate veils that must have cost the earth. Her dress had been plain. Nabeel had wanted a simple Muslim wedding with a few of his friends. Her Uncle Jim had signed the papers. She had insisted on a honeymoon and Nabeel grudgingly agreed to take her down to Florida where he had bummed off with the Italian waiter from their hotel and she had spent the night in tears.

Seated in his father's home, surrounded by luxury, she couldn't care less what Nabeel did or didn't do anymore. Her position in his family was becoming more permanent with every passing day. The baby in her belly would ensure her of that.

She loathed the thought of it feeding off her like a parasite.

Soon it would destroy the figure she loved so much. She wanted a girl but prayed it would be a boy so Nabeel would have to acknowledge it. But it would make Farhan happy to have fathered another son. She wanted that for him; it was the least she could do.

Hanifah gave an exaggerated sigh, dropped the magazine on the floor and picked up a copy of *Newsweek*, drawn to it by the screaming banner on the cover: *SADDAM: DID HE WIN?* Her eyes devoured the print avidly. The last sentence read: *In Saudi Arabia, the.* . . She turned it over only to find the next four pages missing; the censorship boys had struck again. Hanifah screamed, threw down the magazine and stormed out of the room.

'Oh dear. I wonder what it is this time?' Aishah asked, struggling to her feet. 'It's the girl's first baby. . . I wish my English was better. . . I know just how she must feel. Without my mother I was alone too when I carried Sultan. Your father was often away in the early days, but your Uncle Mahmoud was always there and did his best.'

'I'll go and see, Mama,' Maryam said, and Aishah flopped back into her seat, turning her attention back to the TV.

Maryam found Hanifah in the study with her head buried in the *Qur'an*.

'I hope I'm not disturbing you.' She closed the door behind her. Hanifah didn't answer but turned the pages pretending not to have heard.

'Is anything the matter?' Maryam asked.

Hanifah slammed the big book shut. 'Everything is the matter. Can't you see I'm pregnant? Look at me. Just look at me!' she said, jumping to her feet and pulling tight her dress around her belly. 'I'm fat and ugly,' she sobbed, releasing a torrent of tears. 'I hate being pregnant. I hate being here. I wish I was back in America.'

Maryam didn't have any answers or quick solutions. She too was pregnant but no one could know or sympathise with her, not even her mother. She reached for Hanifah's hand and held it in hers. It felt clammy and different from the times when they had strolled through the vineyard hand in hand. Maryam dabbed away Hanifah's tears with her handkerchief and smiled.

'Cheer up. It's not the end of the world,' she whispered, trying to infuse some vitality in to her words. 'You'll have a beautiful boy and look back and say it was all worth it.' Maryam hadn't forgotten Hanifah's indiscretion with her father and wanted to confront her about it, but now was neither the time nor the place. Soon she would be gone and life would continue without her. This was a time to forgive and forget, if such a thing was possible.

Hanifah blew her nose and mustered a smile. 'I'm so lucky to have you as a sister,' she said.

'Have you thought of any names?' Maryam asked.

'That's Nabeel's turf,' Hanifah said. 'He's bound to want to name him after his father if it's a boy.'

'. . . My father will like that. . .' Maryam said flatly.

They kissed and embraced. Hanifah blushed and gave a knowing look that sent a chill down Maryam's spine – her secret was out, but was it safe with this mercurial woman who had made a home in her father's house and heart?

FORTY-SIX

Turki burst into the bedroom, shattering the peace with a toy machine gun glowing red and yellow, spitting *Rat tata tata! Rat tata tata!*

'What are you doing, Turki?' Maryam asked.

'Killing the enemy!' he shouted at the top of his voice, waving the gun in the air and jumping up and down on the bed.

'Stop that at once! Can't you see I'm studying the *Qur'an*?'

'They must die!' Turki screamed, jumped off the bed, flung open the wardrobe and fired at the clothes. *Rat tata tata!* 'I want to be a *mujahideen*!'

'Stop! Come here at once!'

Turki knew from the tone of her voice he had overstepped the mark and made for the door. Maryam got there before him and grabbed him by the collar of his army fatigues.

'Not so fast, young man. I want a word with you.' Turki gave up the struggle. 'Where did you get this?' Maryam asked, taking the gun from him.

'Uncle Nader. . . he gave it to me.'

'And who's the enemy?'

'The *Ameriki* and the Jews. Uncle Nader told me they're all bad.'

'Did he now?' Maryam declared, clenching her teeth.

'He's downstairs. You can ask him,' Turki whimpered.

'Now listen. . . Auntie Hanifah and Dr Joe are *Ameriki*. Are they bad?'

Turki shook his head and tears began to well.

'Do you know any Jews?'

Turki looked embarrassed and shook his head again.

'Well then, how do you know they're bad?'

'But Uncle Nader and Uncle Nabeel said they killed our people and took our land.'

'I'm sure they didn't mean that. Jews are people just like us. Didn't I tell you we must all try to live in peace?'

'Uncle Nader says—'

'Never mind what Uncle Nader says!' Maryam snapped, 'He isn't a solider, *habibi.*'

'But Uncle Nader was a *mujahideen.*'

'Talk to Grandpa. He's a general.' Maryam straightened his military tunic. 'Now go and find Grandma.'

'Grandpa knows everything about everything,' Turki said with pride.

Maryam rushed down the stairs two steps at a time and found Nader and Nabeel in the lounge engrossed in conversation.

'What do you think you're doing?' she asked Nader.

'Drinking tea,' Nader answered with a smirk on his face.

'You're trying to fill the boy's head with hate.'

'Just the truth.'

'You wouldn't recognise truth if it hit you in the face, Nader!' Maryam snapped.

'Ha. . . and I suppose you would?'

'What's this?' Maryam held out the gun and ignored Nader's remark.

'A toy.' Nader said.

'The boy needs a father!' Nabeel shouted.

'And you think you can fill Sultan's shoes? You can't even father your own. . .' Maryam stopped in mid sentence, shaking with anger.

Nabeel jumped to his feet and charged. He threw his hands around her neck and squeezed her throat.

'What did you say, bitch?' He screamed, shaking her like a

doll. Crimson with anger and veins engorged with hate he shouted, 'Let me hear it? What did you say?' Maryam gasped and stared at Nabeel.

Turki rushed in and screamed. 'Let Auntie Miri go!' He kicked Nabeel in the shins and pulled at his *thobe*. Nabeel lashed out with his foot sending the boy flying.

In desperation Maryam swung her arm and the butt of the toy gun caught Nabeel above the eye, splitting open his forehead. The next blow struck him on the back of the head and sent him sprawling, blood oozing onto the floor.

Turki's scream brought Hanifah rushing to the lounge. Grasping the situation in an instant she shouted at Nader as he came at Maryam with clenched fists. 'You lay a finger on her and I swear I'll kill you!'

Nader stopped in his tracks and glared. Dazed, Nabeel struggled to his feet, holding his hand over his wound.

'Don't poison the boy's mind with your venom,' Maryam croaked. 'Take this and get out.' Maryam pulled Nader's ring off her finger and threw it at his feet.

'You'll regret this!' Nader shouted, waving a didactic finger at them. Maryam and Hanifah stormed out carrying Turki.

Forty-Seven

'Have you seen Nader?' asked a voice on the phone.

There was a pause; Aishah tried to put a face to the voice.

'He was here a few days ago,' replied Aishah, recognising the caller. 'Is something the matter, Mona?'

'It's nothing, Auntie Aishah.'

'Are you sure, *habibi*?'

Instinctively Mona replied, '*Alhamdulillah*,' but couldn't hold back the tears. 'Father went away on business yesterday. We were expecting Nader two days ago,' she blurted out. 'Mother's not well. . . There's no one to take her to the hospital. She's really ill, Auntie Aishah, and needs a doctor right away. I think she's going to die!'

'*Maalish, habibi!* I'll send Mahmoud and Maryam over right away,' consoled Aishah.

* * *

Seated in a wheelchair, Khadijah's face was ashen under the soiled cotton veil. An Indian porter wheeled her into Prince Fahad bin Sultan Hospital, Tabuk's foremost private facility.

Maryam and Mona hurried behind to the emergency room. The smell of antiseptic lingered everywhere. A poster shouted out at them as they entered: *Know About AIDS*. The word *AIDS* was in the form of a crumbling red and yellow brick wall,

288

crushed by a hand. On another poster a skeleton lay in a cigarette coffin. Coco, a Filipina nurse with a round face, almond
eyes and shoulder-length hair, appeared swinging a stethoscope.
She wore a white paper hat, the regulation white uniform with
green epaulettes, pink socks with little bunnies on them and
spotless white shoes.

She had a business-like air about her and seemed to know her
job. She moved around a triage cubicle, stuck an electronic
thermometer in Khadijah's ear and wrapped a cuff around her
arm to measure her blood pressure and pulse with a sphygmo-
manometer. Khadijah was too weak to stand up, so she guessed
at her height and weight to fill in the rest of the form. Though
always professional, she didn't really care: her contract was up in
few days and she would be back in Cebu with her son and eating
pork adobo with rice.

The Egyptian doctor glanced at the triage sheet and pushed it
aside. He wore a crumpled lab coat with a row of pens in his
breast pocket that looked like a band of ribbons. Low blood
pressure, weak but rapid pulse and raised temperature all
pointed to a distressed and dehydrated patient. He fired some
questions in Arabic at Mona who didn't know what to say except
'*Alhamdulillah.*' Coco put up a saline drip and the doctor complained about the poor veins in Khadijah's fat arm. He shone a
light into her eyes, muttered something to the nurse and left.

They poked and prodded, teased and tested, x-rayed and
palpitated and pronounced Khadijah 'ill,' a fact everyone knew
from the onset. Dr Francoise Melard, the French gynaecologist,
a willowy woman with placid blue eyes, examined the reports
and the radiographs, punctuating silences with, 'Ah! Bon!'

'Ah! Bon! We need to make more investigations.' Malak, the
female interpreter, jumped in with an Arabic translation before
the doctor could finish.

Dr Ahmed, the Syrian dentist, appeared and examined
Khadijah's mouth with a pencil torch and a wooden spatula. Her
lips were dry, cracked and bleeding. A foul stench emanated

from her mouth. He scribbled his recommendations on the treatment sheet, signed it with a flourish and departed without saying a word to anyone.

Mona stayed behind with her mother and Maryam promised to return in the morning. Swallowing her anger Maryam tried to contact Nader on his pager but got nowhere. Finally, through his travel agent, she traced Uncle Talal to the Happy Hotel in a seedy part of Manila. He was brusque on the phone. 'I'm busy – get Khadijah's brothers to help out – she's their responsibility.'

The next day a little colour seeped into Khadijah's face and Maryam was sure her eyes looked more lively. Mona looked as if hadn't slept. Maryam had brought a basket of fruit, an assortment of biscuits and a thermos of coffee that would keep them going.

Khadijah's day was filled with one test after another. They scanned with one demonic machine, viewed with another and then, when she thought they had finished, they put her in a tube and told her to keep still while they played foreign music. She felt a little better with all the attention she was receiving but didn't recommend the food.

'Ah! Bon!' exclaimed the gynaecologist pulling down the last film from the x-ray viewer and turned to face Mona and Maryam. 'Your mother is not at all well,' she said. 'She needs an operation to remove 'er. . . cancer from 'ere,' and pointed to the uterus, 'and some radiation and chemotherapy for some time. After that she may be okay, it's difficult to say right now.' She shrugged her shoulders and rolled her eyes in resignation, 'Ah! And then it is. . . *Insha'allah*. . . as you say here.'

Malak took over from there, knowing the routine. This was not the first case of cervical cancer she had encountered and rattled off possible scenarios without Francoise's consent. This was her moment on centre stage and Francoise didn't like it one bit, but accepted the fact that the language barrier prevented her from giving the counselling needed in such cases.

'Bon! Before we can make the operation we need 'er 'usband

or 'er son to sign this paper,' she said, handing Mona a consent form in Arabic and English. Mona looked at the doctor in embarrassment and then at Maryam.

'Is there a problem?'

'All men away,' was all Mona could say in her limited English.

'*Merde!* A man must sign 'ere,' pointing at the bottom of the page, 'that's the 'ospital policy. I don't care who signs it but it 'as to be signed!'

Francoise had been in the Kingdom for two months and was tired of what she called 'bullshit protocol,' where a boy of ten had the right to deny treatment to his dying mother because he had a penis hanging between his legs.

Khadijah's condition deteriorated while they tried to find Nader. Her brothers were too busy to come but, '*Insha'allah*', one of them would make it next week. Farhan's authority failed to persuade the Lebanese hospital director to allow the operation to go ahead.

'Hospital policy is hospital policy,' he had whined. 'Believe me, sir, I want to help but my hands are tied.' To add substance to his argument he added, 'I would lose my job and perhaps my liberty if something should go wrong and the family complained to the prince.' Over the years, the 'weasel,' as the staff called him, had learned that by uttering the magic word 'prince' without specifying which one from among the four-and-a-half thousand often got results.

They operated on the fifth day when Nader showed up and signed the form.

'She 'asn't got a chance,' Francoise commented to the Ethiopian anaesthetist, who dismissed her with a curt, '*Allah-hu akbar*.'

The cancer had spread into the wall of her womb, the surrounding soft tissue and lungs. It was only a matter of time, perhaps a few weeks, before the end would come.

FORTY-EIGHT

Maryam finished *Isha* prayer seated on the edge of the bed and was contemplating her life when Turki walked in.

'Are you not well, Auntie Maryam?'

Maryam smiled and nodded. Her whole body ached and her neck was covered in bruises from Nabeel's attack.

'I'm sorry about the gun. Can I help?' he asked.

'Come sit by me,' Maryam said, and Turki climbed up beside her on the bed.

'Grandpa is teaching me how to pray,' he said.

'That's good!'

'I'm going to be a good Muslim.'

'I know you will,' Maryam replied. With her arm around Turki they sat and watched the sky turn deep red and then mauve. Streaks of grey seeped in and one by one the stars appeared.

'Are there bad Muslims?'

'Only Allah can be the judge of that,' Maryam replied.

'Auntie Miri, are you going to marry Nader?' Turki asked.

'Why do you ask?'

Turki pulled a face. 'He's not very nice. I think he's a bad Muslim.'

Maryam remained silent, touched by the boy's concern.

'You don't have to go away now?'

Maryam smiled. 'I want to talk to you about something. But first you must make a promise.'

Turki nodded and smiled. He loved secrets, especially grown-up secrets. He sat with his head resting on his cupped hands watching the light fade and darkness creep in and envelop them.

'You mustn't tell anyone.'

'Cross my heart and hope to die,' Turki replied.

'*Habibi*, where did you learn that?' Maryam asked in horror.

'Auntie Hanifah says that all the time.'

'If you want to be a good Muslim, you mustn't say that.'

'Isn't Auntie Hanifah a good Muslim?'

'She's a young Muslim and has much to learn.'

'That is what Grandpa says.'

'Does he?'

'He says to be a good Muslim you must first understand the *Qur'an* and then let it guide you.'

'You must always listen to the *Qur'an*.'

'Are you going to tell me your secret now, Auntie Miri?'

'It's going to be our special secret. Promise? Maryam said, and Turki nodded. 'Sometimes, *habibi*, we want something but, no matter how hard we try, we can't have it.'

'Grandpa says it's Allah's will.'

'And sometimes what you do doesn't make sense to anyone but yourself.'

There was a long pause. Turki's mind deciphered Maryam's words.

'Tell me you're not leaving, Auntie Miri,' Turki said, and began to cry.

'Hush, *habibi*. It's going to be all right.'

'How can it be all right?' Turki sobbed.

'It's Allah's will.'

'How can it be that?'

'Because it is. I can't tell you why, but it is,' Maryam replied, just as confused as the boy.

'Is it because of Nader and Uncle Nabeel?'

Maryam didn't answer but held Turki closer.

'Is it because of the baby?'

'What baby?'

'This one,' Turki said placing his hand over her belly.

'You know?' Maryam asked in panic.

Turki nodded. 'Mama and Auntie Hanifah look like you except bigger. I haven't told anyone but Hava.'

'Hava?' Maryam exclaimed and laughed.

'I don't want you to go, Auntie Miri. I love you,' Turki said, throwing his arms around her bruised neck. 'Why do you have to go?'

'It's not safe here for the baby and me, *habibi*.'

'Why, Auntie Miri?'

'Remember what I said. Sometimes things just don't make sense. But I want you to know that I will always love you,' Maryam replied.

'How do you get babies? I never want a baby. I want the baby to go away,' Turki said between sobs.

'Hush, *habibi*. Don't be angry,' Maryam whispered, cradling the boy's head in her hands. 'You've got to be strong for both of us,' she kissed his cheeks. They fell asleep holding each other.

294

FORTY-NINE

Aishah sat beside the bed watching blood drip from the poly-thene bag into a tube. With every drop she felt time was running out as Khadijah's life ebbed away.

Khadijah was sedated with pethidine and the sheet rose and fell gently over her chest. An elastic band pulled over her thinning henna-dyed hair, kept the plastic oxygen mask in place over her nose. Grey-green dots tattooed her forehead, a sign of her Bedouin origin. A red line monitoring her heartbeat danced up and down on a screen beside the bed. It gave off a bleep every second. Aishah didn't feel sorry for the woman who had spent the last thirty years living a lie.

'*Khallas!* Madam,' a voice called from the door announcing the end of the visiting hours. Aishah knew the routine. Since the operation four days ago she had visited Khadijah every day, hoping for some improvement in her condition, but there was none and she had left without exchanging a word.

Mahmoud greeted her in the lobby, his eyebrow raised in silent inquiry. Portraits of King Abdul Aziz and his three sons stared down from the wall keeping a watchful eye on the comings and goings of their subjects.

'*Yellah!*' was all Aishah ever said after these bedside vigils, her voice choked with frustration.

'*Insha'allah, bukarah!*' Mahmoud would say.

'*Insha'allah,*' Aishah would echo from behind her veil.

295

Mahmoud went to fetch the Suburban and Aishah waited on the forecourt admiring the December sunset. The climate was pleasant during the day this time of year but the nights got chilly and occasionally there was frost.

A minibus came round the central fountain and screeched to a halt a short distance away. Aishah watched the staff alight and file past her. Many were Filipinas carrying backpacks with fake designer labels slung over their shoulders.

Aishah couldn't explain her feelings towards these girls: there was empathy but envy too. At the end of their contract they were free to return to their far-off countries, their bags overflowing with clothes and luxuries that they would otherwise have done without. But, for the time being, they were like Mahmoud and herself; trapped in a time capsule. With the passing years Afghanistan became an ever-fading memory. Occasionally, Mahmoud would tell her how things were done back home and she would listen, her eyes would moisten, overcome with the longing for her motherland and the family she never knew.

The last nurse alighted and walked towards Aishah, dragging her left foot. She was an older woman, perhaps in her late forties or early fifties, with dark skin. Aishah noticed the chipped front tooth when the woman smiled and shuffled past. There was something familiar about the sound but she couldn't place it in her mind.

The journey home was always the same, slow and in silence. Mahmoud wondered why Aishah wanted to speak to Khadijah, especially as the two hadn't been on speaking terms for as long as he could remember. The roadblocks were still in place but Farhan had given Mahmoud a special pass and the police waved them through with a smile.

Maryam met them in the hallway. Mahmoud shook his head and frowned at Maryam's raised brow.

'Come, Mama,' Maryam said, taking Aishah's hand. 'I've baked you your favourite cookies.' Aishah managed a smile and followed her to the lounge. Zelpha brought in tea and the cookies and Aishah made herself comfortable on the sofa.

'How is Auntie Khadijah?' Maryam asked.

Aishah stared at the wall, oblivious to her question.

'You haven't eaten for days. Have something.' Maryam offered her mother a cookie and a cup of tea. Aishah pushed them away and wept. 'What is it, Mama, why do you weep so?'

Aishah pressed Maryam's hand to her cheek and whispered, 'I want you to be happy, *habibi*. That is all I ask of Allah.'

Fifty

The road snaked north across the plains of Aqaba and zigzagged up the mountains. Convoys of lorries groaned under their burdens and billowed plumes of sooty black smoke as they navigated the hairpin bends and steep gradients. The taxi zigzagged through them along the Kings Highway to Wadi Musa where Joe had an appointment.

Occasionally they passed wrecks that marked the graves of zealous drivers with a love for speed.

'That very, very bad!' exclaimed the taxi driver in a sombre voice, pointing to what had once been a bus. 'Many little children die,' he continued, snapping his fingers with a quick flick of his wrist to emphasise his point. 'May God have mercy,' he crossed himself and kissed the gold cross that hung around his neck, much to Joe's surprise.

'Greek!' came back the reply to Joe's arched brows. 'Don't worry, we are in God's hands,' reassured the driver folding down the sun visor to reveal an icon of the Virgin Mary holding the infant Jesus. The driver took Joe's nod as a sign of approval, smiled and accelerated. 'In Jordan we are civilized,' he said. 'We have Jews, Muslims and Christians living together like brothers, not like there,' he said, thumbing over his shoulder back towards Saudi Arabia.

'Brothers?' Joe laughed.

'Well, perhaps not quite brothers but at least neighbours.'

The taxi mounted the crest of a hill and the town of Wadi Musa lay before them, nestling in a valley.

Joe had gleaned from the guidebook that it was named after Moses who in his travels had passed this way, struck a rock and caused a spring to gush forth. In recent times another miracle had occurred after the Camp David agreement and the once easygoing town was awash with tourist dollars. Construction was everywhere. Hotels, apartments, restaurants and houses clung to the slopes of the valley like limpets. Scrawny horses and donkeys encouraged by a crack of the whip hurried along, dodging pickups and tooting taxis. Bleating goats crossed the road at a leisurely pace and held up the traffic. Children with runny noses waved at him from the sidewalk and windows. 'Welcome, welcome,' was on everyone's smiling lips.

He couldn't get over seeing women wearing headscarves but no *abaya*. They went about their daily chores unveiled and unescorted. He felt relaxed and thought how different Jordan was from Saudi Arabia only two hundred kilometres away.

Joe found the Jordanians a kind and amiable people, always courteous and ever hospitable. Portraits of their monarch and his brother hung everywhere, like in Saudi Arabia. However, in Jordan, the King was a revered peacemaker who had brought prosperity to the country and understood the Palestinian problem.

'Here we are safe, and sound,' said the driver, and pulled up at the hotel entrance in a cloud of dust. The Royal Garden Hotel was a modest establishment run by two brothers, Yahya and Ishmael, under the watchful eyes of their devoutly Muslim father, Mousa. As its name implied, the hotel was surrounded by a garden that in the summer must have over-flowed with flowers but was barren now in midwinter. But there was nothing royal or regal about the single storey, whitewashed building with its unfinished second floor. The travel agent had waxed lyrically that it was only a hundred yards from the entrance to the ancient city of Petra.

'This good hotel,' the taxi driver volunteered with a reassuring grin. 'You be comfortable here,' he added on seeing the disappointment on Joe's face and escorted him into the hotel before he could change his mind.

Collecting a generous tip from Joe and his commission from the hotel after some haggling, he reversed up the drive beaming. 'I come tomorrow, we go to Little Petra and Shobak,' he called out and gave a departing wave.

Sightseeing was the last thing on Joe's mind.

'If you have a problem, Doc, Abdul Karim is the man,' Abdullah the clerk at the Dental Clinic had said just before he left Tabuk. 'He knows everybody who is anybody.'

So early next day, Joe ventured down town armed with a map, a letter from Abdullah and an address. In the narrow streets a troupe of dishevelled children begged for a dollar.

'Gotchya!' Joe said, grabbing the urchin after his wallet, by the arm.

The others scattered in fits of laughter.

'Let me go, let me go,' screamed the boy and the stall keepers laughed, watching the commotion.

'Serves you right, Mansour,' they cried, wagging their fingers. 'Bolice! Bolice!' they said. Mansour struggled to free himself from Joe's grip.

'Okay, you take me here,' Joe said, squatting to show Mansour the address Abdullah had written in Arabic. 'I'll give you a dinar.'

Mansour studied the paper and smiled 'Too far. One dollar.'

'One dinar,' Joe replied.

'*La, La*, no, no, one dollar.'

'Bolice,' Joe said, waving a finger.

'One dinar okay. Come,' said Mansour, and started up the hill.

On the outskirts of the town they turned off the road and took a path through the olive groves.

'Come,' Mansour beckoned and whistled a tune.

'Here?' Joe asked.

Mansour nodded and pointed ahead, Joe followed. Ten minutes later they cleared the olive grove and Mansour pointed at a sprawling mansion hidden behind a wall.

'One dollar,' Mansour said and Joe placed two dinars in Mansour's hand. They smiled and Mansour ran off skipping through the olive grove in his bare feet.

A young man wearing a *kufiyyah* and with an Uzi at the ready met Joe at the steel door. After the usual formalities he was ushered in without ceremony, frisked and escorted to a building that was more a fortress than a house.

Abdul Karim greeted Joe with open arms, the obligatory 'Welcome!' appeared on his lips and an apology for the theatrics. 'You found us. This is my son, Kasim,' he said patting the young man who had met him at the gate. 'These days, you can't trust anyone but family.'

Abdul Karim was a heavy-set man with a barrel of a chest and rounded shoulders that instantly instilled a sense of security. He was an affable sort with a crushing handshake that sorted out the men from the boys. He smiled easily and spoke in a rumbling voice that gave the impression he had considered every word and weighed it for effect and value. His bulldog neck and pencil-thin moustache, together with his thinning sweptback hair, reminded Joe of Marlon Brando in the *Godfather*. In fact, that was precisely what he was if on a minor scale. Abdul Karim was Mr Fixit in these parts.

He had to be around fifty-five, Joe concluded from what Abdullah had confided to him. He had fought in the '67 war and then served the Sultan of Oman as a bodyguard for a few years before crossing the border to Saudi Arabia to work as an interpreter. Before long he was back in Jordan, running a successful 'export-import' business running contraband across the Saudi border.

The two men sipped mint tea and sampled a few dates seated on Italian sofas that would not have been out of place in Beverly Hills. The signature of wealth was all around them in the form of silk rugs from Iran, marble sculptures from Italy, crystal chandeliers from France and embroidered Arabic calligraphy in gold thread from Egypt. Kasim, his gun cradled in his lap, watched over them from a distance and recharged their cups when empty.

'I have eleven children,' Abdul Karim said, beaming from ear to ear, 'the twelfth one is due any day.'

'*Insha'allah*, it will be a boy,' Joe responded, hoping to please his host.

'*Insha'allah!*' echoed Abdul Karim as a matter of habit. Soon the conversation turned to Abdullah. 'How is that rascal?' Abdul Karim inquired of his old friend who had married his niece. 'Is he still out of prison, that no good son-of-bitch?'

'He's well,' Joe replied and fished out the letter of introduction Abdullah had given him. Under the light of the side lamp, Abdul Karim studied the letter through half-moon spectacles resting low on his hooked nose. In silence he considered the contents, periodically stroking the stubble on his chin. Joe waited. Abdul Karim carried out a protracted ritual with his spectacles before returning them to a pouch that had seen better days. Then he gave Joe a knowing smile and returned the letter.

'So you're a tooth doctor?' asked Abdul Karim. '*Alhamdulillah*, I have all my teeth. But my children, keep me up most nights with toothache.'

'Sweets and soft drinks,' Joe replied.

'Children are only children once,' Abdul Karim said.

'*Alhamdulillah*,' Joe said, and returned the letter to his pocket.

'How can I help?' Abdul Karim asked after a while.

'Where do you want me to start?'

'At the beginning of course,' Abdul Karim suggested and listened to Joe's tale of woe, occasionally nodding or shaking his head – all the while feeding the beads from his *misbaha* through his fingers.

Joe sketched a picture and Abdul Karim didn't ask for details respecting his position. Money was what motivated Abdul

Karim; he had learnt during his time in Oman that having principals and loyalties made for a poorer life. He didn't care who the woman was or why she was fleeing, but he had a fair idea. She wasn't *his* daughter; his honour wasn't at stake. But there was one thing that bothered him and curiosity finally won out. Clearing his throat, he poised the question; 'Why a Saudi?'

It was clear from the question that Abdul Karim was not enamoured by the Saudis. Perhaps it had not been such a good idea to come here.

'Does love have boundaries?' Joe asked.

Abdul Karim frowned. He felt troubled by what he heard. He was a businessman who traded in tangible commodities where he could turn a quick profit, not in fickle human emotions. He chuckled at Joe's question in a feeble attempt to disguise his doubts and responded philosophically, 'Love is mysterious.' He looked up at the ceiling and gestured with open hands. 'It is all in the hands of Allah.'

They talked for a while longer. Abdul Karim skirted around the problem without causing offence. Joe had learned that Arabs often had trouble saying no. Saying no was seen as an admission of failure, a loss of face and so, after much small talk, Abdul Karim began, 'Believe me, Joe, I want to help you,' he patted Joe on the knee, 'but kidnapping is not my business. We leave that to the Yemeni,' he added with a dismissive wave of the hand. He looked squarely at Joe. 'Kidnapping is bad for business. Governments, families, tribes, all get involved when it comes to kidnapping and they make things very difficult for us from all sides. You understand how it is? Business has never been better for us and I want to keep it that way.'

Joe took a deep breath and considered his limited options. This was not going to be as easy as Abdullah had said. He remembered Abdul Karim's firm handshake and knew he was not playing games.

'I don't think you understand, friend,' Joe said, shaking his head.

'If you want my opinion, forget this Saudi woman, she's more trouble than she's worth. I can introduce you to a Palestinian or Lebanese girl, all very beautiful. The Syrians are especially sweet I've heard,' Abdul Karim said, kissing his fingers as if he were talking about fruit.

'I'll do it my way.' Joe said, and got up to leave.

Abdul Karim saw the determination in Joe's eyes. He knew then there was something very important Joe had failed to tell him. If he let this mad *Ameriki* stupid enough to fall in love with a Saudi woman go ahead, his business could suffer. The Saudis would increase their border patrols and replace the guards that were covertly on his pay roll – that would make his life impossible. He would lose face with the others, not to mention the money. As a pragmatist he couldn't see a way out but to help Joe – at a price. A more. . . *permanent* solution came to mind, but that would be a last resort.

He broke the silence with laughter. 'Come! Come! Sit down, my friend!' He beckoned to Joe with a twinkle in his eyes. 'I was only testing your commitment,' he said, trying to bluff his way out of a stalemate. 'Do not be so hasty. Life is too short and we have much talking to do. More tea, Kasim,' he called, clapping his hands. 'Now this is what I will do, doctor. If your woman can make it to the border then I may be able to be of some assistance. That is the best I can do under the circumstances.' He wrung his hands. 'I will even send Kasim with you. He speaks English and knows the tribesmen.' Abdul Karim knew that with his son present he would be very much in charge should things take a turn for the worse.

'How much?' Joe asked.

'I'll do that for ten thousand US dollars in cash, payable in advance.' Abdul Karim chewed his lip.

'Ten thousand?'

'Kidnapping is a risky business.'

'I'll need a passport,' Joe said.

'A passport! My goodness you drive a hard bargain, doctor.'

'No passport, no deal.'

'For genuine documents, I will have to grease many palms. . . you know how it is?' Abdul Karim lit a cigarette.

Joe stared at Abdul Karim through the smoke.

'. . . She will need a birth certificate and an American visa. . . they take months to process. . .'

'We don't have months.' Joe said.

'. . . I know someone. . .' Abdul Karim gestured with his fingers how costly it would be.

'Okay, okay, I get the point.' Joe got up and paced the floor, his face flushed with anger.

Abdul Karim drew long and hard on his cigarette – after a thoughtful pause he exhaled. 'You have to marry her,' he said, in a matter of fact tone.

'Marry?'

'No marriage certificate. . . no visa.'

'How much more will that cost?' Joe asked.

'*Insha'allah*,' ten thousand. . .'

'You're kidding!' Joe shouted

Abdul Karim shrugged.

'You've got me over a fuckin' barrel,' Joe said

'*Alhamdulillah*,' Abdul Karim said and offered his hand – Joe shook it in good faith.

Kasim went to fetch fresh tea, leaving the two men to talk in earnest. They pored over an army map and formulated a plan. Abdul Karim knew the region like the back of his hand. These days, he got others to be his mules and risk their lives. The risks were small but they were always there when dealing with temperamental Bedouins who would skin you alive if they took a dislike to you. They valued guns, camels and sheep more than money or human life and most of all they valued their independence.

Joe knew Abdul Karim was right when he said he should not return to Tabuk but wait at the border for Maryam. It would be too dangerous for them both and, if caught, the price would be their lives. The Saudis would have every reason to label him an Israeli spy and he would disappear without trace with a bullet in his head. Late that evening Joe spoke to Maryam from the public phone in the lobby of the Petra Forum Hotel, Wadi Musa's five-star establishment. He faxed a hand-drawn map that was to guide her to the border and freedom.

FIFTY-ONE

'Never!' hissed Khadijah. 'You can go to hell!' She coughed into a tissue and threw it on the floor.

'Hell is where you belong!' said Aishah.

'I'll see you there! Now get out!' Khadijah yelled, coughing again. This time she didn't bother with the tissue and splattered the sheet with blood. Khadijah could feel the end was near – the womb that had denied her a son was going to rob her of life.

'You're the daughter of a bitch!'

'Your mother was a pig!' countered Aishah, jumping to her feet.

'Your son's a faggot!' snarled Khadijah, purple with rage.

'That's a lie! Damn your dead ancestors!'

Having heard the commotion, the duty nurse burst into the room.

'Madam is very ill, you must go now!' she ordered, pointing to the door.

'I'm not going anywhere.' Aishah stuffed a hundred riyal note into the nurse's hand and shooed her out. She realised that a woman who had denied the truth for so long wasn't going to be hectored into a deathbed confession. There had to be another way. The women glared at each other, hatred smouldering in their eyes.

'Leave me in peace,' Khadijah muttered and rolled over to face the wall.

'Talal won't divorce you. He loves you. . .' Aishah began, and sat down.

'If he loved me, why is he in the Philippines?' snapped Khadijah.

'He's there on business,' Aishah said.

'Business? Business? Yes, he's on business all right! He's probably doing business with a whore right now.'

Though anger still consumed Aishah, she knew shouting wouldn't get her very far.

'Do it for yourself,' Aishah urged softly. 'Allah is all-forgiving and merciful. He understands you. It's *haram* for a brother to marry his sister, the *Qur'an* strictly forbids it. . . it is an abomination.'

Indecision crossed Khadijah's face. She turned to face Aishah and nodded. Aishah saw a glimmer of hope. It was the Arab way to shout and gesticulate but when the anger was spent, there was always room for compromise.

'Khadijah, only you can stop this marriage or your soul will be damned forever.'

Through bloodshot eyes the Bedouin woman glared. She knew Aishah was right. 'I'm tired,' Khadijah said, and gave a dismissive wave.

Aishah pursed her lips and held her tongue.

'*Bukarah Insha'allah*,' Khadijah said and coughed more blood onto the sheet. She offered her hand and Aishah grabbed it like a lifeline.

'*Insha'allah*,' Aishah sighed. It had taken cancer to break Khadijah's Bedouin spirit at the eleventh hour and tomorrow there would be a new beginning.

* * *

At eight the next morning the telephone rang.

'Mama is dead! Mama is dead!' Mona sobbed from the receiver into Aishah's ear. The phone froze in Aishah's hand and

308

her mind went numb. Mona continued to weep but her cries went unheard. When realisation came, Aishah's first thoughts were that Khadijah had deceived her; she'd *known* she wouldn't last the night. She had triumphed and was laughing at her this very moment. She let out a howl bringing everyone rushing to her side. She lay on the floor beating her chest, tearing at her hair, rolling her eyes and foaming at the mouth.

'She is dead! She is dead!' she screamed between bouts of wailing. 'She deceived me! The bitch deceived me. She stole my baby!' No one understood what Aishah was saying. Zelpha dashed to the kitchen to fetch some water and Maryam picked up the phone from the floor. Hanifah fanned a copy of a fashion magazine over Aishah's face and released her scarf. Mahmoud rushed in from the garden where he had been planting new bulbs for the next season, his hands covered in dirt.

'What happened?' he asked, and they all shook their heads.

Maryam and Mahmoud took Aishah to the Al Nasser private clinic on Medinah Road where Dr Khan, a young Pakistani doctor, prescribed some sedatives and plenty of rest.

'She's got PTSS,' he said. Dr Khan liked to abbreviate sentences and words, it made him feel important when people asked what they meant. He had seen more cases of PTSS in his six months in Saudi Arabia than in the five years since his graduation from Islamabad Medical School. He could tell from Mahmoud's blank face that PTSS meant nothing.

'What does that mean?' Maryam asked tersely in English, irritated by his arrogance.

The question took the doctor by surprise, 'Nervous exhaustion and shock,' he said. 'It'll pass,' he assured them. 'Plenty of rest.'

* * *

Mona and her sisters prepared their mother's body according to Islamic customs, washing it five times with a solution of camphor and sprinkling herbs and flowers between the layers of the shroud. They wept, not so much because they had lost their mother but because so much had remained unsaid and now there were no more tomorrows. *Insha'allah bukarah* had come to haunt them as well.

Wrapped in white linen, Nader, Farhan, Mahmoud and a few of Khadijah's male relatives took her body in the back of a truck along the Jordan Road to the graveyard on the outskirts of the city. In the old days they would have carried the body but now those days were long gone.

Mona and her sisters could not go as this was a man's duty. They remained at home consoled by Maryam, Hanifah and a few relatives. They tried not to weep. Khadijah was now with Allah and it was time to rejoice.

According to Muslim tradition, Khadijah was buried before sunset. She was placed lying on her right facing Mecca, covered by the dust from which she came. Nader placed a rock to mark the site but that would soon be covered by the shifting sands and Khadijah would be a memory lodged in the consciousness of a few that would fade with time. That was the Arab way, the lore of the desert was harsh, like the unforgiving sun that scorched the earth. Only the tough survived, and not for long.

FIFTY-TWO

Maryam combed her fingers through Turki's hair as he lay asleep beside her. 'I want you to be strong like your father,' she whispered. 'Remember women are your equals. Treat them like sisters, with dignity, and help nurture their dreams.' Maryam paused as emotion welled in her. 'Forgive those who cross you,' she muttered. 'And let the word of Allah guide you.' Her hand trembled. 'I want to tell you so much, *habibi*, but for now I want to ask that you don't judge me for leaving you. I will always love you.' She was unable to control her tears anymore. She kissed the boy's head for the last time.

Her heart pumped with excitement and fear. Her watch said it was midnight. From now on, every minute counted. The further she could go tonight the more likely she would succeed. It would be Saturday before anyone would notice the missing pickup, but she had only eight hours before dawn when Turki would find her gone.

She slipped into the *thobe* purchased from the same tailor that made Turki's *thobe*. It was a size too small and tight around her bosom but the length was right. She fumbled with her hair, plaiting it into a ponytail and slipped it under the collar to keep it out of sight. She tried to coax her swollen feet into the black canvas shoes she had bought a month earlier.

In frustration, she removed the laces and wiggled her toes. This time they slipped in but pinched when she walked. There was only one solution: with scissors from her manicure set she cut slits along the sides and punched the air when her feet slid in without pain. Where there was a will there was a way, she told herself, and a little thing like this wasn't going to stop her.

Turki was fast asleep cuddled up in bed, his thumb in his mouth. He had been running a fever for the past few days but the cough syrup the doctor prescribed had worked wonders.

Maryam felt a lump in her throat. They had become inseparable, supporting each other in their own way. She wished she could take him but that would put his life at risk. He was like his father and would know there had to be a good reason for her to leave.

Maryam slipped on her *abaya* and caught a whiff of the roast chicken she had bought for the journey. At the door she looked back at Turki. Suddenly riddled with guilt she whispered, 'Forgive me. One day, *Insha'allah*, you'll understand.'

With shoes in hand and her bag over her shoulder she crept down the stairs in the dark guided by the banister. At the bottom she stopped and listened. There was no sound.

Moonlight streamed through the kitchen windows throwing rectangles of light across the floor. As a child Maryam found there was something very soothing and enchanting about moonlight. But now it compressed the spectrum into greys, absent of the colours that gave life meaning. At the journey's end they would seep back into her world, giving it purpose and direction.

The full moon slowly rolled across the Arabian sky while clouds raced past like wild stallions. Maryam took a deep breath of winter air. She gazed at the twinkling stars and smiled at the sight of *Shiaara* that Turki had confused with the comet.

Zaki was waiting for her at the back door wagging his tail. Maryam threw him a few morsels of food and watched him devour them. Theirs was an odd kind of relationship where mutual respect overrode fear and distrust. But there was always a distance between them and Maryam never attempted to close it.

With Zaki beside her, Maryam made for the gatehouse at the far end of the compound, taking refuge in the shadows. The night air hummed to an orchestra of a thousand crickets broadcasting their symphony of love. Clouds of bats winged across the face of the moon in search of prey and moths danced around the incandescent bulbs, courting a sizzling death. Squadrons of mosquitoes swarmed overhead and the date palms and grapevines were alive with an army of ants. Scarab beetles crawled out from their burrows to party until the early hours.

As Maryam neared the gatehouse, she could hear a music from the radio: a woman singing of the virtues of her lover to the accompaniment of drums and a flute.

She had tried to escape a week earlier but found Basheer dozing in the gatehouse, his feet on the table. The next day she learned that Basheer had abandoned his tryst with Zelpha in disgust when he discovered she was having her period.

Tonight the door was open and the gatehouse deserted. Basheer had left the radio on to give would-be intruders the impression he was around. She listened for footsteps on the gravel path but heard nothing and raced into the gatehouse, making for the cupboard on the wall where the keys were kept.

They all looked the same. Some were shiny while others looked worn with the brass showing through the chrome. Some had *Nissan* embossed on them; others *Toyota*. She opted for a *Nissan* key that looked new and prayed.

Zaki watched her, cocking his head from side to side. Maryam tried the metal bolt of the gate; it squeaked and came free with a clang, making the gate vibrate like a steel drum. She swung the gate open to reveal the moonlit desert beyond. Zaki barked quietly as if to say *well done* and stuck his nose through the opening, sniffing for adventure. Maryam looked around to see if anyone had heard the commotion, but there was only silence. She shut the gate behind her and prayed Basheer wouldn't notice it unbolted until the morning.

The vehicles were parked beside the wall. The door of the

nearest Nissan truck was unlocked. She jumped in and tried the key. It refused to turn. She rotated it and tried again but nothing happened. She attempted one Nissan truck after another without success. She approached the last vehicle in the line, her heart pounding like the boiler room of an ocean liner.

'This has to be it,' she murmured. The engine came to life. '*Alhamdulillah!*'

The moon hid behind a passing cloud and crisp shadows merged into a uniform grey. Maryam manoeuvred the truck around potholes and boulders not daring to turn on the lights. In the distance she could make out the headlights of cars cutting their way through the darkness on Medinah Road.

The lights of the compound and the world that had been hers for twenty years slipped by like a ship on the high seas. Every turn of the wheels took her further away from her beloved family and her darling Turki. Tears streamed down her cheeks at the thought of never seeing them again. Behind her lay all her worldly possessions. She took with her only memories of the past and dreams of the future.

She saw Zaki's head in the rearview mirror and screamed. He was panting and each breath left a patch of condensation on the window. Maryam slammed on the brakes, flung open the door and ordered him out. Zaki cocked his head and frowned.

'Get down,' Maryam hissed, pointing to the ground and Zaki lay down on the floor of the truck. 'Get out now!' Maryam implored, but Zaki remained defiant. Maryam had never touched the animal before but she reached nervously for his collar and tugged. 'Come on, Zaki, get down.' Zaki licked her hand. Maryam recoiled in horror and shrieked. The dog didn't move. Maryam looked into his brown eyes and felt ashamed; he was also Allah's creation. She patted his head without fear, remembering the story of Androcles and the lion and climbed back into the cabin.

Dust danced in the beams of the headlights when she switched them on. She approached the ramp leading on to Medinah Road and eased the truck into second gear. The engine stalled. She hit the clutch and the truck rolled back down the ramp out of control.

'Shit!' Maryam slammed the brakes. The truck jolted to a halt. Zaki leaped to his feet and barked. Quickly Maryam turned on the ignition, gave plenty of gas and released the clutch. The truck shot up the ramp like a sprinter bursting from the blocks and lurched on to the road before coming to a halt on the verge.

'Phew! That was close,' Maryam exclaimed. She threw off her *abaya* and donned the checked *gutra*, adjusting the *agal* using the rearview mirror. She laughed at the beardless face that stared back and pulled the corners of the *gutra* over her chest to hide her bosom. Zaki watched through the rear window with interest.

Maryam spotted a pair of taillights speeding away, otherwise Medinah Road was a plain black ribbon that stretched ahead. The lights of Tabuk stretched across the horizon, and above them the comet streaked through the heavens.

Tiny lights bobbed along the wayside. They were the eyes of desert rats like the one Sultan had kept as a pet – until Uncle Mahmoud found had out and set it free.

Feeling more confident, Maryam eased into third gear and then into fourth watching the speedometer creep up and hover at forty-five. With every passing kilometre she felt the tension double in the small of her back.

She passed a compound hidden behind a high wall surrounded by concert blocks the size of cars to prevent suicide bombers. The military police kept watch, armed with submachine guns and looked very imposing in their khaki uniforms and red berets. Since the latest bombings the Americans had moved there from the city where they could be protected.

Flashing billboards adorned by fairy lights and advertising Turkish restaurants slipped by, then a mosque – little more then a tin shack with white walls and green roof crowned by the crescent moon. Batteries of auto workshops, a hive of activity during the day, stood silent. Cement factories, auto showrooms, builder's merchants all rubbed shoulders along Medinah Road with farms and agricultural enterprises.

A sign warned of a checkpoint. Maryam saw the white oil drums in the middle of the road and her heart quickened. She glanced at her watch; it was one thirty in the morning. As she slowed, she made out three men in khaki uniforms sitting cross-legged on a threadbare carpet playing cards next to a wood fire. Their teacups glowed amber in the light of the dancing flames and food debris lay scattered around them, attracting ants. A *shisha* pipe gurgled. The men cast an annoying glance in her direction.

'Mustapha, it's your turn,' a voice called out. A portly man grunted and heaved himself up. Maryam adjusted the *gutra* to shield her face and held her breath. The man ambled towards her, cleared his throat and spat.

He spotted Zaki and froze. A tense moment passed. Zaki snarled.

'*Yellah, Ro! R*o – Go! Go!' shouted Mustapha and waved them through. Maryam hit the gas pedal and accelerated away.

'Bloody Bedouins and their mongrels!' Mustapha cursed, and rejoined his pals.

'Well done, Zaki!' Maryam called over her shoulder and relaxed a little. With Zaki there she didn't feel alone or vulnerable anymore. Without warning the truck rattled, the glove compartment sprung open and a torch fell out.

'Shit!' Maryam gripped the wheel. Then two more speed bumps followed, marking the end of the highway.

Maryam navigated the traffic island topped by the giant crown. As she took the exit marked *Jordan and North* she noticed the walls of the Sahara Hotel draped in purple bougainvillea. She thought of Joe and smiled. The hotel would always hold a special place in her heart.

The road swept past the city dump and headed north towards the industrial sector of Tabuk. A construction site gave way to desert peppered with picnic areas, each with a bright canopy, swing, spring-mounted horse and merry-go-round. On the horizon, Maryam made out the silhouette of two monolithic hands ten stories high, sitting on a table of grass the size of a dozen football fields. Nader had called them 'the begging hands of the Al Sauds in one of his sarcastic moods.

From the avenue of date palms and acacia, Maryam recognised the three-lane highway they had often taken to Haql. This was the Jordan road that passed the vast Saudi ARAMCO complex. Squat white buildings with flat roofs looked like matchboxes besides the petroleum tanks. Black and yellow curb stones lined miles of road and barbed-wire fencing ensured everyone knew this was a security zone.

A few kilometres down the road, a giant clam-like structure materialised into a football stadium, a monument to the country's obsession with the game. The moonlight bounced off the orange seats that were the sole preserve of men. Sultan had represented his squadron on the field but she had not been allowed to watch; the *mutaween* had declared it unhealthy for women and therefore *haram*.

The truck bobbed like a boat over islands of sand left behind in the last sandstorm. It was the season of fierce winds that whipped up the sand into trillions of missiles that frosted windows, blasted the paint off cars and choked the air-conditioning.

In the wing mirror Maryam saw the city lights shrink as a triangular tower with a roof that looked like a three-cornered hat appeared in front. A complex of Mediterranean-styled houses, each with its own patio and balcony all in chocolate brown, loomed ahead. Sultan had told her this was where the boys from the 'dirty brigade' – the Ministry of the Interior – lived; away from the rest of the world, with their own supermarket, medical centre and countless mosques.

Maryam approached a small roundabout and five interlacing arches that cut the heavens into neat crescents. These were the city gates. The sign, her sign, blazed magically across the sky framed by the central arch like a photograph and Maryam knew she was headed in the right direction.

For Jordan.

The road shrunk to a single lane and deteriorated into a series of cracked asphalt. A mock castle the size of a house, with a string of fairy lights laced around the battlements and turrets, stood between her and the open road.

She crawled towards it, looking out for the guard, and spied him sleeping on a mattress as she cleared the last set of drums. Now only seventy-five kilometres separated her from Joe and freedom.

The road opened up again into a three-lane highway meandering past farms and tin shacks like a silent river. The odd mosque and gas stations surrounded by the mangled remains of cars and trucks slipped by, replaced by a wall of darkness. A three-metre-tall carton of milk stood at the entrance to the Al Hemidi farm that supplied Tabuk with dairy produce. Impatient cars tooted and sped by, exceeding the speed limit. Maryam's destination drew closer and the reality of her freedom crystallized in her mind. According to Joe's map she would soon pass ASTRA farms and the halfway mark.

A sudden flash of light flooded the cabin through the rear window. Zaki barked a warning. Seconds later a mammoth SAPTCO coach roared past and cut in front of her. She now understood why there were so many deaths on Saudi roads.

At the gates of ASTRA farm, a lorry crammed with sheep gave a penetrating blast and mounted the road leaving a cloud of dust. Her father had told her ASTRA farm had grown fat supplying rations to the armed forces during the Gulf War.

The road narrowed to single lane through the village of Bir ibn Hirmas at the crossroads of the Jordan Road and Haql Road. Maryam could make out mountains of rusting cars contorted beyond recognition, each twisted piece hiding a macabre tale of sudden and violent death. Camels with an air of superiority shared their pen with goats, sheep and donkeys.

Bir ibn Hirmas had grown around the Hijaz railroad that cut through the village, but when the railroad closed, the village somehow lost the will to live. A fleet of white Land Cruisers, with a distinctive green band and a comb of red, blue and yellow lights, stood like horses parked under the eucalyptus trees outside a police station bristling with antennae.

Maryam passed the village gas station set back from the road. Following Joe's instructions she reset the odometer to zero. Cables stretched between pylons measured her progress. As the odometer clicked to ten, she spotted the solar-powered telephone, marked 008 on the map, and pulled up beside it. She picked up the torch that had fallen on the floor and climbed out of the Nissan.

'The numbers have to be here somewhere,' she muttered to herself and found them in the shadow of the solar panel.

'*Alhamdulillah*,' she declared, and got back into the truck.

Following the map Maryam turned off the paved road and trundled along the dirt track. Her heart pounded, knowing the border was only twenty kilometres away. She had barely covered fifty metres when the truck shuddered to a halt. The engine groaned and died.

'Shit!' Maryam screamed and stamped her feet. She turned on the ignition and slammed down the gas pedal. The rear wheels spun and threw up a plume of sand, covering Zaki, but the truck didn't budge.

A car heading for the border, piled high with belongings and crammed with Egyptians shouting abuse at Saudi Arabia, slunk past. Maryam realised she had to get away before someone stopped to help – or until dawn put in an appearance.

She searched in the back for a shovel but found none. There was no way out but to dig with her bare hands. Zaki watched Maryam for a moment cocking his head one way, then another. Maryam scooped out a handful of sand but more would fall.

'It's no use,' Maryam muttered. Zaki came to her rescue

wagging his tail. They laboured together and within minutes both wheels seemed to be free.

'We've done it, Zaki!' Maryam said. She jumped into the cabin and started the engine, but still the truck refused to move.

'*Shaitaan!*' Maryam cursed and punched the steering wheel. The truck's horn blared like a foghorn, piercing the night.

'Stupid piece of junk. A donkey could do better,' she said turning off the engine. She flopped back into the seat and tried to recall how Sultan and Khalid freed themselves from the sand. She could see them now, their muscular bodies, *thobes* gathered around their waist, rocking the truck, pushing sand under the wheel with their feet. Inspired, she rushed out and followed their example pushing with all her might, but the truck remained steadfast.

'You're doing this because I'm a woman,' Maryam gasped and lent against the truck, physically and emotionally drained. Zaki cocked his head, lay down at her feet and made a low growling sound as if voicing sympathy.

Her baby kicked, reminding her she was not alone, as if she needed reminding. She was in this wilderness breaking every law in Saudi Arabia for the safety of her baby and her love for Joe. Every kilometre towards the border would take her further away from her doom and bring her closer to the man she loved.

FIFTY-THREE

A faint glow in the east warned Maryam her dawn was near and time was running out. She risked discovery, stranded so close to the road, and almost certain death if she remained.

Under the glow of the courtesy light above her head, a cloud of sand flies performed their ritual dance. Maryam focused on the map Joe had faxed from Jordan late one night while the rest of the house had slept. She had pored over it in the sanctuary of the toilet with the thrill of a girl reading a love letter. Later she had hidden it in the holy *Qur'an* where no one would have dreamt of looking.

She followed a black line across the folds of the paper, as barren as the landscape outside. According to the map, she was only a few kilometres away from the village of Zat al Hajj on the old railway line.

In the distance under the moonlight Maryam could make out the silhouette of houses and the block of blackness that was the fortress. 'That must be Zat al Hajj,' she muttered to herself. Beyond it lay freedom and Joe. The thought of Joe brought a smile to her lips, filling her with determination and purpose. She called out to Zaki, grabbed her bag and slammed the door in disgust.

The dirt track still stretched ahead, disappearing into the darkness. Zaki returned from another wild foray away from the path, basking in his freedom. Maryam looked over her shoulder one last time at the distant pickup truck, trapped like a horse in quicksand.

Her bag grew heavier with every step, forcing her to rest. She wondered if she was carrying the burden of her crime and the guilt of thousands of women who had sinned before her. Zaki stopped and waited, looking back at her and whining as if to convey the urgency. As they drew closer, individual trees materialised from a forest of palms and, in the distance, a shape grew to dominate the squat buildings of Zat al Hajj.

'That must be the Turkish fortress Joe drew on the map,' Maryam told Zaki. She drew comfort from the streak of light beyond the village and felt that each step she took was a step in the right direction. Suddenly Zaki froze and stared into the night. He sniffed the air and twitched his tail.

'What is it?' Maryam whispered, suddenly fearful. Zaki cocked his ears from side to side and snarled. Somewhere in the darkness, danger lurked. Maryam hurried behind the dog, trying not to make a sound.

They were a hundred metres from the village and the fortress when she saw them over on the rise. Framed against the bleached sand, a pack of wild dogs came bounding towards them. With every leap, a cloud of sand vaulted into the air like puffs of smoke. Zaki barked and urged Maryam to run.

The end would be slow as flesh was torn off their bones by merciless fangs. They would rip out her child from her womb and fight over it like a rag doll. The thought sent a shiver through Maryam and spurred her towards the sanctuary of the buidings. The bag was slowing her down and so she threw it over the wall of the first derelict shack she passed on the outskirts of the village.

Rounding a turret, Maryam saw an archway and ran to it. Once inside, she knew she would be safe. She drew closer and saw a wall of bricks where once there had been an entrance. Her heart sank.

Zaki barked and scurried towards another tower, which had

once served as a water tank fuelling steam engines. At the base there was a crude wooden door. Frantically, Maryam laboured with the rusty bolt until it shot back and she tumbled into darkness. She slammed the door behind her and waited for the attack. The pack circled the tower, howling.

Inside, the stench of dung mixed with straw assaulted her nostrils and bleating of goats competed with the yelping of the curs outside. Through the slats Maryam saw the pack leader approaching and braced herself against the door. Standing on his hind legs the beast clawed at the wood, driving fear into her heart and sending the goats cowering to the far end of the room.

The beast's breath made her retch and his bark jarred her nerves and left her ears ringing. She stared into the beast's eyes and saw evil in the empty blackness. She screamed. He was a muscular beast unlike the Saudi saluki. His huge head bore the scars of many battles and his rubbery black lips glistened in the moonlight, dripping with saliva.

They glared at each other only a hand's breadth apart. The nightmares she experienced soon after discovering her pregnancy had come true. Pushing against the door her arms ached and knees felt weak. He could smell her fear, the door gave a little and the beast knew victory was in sight. Maryam grabbed the disc around her neck without knowing why.

There was a flash and a bang and suddenly the pressure against the door was gone. Maryam heard voices and saw two men carrying guns and a lantern. Seeing them, the hounds scurried off into the darkness.

Maryam held her breath and watched the men through the slats. They were in their twenties, Maryam surmised from their lean bodies and boyish bravado.

'We must hunt down these hounds before we lose our goats,' shouted one and the other grunted in agreement. 'Where's Hassan, that lazy son of a bitch?'

'We gave him a job and this is how he repays us,' complained the second man.

'Can't trust the Sudanese. Remember the motherfuckers backed Saddam.'

'That black bastard must go,' declared the second man in a voice that strangely lacked conviction. Perhaps he knew without Hassan they would end up having to do all the dirty work.

Maryam listened to them cursing Hassan in the way only Arab men know how. Insulting first his mother and then his sisters, calling them names of animals in the crudest fashion.

'They fuck like animals, those black whores,' said the first man, gesturing with his hands and hips. He flicked a plastic lighter into life and drew hard on what looked like a cigarette until the end glowed.

The men held hands and shared the cigarette between bursts of conversation interspersed with laughter. The smoke wafted through the slats and evoked memories of the day she had happened upon Nabeel and Nader in the vineyard. They had turned on her like wild animals and admonished her for straying from the house. Funny how smells could resurrect memories, she thought to herself. How could she forget that day? It was the day the sun had streamed through her clouds of doubt and she had decided to confront the hypocrisy of the culture in which she was trapped.

'Strong stuff!' The man drew one last time and sent the stub spiralling into the night with a practiced flick of the finger.

'Yeah! Found it in Hassan's room.'

'Does he know?' The question hung in the air for a moment awaiting a reply.

'He loves his head too much to complain.' They giggled like schoolboys.

Maryam's heart pounded in her ears and she was sure the men outside could hear it too. What if they decided to enter? What would be her fate? Maryam squeezed the disc in her hand and shut her eyes tightly.

'Let's go,' said a man and lit another cigarette. 'The fucking dogs won't be back.'

'*Insha'allah*,' replied his friend, and made towards the door. 'I'll just check the. . .' A bark stopped him in his tracks. Maryam recognised it at once. Zaki was alive and had been watching over her. The men spun around and gripped their guns.

'Let's get one of them!'

'Yes! We'll hang him from the tower with his guts hanging out as a warning to the others.'

* * *

Moonlight streamed into the tower through a window high above the ground and spread a rectangle of light on the straw-covered floor. Recognizable shapes emerged. A dozen goats stared at her while munching away at the straw. A rusting fire-place bolted to the wall sent a conical chimney into the darkness above.

Thirst and fatigue surfaced. The chamber spun about her, the walls rocked on their foundation and then there was stillness. She slipped to the floor and drifted into sleep, huddled against the door.

* * *

The call to the faithful entered Maryam's subconscious. The first rays of sunlight streaked across the rose-tinted sky and over the derelict village. The stone floor felt cold and uncomfortable against her stiff thighs. The *agal* was on the ground beside her like the halo from a fallen angel. She lay there looking up at the underside of two rusty tanks blackened by soot. Like Tibetan monasteries hanging to a cliff face, colonies of hornet's nests clung to the archway that divided the building. Behind the chimney a crude ladder made of giant staples fixed to the wall led to a triangle of sky in the ceiling. A few stars were still out but soon they too would be gone, driven off by the sun as it rode across the heavens.

Thirst gripped her by the throat and hunger grumbled in her belly. Wide-eyed goats crowded round her, pushing and shoving like children. Their ballooning udders beckoned to her. If only she had a bowl, she could quench her thirst, she told herself.

A chorus of '*Allah-hu akbar*' brought the *Fajr* prayer to a close. Maryam watched a handful of men collect their *ship ship* and disperse. The mosque was only a few years old and looked out of place among the decaying buildings.

Perhaps now was the time to retrieve her bag and leave while the village slept. There she had water and food together with a wad of money and jewellery in case she had to buy her way out of trouble. She hadn't heard any shots, so was Zaki safe? Perhaps he was watching over her this very moment and that thought pleased her.

Maryam pulled herself up using the door for support. Her whole body ached. The baby kicked as if to remind her of its existence. *The child must live.* Sultan's words echoed in her head even now when all she wanted was food and water.

A movement caught her eye through the slats. A statuesque man came towards her carrying a vessel. His turbaned head and youthful face reflected the morning light. This must be Hassan, the Sudanese herdsman the men had cursed in the night. He whistled a stange melody presumably from his beloved Sudan. Panic gripped her. The only way out was up the ladder and she scrambled up it to the opening in the ceiling. Hassan entered the tower and stopped whistling, surprised to find the door open. Maryam froze and gripped on to the metal rung until her knuckles turned white.

Hassan made clicking sounds from the side of his mouth and the goats gathered around him bleating their own greeting. It was as if they told him of their ordeal and about the stranger who spent the night with them. Hassan began to work, coaxing the milk from the udders with a rhythmic motion. Maryam looked down at the inviting milk and almost lost her footing. The metal rung dug into the soles of her feet causing her pain. It was getting lighter and soon her *thobe* would stand out against the dark walls.

'*Ya*, Hassan!' called an angry voice.

'*Nam!*' Hassan replied.

'*Tal henna!* Come here!' As Hassan made for the door, Maryam recognised the voices from the night.

'Where were you last night, nigger, when the dogs came?' goaded one of them. Before Hassan could reply the other waded in.

'We lost two goats,' he said, lying.

'You'll pay for them from your wages,' added the first man.

Maryam looked down at the bowl of milk and climbed down; she didn't care if she was discovered. The warm milk rushed down her throat like a mountain spring, some of it splashed over her chest and soaked into her *thobe*. Nothing mattered so long as the void in her stomach was filled.

She wiped her face with her sleeve and climbed onto the terrace, keeping low and out of sight. She heard Hassan apologise for a crime he hadn't committed.

'It won't happen again, I swear on my father's grave.'

The men accepted his utterance. That was the Saudi way, where a man's feelings were kept in check lest they be misconstrued as a sign of weakness.

'*Yellah!* Go back to your work,' ordered the first man.

'May our Allah have mercy on you!' added the second and Maryam heard them shuffle away. Their parting words tore at Maryam's conscience. To her, all Muslims were equal in the eyes of Allah.

Downcast and defeated, Hassan returned to his goats, a broken man. He wanted to leave this cursed land that very moment but he needed the job to feed his family back home. He could see their happy faces waving at him by the runway. He carried their hopes and aspirations and this job was to be the beginning of a new and better life for them all. He came also to perform *Haj* for himself as willed in the Holy *Qur'an* and for his

327

parents and the village elders who were too poor and frail to travel. In a way he was their saviour, their path to salvation. So they had scraped together some money to send him to the Holy Land to pray for them at the Great Mosque in the shadows of the Al Kaaba. They looked upon the Saudis as a virtuous people, but that illusion was shattered for Hassan at Jeddah airport where he and other workers were herded like animals. It dawned on him he was just another slave tolerated in the name of Islam.

A tear saturated with hatred fell from his cheek onto the holy soil of Arabia. In his anger, he didn't notice the empty bowl but immersed himself in his chores, thinking of his family back home in his war-torn country. They were the real victims, and he swore one day he would have his revenge.

FIFTY-FOUR

At night Khadijah's face came to haunt Aishah, spitting blood onto her face. She would sit up in bed burning with fever. Some nights the nightmares would return from the deep past. She would hear a baby cry and see saucer-shaped lights and smell the antiseptic. Sometimes she would hear a woman's voice call out, '*Waled!* Boy, Madam! *Waled! Alhamdulillah*,' in a foreign accent and then there was darkness and a wall of silence. Occasionally she would hear angry voices that she didn't understand and then there was the sound of shuffling, a peculiar sound like foot dragging, that grew faint until it was no more and the crying of the baby died with it.

Khadijah's face would return to torment her with demonic laughter that penetrated her skull and bounced off the walls, echoing forever.

'*Bukarah, insha'allah. Bukarah, insha'allah.* Ha ha ha!'

The medication dulled the senses. Sounds and voices became telescoped and distorted. Days and weeks rolled together. Aishah lost her appetite and grew weak. That depressed her even more. Outside, the state of emergency was at Level Red and Farhan spent most of his time on the military cantonment. The doctors didn't know what to do but kept reassuring the family that all would be well in the end. Post-traumatic shock syndrome they called it and dismissed it at that: 'happens when there has been a death in the family or of a close friend.' Mahmoud wasn't impressed by their diagnoses. Khadijah was neither family nor friend and decided it was time Aishah was open with him.

'Aishah! Aishah!' Mahmoud called and shook her by her shoulder. Aishah lay on the sofa with her feet tucked under her dress. The television flickered in her glazed eyes but registered no emotion.

Warped by drugs, her name sought recognition in her subconscious. A blank expression hung on her face like an empty canvas.

'What is it?' she inquired after a while, her speech slurred.

'We must talk,' Mahmoud said.

'Talk? About what?' she asked like a child.

'Khadijah.'

'Who?' Aishah asked.

Mahmoud shook his head in despair. 'Khadijah? Nader's mother! Aishah, Aishah!' Mahmoud muttered something in Pashtu.

Aishah suddenly sat upright and shrieked. Her face paled and her eyes bulged in their sockets as if she had seen a ghost. She gasped for breath and shook her hands.

'She's back, she's here,' Aishah screamed.

'Who?' Mahmoud frowned.

'Her! I swear it was she.'

'Aishah, she's dead.'

'I swear upon our mother's grave, she's alive,' Aishah cried.

'You're not well, Aishah. Don't bring our mother into this.'

Aishah sobbed and hung onto Mahmoud's arm. 'I saw the woman who stole my baby!' she mumbled. 'The one who took my boy! She's here in Tabuk.'

'Which boy?' shouted Mahmoud.

'My boy! The boy who died. . . I mean. . .'

'It was a girl! I bathed her myself,' Mahmoud replied.

'No! No! It was a boy. I swear upon the Holy Book it was a boy. And she took him away! Don't you remember that night?'

Mahmoud nodded and muttered something under his breath,

remembering all too well. How could he forget the night they almost lost Aishah?

'I was conscious when I gave birth. They had given me this injection in my back to kill the pain. The midwife showed me the baby all covered in blood and I remember her saying, 'It's a boy, Madam! It's a boy!' To this day I can see his little face and hear his cry.'

'What are you saying?' Mahmoud asked

'I must have passed out but a few days later, when I awoke, they told me my baby had died.'

'Yes. Farhan and I buried the child,' Mahmoud said.

'I questioned them,' Aishah continued, 'but they said they knew nothing and the midwife was never seen again.'

'And this woman is back?' Mahmoud asked

Aishah nodded vigorously.

'How do you know?'

'I didn't recognise her at first but I knew there was something very familiar about her face and the way she walked. She is older now but when you called her name, it all came back.'

'I called her name?'

'When you called my name, it sounded like hers.'

'What do you mean it sounded like hers?' Mahmoud demanded, throwing his arms in the air. 'What's her name?'

'Asha, I think.'

'How can you be sure? It was thirty years ago.'

'I remember she said it meant hope or something like that.'

Mahmoud's analytical mind understood everything. The names were so similar they could easily be distorted by a mind warped by drugs.

'I must talk to Farhan at once,' Mahmoud said.

'Wait! First we must confront the woman. Only her testimony will convince him. He avoids me these days, thinks I'm mad.'

'I know,' Mahmoud murmured brushing his moustache with the back of his hand. He too had noticed the change in Farhan since the bombing and Hanifah's conversion. They didn't talk as they used to. 'You should've spoken to me. . . I would've listened.'

'I had no proof. Khadijah wasn't going to confess, fearing divorce, and the midwife had fled the country.'

'What's Khadijah got to do with this?' Mahmoud asked, raising his voice.

'Don't you see? It was Khadijah's child you buried. . . the girl.'

'And you want me to believe Khadijah took your. . .' The words choked in Mahmoud's throat. 'This is too fantastic. . .'

'She stole my son. . . she stole my son!' Aishah sobbed.

Mahmoud couldn't believe his ears and shook his head. 'You're possessed by a *Jinn*!'

'She was desperate for a son.'

'Khadijah was your friend.'

'A boy meant more to her. He saved her marriage.'

'May Allah have mercy!' Mahmoud exclaimed. 'So Nader's. . . ?'

'He's my baby!' Aishah declared. 'He has my eyes. You've said that yourself many times.'

Mahmoud clasped his head in his hands and shook in disbelief.

'You believe me, don't you? I beg of you,' Aishah pleaded. Mahmoud remained silent.

'Do you know what you're saying?' Mahmoud asked after a while.

'May Allah strike me dead if I've lied!' Aishah replied.

Mahmoud nodded, placed a reassuring hand on his sister's shoulder and walked out.

*　*　*

Mahmoud lay awake in bed as night dragged her feet. The events of the past few days rushed through his brain like a rollercoaster. Just as he was beginning to understand everything, another question would rear its head like a demon, leaving him confused.

Thirty years before, both Aishah and Khadijah were in King Khalid Civilian Hospital giving birth and since then relations between them had deteriorated.

Where there had been friendship and sisterly love, animosity and hatred reigned. They waged a war of words and petty back-stabbing in a fashion only women know well. It was also true that Nader and Aishah's two sons looked so alike that they were often mistaken for brothers. True too was the fact that Khadijah was distraught with fear, knowing Talal wanted a son and had talked of taking a second wife. Nader's birth had saved her marriage and the humiliation of being displaced by a younger woman.

So many questions remained unanswered. How were the babies switched? Was the baby girl a stillborn or was she murdered?

Fajr prayer beckoned a day that would end thirty years of torment for Aishah and dissolve Nader's engagement to Maryam. He couldn't marry his sister.

* * *

Dr Muneer Al Hawash, Director of Prince Fahad Bin Sultan Hospital, ushered them into his office where the temperature never strayed above twelve degrees Celsius. Over the years he had learned that, like reptiles, people became lethargic in a cooler environment. Those who entered his office angry, departed refreshed having unburdened their minds and quenched their thirst on mint tea.

He was no more then five feet four, with close-cropped hair greying at the temples. He had a permanent smile on his waxy face and piggy eyes. A black tie hung around the collar of his lemon shirt and the lab coat that almost touched the floor gave him the appearance of an Emperor Penguin, shuffling about in black shoes.

He welcomed them with the customary '*Ahlan*,' repeated

several times to emphasise his delight at receiving such important guests. They sat making small talk, mainly about how grand the hospital was.

'We're going to computerise the appointment system,' he said proudly, pointing at the monitor taking up most of his desk. Mahmoud reflected on the fact that all the computers in the world couldn't predict when the new moon would be sighted to mark the beginning of the *Hijarh* calendar and no Pentium processor was going to change the Saudi's perception of time.

'We have ten new graduates in our Saudisation program,' Dr Al Hawash continued, but failed to mention that only one had put in an appearance so far. It all sounded good and a Saudi clerk sitting at a keyboard did wonders for public relations even if he screwed up the system on the days he chose to show up.

'So how can I be of service?' Dr Al Hawash asked.

Mahmoud explained the purpose of their visit and Aishah nodded from behind her veil. With arms folded across his chest, Dr Al Hawash clicked with his ball point pen.

'This is incredible,' he said after Mahmoud had finished.

'It's true,' Aishah nodded.

'Yes, but. . .'

'There is no but!' Mahmoud snapped, annoyed by the clicking pen.

'Is this woman working here?' Dr Al Hawash asked.

Aishah gave an emphatic, 'Yes.'

'How can you be so sure?'

'I saw her with my own eyes.'

Dr Al Hawash wasn't impressed. In his world a woman's word was only worth half that of a man's.

The clicking grew more frequent as Dr Al Hawash's mind went into overdrive. These were influential, powerful people. On the other hand whatever occurred happened at another hospital some thirty years ago, so how could he be held responsible?

'We need to examine this,' he said picking up the phone and jabbed at a key on the keypad marked DON. 'Maggi, do we have anyone called Asha?' he asked the director of nursing without any pleasantries.

'Yes, two.'

'Personnel files, please.' He hung up just as tea arrived, followed by the two olive green files.

Aishah turned away from Dr Al Hawash before lifting her veil to squint at the two passport-size photos.

'That's her!' Aishah gasped, overcome with emotion. 'She's the one. The one who stole my boy.' She pointed an accusing finger at one of the photos.

'Are you certain?'

'As Allah is my witness,' replied Aishah.

Dr Al Hawash wasn't going to argue with Allah. All he wanted was this episode to come to an end. He spoke again on the phone with some urgency and hung up. Waving a sheet of paper he said, 'We'd better talk to this person and get to the bottom of this. I'm sure there's a simple explanation.'

Ten minutes later, a bewildered Asha shuffled into the director's office in her green midwife's uniform. Once the niceties were over, Dr Al Hawash got to the point.

'I have a few questions to ask you. You're a midwife?'

'Yes sir. Thirty-two years this year.'

'Have you worked in the Kingdom before?'

'In Dhahran, Jeddah and Tabuk, sir!'

'Tabuk?'

'At the civilian hospital, sir!'

'King Khalid Hospital?'

'A long time ago.'

'Why did you leave?'

'My son had an accident.'

'What kind of accident?'

'Car accident, sir. He was only ten.'

'Was he okay?'

'He died.'

'So you know what it's like to lose a child.'

'That I do, sir.' Asha replied in a tone of desolation. As a mid-wife she witnessed the miracle of birth but also saw the dark hand of death, but nothing had prepared her for the loss of her boy. Yes, she knew just what it was to lose a child.

Aishah looked at the woman and felt pity. The anger had died with Khadijah and sadness filled the void. The past couldn't be changed. Only Maryam and Nader's future remained to be saved.

'We want the truth,' said Dr Al Hawash.

'Truth, sir? What about?'

'The Madam here says you swapped her baby some thirty years ago.'

A curtain of fear fell across Asha's face. She shifted her weight from one foot to the other. There was a palpable silence. All eyes focused on Asha for an answer.

'We only want the truth, Asha.' Dr Al Hawash asked, putting on his best bedside voice.

Aishah and Mahmoud nodded. 'We're not here to judge,' Aishah said.

Asha fidgeted with her fingers and stared at Aishah's veil. She didn't need to see her face; it was etched in her mind with the acid of guilt. She remembered the tearful face, pained by incomprehension.

'My little boy was dying,' Asha mumbled.

'What happened?'

'I needed the money.'

'Tell us what happened at the hospital.' Dr Al Hawash asked, clicking his pen again.

Asha paused and composed herself. She blew her nose and dabbed her moist eyes with a tissue. 'My son would be forty now,' she said.

'We need to know. . .'

'Two madams came in for delivery. They were friends, I think. . . it was a long time ago. One had a boy and the other a girl.'

'Go on. . .'Aishah encouraged.

'The girl died after a few days.'

'How?' Dr Al Hawash snapped.

'Honest to God, I don't know, sir. I found her dead in the cot during the night.'

'What happened next?' Aishah asked, nodding her head.

'When I told the madam, she went crazy and ordered me to swap the babies.'

'Did you ask why?'

'I had no choice. . . the crazy madam threatened to tell the authorities that I had killed her child.'

'But you hadn't?' Dr Al Hawash asked, putting the pen down.

'No, sir. I wouldn't harm an ant. I'm a Buddhist, sir, we believe—'

'What happened?' Mahmoud pressed.

'The boy's mother was at death's door and wasn't expected to live.'

'So you swapped the babies to save your neck?' Dr Al Hawash asked, pointing an accusing finger at Asha. The question hung in the air.

'The madam offered me money,' Asha replied after a while, looking ashamed. 'My boy was *dying*. I needed money.'

'Ah, now we're getting there!' Dr Al Hawash smirked.

'Honest to God, it wasn't the money.'

'But you took it anyway.'

'For my boy. . . you have to understand, sir,' Asha pleaded.

'We've heard enough, doctor,' Mahmoud interrupted.

'Wait a moment, Mahmoud,' Aishah interrupted. 'How did the baby die?'

'I don't know, Madam. That's the honest truth. I only found her, I swear on my son's grave I never touched the sweet girl.'

'I believe you!' There was no anger or pity, just sadness in Aishah's voice.

'Forgive me, Madam, I am so sorry,' Asha whispered and wept, letting go thirty years of guilt. She didn't care what happened anymore, God had taken her son and that was punishment enough.

Aishah got up and hugged Asha. 'Thank you,' she said. 'Thank you for giving back my son.'

Dr Al Hawash picked up his pen and clicked away, happy with the resolution.

Mahmoud sighed. Everything fell into place in his head, reinforcing his faith in Allah and his sister. Taking Aishah's hand he led her away, tears of happiness in her eyes.

FIFTY-FIVE

Turki yawned, stretched his arms and rubbed the sleep from his eyes. 'Auntie Miri,' he called, but there was no answer. He turned over and fell asleep. Two hours later a knock on the door awoke him.

'Is anybody home?' Hanifah asked, peeking round the door. Turki hid under the covers and kept still.

'I can see you,' she called. She tickled his feet and made him laugh.

'How's your cough today?' Hanifah asked. 'Is it better?'

Turki nodded. 'Where's Grandma?' he asked.

'She's gone to the hospital with Uncle Mahmoud.'

'Is Grandpa back?'

'He'll be back today,' Hanifah replied. Farhan had been in Riyadh for a few days. He had flown back on the early morning flight but had gone to his office to meet with Colonel Nasser, even though it was Friday.

'Where's Auntie Maryam?' Hanifah asked. 'We have been waiting for you both at breakfast.'

Turki shrugged his shoulders and looked blank.

'Maybe she's gone to the hospital too?' Hanifah muttered. 'Looks like we're going to be all alone.' They made their way to the dining room for breakfast.

'What are you going to do today?' Hanifah asked after they had been seated a while.

'I want to make a kite,' Turki said, licking the honey off his fingers. 'Uncle Mahmoud showed me how.'

'Can I help?'

Turki nodded and gulped down the mango juice Josi had made.

'You look like a clown,' Hanifah laughed.

Turki grinned and licked the orange moustache around his lips.

*   *   *

Aishah and Mahmoud returned at midday.

'How was it at the doctor's?' Hanifah asked, noticing a change in the air.

'We've solved the problem,' Mahmoud answered.

'Look what I made, Uncle Mahmoud!' Turki shouted, rushing into the lounge with his kite.

'We'll fly it this evening,' Mahmoud said, inspecting Turki's handiwork.

'Auntie Hanifah helped,' Turki added.

'Where's Maryam?' Hanifah asked.

'She's been moody of late. Mahmoud go fetch her,' Aishah ordered. 'My appetite's returned. I'll organise lunch. Turki, call Uncle Nabeel!'

'He's away camping,' Hanifah said.

'That boy should get a job now that he's going to be a father.' Aishah tisked.

Mahmoud searched for Maryam in the library and then headed for the stables. Basheer came running to him in the Vineyard.

'Zaki has vanished,' he said out of breath. 'I found the front gate open this morning.'

'How did that happen?'

'I don't know, sir, but a pickup is missing too,' Basheer said.

'Nabeel's probably taken it and the dog's chasing rabbits. He'll be back when he's hungry,' Mahmoud replied.

He returned to the house stroking his beard, deep in thought. Perhaps the maids had seen Maryam? He headed for the kitchen to find Zelpha in tears.

'I found this under Madam Maryam's pillow when I made the bed,' she said, handing him an envelope.

'What is it?' Aishah asked, seeing Mahmoud's sombre face. Mahmoud showed her the letter. The teacup fell from her hand and crashed to the floor. 'Nabeel's guilty of this,' Aishah screamed.

'What's the matter?' Hanifah asked. 'What's he done?'

'Maryam's gone,' Mahmoud muttered.

'Gone where, Uncle Mahmoud?' Turki asked, and searched their faces for an answer. Hanifah held him close.

'Read!' Aishah commanded, handing Mahmoud the letter.

Maryam's words spilled from Mahmoud's lips. *'I have brought shame upon our family sharaf. I didn't mean to hurt anyone. Forgive me.'*

'What has she done?' Aishah demanded.

Mahmoud continued. *'Let Allah be my judge. . . I beg your forgiveness. Please try and understand. I will always love you but now I must leave you.'*

'Enough! Enough!' Aishah shrieked and covered her ears. She slapped her head and wailed.

Turki clung to Hanifah and began to cry.

'Hush, baby, it's all right,' Hanifah comforted, tears running down her cheeks.

'I want Auntie Miri,' Turki sobbed. 'She promised she'd never leave me.'

'She'll be back.'

'Auntie Maryam is not coming back!' Turki snapped.

'Would you like to fly your kite?' Hanifah asked.

'No! I only want Auntie Miri!' Turki said, and ran out of

the room. Hanifah made to follow but Mahmoud stopped her.

'I'll talk to him later,' Mahmoud said. 'He needs time.'

*   *   *

The phone rang, Nader swore. 'It's Friday morning,' he grumbled.

'Answer it,' Lo said, and tucked her head under a pillow.

'*Nam!*' Nader barked, nursing his throbbing head, promising never to touch the whisky again.

'Nader?'

'Who's this?'

'Nabeel.'

'Why are you ringing so early?'

'It's three in the afternoon.'

'Shit! My head hurts. What do you want?'

'She's gone!'

'Come back to bed,' Lo called, poking Nader's back with her toe.

'Shut up!' Nader shouted and threw a pillow at her. 'I'll kill you if you touch me with your feet again.' Nader twisted Lo's toe and made her scream.

'She's gone,' Nabeel repeated.

'What are you talking about?'

'Maryam's disappeared. Left home. Run away.'

'When?' Nader asked, holding his head.

'I don't know, I just got back.'

'With whom?'

'Alone, I think.'

'She can't go far alone.' Nader scoffed.

'You're right,' Nabeel replied.

'Keep me posted.' Nader slammed the phone down. 'You haven't seen the last of me, bitch,' he seethed, punching the bed. Lo ran out of the room clutching her clothes. 'I'll get you if it's the last thing I do. Jew lover!' he continued, and smashed the bedside lamp against the wall. 'If I can't have you, no one will!' He gritted his teeth and buried his throbbing head in a pillow.

* * *

Hava munched away at the carrot, watching the boy's every move.

'You like that, don't you?' Turki said, and fished another carrot from a plastic bag. The horse nodded his head as if to say yes.

'Are you happy?' Turki asked and stroked Hava's chin. 'Auntie Miri's gone but I guess you know. Grandpa says animals can feel things. Can you?'

Hava shifted his weight to another leg and snorted.

'I wish I knew where she is. Do you miss her, Hava?' Hava shook his head, rattling the chain, and bit into the carrot.

'I miss her so much. I miss her more than Mama,' Turki said, trying not to cry. Hava stared at the boy and turned his ears to listen.

'I wish you could talk,' Turki said, offering another carrot. 'Grandpa said horses understand. Do you understand?' The horse nuzzled up and rubbed his nose against Turki's shoulder.

'I am so sad. Auntie Hanifah has been nice to me but I'm afraid she might go too.' Tears welled and streamed down Turki's cheeks. Hava looked at the boy and stopped chewing.

'Will you go one day too? Who will I talk to if you go? I'll get Grandpa to promise never to send you away. Would you like that? You're a good boy.' Turki patted the horse's neck and sobbed. Hava swished his tail and continued chewing.

'Do you think I'll see Auntie Miri again? She is so special. You are special too but in a different way,' Turki whispered in the horse's ear.

'I want to tell her about my adventures. I want her to see how we jump and canter.'

'Do you think she would be happy if she knew I was not angry with her? Oh, I do wish you could talk, you big silly horse.' Turki patted Hava's shoulders. 'I know you're wise like Uncle Mahmoud, you just pretend to be dumb.'

Turki ran his fingers through Hava's mane, picking out the straw.

'I have to be strong,' Turki mumbled, resting his head against the horse. 'I promised to be strong for Auntie Miri too.'

'Have some of these,' Turki said, and produced some sugar cubes from his pocket.

'Now don't you go telling Grandma 'cause she says they are bad for your teeth.' Turki stroked Hava's head and gazed into his big warm eyes.

'Oh, I forgot, you can't talk, so we are safe, aren't we, Hava?' Turki laughed and brushed away his tears with the back of his hand.

'I love you, Hava.'

FIFTY-SIX

The two men saluted, shook hands and embraced in the customary Arab way, kissing the left cheek once and then the right cheek twice, all the while shaking hands. Farhan welcomed Colonel Nasser to his office at the Area Command headquarters in the King Abdul Aziz Military City. He beckoned him to the Louis XV chairs surrounded by modern furniture. They exchanged greetings again and again, rephrasing the same sentence in different ways. There would be a pause and the ritual would begin again until they were satisfied that the other was indeed well and an unwritten period allocated to this performance had lapsed. A lieutenant appeared with cups of tea on a silver tray, a plate of Farhan's favourite dates and a coffee dispenser that doubled as a thermos flask.

Nasser was brother-in-law to Eid's wife but from a different tribe. They had known each other since their college days, but one had chosen the army and the other the police. They exchanged news and complained they hadn't seen each other for so long. The families must get together soon, they agreed with an '*Insha'allah*'. The last time they met was when Nasser's nephew, Yahya, was found behind the Armour Institute floating in the reservoir. Social life in Tabuk, and for that matter in Saudi Arabia, centred around the family, and distant relatives or friends never crossed the threshold uninvited. It was another way of keeping the wolf away from the sheep and preserving the all-important *sharaf*.

345

They watched the news footage of the American Ambassador together with Madam Secretary, Farhan, Nasser and a battalion of lesser officers. They all looked important with their peaked caps and khaki uniforms, displaying their ranks and honours, picking their way through the rubble of the bombed head-quarters of the US military training mission. Several high-ranking princes were visible, led by the Foreign Minister wearing a solemn face for the occasion. It was a serious matter; this time it was American blood but tomorrow they dared not ask whose blood it would be.

Keeping with custom, Nasser waited a while before broaching the purpose of his visit. By nature he was frugal with words but made an effort at small talk. This was a delicate mission. He felt uncomfortable in a room four times the size of his. But this was to be expected for the office of the area commander of the Tabuk region.

Against one wall, two flags of Saudi Arabia flanked the smaller ones of the three branches of the armed forces and the king and 'the three wise men' looked on from the opposite wall.

Three canvases of black velvet embroidered in gold calligraphy proclaimed the faith of the nation. A bank of photo-graphs covered a wall like a patchwork quilt documenting Farhan's journey through the palaces of power. There were pictures with the past three kings and countless senior princes, but the one that made him most proud was the one with his friend Norman Schwarzkopf who had commanded the allied forces during the Gulf War.

A collection of 1/72-scale models of tanks, aircraft and frigates jostled for space on a tinted glass table with chrome legs.

'That's my favourite,' Farhan said, seeing Nasser eyeing the model of the Bradley fighting vehicle. 'Great for desert warfare, manoeuvrable, fast and dangerous. Don't let the size of the cannon fool you. It's as deadly as a sidewinder and as swift as an Arabian steed. It's the equivalent of our old cavalry but a thousand times more effective.'

The lieutenant returned with a silver *mabkhara* and they fanned the plume of smoke towards them and inhaled, muttering '*Bismillah.*' After another round of coffee, Nasser decided it was time to get on with the business that had brought him.

'Do you recall that they found my nephew floating in the lake?'

'A real tragedy,' Farhan replied.

'We think we know who the killers are.' Nasser watched for a reaction.

'Didn't he drown?'

'That's what they wanted us to think and we let them think it.'

'There was more than one killer?'

'Five to be precise.'

'Five?'

'We identified four by their DNA and prints.'

'Why DNA?' Farhan asked.

Nasser clenched his jaw.

'May Allah have mercy!' Farhan exclaimed.

'The fifth from prints and photo. We believe he's the mastermind. . . probably had nothing to do with the murder – but ordered it.'

'So what are you waiting for?' Farhan asked.

Nasser didn't answer but slipped the cassette into the VCR and pressed play. They watched the recording of the US military training mission taken by a security camera from the adjoining building.

'I want you to watch this,' Nasser said. They saw a figure alight from a pickup decked with watermelons and make a getaway. 'The number plates were false, probably from a car dump. This is an image of the bomber taken from the video.' Nasser handed Farhan a 12 x 8 photograph. 'The CIA helped us on this. The *gutra* and the beard obscures much of the face.' Nasser sipped his tea, craving a cigarette. He knew Farhan didn't approve of the habit. 'That's what we had until we provided them with a picture of the killer and, *Alhamdulillah*, the computer came up with a positive ID.'

'Wonderful things, computers. Where would we be without them?'

'Herding goats,' Nasser responded with a nervous laugh. In his line of work there was no fear of that happening. There were many ways to catch a criminal and get a confession.

'So the killer and the bomber are one and the same?'

'Indeed so,' Nasser said.

'Where did you get a picture of the killer?'

'A driving license,' Nasser replied. 'You remember the road-blocks people complained about. It was a long shot but we thought that if the killer's driving license expired he would have to renew it or risk a fine or imprisonment and so we put the pressure on at the roadblocks.'

'Good thinking.'

'As luck would have it, that's exactly what happened. We dusted every license for fingerprints and fed them into a computer to match with the prints we had lifted from Yahya's wallet and ID cards.'

'That's a lot of work.'

'We had a team of ten working flat out.'

'Well done! I could do with such dedication on my team.'

Nasser thanked Farhan for his compliments and continued. 'A few months ago, we caught a Filipino peddling heroin down-town. It was concealed in antibiotic capsules. He sung like a nightingale when we spelled out his options, or rather, the lack of them, given our policy on drug traffickers.'

Farhan smiled and sipped his tea.

'He said a friend had bought a jar from the pharmacy at the Military Hospital.'

'My hospital,' Farhan asked, looking annoyed.

Nasser nodded. 'We caught up with his friend who didn't know much either but led us to a certain Dr Ali who wanted to finance his gambling. The funny thing is that he didn't even know what he was selling, only that it was contraband and saw a quick profit.'

'Deserves to lose his head!' Farhan said. He couldn't understand the fascination for drugs although he was partial to a good beer and Johnny Walker.

'We're letting him live for the time being to catch the bigger fish.' Nasser explained the ingenious method that was employed to get the drugs past customs. 'The Swiss are looking into their side of things and putting their house in order.'

'They must have been shocked to find a drug ring operating from within one of their pharmaceutical companies.'

'It took a lot of convincing. You know how the Swiss are. They think they are beyond reproach. Yesterday the president of the company was found hanging in his garage.'

'This Ali. . . is he talking?' asked Farhan.

'He's more than talking, he's identified the—'

There was a knock at the door and the lieutenant entered looking flustered.

'It's your wife, sir! She says it was urgent and insisted—'

'Women are the curse of men!' Farhan exclaimed.

'But where would we be without them?' Nasser laughed.

Farhan mumbled an apology and excused himself.

Farhan took the call in the adjacent room and listened to Aishah's wail.

'*Who's* missing?' Farhan asked, trying to keep his voice down. A muscle twitched in his clenched jaw. Ever since Khadijah's death, Aishah's behaviour had irritated him and now she was imposing herself at his work place.

'He's *my* baby, I have proof, *Allah-hu akbar!*' Aishar cried.

'Proof of what?'

'My baby!'

'You don't know what you're saying, woman. I'm too busy for your nonsense. Let me speak to Maryam!' Farhan ordered.

'Maryam's gone!'

'Gone where?'

'Nobody knows.'

'Someone must know. She can't just vanish. Let me speak to

Mahmoud or Hanifah!' he ordered. Aishah banged the phone on the table and called out to Mahmoud. Minutes passed. Farhan watched a soldier through the window checking the IDs at the gate to the cantonment.

The earpiece crackled into life and Mahmoud came on the line. Before Farhan could utter a word Mahmoud's voice demanded a hearing. Farhan respected the soft-spoken Mahmoud and knew that when he spoke it was time to listen. This was one of those moments. Mahmoud was economical with his words but said enough for Farhan to understand there was an earthquake shaking the foundation of his family. Boiling with rage, he returned to his guest.

Nasser knew not to ask about the family; this was not a social call and he was there to do a dirty job. He craved for a cigarette but sipped tea instead. Perhaps this was the wrong time, but then any time would be a wrong time.

'We supplied the CIA with the photo from the license and their computer recognised ninety eight points. That's as close a match as you can get.'

Farhan listened but his mind was with his family. He fidgeted with a dagger that was his letter opener.

'This is our man,' Nasser said, handing Farhan a photograph and watched Farhan's face turn pale.

'There must be some mistake, Nasser,' Farhan laid down the dagger absently.

'No mistake I assure you.'

'I've known him since he was a baby.'

'Children grow up.'

'He comes from a good family.'

'Not all the fingers of the hand are the same,' Nasser quoted an old Arab proverb.

'He's going to marry my daughter!' Farhan shouted.

'That's why I've come to you.'

An awkward silence descended between them.

'How sure are you?' Farhan whispered.

'A hundred percent.'

The photograph shook in Farhan's hand and his mouth felt dry. He sipped some tea, fighting to control his rage and humiliation. How could he have made such a blunder? He should have seen the writing on the wall. The diatribe on the monarchy and the fanaticism for Islam should have alerted him. Why had he let himself be blinded by friendship and let his heart rule when the family's *sharaf* was at stake?

'I want to offer you the opportunity to resolve the problem because of our friendship. Only I know all the facts.'

'What of the CIA?'

'The Americans know nothing of value. To them one bearded Arab looks the same as another, much like the Filipinos are to us.'

'So the murder, drugs and the bombing is the work of this man,' Farhan summarised stabbing at the photograph.

'Four or five men are involved in the drugs and murder but the bombing. . . well that's another story. We believe that's more organised and I smell the stench of the Brotherhood.'

'*Ikhwan!*' Farhan exclaimed.

'I also believe this man is a leading light in the movement and possibly a future leader.' Nasser explained, pointing to the photo. 'We have it from a reliable source that he met with their leader a few weeks ago in Jeddah.'

'The one they call the Father.'

'The very same.' Nasser nodded.

'Give me some time and I'll clean up this mess,' Farhan said. There was no other solution to the problem. As the Area Commander it was his responsibility to preserve the security of the area. This cocktail of murder, drugs and terrorism would bring about his destruction and everything he had worked for. Heads would roll and his could be the first to hit the ground if something wasn't done and done quickly.

'Seven days. After that it'll be out of my hands. Do you recognise this person?' Nasser said, handing Farhan another photo.

'It's my daughter.'

'Maryam?'

'You know I only have one daughter. Where did you get it?'

'From a wallet.'

'She must have given it to Nader.'

'Do you know this man?' Nasser said, pushing another photo across the desk.

Farhan examined the picture and shook his head. 'Should I?'

'We found your daughter's picture in *his* wallet,' Nasser said.

'What are you saying, Nasser?' Farhan exploded, narrowing his eyes.

'Nothing, just tying up some loose—'

'Who *is* he anyway?' Farhan snapped, his patience wearing thin.

'An *Ameriki* doctor.'

'Dr Joe?'

'So you know the doctor?' Nasser asked in surprise.

'My grandson mentioned his name.'

'Your grandson?'

'He's Turki's dentist.'

'Ah, now I am beginning to get the picture.' Nasser took a sip of tea, longing for a cigarette.

'How did Maryam's photo get into the doctor's wallet?' Farhan asked, glaring at Nasser.

'With your permission I'd like to talk to her,' Nasser said, gathering up the photographs.

'That won't be necessary. Leave it with me. I'll get to the bottom of this.' Farhan stood up to end the meeting.

The two friends shook hands, wished each other good health, saluted and parted.

FIFTY-SEVEN

The midday sun blazed mercilessly. A pickup had trundled through a few hours before but otherwise nothing had moved. Maryam squatted against the tank in a sliver of shade and wondered what to do next.

From her vantage point she could see the whole village and the rail track that disappeared in the distance. A forgotten fortress dominated one end of the ghost town with its crumbling walls. The sand was now piled up in caverns that had once been the homes of Ottoman soldiers. The mosque, a new building, took centre stage beside the police station, bristling with antenna and flying the national flag.

To leave now, in broad daylight and in the scorching heat, was dangerous, Maryam told herself, and she pored over the map, wishing the black lines would shrink, bringing her closer to Joe. Hassan had made several visits to the tower bringing fresh hay and water for the goats. On one occasion he sat talking to himself, bursting into song with the animals gathered around him. The words were foreign to Maryam's ears but the love song needed no translation. Love was in everyone's heart and it was the sum of this love that kept the world spinning in the right direction, she thought.

Thirst reared its head again and hunger clawed inside her stomach while her baby kicked, restless in the heat. Although winter, the heat was still formidable away from any cooling breeze. Maryam's thoughts turned to Zaki. She hadn't seen or heard from him. Perhaps, driven by hunger and the taste of freedom, he had abandoned her.

She knew Joe would still be waiting for her across the border. He was one person she could trust and felt ashamed that she had not to come to his aid in the souq that day when their nightmare began. He would wait for her till eternity, he had told her on the phone. Those words helped dispel her thirst and calmed her hunger, feeding her with the determination to succeed. According to the map, the border was only fifteen kilometres along the rail track through the village of Halat Amar. She would begin her journey at dusk when the men were occupied with *Isha* prayers.

Her thoughts turned to Turki. Finding her absent he must have raised the alarm. They would be looking for her, scouring the farm and surrounding areas, thinking the worst, knowing the dog was missing too. Once they discovered the pickup gone they would widen their search. She was sure Hanifah would add two and two. . . but would she hold her tongue?

It wouldn't be long before they found the truck by the roadside and then they would swarm like locusts over the area.

Voices drifted over the wall and interrupted her thoughts. She could hear the sound of shoes on the gravel until they stood below her and she strained to catch their conversation. She recognised Hassan's voice but not the others.

'No, I haven't seen anyone acting suspicious but, *Insha'allah*, I will let you know if I do.' Maryam heard Hassan say. With that assurance the men left.

From the few words that reached Maryam, it was clear the truck had been found. Why else would they be probing the village? Hopefully, with Hassan's assurance, they would confine their search to the main road. She felt grateful to Hassan but wondered why he hadn't told them of the *agal* he had found on the floor that morning or the milk that had gone missing.

The sun passed its zenith and began to slowly tumble from the heavens. The shadows emerged from under the rocks and stones and stretched out. Not a soul moved, only the whine of the flies came from below. Numbed by inactivity, her legs felt stiff and hunger returned with a vengeance, gnawing at her inside like rats. Her thoughts turned to the bag she had abandoned.

Perhaps now was her chance for freedom? She made a mental rehearsal of her descent down the ladder. It would be safer under the cloak of darkness but it could end in tragedy should she lose her footing. She made up her mind.

She peeked over the wall and looked around before climbing down the ladder, taking her time. As soon as her feet touched the ground the goats came to her.

'Shush,' she whispered with her finger across her lips, but they took no notice. She found the door bolted and swore. How could she have allowed herself to be trapped? She tried to reach for the bolt through the slats but it was too far, she only succeeded in taking the skin from her knuckles. The only way out was through the window, but that was three metres above her. She sat on the floor and wept.

Tired and hungry, her body gave into exhaustion and she escaped into sleep. She woke with a start at the sound of the bolt being drawn and Hassan's voice. The goats gathered at the door bleating their hearts out. Maryam retreated to the far corner but there was nowhere to hide. Stepping from the sunshine, Hassan's eyes took a while to adjust to the gloomy interior. He spotted a figure behind the chimney and stopped singing.

'Ya. Omar is that you?' he called out. 'What are you doing here?' he asked.

Maryam took the initiative. 'I'm not Omar,' she replied with authority.

'Who are you? Are you a *jinn*? How did you get in?' Hassan asked, with fear in his voice.

Maryam stepped from the shadows and Hassan fell to the floor covering his face with his hands, shielding his eyes.

'Don't hurt me, I'm only a poor herdsman, I never did anyone any harm. May Allah have mercy!'

'I won't hurt you,' Maryam said.

Hassan spied through his fingers and reached out and touched her hand.

'*Alhamdulillah*, You're not *jinn*,' he said. 'How did you get in here? Why are you wearing a *thobe*?'

'Fetch me some food and I'll tell you,' Maryam commanded, and sat down on the straw covered floor.

Hassan bowed and left and returned with food and water. 'I'm sorry the *khoubz* is not fresh,' he said, bowing again.

Maryam dived into the biscuits like a savage, till only the wrapper and crumbs remained. She attacked the *hommos* with bits of bread until that too was gone.

Hassan watched from a distance. 'You were hungry.' He smiled, flashing his white teeth.

Maryam nodded and gulped down the water, letting it splash over her face. She wiped her mouth and told Hassan how she had come to be trapped in the tower. Hassan sat on the floor, surrounded by his goats, cradling a kid, combing his fingers through its coat, listening to Maryam's incredible story. He didn't ask any questions.

'Will you help me?' Maryam asked.

Hassan looked surprised. 'How?'

'Fetch me my bag. I threw it into a shack at the edge of the village.'

'Men came yesterday, they asked many questions.'

'They'll be back. You mustn't tell them I'm here,' Maryam said.

'Don't worry, I understand. Like you I too am a long way from home, away from my loved one,' he said and left, bolting the door behind him.

Half an hour passed and still there was no sign of Hassan. Maryam tied knots in the straw and threw them in the corner. She paced the floor and spied through the gaps in the door.

Where are you, Hassan? She asked. Had she been foolish to tell him about her bag filled with money and jewellery? Had he gone to the police? Was she his prisoner?

Two hours later Hassan appeared with a hessian sack filled with straw.

'What took you so long? And where's my bag?' Maryam demanded.

Hassan emptied the straw on the floor and handed Maryam her bag. 'I had to throw the chicken. . .' He pinched his nose.

Maryam giggled and thanked him.

'I'll get you food and water after *Isha* prayer and then you must leave before they come looking.' Hassan left, bolting the door. Their fingers touched through the slats and he walked away singing to himself.

As the day wore on, the sky slowly turned crimson and then an ever deepening shade of mauve before a star-studded veil was drawn across the heavens.

* * *

A curious stillness filled with the hum of insects descended on the village. Through the slats Maryam watched a red moon float into the night sky like a balloon. The sight brought tears to her eyes. She remembered Sultan telling her how particles in the atmosphere made the moon red. Suddenly Maryam didn't feel alone anymore. Sultan was with her and somewhere, a few kilometres away, Joe too was seeing the moon rise and they were united in that moment.

After *Isha* prayer, Hassan returned with food and the *agal*. In the light of the moon, Maryam ate and Hassan went about his chores, milking the goats.

'*Ya*, Hassan!' Omar called and Hassan rushed out, motioning Maryam to keep silent.

'Make sure you shut that door. If we lose another goat, we'll feed you to the dogs.'

Hassan returned muttering to himself and shaking his head. The village turned in for the night and Maryam decided it was time to leave. Hassan gave her another chicken for the journey, shook her hand, pressed it to his heart and bowed.

'Why do you bow?' Maryam asked. Hassan gazed at Zubaida's disc around her neck.

'It is from my land. You're one of them... the Women,' he said.

'I've left you something in the furnace. Go back home to your family,' Maryam said.

Hassan fell to his knees and whispered something.

Zaki wasn't there to greet her when she stepped from the tower. She felt disappointed, alone and vulnerable.

Maryam donned her *abaya* to take advantage of the darkness and made her way west through the village, hugging the shadows until she cleared the last ruin. The rail track stretched before her like a giant ladder.

Her confidence grew with every step. She missed Zaki panting at her heels and wished he were there. Frequently she stopped and surveyed her surroundings, fearful of the beasts. The lights of Zat al Haj grew faint and disappeared altogether. The moon climbed into the sky and the shadows sharpened.

She stumbled upon a dead camel and shrieked when a bird fled from its belly disturbed by her footsteps. It lay with its neck contorted and legs still hobbled together by rope. The skin stretched over the bones like a tent and moonlight bounced off the teeth from a face frozen in a grimace. Maryam recoiled and hurried on.

The ground rose and fell around her but the track continued level oblivious to its surroundings. Maryam knew every step brought her closer to Joe and that made it easier to take the next one. At midnight, the lights of Halat Amar appeared on the horizon. She knew beyond them lay the sanctuary of Jordan and beyond that America and a new life for herself, Joe and their son. The thought pleased her and she smiled.

She passed another railway station with curved arches standing alone beside the track, awaiting the train that would never come. She looked at the horizon visualising Joe and continued on. Ahead, a dark form materialised and grew into a mangled steam engine lying on its side like the dead camel she had passed earlier.

She remembered it from her childhood when the family had picnicked there one winter's day. Her Father had told her it was one of the Turkish locomotives that the Englishman, Lawrence, had blown up around the time of King Abdul Aziz. They had clambered over it, crawled inside to explore the boiler and hidden in the furnace while playing hide and seek. Her mother scolded her when she emerged with her pretty frock covered in soot, looking like a chimney sweep. Now it was a monument to her memory of her brothers and a happy family outing.

Choking back the tears, she pushed ahead with her head bowed in silent homage to her past. Suddenly, a blood-curdling howl reached out from the darkness leaving her rooted to the ground. She should have known the beasts would be back like they had come in her dreams time and again. She couldn't see them but they were close, toying with her, knowing this time she had nowhere to hide and no one would come to her aid.

Another howl echoed into the night and soon there was a chorus. A dominant growl silenced the commotion and the leader materialised a hundred metres along the track. He seemed in no hurry and fixed her with his stare, watching her every move, seeking out her weakness.

In some, fear shuts down the process of thought but in Maryam it galvanised her. She wasn't going to let some dogs get in the way of her freedom. Not today, not anytime and not when it was within her grasp. She wasn't going to give up her love or her baby without a fight. She stared back, remembering what the farm workers had said when she had stood her ground with Zaki. *Never show fear, they can smell it.*

She took a step back and then another, watching the beast watching her. He didn't move, but all the while Maryam retreated with confidence, step by step, knowing what she was doing, where she was going. She couldn't see the pack but felt their eyes.

She was about ten steps from the locomotive when the leader snarled and tore down the track. Maryam turned and fled, seeking out the opening to the furnace. She threw in her bag and squeezed in. She pulled on the door but it refused to close all the way.

The leader thrust his snout through the gap and snarled. Once again his breath made Maryam's stomach heave.

The pack circled the engine looking for a way in. Soon the yelping died and they laid siege. Every now and then a beast would come and sniff at the door, snarl and return to his position.

As a child, the belly of the furnace had seemed cavernous. But now the sand had claimed some of the space and as a pregnant woman she felt the walls closing in on her. In the darkness, her fingers found the grill that led to the boilers and soot-covered wall studded with nuts. She felt like the bird she had disturbed from the belly of the camel. Only she had nowhere to flee. Her fingers went numb holding onto the iron door and her grip weakened. She wasn't sure how long she could hold on.

The faces from her nightmares came to hound her as before but now the beasts were real. They could smell her fear and she was sure this time they wouldn't leave when daylight broke. Her journey so far had been a string of disasters and they'd progressively gotten worse. She stared at the fangs only inches from her face and her belief in herself and her destiny began to fade. Sultan had promised he would be with her, walking in her footsteps, but was nowhere to be seen.

Remembering Zubaida's words, *It will give you strength to ward off the* jinn, Maryam grasped the stone around her neck and prayed, not knowing what she was saying or to whom.

Suddenly the head vanished, letting in a shaft of moonlight. A black form came bounding across the sand. Maryam's heart leapt recognising Zaki's familiar shape. It was like the Egyptian actor, Omar Sharif, galloping across the desert on his horse.

Zaki and the beast clashed. Engulfed in a cloud of sand and

fur, a snarling tornado raged for supremacy. Maryam gripped the stone and willed Zaki to victory. It felt cold in her hand, an island of tranquillity. Like boxers, the dogs fought in bursts of brutal fury, watched in silence by the pack gathered in a circle.

The fight ended abruptly. The sound of savagery was replaced by whimpering and then silence. Maryam listened with bated breath. She didn't have long to wait. Out of the dust Zaki emerged, wagging his tail.

One by one the members of the pack showed allegiance to their new leader by barking while rolling on their backs. Maryam watched with admiration; Zaki was now free from the shackles of men and had his own tribe.

He limped towards her, covered in blood. Maryam pushed open the door and stepped out. Zaki cocked his head and barked as if to say, you're safe now, have faith.

'Let me have a look at you,' Maryam said. Zaki looked at her and then over his shoulder at the pack and again at her. He stepped forward and was beside her.

'Thank you, Zaki,' Maryam whispered and hugged the dog. 'Let me take this off,' she said unfastening his blood-soaked collar. 'You're free now, Zaki,' Maryam said, and threw it into the desert.

Zaki licked Maryam's hand, barked and limped away, melting into the darkness, taking his new tribe with him.

With tears in her eyes Maryam dropped to her knees and punched the sand in frustration. 'Oh, why do I have to lose everyone I love?' She kissed the stone and slipped it under her *thobe* to rest close to her heart, as it had rested against Zubaida's and all the Women before her since the beginning of time.

FIFTY-EIGHT

The Land Cruiser skidded on the gravel and came to a halt in a cloud of dust. Farhan slammed the door and stormed into the house. Aishah and Mahmoud met him in the hallway, searching his face for news.

'Have you found her?' Farhan snapped.

Aishah sobbed and shook her head.

'We've searched everywhere,' Mahmoud replied. 'The night watchman says a pickup is missing and the dog's gone, too.'

'Are you sure she hasn't been kidnapped?' Farhan asked.

'The gate was unlocked from the inside and there's no sign of a struggle.'

'Where was the watchman?'

'He said he was doing the rounds. There is nothing missing besides Maryam's jewellery.'

'Clothes?' Farhan asked.

Mahmoud shook his head.

'Money?'

'I don't think so,' Mahmoud said.

'What about the Shamrani girls?' Farhan barked.

'They haven't seen Maryam in weeks.'

'It's all Nabeel's doing,' Aishah sobbed into her hands.

'What has he to do with this?' Farhan looked puzzled.

'He attacked her, almost killed her. Ask Hanifah,' Aishah said.

'Attacked her? Why?'

'I don't know. Nader was there too.'

'Nader!' Farhan fumed and clenched his teeth.

'Nader's our son,' Aishah said. 'We have proof, the midwife confessed. Ask Mahmoud.'

Mahmoud nodded and stroked his beard. Farhan, looking pale, led the way to the library and Mahmoud followed. With the eloquence of a sledgehammer, Mahmoud told Farhan what had happened at the hospital. Farhan listened, playing with his ring, lost for words.

'I can't believe I had another son all these years. I should have listened to Aishah,' Farhan sighed and cradled his head in his hands when Mahmoud had finished.

'So should I,' Mahmoud added.

'Where could Maryam be?' Farhan asked, seating himself behind his desk.

'She was very unhappy.' Mahmoud brushed his moustache.

'I'm her father. She should have come to me,' Farhan said looking puzzled.

'She did.'

'Yes, and I listened.'

'Like you always do. But did you hear?' Mahmoud asked raising a brow. 'I think she was afraid.'

'Of what?' Farhan asked, throwing open his hands.

'You, herself, the world. . . but mainly you.'

'How did it come to this Mahmoud? How could this have happened?'

'Fear,' Mahmoud said, and shrugged his shoulders.

'Fear?'

'Yes, fear. Fear of loving. Fear of the police, the state and the family. Fear of you.'

'What are you saying, Mahmoud? How did I fail her?' Farhan wrung his hands in frustration.

'She didn't want to disappoint you or break your promise to Talal.'

'I thought I was doing the best for her.'

'A river must find its own path from the mountain to the sea.'

'How could I have been blind? I gave her everything.'

'Did you?'

'Why do you question me?' Farhan scowled, slapping his hand on the desk.

'I should have done so a long time ago,' Mahmoud replied, returning Farhan's glare.

'Where is Turki?' Farhan asked brusquely. He knew Mahmoud was right. He should never have promised his unborn daughter in marriage and let pride and honour influence his judgement.

'He'll be in the stables.'

'He loves that horse. How's he taking it?' Farhan asked, mellowing a little.

'He'll live,' Mahmoud replied, stroking his beard.

'Does he know anything?'

'Probably. He's been through a lot and is growing up fast.'

'He's strong like Sultan.'

'Don't let him down, he looks up to you,' Mahmoud said, as Hanifah entered the library looking distraught.

'I know,' Farhan replied.

'I'll go find Turki,' Mahmoud said and left, closing the door behind him.

'Any news?' Hanifah asked and came over to the desk.

Farhan shook his head, his lips pursed in bitterness.

'I feel real bad,' Hanifah said, putting her hand on Farhan's shoulder and giving a squeeze.

'Why?' Farhan glanced sharply at her, twisting his ring round his finger.

'I taught her to drive.'

'What possessed you to do that?' Farhan exclaimed, banging his fist on the table.

'She asked and I thought nothing of it. We all drive in my country, I thought it was a bit of fun.'

'Fun? Look what your fun has brought!'

'The *Qur'an* does not forbid it.' Hanifah adjusted her scarf around her forehead, tucking in a strand of hair.

'That may be but the law forbids it,' Farhan growled.

'I thought the *Qur'an* was the law.'

'*Habibi*, it is dangerous to question a *fatwa* from the Grand Ulama,' Farhan explained.

'I'm sorry.' Hanifah bowed her head.

'You were not to know, were you?' Farhan raising her chin to look into her blue eyes.

'Know what?' Hanifah asked, studying Farhan's solemn face.

'That she would run away.'

'Of course not,' Hanifah replied, turning away. 'You know I wouldn't do anything to hurt you. I miss her too,' Hanifah said and began to cry.

'Maryam had a fight. When did this happen?'

'A few days ago while you were away,' Hanifah sniffed.

'Why wasn't I told?' Farhan snapped.

'You've been under so much stress. I didn't want to trouble you.' Hanifah blew her nose.

'What do you know of Dr Joe?'

'Dr who?' Hanifah looked startled by the question.

'Are you telling me everything, *habibi*?' Farhan asked, putting his arm around her, holding her close.

'What are you going to do?' Hanifah ignored Farhan's question.

'I have no choice.'

'You're frightening me, Farhan.'

'It is a family matter.'

'What's that supposed to mean?'

'It is about *Sharaf*.'

'I don't understand,' Hanifah said, shaking her head in despair and leaning against the desk for support. 'What's *Sharaf*?'

'It does not concern you.' Farhan brushed his beard as anger simmered in his eyes.

'I'm carrying your child. Doesn't that count for anything?' Hanifah whispered, tears running down her cheeks.

'*Sharaf* is a man's honour, my honour, my family's honour.'

'We live in a modern world, Farhan. Promise me you won't hurt her?'

'I've ordered a search. We'll hunt her down.'

'Answer me, damn you!' Hanifah sobbed.

'She won't get far.'

'She's your daughter, Farhan, not an animal. She is Allah's child like you and me.'

Farhan glared at Hanifah and turned away. 'We have our ways,' he muttered.

'You gave her life. She's your baby. Like this one,' Hanifah said, placing her hand over her belly. 'If you love me, promise me you won't harm her.'

'Dry those tears and find Nabeel,' Farhan ordered, his jaw set hard.

Aishah sat in the lounge wailing with a pile of crumpled tissues at her feet. Every so often she stopped and blew her nose. She didn't care that her head was uncovered showing greying hair that had not been brushed for days. Looking pale she mumbled to herself repeating '*Allah-hu akbar*' and slapped her forehead with her hands.

'What did Farhan say, Mahmoud?' Aishah asked as he entered the lounge. Mahmoud sat on the edge of the sofa beside his sister and shook his head in silence. Zelpha entered carrying a tray of tea, put it on a side table and rushed out crying.

'What's he going to do?' Aishah asked between sobs.

'I don't know.' Mahmoud stood up and looked down at his sister.

'Is he going to. . .' Aishah began, squirming on the seat.

'He hides his pain well,' Mahmoud interrupted, pacing the floor.

'Talk to him. He listens to you.'

'He keeps his own counsel these days. Things have changed.'

'How?' Aishah asked looking bewildered.

'They just have,' Mahmoud replied, catching a glimpse of Hanifah leaving the library. 'I'll go and find Turki.'

'Yes, the boy needs you,' Aishah said.

Hanifah found Nabeel in the men's lounge.

'How can you watch television when your sister's gone missing?' Hanifah shouted, venting her anger.

'She hasn't gone missing. She's run away. But she won't get far,' Nabeel said nonchalantly.

'How do you know?'

'She's got nowhere to go.' Nabeel laughed.

'She's your sister. How can you be so callous?'

'What do you care, slut? You only love money.'

'Don't you dare talk to me like that, you worthless piece of shit!'

'You won't fool the old man forever.'

'Yeah, what are you going to do? Kiss my ass!'

'Fuck you!' shouted Nabeel and flicked between the channels.

'Your father wants you in the library, asshole!'

Nabeel cursed, slammed the remote on the side table and stomped out. He knew this would come.

Farhan sat in stoic silence waiting for Nabeel. He thought about what Hanifah had said. She had changed so much from the person he had met only a few months earlier. Perhaps he had been too hard on her. She was right; Maryam was his flesh and blood. . . but how could she understand their ways? There could be no going back from what had to be done.

'Why did you fight with Maryam?' Farhan erupted as Nabeel entered the library.

'What difference does it make? She's brought shame on the family.'

'You drove her to it!'

'The hell I did. Didn't you see her belly?'

'What are you saying?' Farhan asked, getting up from the chair.

'Do I have to spell it out? She is pregnant,' Nabeel replied with a smirk.

'That can't be!' Farhan muttered, glaring at his son's smiling face. 'Whose child is it?' Farhan shouted, gripping Nabeel's *thobe* and almost lifting him off the ground.

'Why don't you ask your whore?' Nabeel shouted.

The back of Farhan's hand caught Nabeel across the face knocking him off his feet. 'Leave Hanifah out of this and don't call her that again, she's a good Muslim!'

'How can you be so sanctimonious, Father?' Nabeel cried, getting to his feet. Blood trickled from the gash on his cheek.

'You always preferred boys!'

'That doesn't give you the right to sleep with my wife!'

'Wife? You bought her like you buy your friends! I know all about your cosy arrangement.'

'Does my mother know? She thinks Hanifah carries my son.'

'Get out of my sight before I kill you.'

'Better you kill Maryam. And save at least some of the family honour!' Nabeel stormed out of the library to leave Farhan fuming.

* * *

Turki stood on a stool and combed Hava's mane, untangling the hair.

'What have you been doing to get in such a state? I hope you haven't been fighting with the others? And it's no use turning your head away, Hava, I know when you've been naughty. Auntie Miri says it's rude to turn your head away when someone is talking to you. Do you remember Auntie Miri, Hava? I suppose you don't. I miss her very much but I am going to be strong. *Insha'allah*, I will see her again one day.'

Mahmoud entered the stall, gave Hava a pat on the back and asked. 'What has Turki been telling you?'

Turki blushed and looked away.

'Come, let me give you a hand, otherwise we will be here all day.' Mahmoud picked up a body brush and began grooming Hava's neck, working his way down towards the shoulders. They both brushed in silence for a while.

'Uncle Mahmoud?' Turki said.

Mahmoud grunted an acknowledgment from the other side of the horse.

'Uncle Mahmoud, do you know where Auntie Miri is?'

Mahmoud looked over Hava's back at Turki and shook his head.

'Does Grandpa know?' Turki asked.

Mahmoud shook his head again.

'I thought Grandpa knew everything,' Turki said, dismayed.

'I've finished. Have you?' Mahmoud asked, and Turki nodded. They put away the grooming equipment, said goodbye to Hava and strolled out into the sunshine. Together they checked on the other horses, making sure they had been fed and watered.

'I miss her too,' Mahmoud said.

'But why did she leave?' Turki asked, looking up at his great uncle.

'She must have been unhappy,' Mahmoud replied. The pair walked out of the arena and Mahmoud shut the gate behind them. '. . . and I should have known.'

With pursed lips Turki looked up at him and then turned away.

Mahmoud smiled, recognising the boy's attempt at bravery. He knew how tormented Turki was, just as he had been when he had lost his parents. '*Insha'allah*, she'll come back,' he said, ruffling Turki's hair with his huge hand.

'*Insha'allah*,' Turki replied, gazing up at his uncle and putting on a smile. He looked at the stones along the path on the way home and remembered the game he had played with his aunt. In life you step from one stone to another, he told himself.

FIFTY-NINE

Maryam watched the pink dawn streak cross the horizon and fill the sky with colour and saw it as a promise of hope. She could feel it in her bones and stretched her arms and flexed her fingers. She knew Zaki's victory was an omen too. Soon she would be united with Joe and nothing was going to get in her way.

She had rested as well as she could on the bed of sand inside the furnace and the biscuits and dates had sustained her body, while Zubaida's memory and Sultan's voice had kept her spirit buoyant. Two long days had passed since she took the first steps towards freedom and now she strode purposefully towards Halat Amar. She abandoned her dirty *abaya* to avoid drawing attention and hid it under the locomotive where no one would think of looking.

Skirting round the village she took the dirt track marked on the map and headed south away from the town. She avoided the Bedouin campsite, its tin shacks built from corrugated panels, the spaces between littered with debris. Sheep and camels ignored her and continued their chewing. Soon she was clear of the village and trekking along the winding path towards the craggy mountains in the distance.

* * *

A rookie soldier watched the man's progress as he pissed, kneeling behind a thorn bush. He was surprised he wasn't wearing an overcoat on such a chilly morning but these Bedu were a hardy bunch, he told himself as he pulled up his pants and buckled his belt.

This was his first night on border patrol when he should have been tucked up in bed with his new fourteen-year-old bride, getting his money's worth. He had given her a dowry amounting to five years of his salary and had borrowed the money from his uncle, his wife's father. It would have been cheaper to get an Egyptian or Yemeni girl but his father wouldn't have any of that.

'You have to marry your cousin!' His father had bellowed – and now he was in debt up to his eyeballs.

His seventy-year-old grandfather, who had had seven wives, told him that in the old days it had been easier. But those were the days before oil. When they found oil, everyone got rich and prices went spiralling up, including the price of the dowry. Now young men like him had to beg, borrow or steal to put together enough money to get married. He cursed the system that had failed him and so many others.

The radio crackled into life in the cabin of the Nissan Patrol.

'Anything to report?' an irate voice inquired.

'Nothing stirring except an old Bedu!' the rookie soldier shouted into the microphone feeling important.

'You don't have to shout! Bedu, you say?'

'Yeah. An old codger.'

'Speak to him?'

'No. Just saw him from a distance going down the track towards the mountains.'

'Old you say?'

'Yeah. The bugger walked real slowly. . . might have been carrying something.'

'Like what?'

'Probably his rifle. . .'

'Most likely. . . up early hunting for hares. . . keep your eyes

371

peeled, there's a big reward out. . . comes all the way from high command.'

'How much?'

'Don't know. Just check everyone and report anything unusual.' The recruit signed off and reached for his standard issue binoculars to take a closer look at the old Bedu disappearing in the distance. He could certainly use the reward whatever the amount. He adjusted the focus and squinted at the figure for a few minutes and wondered why he wasn't wearing the *abia*, the traditional winter coat. What bothered him most was the black bag the man carried. And where was his rifle? He peered again, just as the figure reached the crest of the rise and looked back.

For a moment the rookie couldn't believe his eyes and looked again.

'*Ya*, Allah!' he exclaimed, staring at a beardless face. It was impossible, women were forbidden to dress as a man. He fumbled with the handset and babbled into it without following protocol.

'I think I've seen our man. . . I mean a woman.'

'Come again?'

'The old Bedu. He's a woman.'

'Calm down and start again.'

'It's a woman dressed as a man.'

'You've had pussy on the brain since you married that little nymphet!'

'I swear I saw a woman in a *thobe*!'

'Yeah, and a black sheep in an *abaya*.'

* * *

Nader jabbed at a dust-covered knob and the car radio came to life. He listened for a few minutes to the police controller jabbering about nothing to his friends.

This was Nader's morning ritual on his way to work.

The airways were always alive with gossip but not today. He

stabbed at another button and tuned into the military band. Since the bombs, this was always humming with activity but again there was nothing happening.

He switched to the frequency of the border patrol and recognised the controller's jocular voice. He listened to his banter for a few minutes. Suddenly, he bolted upright as if struck by lightning.

'Dumb fools! You've found the whore!' he shouted at the radio and slammed the breaks. The pickup lurched from side to side and came to screeching halt in a pall of acrid smoke. He made a squealing U-turn and headed for the border, his blood boiling with rage as the memory of the *Ameriki* slut's irritating accent burned like battery acid in his head: *She chose a real man, creep!*

*   *   *

Farhan slammed the phone down as soon as the call from Colonel Nasser ended. 'Get me a chopper!' he barked into the intercom.

He should have known she would travel dressed as a man. After all this was a man's world and only a man could get as far as she had. He tried to stifle the pride he felt at her courage; but in thirty minutes he would have her in his sights and put an end to the shame she had brought him and the family. He couldn't bring himself to say her name. His mind had already started to close the door on the memories of his daughter. He had given her everything, but still she had betrayed his trust and broken the unwritten laws of the family, the tribe and of the nation. 'She must pay the ultimate price. . .' he muttered to himself as he strode out to the whirling helicopter.

*   *   *

'They have found your woman!' Kasim said, after turning off the handset of his satellite phone.

'How do you know?' Joe asked.

'I spoke with a guard across the border, one of my father's men. She is as good as dead, we can go home now,' he said dismissively. Their Bedu companion nodded in agreement.

Joe couldn't share Kasim's fatalism. He had waited three long days and he would continue to wait for as long as it took. Maryam had made it this far and, God willing, there had to be a chance she would make it across the border with a little help.

'I'm going over,' Joe said.

'The hell you are.'

'We had an agreement. Where is she?'

Kasim remained silent. He had orders to waste this lovesick *Ameriki* if push came to shove and he wasn't going anywhere.

'Damn you! Tell me where she is or I'll kill you here and now!' Joe exploded, gripping Kasim by the throat. In a second, the Bedu was up and his revolver jammed into Joe's ribs. Kasim's face turned purple struggling for breath. Another sharp prod from the revolver brought Joe to his senses. He would be of no use to Maryam dead. He released his grip.

'You are mad!' Kasim croaked. 'You will pay for that.' With his Uzi in hand he stood looking smug and satisfied. 'We are going back,' he said, 'but you can stay... in your grave!' He threw Joe a shovel that was in the back of the truck and shouted, 'Dig, *Ameriki* bastard!'

Joe realised he had been duped. They had intended to kill him all along. He had to think fast. 'You want more money? I'll give you more,' Joe offered, hoping greed would sway their judgement, but they only laughed louder.

'We will take it when you are dead,' Kasim mocked.

From the shade of the tent the two of them watched Joe labour. They laughed, jabbing insults at him in Arabic that he didn't understand and spat in his direction.

The ground was baked hard by the unforgiving sun. The sweat dripped off his face and soaked into his *thobe*. His soft hands protested at the hard labour. There had to be a way out. Maryam and their child's life depended on him. He realised with every scoop of dirt he dug *his* time was running out – the only option was to fight. His mind went into overdrive.

'Water!' Joe shouted, in the direction of the tent, wiping the sweat off his face with his arm.

'Dig, *Ameriki* dog! Dig!'

'I am through with this!' Joe shouted. He threw down the shovel and climbed out of the hole.

Kasim and the Bedu laughed and ambled over to have a look.

'What do you think?' Kasim asked, looking at the Bedu.

The Bedu gave a toothy grin and drew his revolver, a Colt 45, from the holster on the belt around his waist.

'Get in!' Kasim ordered, pointing the Uzi at Joe's head. 'Hasta la vista, baby!' Kasim smirked, mimicking his hero, Arnold Schwarzenegger whose movie, *The Terminator*, he had watched repeatedly until the video tape had snapped.

Joe glanced swiftly at Kasim and then the Bedu and back to Kasim again. It was now or never. In one swift movement Joe picked up the shovel and flung a scoop of dirt at Kasim's face and then launched it at the Bedu, hitting him squarely on the chest.

Kasim tried to dodge the dirt and lost his footing on the gravel. The Bedu's revolver went off with a bang. Joe hit Kasim with a football tackle. They rolled in the dirt, Kasim kicking and biting, screaming for help. The Bedu rushed over looking pale, the revolver shaking in his hand as he tried to get a clear shot at Joe. Suddenly the Uzi spat lead, bucking like a bronco in Kasim's hand as the two fought over it.

A volley of bullets ripped across the Bedu's chest, turning his *thobe* red with blood. He groaned and fell. The Colt landed with a thud by Joe's side. He grabbed it by the barrel and smashed it into the side of Kasim's head. The Uzi fell silent and dropped from Kasim's grasp. Joe kicked it away, straddled Kasim and pinned him down. Kasim's left eye was squinted shut against the blood that was flowing into it from the fresh gash to his temple.

'Now, boy. . .' Joe gasped, 'let's see what you amount to with-out your toy. . .'

'Fuck you!' Kasim hissed and spat in Joe's face.

Joe's fist smashed into Kasim's jaw. 'Where is she?' he shouted.

'Go and fuck yourself, infidel!' Blood trickled from the corner of his mouth – he didn't like the taste.

Joe's elbow caught Kasim's proud nose and probably dis-figured it for life.

Kasim screamed out in pain.

'Tell me!' Joe commanded and raised his fist to strike again.

'No more. . . No more!' Kasim whimpered. 'She is over the ridge.'

'How far?'

'I don't know. . . Maybe two kilometres. . . maybe less."

Joe could tell from the expression in Kasim's eyes he was scared out of his wits and probably telling the truth.

'You are a dead man! You are fucking dead! My father will kill you for this!' Kasim bawled, cupping his bleeding nose with his hands.

'Yeah, I'll see you in hell.' Joe tore Kasim's *gutra* into strips and gagged his mouth and bound his hands and feet. 'You'll live. I'll deal with your father when we get back.' Joe said.

Kasim said something that was unrecognisable.

The Bedu lay face down in a pool of congealed blood. Joe felt for a carotid pulse and found none. He was way past dead.

With his *thobe* hitched around his middle, the Uzi slung over his shoulder and a pair of binoculars around his neck, Joe ran along the wadi floor. He clambered swiftly up the slope to the crest of the ridge. A kilometre across the dunes he could make out two parallel coils of razor wire separated by a hundred metres of no man's land. On the other side of this was Saudi Arabia.

A few days earlier, Kasim had pointed out the whereabouts of the camouflaged tunnel beneath each coil through which they smuggled Saudi criminals on the run. Abdul Karim had marked these on the map he had faxed through to Maryam. Joe found them and crawled under the razor wire, across no-man's land and entered Saudi Arabia undetected.

Sixty

From behind a rocky outcrop, Joe scanned the Arabian landscape through the binoculars. The undulating dunes, peppered by clumps of grass and clusters of rocks, stretched before him until they kissed the sky.

Dust devils danced like whirling dervishes under the midday sun to the sound of the wind whistling through the tamarisk bushes. In the distance, to his left, he could make out the ramshackle town of Halat Amar, a jumble of buildings with corrugated roofs, an assortment of television antennae and white walls. He panned across the terrain and followed a lorry going east towards Tabuk billowing smoke. A white dot in the distance inched closer and materialised as a pickup.

Where are you Maryam? Joe thought to himself, *I'll go back and kill that bastard Kasim if he's lied.* He scrutinised the scene again, taking his time. Nothing moved in the heat even though it was winter. He watched the pickup turn off the main road and head his way, sending up a plume of dust.

Probably a Bedu returning home, Joe thought. A glint of light above the horizon caught Joe's attention. He stared hard but saw nothing and then suddenly he spotted a black speck in the sky. It seemed stationary but he could be wrong.

On an adjacent dune Joe saw a sidewinder snaking away, leaving its signature grooves in the sand. A lizard basked on a nearby rock soaking up the heat, every now and then flicking out its forked tongue and bobbing its head. A passing jet left a vapour trail across the pristine blue sky – but still no sign of Maryam. Maybe she'd already been caught. A sudden gust of wind whipped up sand onto Joe and the Uzi. He swore, shook his head and spat out the sand.

A chequered *gutra* bobbed up and down in the distance. With the intensity of a lion stalking its prey, Joe watched it weave between the dunes, disappearing for a while only to reappear a little later. He gripped the binoculars and stared, trying not to blink. A rhythmic pounding thundered in his chest. He watched the pickup pass the Bedu settlement and head his way.

'Who the hell is that?' Joe asked aloud and licked his dry lips. The speck in the sky had grown into an army chopper; he could hear the *tat-tat-tat* of the rotor blades getting louder by the second.

'Shit! That's all I need!'

The lone figure reappeared suddenly between two dunes about a kilometre away and in an instant he recognized Maryam. His heart pumped a river of adrenaline. He exploded from his hiding place and charged towards her waving like a madman.

He scrambled up the dunes on all fours and tumbled down them, sprinting across the flat islands of land between them. There was no time to waste. Whoever was in the pickup and the chopper were closing in fast.

And he had no doubt they were coming for Maryam.

* * *

Maryam heard the grunt of an engine and the rattle of a vehicle. Masked by the dunes, she couldn't tell from which direction the sounds were coming but they were getting louder.

She saw the chopper, a dot at first in the eastern sky but growing bigger by the second and knew her father was coming to exact the price of his *sharaf*.

'Where are you, Joe?' Maryam sobbed, and searched the

horizon in the direction of Jordan. Where was Sultan who had promised to be with her? She knew the border was just beyond the giant dune that stretched before her. She gripped the disk through the *thobe* to squeeze out an answer.

'As long as I am breathing I won't give up,' she said. Placing one aching foot in front of the other she began the ascent. After every fall, she picked herself up and pushed ahead, puffing hard. 'I want to live!' she shouted between gasps. 'I want to see my son! I want to see Joe!' Tears streamed from her eyes.

She thought she heard her name and spun round but there was no one there.

Suddenly on her left, from the direction of Halat Amar and the highway, a white pickup materialised over a dune and halted about forty metres away. It looked menacingly familiar. The door opened and the red of the crescent – the hospital emblem – caught her eye. At once she knew it was Nader. 'Why was he here?' she asked. Panic dug its claws and spurred her on.

I will live. . . I will see my son. . . I will be reunited with Joe!

She heard her name again before it was drowned by the whirling blades of the chopper hovering above in the eye of the sun like a falcon about to swoop for the kill. She saw the silhou-ette of a man carrying a gun framed against the skyline – now coming down the giant dune towards her.

Once more, she felt like a wounded animal circled by hounds, baying for her blood. The nightmare had begun, she thought. Then she heard her name again and recognised the voice. It was Joe.

'Joe! Joe!' She screamed, and scrambled towards him with renewed vigour. If he could be with her, she knew she would be safe. He had come to rescue her. She felt ashamed for thinking he might not.

The chopper's shadow grew and its engine drowned even her pounding heart. Sand swirled, earth, machine and shadow came together on a flat piece of dirt at the base of the dune about fifty metres to her right and the engine cut out.

She glanced behind her to see Nader jump out of the pickup and bound towards her, wielding a gun. He was close enough for her to see that his face was contorted with rage.

Joe was now only metres away and scrambled desperately toward her. Her foot caught in the *thobe*; she stumbled. Joe reached her in time to catch her.

Farhan materialised from the swirling dust in his khaki uniform. 'Stop! Stop!' he shouted, in Maryam's direction.

Nader was twenty metres away; hatred burning in his eyes. 'I'll kill you with my bare hands, whore!'

'Help me, Joe!' she gasped. Fear seeped into her brain clouding her mind. She knew the end was near. No one could stop what was about to happen – not even Joe.

Three sharp shots pierced the air, Farhan's pistol spat out the brass casings and then there was stillness. No one moved.

Nader broke the silence. 'Kill the bitch!' he yelled, pointing at Maryam. 'Kill her! The whore's brought you shame!'

'So have you!' Farhan snapped.

'Me?' Nader asked, stabbing a finger at his chest looking indignant.

'Yes you! I know all about you, Nader!' Farhan shouted.

'The hell you do! Kill the whore or I will!' Nader raised his gun.

'You bombed the *Ameriki* and the innocent died.'

'The infidels trespassed on our Holy Land. They got what was coming!'

'You had a boy murdered. I know about that too.'

'Boy? What boy?' Nader pointed his gun at Farhan and then at Maryam and at Farhan again.

'We know about your operation.'

'You know nothing, old man!' screamed Nader and took aim.

'I'm your father. Go on shoot me,' Farhan yelled, glaring at Nader.

'You're insane!'

'Khadijah stole you.'

'Stole me?'

'From the hospital where you were born! Aishah is your mother!'

'You've lost your wits. Kill that bitch or I will!' Nader said, turning to Maryam.

'She's your sister. You're my son.'

The words exploded in Maryam's head and all the pieces of the puzzle fell into place: they explained why her mother didn't approve of the marriage. She had known all along Nader was her brother, not Talal's son.

'She carries this Jew's child!' Nader erupted, pointing at Joe. 'Kill her. . . kill him! If the whore is my sister then she has sullied my honour too. Kill her! Or I will do it!'

Maryam looked at her father's angry face and then at Nader's consumed by hate. One was bent on tribal justice and the other on revenge. Her mind spun and she felt weak. She looked up at Joe and then crumpled to her knees. She saw Nader raise his gun and heard Joe's drawn our scream, 'Nooooooo!' Joe threw himself between her and Nader.

There was an explosion that echoed forever in her head and then there was stillness.

Nader lay in a heap with half his head blown away and the sand splattered with his blood and brains.

Maryam saw a smoking gun in her father's hand. She gasped. 'You've killed him. You've killed your son!'

Farhan's face was a mask of pain and his eyes were wells of desolation. He glared at them in silence from ten metres away, breathing hard. Muscles twitched in his jaw, as a battle raged within him between love and pride. Long seconds coalesced into minutes and Maryam knew the time had come. Instinctively she reached for the disc around her neck and for Joe – their hands touched and eyes met, declaring their love for each other.

Joe cocked the Uzi and prepared to fire.

'No, Joe. . . let my father have his honour,' Maryam said, and pushed the gun down. 'I am ready to die now with you by my side,' she whispered, and kissed the disc.

Farhan raised his arm and Maryam looked down the barrel of the gun pointed at her head. His hand trembled. Father and daughter locked eyes for a second and twenty years of memory was erased from his consciousness.

'*Bismillah*,' mumbled Farhan. Suddenly an angry gust of wind, whipped sand into his eyes as he squeezed the trigger three times, the sound of the shots pounded in Maryam's head.

Farhan rubbed his eyes and saw the emptiness of his deed; none of his remaining bullets had found their mark.

'Forgive me, Father!' Maryam cried, reaching out to him.

Farhan turned and walked silently away. To him she no longer existed, he never had a daughter.

'I'm your flesh and blood!' she sobbed crawling after him. 'It doesn't have to end this way. Father?' She wailed, punching the sand. 'I love you Father, I love you all. Please forgive me.'

'His pride blinds him,' Joe said. He knelt down beside Maryam and held her close.

'*Sharaf* is the curse!' Maryam sobbed into his chest. 'I love him so much. I may have died in him but he will live in me forever.' She looked at Nader's lifeless body sprawled across the sand. 'He was my brother, we shared the same womb. How could that be?'

The chopper rose from a cloud of dust, hovered for a moment and banked away. They watched in silence till it was a speck in the sky and no more.

With tearful eyes Maryam looked across the dunes, grabbed a fistful of sand and let it trickle through her fingers to be carried away by the wind. 'This sand is in my blood, my heart belongs here,' she whispered. Tears of sorrow fell from her cheeks and soaked into the dust of Saudi Arabia.

'Meet our son,' Maryam said at last, turning to Joe and placing his hand on her swollen belly.

'I love you,' Joe replied as they embraced and he brushed the tears from her cheeks. Then they climbed the dune hand in hand. To freedom and a new beginning.